TALES OF THE SHADOWMEN

Volume 17: Noblesse Oblige

also from Black Coat Press

Tales of the Shadowmen 1: The Modern Babylon (2004)
Tales of the Shadowmen 2: Gentlemen of the Night (2005)
Tales of the Shadowmen 3: Danse Macabre (2006)
Tales of the Shadowmen 4: Lords of Terror (2007)
Tales of the Shadowmen 5: The Vampires of Paris (2008)
Tales of the Shadowmen 6: Grand Guignol (2009)
Tales of the Shadowmen 7: Femmes Fatales (2010)
Tales of the Shadowmen 8: Agents Provocateurs (2011)
Tales of the Shadowmen 9: La Vie en Noir (2012)
Tales of the Shadowmen 10: Esprit de Corps (2013)
Tales of the Shadowmen 11: Force Majeure (2014)
Tales of the Shadowmen 12: Carte Blanche (2015)
Tales of the Shadowmen 13: Sang Froid (2016)
Tales of the Shadowmen 14: Coup de Grâce (2017)
Tales of the Shadowmen 15: Trompe l'Oeil (2018)
Tales of the Shadowmen 16: Voir Dire (2019)

Shadowmen: Heroes and Villains of French Pulp Fiction (non-fiction) *(2003)*
Shadowmen 2: Heroes and Villains of French Comics (non-fiction) *(2004)*

TALES OF THE SHADOWMEN

Volume 17: Noblesse Oblige

edited by

Jean-Marc & Randy Lofficier

stories by

Matthew Baugh, Atom Mudman Bezecny,
Nathan Cabaniss, Matthew Dennion,
Brian Gallagher, Martin Gately, Travis Hiltz,
Randy Lofficier, Nigel Malcolm, Rod McFadyen,
Christofer Nigro, John Peel, Frank Schildiner
and **David L. Vineyard.**

cover by

Mandy

A Black Coat Press Book

Visit our website at www.blackcoatpress.com

ISBN 978-1-64932-024-7. First Printing. December 2020. Published by Black Coat Press, an imprint of Hollywood Comics.com, LLC, P.O. Box 17270, Encino, CA 91416.

Table of Contents

Our regular contributor Matthew Baugh usually opens each volume of Tales of the Shadowmen *because his name is first in the alphabetical order. However, his position has never been more justified than with this year's contribution, in which The Little Prince—a character only used once before, by the editors in Volume 2—weaves a parable of science and faith, logic and emotion, in this little gem appropriately entitled...*

Matthew Baugh: *The Cubic Displacement of the Soul*

Asteroid B-612 - October 1890

The professor stared at the smiling blond boy framed against the starry sky and wanted to scream.

"Are you feeling better?" the boy asked. His manner was polite and calm, something the professor found baffling considering the two of them stood on a house-sized chunk of rock that seemed suspended in the depths of space.

"Madness! This is madness!" he whispered.

The boy cocked his head to the side, a gesture the professor thought might mean curiosity.

"The doctor said you might feel like that." He held out a teacup full of a dark, steaming liquid.

The professor took the cup and sniffed at its contents. The odor, something between fresh coffee and wet dog, made him wince.

"What is this?" he demanded.

"Black hellebore tea. The doctor said it would settle your mind and clear your thinking."

"I do not care for the aroma. You said hellebore?" The professor shuffled through his encyclopedic memory. "That's the flower commonly called Christmas rose, I believe, and it is toxic. Are you trying to poison me, child?"

"Poison?" The boy seemed bemused by the question. "Of course not. Here, see?"

He raised the delicate porcelain cup to his mouth and took a long sip. When he lowered it, the professor saw that about a third of the contents were gone.

"It is perfectly safe," the lad said. "You don't have to drink it if you don't want to, but I think it will make you feel better."

The professor took the cup and raised it to his lips. The tea tasted as strange as it smelled, but he drank it without any further reservation. He didn't know much about children, but he knew a great deal about deception, and he was confident the boy hadn't lied. Besides, it would be absurd to stage this elaborate setting just to poison him. The professor knew even more about crime and didn't think this could be a scheme to harm him. No, this boy and the doctor wanted something else, he just hadn't yet figured out what.

To his surprise, the tea helped. His questions didn't vanish, but they shrank to the level of manageable curiosity. The overpowering sense of unreality dwindled to a feeling of irritation. He still didn't understand his situation, but he could accept it.

"That did help," he said. "I suppose I should thank you."

"Thank the doctor," the boy said, beaming. "He was the one who gave me the tea."

"I think he lied to you about its contents. I have a comprehensive knowledge of vegetable toxins."

"The doctor told me it was the same medicine that cured Heracles of his madness."

The professor snorted. "Heracles is a myth. A baseless fantasy for children. In the real world, hellebore has no such medicinal properties."

"Oh, but the doctor didn't get his hellebore from your world. He said it came from Pollux IV."

"Not from my world?"

"Not from your planet," the boy replied. "I think that's the better way to say it."

The professor looked around again. Aside from the boulder on which they stood, there was nothing but black sky dotted with stars. Only one of these stood out, a yellow light several times larger and brighter than anything else.

"The sun?" He whispered.

"It looks smaller from my planet, doesn't it?"

"This can't be another planet!" the professor said. "It's some clever illusion, but that's all. If I just walk away, that will quickly become apparent." Without waiting for a reply, he strode off.

He was back in less than two minutes.

"It doesn't take long to walk around my planet," the boy said.

The professor didn't reply. Turning 90 degrees, he set out toward a different horizon. He did this several times before accepting that he was, in fact, on a tiny planet. It was a pretty world with three tiny volcanoes and an abundance of green plants. None of which made any sense.

"Very well," he said, returning from his sixth circumnavigation. "I admit I am on your planet. I have some questions, but I suppose introductions are in order first. I am Professor James Moriarty, mathematics tutor."

"I'm very pleased to know you, professor." The boy made a graceful bow. "I'm afraid I don't have a proper name. Living alone on my little planet, I've never had much use for one. However, the doctor calls me the Prince, so that will have to do."

"Ah, the doctor. Would that be Doctor Omega?"

"Indeed it would," the Prince said, his smile broadening. "Are you also a friend of his?"

"Not a friend," Moriarty replied. "But I have met him."

Moriarty had come to Paris, looking for an advantage. He didn't know what he wanted, but the detective, Holmes, had grown from nuisance to a real threat, and nothing the professor did could shake him off the trail. Usually, Moriarty would not have turned such outré methods, but his sometime colleague, Nikola, had recommended this place, and Nikola was someone to be respected.

He turned onto the old street; his collar turned against the drizzle that had driven most of the traffic from the roads. There, between two stone houses, sat the *Bureau d'Echange de Maux*.

"Excuse me, my good fellow."

Moriarty turned toward the voice; a man in what looked to be his eighties stood there, dressed in black cape and astrakhan. His severe expression and shock of unruly white hair gave him the look of a stern schoolmaster.

"Yes?" Moriarty said.

"I see you're headed toward the Bureau."

"What of it?"

"I would not recommend it."

"Frankly, sir, I don't see how it is any of your concern."

"Oh, but it is," the older man said. "In that place, you can trade a good for an evil, but the price is never worth it."

"Again, that is my concern, not yours."

"I have made it my concern to prevent the spread of the sort of evils that are this place's specialty. My name is Doctor Omega; allow me to buy you a brandy and tell you more."

"I see no reason to oblige you. Good day, sir!"

Moriarty turned but had only gone a few steps when the man called out.

"Come, come, Professor Moriarty. You really should listen to me."

He turned slowly, scanning the street as he did. The stranger was alone; he was certain. He was equally sure the man was not Holmes in disguise.

"You know me, sir?"

"I attended a lecture you gave on binomial theorem several years ago. I must say, you are one of the great minds of the century."

Moriarty's mind raced. The fact the man knew him and was aware of the Bureau's dark reputation was a complication. He would have to be eliminated, but it would be best to learn what else he knew first. He forced a smile.

"On second thought, I'd be delighted to have a drink with you."

"So you see, anything you get from that place comes with a terrible consequence," the man—who called himself Doctor Omega—said. "It's a sort of Faustian bargain if you will."

"I don't see any such thing," Moriarty replied. "First, while you have told some harrowing stories of deals others have made at the *Bureau d'Echange de Maux*, you have no evidence that they are true. Even if they are, I see nothing wrong with a bargain like Faust's."

"Nothing wrong in selling your soul to the devil? That seems most peculiar."

"You are an educated man, doctor," Moriarty replied. "You possess an advanced degree, so I will do you the courtesy of assuming you are no fool. Surely, you can appreciate my point of view. First, there is no such thing as a devil. That is a superstitious conceit of humanity with no empirical basis whatsoever."

"Ah, but what I said is metaphorical," Omega said. "Surely, you can see that mortals can assume the traditional role of Satan, tempting us to evil with rich rewards."

"Even so, you depend on intangible, irrational concepts. You must know that evil has no objective existence. It is a quality that we humans give to things for purely arbitrary reasons."

"If the proprietor of the exchange gives you something that will harm you, would you agree to call that 'evil?'"

"I might, but it makes little difference. If this man is Mephistopheles, as you suggest, he is still offering me something of worth in return for my soul. That is to say; he offers something for nothing."

"You do not believe in the soul either, I see," Omega said.

"Of course not," Moriarty snapped. "Why should I believe in something that cannot be seen or touched? The soul is a human invention. Philosophers use it as a way to hide from the reality of death. Clergymen create visions of eternal rewards and punishments that they use to control the gullible."

"I must disagree," Omega said. "The energy that animates all living things is genuine. I have seen it many times in my travels."

"Really?" Moriarty took a sip of his brandy as he wondered if the man was a common lunatic. He had decided mainly against it. Doctor Omega was undoubtedly mad, but there was nothing common about him.

"Tell me, doctor, how might I determine for myself the reality of the soul? What properties does it have that can be measured? Does it have mass? Does it occupy space? If it is real, it must have real properties."

"Oh my, you are a keen one," the doctor said, laughing. "As it happens, one of your country's finest thinkers has established just that. She tells her beloved, 'I love thee to the depth and breadth and height my soul can reach.' Three dimensions, Professor Moriarty. The soul has cubic displacement."

Irritated, Moriarty rose from the table. "Really, doctor, it you're not going to take this topic seriously"

"Tut, tut," Omega said soothingly. "Please forgive my sense of whimsy, but it seems to me that poets and mathematicians have a great deal in common.

You each use special language to help people understand things that they cannot see or touch."

"Absurd! Poets deal with fantasies and dreams. Mathematics represents the physical universe."

"You are the author of the *The Dynamics of an Asteroid*, aren't you?"

"I am." The abrupt shift of topic made Moriarty wary.

"A magnificent work," Doctor Omega said. "I daresay you are Britain's foremost authority on the topic."

"I daresay the world's foremost," Moriarty replied dryly.

"Yet you have never touched an asteroid, and never even seen one without a telescope. You know about asteroids, but you do not *know* asteroids."

"You are playing semantic games, doctor."

"No, no. I am very serious when I tell you that I can introduce you to someone who knows asteroids far more intimately than you and can show you things that defy your narrow understanding."

"I would say I've wasted enough of my time here."

He turned to leave and found himself facing a large, muscular man with a pleasant face. Moriarty cursed himself silently for allowing the man to come upon him undetected. The man grabbed the professor, spun him around, and pinned his arms to his sides with hands that seemed as strong as steel clamps.

"Thank you, Fred," Doctor Omega said. "I'm dreadfully sorry for this, professor, but I cannot allow you to go to the *Bureau d'Echange de Maux*. The deal you would make there would destroy not just you, but thousands upon thousands of others."

"Fool! You are both dead men for laying hands on me!" Moriarty said, snarling. "My men are always close at hand. You will not leave this building alive."

"Yes, yes," the doctor said pleasantly. "Ah, there it is."

He produced a silver wand with a red light at the top.

"Just watch the Baltian neuralyzer," he said.

There was a flash of light from the device.

"The next thing I knew, I was on your planet, or rather, your asteroid," Moriarty said. "I have no memory of the passage."

"Well, I am happy for your visit anyway," the Prince said, smiling. "Not many people come to my planet."

"Yes," Moriarty replied, then, "Are you the expert on asteroids that the doctor mentioned to me?"

"I know my planet very well, I suppose," the Prince said. "Would that make me an expert?"

"Perhaps, if only in the mind of that doddering madman."

"But you wrote a book about asteroids. Perhaps you could tell me something about my planet."

"I could, yes. It would take some months of observation, but I could describe its mass, orbit, and rotation down to the smallest degree. I could tell you its density, composition, and a million other facts."

"That would be wonderful!"

"It would take several hundred pages, and would require a level of understanding that even most mathematicians could not grasp."

The Prince thought about that for a moment or two.

"Couldn't you tell me about my planet in some way that would be easier to understand?" he asked. "Perhaps you could draw a picture?"

Moriarty drew himself to his full height.

"Young man, I occasionally make diagrams. I never make drawings."

"That is too bad," the Prince said. "But, could you answer a question I have?"

"What is it?"

"I tend the plants here, and there are always weeds, especially baobab shoots. I have thought that, if I went to Earth and got a sheep, it could eat the weeds for me."

"I am not an authority on sheep," Moriarty said.

"I see. But my question is really about asteroids. If I were to leave and be gone for a long time, would my planet be lonely?"

"A planet is an insensate mass of minerals. It cannot feel lonely. Only living beings have emotions."

"You are saying my planet is not alive?" The Prince seemed shocked by the notion.

"Everyone knows that planetary bodies are not alive," Moriarty said. "The scientific community is in absolute consensus about this. At least, except for George Challenger, and he is a crackpot of the first water."

"I just thought that I would miss my planet, so it made sense that it would also miss me."

"That makes no sense. Then again, there is a great deal about your world that makes no sense. For example, how is there an atmosphere around this rock."

The Prince rubbed his downy chin thoughtfully.

"I suppose that is because, if there were no atmosphere, I would not be able to breathe."

"That is no answer," Moriarty snapped. "Things don't happen just because we need them to. A planet must have sufficient gravity to hold an atmosphere, and for that, it needs sufficient mass. For that matter, why do I feel like I weigh the same here as on Earth? On such a tiny ball, I should be able to leap out into space. What is it that holds me to the ground?"

"I have always assumed that we were held to the planet by love," the Prince said.

Moriarty snorted.

"You sound like Empedocles, or Augustine, or one of those other learned fools of antiquity who thought that gravity was the same as love. It is not!"

"What do you think holds us to the planet," the Prince asked in perfect innocence.

"Something else!" Moriarty's voice had risen almost to a shout. "Some natural, measurable phenomenon!"

Moriarty fell silent, and the Prince watched him quietly for a while. The boy was not frightened, he could tell, but seemed puzzled and a little sad. Finally, he spoke.

"I think I understand why the doctor brought you here," he said. "You don't know my planet."

"I know more about asteroids than anyone on Earth."

"But how can you know someone if you've never met them? How can you ever become friends if you just watch them from far away?"

That caught Moriarty off-guard. He had many associates, some of them he valued highly, but none that he would call friends. His towering intellect had always made human intimacy difficult. He had only encountered one man in his adult life who could talk with him on an equal basis, and that was his deadliest enemy. He had watched Holmes from a distance for several years but had never yet met him face-to-face. What if he did? Was this a chance to know another human being and to be known in return?

"Nonsense," he said, though he kept his voice gentle this time. "I don't see much value in your way of 'knowing' things. My ways are more logical."

"Still, we don't need to agree to be friends," the Prince said. "You are welcome to stay as long as you like."

"Thank you, Your Highness." Moriarty found the offer somehow touching. "I must go, though. I have pressing business back on my planet."

Doctor Omega's ship, the *Cosmos*, arrived several hours later. He didn't try to land, for the vessel was nearly the size of the little planet. Instead, the ship went into a stationary orbit, and Fred lowered a rope ladder, which the professor climbed to the ship.

"How are you, my good professor?" Omega said when he was safely on board.

"Unchanged," Moriarty replied. "I shall need some more of your hellebore tea if you are going to show me more impossibilities, but nothing will sway me from my purpose."

"I'm afraid this calls for something more than hellebore," the doctor said. He raised the silver wand in front of Moriarty's face again.

Professor Moriarty stood on the ancient street in the clear Paris evening, trying to remember how he had come there.

"Professor!"

He turned to see Sebastian Moran running toward him. His lieutenant wore a relieved expression.

"Where have you been?" Moran said, stopping next to him. "We've been looking for you for hours.

"I don't remember," Moriarty replied. He had the vague sense that he had traveled somewhere, met someone. He couldn't capture the details.

"Did you find what you were looking for at the *Bureau d'Echange de Maux*?" Moran asked.

Moriarty looked at where the shop had been. Now the houses that had flanked it stood together, sharing a common wall. It looked like they had existed that way for many centuries. He had the unsettling idea that the Bureau had gotten tired of waiting for him and moved on. He felt angry at himself.

"I was deceived," he said. "There is clearly no such place."

"What do we do now, professor?"

Impossible ideas drifted into his head: traveling the stars, living on an asteroid, becoming a friend of Sherlock Holmes. Angrily, he swept these fantasies from his mind to focus on the practical.

"Back to London," Moriarty said. "I have a murder to arrange."

Atom Bezecny revisits a theme that has often seduced our contributors—that of the relationship between two dark-clad vigilantes, Judex and the Shadow. While no one has ever thought Walter Gibson was influenced by Feuillade & Bernède's creation—if anything, he admitted having The Phantom of the Opera *in mind when he created* The Shadow*—the similarities are such that, when* The Shadow *comic-strip was published in France, it was simply retitled* Judex.

Atom Mudman Bezecny: *Walking on Foreign Ground, Like a Shadow*

New York, 1928

Judex was in New York. A family friend had called him out here from France. His mother, Julia Orsini, was friends with the parents of Kent Allard, the American vigilante who was Judex's contact. The two vigilantes were similar in style—they were fond of the dark. Their clothing seemed shaped from darkness itself, and the night was their ally. The two were so similar, in fact, that a slight modification to Judex's outfit made him a double of the Shadow. He had come here to play that part, in an effort to confound a plot against Ken Allard and his organization.

"An assassin, a gangster named Tony Rico, has learned that I possess the twin jewels of the Russian Czar. He has decided to eliminate me and steal the gems in one fell swoop."

The Shadow had made copies of his signature jeweled rings for Judex to wear.

"However," he continued, "the information he received from my old enemy Benedict Stark also revealed to him my close association with one of my agents. You know the one I speak of?"

Judex nodded. If he recalled correctly, his friend was a little sweet on the woman in question.

"In order to convince Rico that he's facing me, you must utilize a female associate," continued the Shadow. "One who will pose as my assistant. Fortunately, I have taken the liberty of finding someone for you. I believe that the Gillespie Circus has recently toured Europe?"

"That is correct," said Judex.

"The owner of that circus, Mary Gillespie, will be your assistant. Her father was Colonel Gillespie, a friend of mine and an adventurer of no small renown. Coincidentally, she is friends with the woman she is impersonating."

"What can this woman offer me?"

“Mary Gillespie once defeated a criminal operation which threatened her circus, so she possesses prior experience as a crime-fighter. Similarly, carnival skills are valuable outside of their intended use—magic tricks, knife-throwing, and animal handling are all useful in our work. Finally, her father left her with an extensive blowgun collection.”

Judex nodded. His counterpart handed him a card with an address.

“Gillespie knows you’re coming. Meet with her at once, and do all you can to flush out this killer. I do not intend to allow him to interfere with my work.”

Tony Rico was proud of himself. He’d been very thorough. No loose ends.

The lights of Manhattan shone down on him through the night-dark window of his limousine. Theaters and casinos rolled past him, overflowing with rich and poor alike. He found himself admiring his cufflinks.

“So give it to me again, boss,” Otero said, from the driver’s seat. “You bringin’ *both* of those scientific gizmos with ya?”

“This is power, Otero, for defense and offense alike. I’m not a little man anymore. Soon I’ll overtake the big guys and get me a long-overdue majority share of the pie. An’ you’ll get your cut, rest assured.”

“Well, thanks, boss. Gee, it’s really somethin’, you havin’ that super-laser *and* being able to make it so fellas can’t see ya.”

“Yeah, and it weren’t easy to get, either.”

Rico stared at his reflection in the window and thought over how it had all gone down... the first tip he’d gotten was learning about Stanford Marshall. Under the name of the Black Tiger, Marshall had used an invisibility belt invented by a pair of scientists named Stanfield and Van Dorn. The belt had worked perfectly for the Black Tiger until Rico had caught him sleeping one day.

A knife across his throat was more than sufficient. Rico wouldn’t have taken the chance to snuff him if he hadn’t believed the tip about the belt. Once he had it, and proven it worked, it had just been a matter of using it to sneak behind closed doors to learn the secrets of New York’s underworld. How he’d learned about the Czar’s rubies was a whole other deal. He wasn’t the first one to try to steal those jewels.

In addition to creeping in on fellow gangsters, Rico had also looked at laboratories for a source of profit. Blackmailing crooks was one thing, but here was the opportunity to steal secrets he could then sell to foreign buyers. He could spin world governments around his finger, if he tried hard enough—just on account of this belt and his good sense of hearing.

But one day he’d made a mark of a Professor Adam Strang. Strang was a quiet man, preferring slow nights where he could casually read a Reggie Ogden novel. But he had a history to him—his notes hinted at a caper which had been hushed up by the police. Supposedly, a criminal engineer by the name of “Sparks” had used a machine to kill people by radio control, in an effort to get his hands on the Czar’s jewels. The machine he had used was based on television technology invented by a Dr. Houghland, an associate of Strang's. Knowing Strang would never talk to a stranger, and having never been a patient sort, Tony had dragged Strang back to his hideout and tortured him for information. He wanted that death-machine—and furthermore, he planned to continue Sparks' quest for the Czar's jewels.

He knew they were around here somewhere. Out on these streets. With his last breath, Strang had revealed who owned those jewels. Other men might have paled upon hearing the name, but Rico had only laughed. His new target was armed, yes, with twin pistols—he was a keen fighter too, and he was smart as hell. But that costume he used to cow lesser men made him noticeable. He was said to have a talent for disguise, it was true, but then, there was the girl. It would be a miracle if there was a dame half as enticing as her—he'd spot her in an instant. If he hit his agents, then, in due time, he'd wipe out the big guy. He'd claim those jewels both for their financial value and as a trophy, proof of the work he'd put in to become a big shot.

"Keep your eyes peeled, Otero," he murmured, returning at last to the moment. "It's a Saturday night. He follows crime, and crime won't be staying in on a weekend..."

In the restaurant known as Rusterman's, Judex found his way to Mary Gillespie's booth. He could tell her hair was dyed, but was only to complete her startling resemblance to the Shadow's agent. They really could pass for sisters.

While he did not cloak his face in red fabric as Allard did, Judex had come to the restaurant in his dark clothing, and that, along with the look in his eyes, had given him away to Mary.

She fast proved herself an observant girl. She was pleased to hear that her old college roomie was doing well, even if she kept strange company. After finishing her beer and her cigarette, she started talking business.

"I remember hearing about Tony Rico," she said. "You hear a lot in the circus business—people gab and they think you don't listen. Rico is a small fry who wants to climb the ladder. He's mostly talk, but his ambition makes him dangerous. He's liable to do some crazy stuff if he's mad enough."

"You are unconcerned about joining me against this man?"

"Sure, I've seen chumps like him before, and knocked them over. I'm not worried here."

She began to file her unpainted nails. Her shimmering black hair trailed down her shoulder. Judex, as a professional and a happily married man, observed her beauty only aesthetically; but many other individuals in this restaurant found their heads turned by the gorgeous ringmaster. She went on:

"To give a specific example, Monsieur Judex, I've been married. Marriage is a tough trial for any woman these days, mark my words, but my man took the cake. My Jim was sweet and cute till he *had* me, and then things went downhill. You'd think after running away from a hard-swilling, hard-fisted deadbeat, I'd want to stay far from anything even somewhat similar to danger. But the opposite's been true. When your friend recruited me on account of knowing my father, I jumped at the chance. Fancy that."

"My congratulations to you, Madame, for surviving such peril."

"*Merci beaucoup*," she nodded.

Judex noticed that she was looking at something behind him, while she worked on her nails.

"Do you have any leads?" Mary asked him.

"No," he replied, "but I can tell that you do."

"Oh, a mind-reader—that's cute. I suppose I made it pretty obvious. I'm just spotting out my lead. There's a reason why I met you here of all places. This is where Rainbow Benny likes to hang out."

Slowly, Judex turned, as if sweeping the room for a waiter to flag down. His eyes locked only briefly on Mary's target, a thin, nervous-looking man. He distantly remembered an American crime file on "Rainbow" Benny Loomis, who was involved with petty horse-bet schemes. He looked back at his aide.

"What are you waiting for?" she asked. "Let's give him an interview."

The two rose and walked over to Loomis' table; he dined alone. He gulped upon seeing them.

"H-hello, Mary. I didn't think I'd see you here."

"Hello, Benny. I wonder if you can give my friend and me some information."

"Your friend...?"

"You've heard of him," she said, grinning. "Carries two automatics—prone to laughter, too. He's in disguise of course, just as I am."

"Wait, Mary, you mean, this guy—this guy is...?"

"Exactly."

Benny stared at Judex and paled.

"Please don't kill me, mister," he pleaded. "I've had buddies who've gotten your handiwork. I don't want none of the same. I'll tell you whatever you want."

"Thank you for being reasonable," Judex intoned. "We need to find Tony Rico."

"Tony Rico! He thinks he's the new Enrico Bandello. That's why he took the name Rico—his original name was Chris Jorgenson. But he might be a big shot someday if he stays as cutthroat as he is..."

"We want to know about him," Judex interrupted.

"Of course, of course... Well, I don't know where he's staying right now... He's burned a lot of his old joints when they got too hot. But he's got a limo these days—I know the plate number!"

Judex passed him a napkin and a pen, and Loomis scrawled a handful of digits. The avenger nodded and rose to leave.

"Thank you, Mrs. Gillespie, you've proven very useful. As for you, Benny—stay out of trouble."

He turned to leave, and Mary joined him. They both memorized the license number, and began to stalk their prey. They disappeared in the dream-sea of buzzing lights and rushing noises. As they departed, however, they did not notice eyes watching them from the dark.

Rainbow Benny would not be alone at his table for long. He knew he'd had too much, but he'd never seen a chair move on its own before. He heard a man sit down across from him but there was no one he could see.

"Joint's haunted," he murmured, but a voice came out of the air:

"No ghosts, Benny." He knew that voice: it was Tony Rico's. "Listen, Benny. I heard a rumor—got a lot of ears—that you had a couple of guests down here tonight. Guests I'm real interested in meeting. And I know you've been doing stoolie work. Who did you meet with, and what'd you tell 'em?"

"Tony, what's going on here? Wh-why I can't see ya...?"

"Never mind that. I'm sure you'll trust me when I say I could shoot you dead in an instant."

"I-I know you could, Tony."

"So tell me, then. What's happening?"

Benny sweated—somehow, this was terribly real. Like a lot of stoolie he wasn't a great liar, so he didn't bother trying.

"There was one of them cloak people in here. You know the one." With his hands he gestured two guns and gave a thin impression of The Shadow's laugh. "I-I told him—"

"You told him what?"

"Look, Tony!" He felt like he was screaming but his voice was weak. "He was looking for you, and so I gave him your limo's license number! But you wouldn't bump off a pal, would you? Much less a pal who's sittin' in a public place..."

There was a long pause. Because he couldn't see him, Benny had no idea if Tony was even still there. But at last he spoke:

"No, you've actually done me quite a big favor, Rainbow. You've given me a good idea. I think I'll let you live—for now. But no more squealing about me to cloak types, OK?"

"Y-you got it, Tone. You don't have to worry about me!"

There was a hint of a laugh, and for a long while Benny didn't dare to move. After long minutes, however, he reached out for where Tony's voice had come from. There was nothing but empty air.

Rainbow Benny wiped his sweat-slick forehead and lit a cigarette.

"These are the times that make a fella wanna run up the tab another six hours..."

Many hours passed, during which Judex and Mary doggedly searched the city. But even with their keen eyes, they had no luck—they could only hope that the Shadow and his lady-friend, Margo, had better chances. Of course, these sorts of investigations were often not the work of a single night.

They were ready to return to base when Mary Gillespie spotted something that made her rub her eyes in disbelief. This gesture was enough to get Judex's attention, so he scanned the street until at least he saw it—it was a short limousine, a modest one, but it was unmistakable. The license plate was perfectly right. Mary started off towards the car, but Judex grabbed her shoulder.

"Wait. The windows are too tinted to tell if someone's inside. You'd best let me handle this."

"What? Because I'm a girl? Don't forget, friend, I've got my father's blowguns."

"I insist on going first. Perhaps you could use your blowguns to cover me?"

He strode over the car. He had disguised himself as the Shadow, as per their plan, which amounted to covering his mouth with a red cloth and arranging his coat and cloak slightly differently.

He peered into the car with steely eyes, hoping perhaps to catch Rico off-guard. But it soon became clear there was no one in there. Judex's eyes narrowed. Something was wrong. He became suddenly aware of how exposed he was—how the car had been parked to place him directly under the center of the streetlight...

There was a burst of light and noise, and out of one of the nearby alleys something flew towards him. He dove out of the way and watched in amazement as part of the car turned red hot and ran down onto the street, reduced to a bubbling fluid. In an instant, the detective's mind assembled one simple fact: Tony Rico had access to a weapon unknown to the ordinary criminals.

Judex looked for any sign of the gangster, but to no avail.

A second shot rushed out of the darkness. Judex saw where it came from, but he had no idea now if Tony had been responsible for it. It seemed as though it had come out of thin air. He evaded the shot, but he needed to get close to its point of origin if he was going to figure out what was happening. It would take him a few seconds to reach that alley, and that was too long.

Mary Gillespie had been paying attention too. She dashed for the alley and was surprised when she collided with something.

"What the hell...?"

The thing in her arms struggled against her, and she punched at it.

"Listen, whatever you are," she shouted, "I've wrestled with elephants, lions, and city permit officials! I'm not scared of you!"

Just then something came out of the air—and it was made of metal. Mary couldn't see it, but it still smacked her temple. She saw stars, but refused to let go of the grip she'd forged on her invisible foe. By now Judex was over to where they were. His voice spat out hot:

"Leave her alone, Rico!"

"You won't get me, creep!" came Tony Rico's voice. "I want those rings, and if I have to pry 'em off a heap of barbecue I'll do it!"

Mary rallied her strength and looked for an advantage. She realized that she had another metal object in her hand. It seemed to curve around Rico's body. She pulled hard at it, making him cry out.

Judex's fist came in hard, seeking the source of that cry, and he connected, knocking the invisible Rico down even as Mary tore off the thing she'd seized. It was a belt—she could see it now. And she could see Rico, lying prone on the sidewalk. In one hand he held an enormous metal box of some kind, which had the grip and trigger of a handgun.

Before Mary or Judex could react, he aimed the device at Judex and squeezed the trigger.

Once more, a flash of light split the darkness. The strange bolt flew towards Judex, but he had employed a trick Allard used often: by swirling his cloak, he had made it hard to tell where his body was. The smell of burning fabric hit Judex's nose, but he was unharmed.

As he moved his body to avoid the shot, he dove towards Mary to get her out of the way. She fell to the ground, but he stood between her and Rico while she recovered.

With eyes crazed with rage, Rico pointed his weapon at Judex and fired again. The avenger dashed back, but this time, his cloak was set ablaze. He had to work his way out of it before he roasted, but as he did so he was left a sitting duck.

Suddenly, there was a sharp hiss, and something flew over his shoulder. It was a dart, and it jabbed Rico straight into his shoulder. He cried out, and Judex already knew that behind him, Mary had one of Colonel Gillespie's blowguns between her lips.

"Damn dame..." Rico murmured, as he tore the dart out. "Y-you've poisoned me..."

"Get ready to wake up in jail, Rico," Mary intoned.

But Rico growled, and raised his energy-weapon. Judex frowned and cried:

"Look out, Mary! He's not done yet!"

Rico charged at Judex and whipped the gun back over his shoulder. He laid down a crushing blow on the vigilante and, though Judex dug his heels in, he fell out of the way. Rico now had the gun pointed squarely at Mary.

"I-I can at least get the dame who busted me before they send me up..." he slurred.

His fingers inched down on the trigger. Mary Gillespie was not afraid. She closed her eyes and clenched her fists, and was ready to go out with dignity.

However, twin shots suddenly rang out, and a pair of bullets hit Rico. He dropped his death-ray at once, leaving it smashed on the pavement. His blood splashed over the innards of the machine. But even as he died, his hands reflexively squeezed the trigger, and the heat-bolt discharged towards his intended target.

Mary gave a cry and fell. Judex ran to her. Kneeling down, he saw she had been caught in the ripple of the blast striking the sidewalk. Her legs were burned, but not seriously. He looked up to where the shots had come from.

The Shadow approached him slowly; Mary's double, Margo Lane, was with him. She ran to Mary and knelt down. Mary grinned and took her friend's hand.

"Thanks for the exercise, Margo—I'm glad I took you up on it. I haven't worked out like that since my trapeze days."

"Mary Gillespie," the young woman said proudly, "I always knew you were brave, but you took it a hell of a lot better than I did my first time... and God, you got hurt doing it! We have to get you to a doctor."

"I'll be alright," Mary replied. "My uncle Leonard's in town, and he's a doc. He'll look me over without my having to sweat a bill."

Margo helped Mary to her feet. As they began to talk, Judex and his comrade looked down at the corpse of Tony Rico.

"We can't linger long," said the Shadow. "I will recover what remains of the Houghland machine, and place it in one of my warehouses. Thank you, Jacques. You've done me a great favor."

Judex did not grin—he hardly ever did, much like his friend. But there was the faintest hint of something in his voice when he spoke, and it would require a detective of their skill to discern that something.

"You could have handled this two-bit thug by yourself, yet you chose to call me over across the sea. You made me a guest in your home, which you rarely do for others."

Allard stared at him, with a particular light entering his eyes. Meanwhile, Mary and Margo were talking idly, as if there wasn't a corpse just a few feet from them. In the distance, police sirens sounded.

The Shadow locked eyes with Judex.

"I have learned that this life we live can be lonely," he said. "My associates are not my family—they must never be. But you are a part of my past. I have observed you and your wife, Jacqueline, and though I'm gladdened by your happiness, I've felt my loneliness deepen. I intend to spend time with what family I have before—"

"Before?"

And he said nothing then; for he knew what his friend spoke of. There was never a guarantee of tomorrow. But they'd bought one more, at least.

Taking up the remains of the machine, Judex and his three friends disappeared into the night. Running under the canopy of a nearby alley, they were nothing but shapes in the night. Shadows.

They say great minds think alike... This story by our regular contributor Nathan Cabaniss is echoed by that of Martin Gately, in that they both use the fascinating character of Robur the conqueror, created by Jules Verne. Like his better known counterpart Captain Nemo, Robur—whose name is Latin for "hard timber" or "oak," and, by metaphorical extension, "strength" —is a mystery wrapped inside an enigma. Verne eventually gave an origin to Nemo and belatedly had him repent on his death bed, but there was no such redemption for the would-be "Master of the World"...

Nathan Cabaniss: *Master of the Six-Gun*

The American West, 1896

The music began at roughly three in the morning.

Everything in town was closed for the night, doors locked and lamps doused... Even the whorehouse had long since gone quiet. It started as little more than a murmur in the distance, a soft hum carried gently by the wind. But the sound grew in timbre, barreling down on the town like a stampede or a freight-train, or just plain ornery tornado.

By the time the townsfolk grumbled awake, wondering just where the hell that racket was coming from, and just who the hell was staging a parade at three o'clock in the goddamn morning anyway, the crashing cymbals and blaring horns reached their crescendo.

There was no mistaking it: someone was playing Beethoven's Fifth Symphony.

Those that bothered with trousers yanked them on hastily and gathered in the street outside, but their grumbling ceased once it became apparent that the music wasn't coming from the saloon, or a traveling musical troupe, or any other earthly location; it was coming from the sky.

What appeared to be a great, black cloud descended from above—first blotting out the stars, then the half-moon. It dwarfed the town, enveloping everything in sight in its all-encompassing shadow. Everyone froze where they stood, befuddled at the impossible sight before their eyes.

Brilliant flames briefly illuminated its side, followed quickly by a series of dull thuds. A scream shot through the air, starting as a whistle before letting loose in a full-tilt banshee shriek. The roof of the stables collapsed, going up in an explosion of gunpowder and splintered wood. More screaming whistles cut through the breeze, bearing down on the town like a horde of angry train whistles...

By the time they realized what had happened, it was too late—the entire town was wiped from the face of the earth in the space it took to empty a piss-pot.

"Stay back... *I'll kill 'er!*"

A gunshot tore through the open window of the tavern, found a space in the dirt road between the sheriff's feet.

The sheriff jumped behind a covered wagon, almost losing his bladder's contents in the process. He cursed himself the allowance of a third glass of tea at lunch.

"What do you think, Reeves?" the sheriff asked the man next to him.

"Listen up in there," Bass Reeves called out, ignoring the sheriff. "You kill that woman if you want, but you might as well be signin' your own death warrant if you do. Only way you're leavin' this town alive is if you walk out here and surrender yourself."

"Are you…?"

Reeves held up a hand, silencing the sheriff.

"You want me," the voice from inside called in reply, "then you come on in and get me!"

Reeves wiped the sweat from his mustache, rubbed his stubble as he thought.

"Well?" the sheriff asked, unable to take the silence anymore.

"I'm gonna have to go in after him," Reeves said, unholstering his revolver. "Keep yelling at him—anything to keep him talking. I'll try to sneak in the back..."

"What the hell am I supposed to say?"

"Anything. Ask him about his favorite opry..."

The sheriff stared back at Reeves, in disbelief.

"This is the best plan the famed U.S. Marshal Bass Reeves has to offer? A discussion of fine arts with a wanted felon?"

"Don't you worry none, sheriff. I always get my man."

With that, he slipped away, disappearing into a back alley before the sheriff could offer any protest. The sheriff took off his hat, fanned his sweat-soaked brow. *How the hell was he going to explain* this *one if it went south?*

"Uh, say in there... What's your favorite opry?"

There was a long pause before the felon answered: "*What?*"

Reaching the back of the tavern, Reeves slipped beneath a window at the building's rear and wedged his fingers between the panes. The window gave way. He hoisted himself up into the backroom, and eased the hammer back on his revolver. He crept his way towards the front, where the felon "Devil" Bob Canyon was trading loud insults with the sheriff (and getting the better of him, at that).

Reaching the door leading into the main entryway, Reeves peeked around the corner to get a survey of the room. A fancy-dressed man was already dead on the floor, a line of red trailing down his eyes from a hole in his temple.

Devil Bob had his back turned to Reeves, yelling out the door until he was red in the face. He kept a tight grip around the woman's waist, his pistol cocked and pressed firmly into her cheek. Tears ran freely from her eyes, but she did her best to keep her sobs to herself, not wishing to draw further ire from the man holding a loaded gun to her head.

The only other person in the room was some old Granny, bundled up in a poncho and large hat with dead flowers that covered most of her face. She didn't seem especially bothered by any of the goings-on around her.

Reeves put a thumb to the hammer on his revolver and eased it back down; convinced he could now take Devil Bob in alive, he wouldn't have to bother with shooting. It would still be risky, what with the loaded gun to the woman's head, but Reeves wanted to bring the man in alive, if he could. All it would require was a sharp crack to the side of his head, and Devil Bob would be out cold.

Carefully, Reeves slid out of his boots and padded his way into the room, barefoot. Out of nowhere, the Granny shot up from the ground, as if something had suddenly startled her awake. Reeves was about to motion for her to keep quiet, but then he saw what was in her hand—a large Navy Colt revolver.

Before he could say anything, she threw the hammer back and pulled the trigger in the same blurred motion. A loud boom filled the room, and Devil Bob stiffened. His arm fell from the waist of the woman, who ran outside, screaming her head off.

The Granny knocked off her hat filled with dead flowers—turned out she wasn't a granny after all, but a man. He threw off the poncho, revealing a figure that wasn't especially big or tall in any meaningful way, but imposing all the same. He wore all black, except for the Indian breastplate of bead and bone that hung from his neck. He put his Navy Colt back in its holster on his belt, opposite from where an ornate tomahawk hung on the other side.

"Howdy, Bass," Mordecai Jefferson said, retrieving a black hat from the ground, notable for the feather of a red-tailed hawk jutting out from its snake-skin band. "Good to see you're in town... You can pay me the bounty on this feller now, and save me a trip."

Reeves stood over Devil Bob, now deader than Wild Bill Hickok.

"I been trackin' this man for near a week," he said, holding his revolver so tightly it caused his hand to shake. "Sleepin' less than three hours a night, fore-going a fire so's he wouldn't see me on his tail..."

"Well, he ain't going anywhere now," Mordecai said with a grin. "I saved us both the trouble."

Reeves hauled off and slugged him, knocking Mordecai right off his feet.

The last embers of the fire were winking out right as the sun began to sink at the horizon, coloring everything in a horrid pink sheen. The gang that made it hadn't bothered to stop and sleep for the night, only starting the fire to cook a fast meal and quickly be on their way.

A giant hand rustled through the ashes, found the butt of a thin cigar. Pinched between fingers that were each roughly the size of a railroad spike, the hand brought the cigar up to a wide-set nose that instantly recognized the scent of the man who smoked it scant hours before.

The hand threw the cigar back into the pile of ash, moved up to shade a pair of eyes hidden beneath a massive brow as they looked towards the sun setting over the horizon. The figure standing at the dying fire guessed that the men he was after had already traveled a good ten miles, if they were still riding as hard as they had been the past two days.

He'd hoped they would have stopped here and made camp, allowing him to ambush them while they slept. But alas, he wouldn't be doing any ambushing this night... The strange, hulking figure resigned himself to the fact that it would be many more days until he could catch up with them again. His sheer size prevented him from travelling by horseback, and most horses were frightened of him, anyway. Those that let him sit in the saddle couldn't carry his weight for as long as they could an average man... because he wasn't really a man. In truth, he didn't know what exactly he was. The man who might as well have been his father had called him O'Neil, and that was good enough for him.

That man had taught him everything he knew. Most importantly, he taught O'Neil how to shoot, which came in handy when O'Neil avenged the man's death after catching up with his killers. It turned out O'Neil was quite good at shooting, indeed, and soon thereafter, he took to hunting down bad men and collecting the bounties on their heads. It was an agreeable lifestyle, for it allowed him to spend most of his time on the trail—in the deserts and the mountains and the forests, away from the large gatherings of people one would find in towns or other civilized settlements. It was always a dodgy proposition whenever he'd visit such a place—because of his appearance, he was often shunned or ran out of most towns he dared step foot in.

All except for the little town of Sweetwater, Texas. The townsfolk there didn't seem to take exception to his appearance. He didn't have to wear a bandana to cover his face or pull his hat low to try and pass for normal. They didn't care that he couldn't speak properly, that he only communicated through written missives and hand gestures. The postmaster and his daughter were always friendly and amiable, and the sheriff often bought him a drink at the saloon whenever he'd bring in a wanted felon alive. He was always welcomed by the two-dozen or so citizens who called Sweetwater home with a wave and a grin, and treated well enough to make him think he might build a house there someday and settle down once he'd earned enough money.

And then, O'Neil came to Sweetwater one dusty morning to find it leveled to the ground. All of them, the sheriff, the postmaster and his daughter, the two-dozen or so citizens who were always so kind... they lay dead in the smoking ruins of their town, never to smile or wave or do much of anything else again. Reaching the burned-out ruins of the church, O'Neil fell to his stubby knees and cried like he hadn't since the man who might as well have been his father died. He'd made those men pay... he'd make whoever was responsible for this atrocity pay with the same bill of goods, dealt in hot lead.

After doing some eavesdropping at the next town's saloon, O'Neil learned of a certain party seen riding into Sweetwater right before it was burned to the ground. He didn't know if they were the ones ultimately responsible, but one thing was certain—they were a band of thieves and outlaws, men wanted on charges of robbery, murder and worse. When he finally caught them, he would see them brought to justice, and would uncover the truth of what happened at Sweetwater.

"*Whooo-wheee*," a voice called from behind, causing O'Neil to nearly jump out of his skin.

The voice echoed from a rocky outcropping next to the dead campfire. The sun was completely gone from the sky now, replaced by the snow-white glow of the moon and stars casting long shadows in the night. A figure materialized from one of those shadows, took the vague shape of a man.

"You're a big one, ain'tcha?"

O'Neil put a hand to the revolver at his belt, a large firearm custom-built to fit his oversized, stubby fingers.

"Easy now, partner," the stranger said. "We're only here to talk..."

More forms slid out from the shadows, had O'Neil surrounded before he knew it. Soft giggles tickled the night, along with sounds of guns being drawn and knives being unsheathed.

Their leader stepped into the moonlight, revealing himself to be a man with scars all up and down his body, giving off the impression that his skin was patched together like an old quilt. He grinned at O'Neil, let the hulking brute get a good look at the pistol he held in his hand.

"Me an' my pards were just curious as to why you've been doggin' us worse than a bad case a' the clap..."

O'Neil kept his hand on his gun. He tried to count the men around, do the math of how many rounds it would take, but they kept crawling out of the darkness, enclosing on him like a pack of wolves.

"Wait a minute," the leader said, getting a better look at O'Neil now that he was up close. "You ain't even a man. You're a goddamn…"

He never finished the sentence. Gunfire filled the night, followed by a deathly silence.

Mordecai Jefferson poured a generous shot of whisky into his glass and gulped it down in the same motion. He winced—the shiner on his cheek flared up at the simple act of drinking. Angered, he poured another, even more generous shot.

He felt someone approach his table at the back of the saloon. He deliberately kept his eyes on the bottle as the man pulled a chair over and took a seat.

"Best not to be around me now, Marshal," Mordecai said. "I can't be held responsible for my actions when I'm in my spirits..."

"You're rarely not in your spirits, from what I recollect," Bass Reeves said, taking the bottle from Mordecai and helping himself.

Mordecai leapt from the table, putting a hand to his Navy Colt.

"You can sucker-punch me all you like, but I will not abide another man stealing my liquor..."

Reeves met the threat in Mordecai's eyes with one in his own. "I needed Devil Bob *alive*."

"And I need my twelve-hunnerd dollars."

"That's why I'm here," Reeves said. "Got a proposition for you..."

"Not interested."

"What if I told you you'll get your twelve-hundred, plus another two afterwards?"

This gave Mordecai pause. He took his hand away from his revolver, and slumped back into the chair. "I might be a bit interested..."

Reeves tilted the bottle into Mordecai's glass, filling it to the brim.

"Before you shot him, I was hopin' to talk to Devil Bob 'bout a gang he used to ride with..."

"Way I hear tell, Devil Bob ran with many a gang..."

"Yeah, but this one's special. Towns they've been spotted riding towards have been flattened not long after."

Mordecai stopped before his glass could touch his lips.

"*Flattened?* The hell does that mean?"

"Exactly what it sounds like. Where a town once stood, there's nothing left but dead earth."

"How does an entire town get to be like that?"

"Don't know. One of the many things I hoped to ask Devil Bob."

"How many's in the gang?"

"Not sure of that, either. Another thing I hoped Devil Bob could elaborate upon."

Mordecai took a deep sigh. "I don't know. This is soundin' like more trouble than it's worth, even at thirty-two hunnerd."

"I need you on this one, Jefferson. Much as I hate to admit it, you're a good shot, and useful in a scrap," Reeves said. "Besides, I saved your life back in that affair at San Antonio, so you owe me even if I'm not payin' you."

Mordecai thought long and hard before he answered: “OK. But you’re keepin’ me in bullets and liquor for the duration of my services.”

“I’ll pay for your bullets, but your liquor’s on your own tab.”

Mordecai thought on it again before responding: “Deal.”

The grim man checked the readings from his cabin below-decks. They would be upon the next target in fifteen minutes. It was time to make the evening’s music selection. He got up from his chair and went over to the shelves of gramophone discs.

“Mozart this time, I should think,” he said aloud, to no one in particular.

He had begun to speak to himself more often these days, finding it a soothing way of sorting through his many thoughts. He would never confess as much to anyone, but he had grown to prefer this greatly to conversation with others—after all, it was easier to communicate when he didn’t have to filter his speech in a way that made it more palatable for lesser minds to understand.

He had always had trouble explaining the true extent of his ideas to the world outside. The small-minded fools of the Weldon Institute had mocked him, chased him off their campus for daring to suggest that heavier-than-air craft was the future of air travel. He had proven them wrong, of course, taking them aboard his *Albatross* and traveling around the world in a mere three weeks. Still they plotted and schemed behind his back, destroying his airship in the process. That was the problem with small-minded men—they always sought to destroy what they did not understand. “Robur the Conqueror” was the name jokingly bestowed upon him. How little they still did not understand...

Right as he was about to lower the stylus into the groove of the gramophone disc of Mozart’s *Requiem in D Minor*, there was a knock on his cabin door. Annoyed, Robur told them to enter.

His ground lieutenant opened the door, holding his grey hat in his scarred hands. They ran up and down his body, giving the man the appearance of a rag-doll that was long past its prime, held together by the last tatters of an old quilt and frayed yarn. He was a bushwhacker in the Civil War, a man so violently ill-tempered not even the rebel army would officially enlist him. William T. Anderson was so vicious in his methods that he soon garnered the nickname “Bloody Bill,” a moniker he did everything in his power to ensure was well-earned.

He was killed in the war, but his body was recovered after being buried in an unmarked grave. Wealthy Confederate sympathizers had acquired the means of reanimation pioneered by the late Victor Frankenstein, and used it to bring their cruelest son back to lead a second secession of the southern states. Those plans never came to fruition, however, and the revived Bloody Bill found himself adrift in the lawless lands of the American West—a soldier without country or cause. Robur found him entertaining a gathering of degenerates in a horse stable late one evening, fighting three starved Rottweilers barehanded for the sum of fifty dollars. He proved to be exactly the type Robur required, and before long had gathered a posse composed of former bushwhackers, bandits and other such dregs and derelicts, which he led with skillful aplomb. Robur had no love for the man or his methods, but there was no denying his results. Sometimes a rabid dog was exactly what was required to do the job.

"What is it?" Robur asked of his lieutenant.

"We've got a problem..."

Robur had little patience for suspense. "*What?*"

"Engineers found it in the munitions storage. A pound of dynamite, fuse set to go off with the first cannon shot. We hadn't a' spotted it, it woulda set off the whole kit'n'kaboodle."

Robur felt a pain growing in the space between his eyes, the first wink of a headache. *More treachery...* "The culprit?"

Bloody Bill raised an eyebrow, conspiratorial. "It's just as you thought."

Robur's lips curled downward. "Bring her to me."

The sun was just beginning to set over the horizon as the woman made her way to the observation deck.

It was rapidly growing colder, and she wasn't wearing a breathing mask, but the *Conqueror* had lowered its altitude in preparation for an attack run, so she didn't have to worry about facing the elements. Besides, she wanted one last view of the setting sun from this angle for what she was certain would be the last time.

It was a truly remarkable thing, traveling amongst the clouds. She had witnessed several take-offs of hot-air balloons before, but this was something entirely different. A mastery of the elements, seeing the world from a vantage point previously thought impossible... the view alone almost made her forget the insane mind that steered it.

He was little more than a nuisance during the affair at the Weldon Institute, but the Agency took an interest in him, nonetheless. His heavier-than-air craft was a threat previously undreamed of in the world before, and the Agency had wanted someone on the inside—someone unassuming and unthreatening. So of course they picked *her*... who else but a woman could pass through the world of men undetected? Bringing trays of coffee and cake while the menfolk talked of their secrets and plans, never once assuming the quiet secretary who refilled their teacups and picked up their dirty plates could maim them all five different ways from where she stood...

It was equally satisfying and humiliating in the same breath.

It was also a situation that was quickly spiraling past her control. Not even a scant few weeks into her tenure as Robur's secretary had the man started bombing whole towns, wiping them off the face of the Earth for little more than being inconveniently placed. She felt powerless, stranded on this hunk of flying metal with no way to contact the Agency, no way to call in the cavalry and put an end to Robur's mad scheme. In her desperation, she had no other choice but to resort to reckless action...

Just then, she felt them approach behind her.

"Ms. Adler," the Missouri-born voice called out in an even tone. "We're going to have to ask you to come with us, Ma'am."

Irene Adler didn't turn around to face Robur's scarred dog. She could still get out of this. Everything had gone according to plan so far.

"And if I don't?" she said, remaining perfectly still at the deck's handrail, her mind racing through various scenarios...

She then heard the heavy click of a revolver.

"It's not a request."

"How did you know?" she asked, attempting to stall for time.

Irene kept a derringer tucked away in her bodice, but that would prove ineffectual—bullets didn't seem to have much effect on the resurrected Bloody Bill, and there wouldn't be enough shot to deal with the posse standing behind him, anyway. *There had to be another way out...*

"The Captain had his suspicions. Been watching you extra close for a time now..."

Just then, her eye fixed to the loading dock on the platform beneath them. The rope-and-pulley system used to load cargo swayed in the air roughly eight feet from where she stood. The cargo hold was on the platform about fifteen feet above them. She finally turned to look Bloody Bill in his scarred face, deftly moving her hands to grip the railing behind her. It was a long shot, but what other choice did she have?

"Are you going to kill me?"

"Can't say as I know, Ma'am. It's up to the Captain."

"But if he ordered you to kill me, you wouldn't hesitate, would you? That's how you got your *nom de plume*, after all."

His scars seemed to flare, turning a bright red as the blood rushed to his face. "It was war. Lotsa folks do things they aren't proud of..."

"'Lotsa folks' don't take to it the way you did, though, do they? How many do you think you've killed, if you had to place a number on it? Would it be in the triple digits, I wonder?"

Without thinking, Bloody Bill marched towards her.

"I was gonna be nice about this," he said, eyes growing wide with rage. Men were so easy to manipulate, as long as you knew the right buttons to push...

With that, Irene leapt onto the railing and launched herself at the tow-line. Bloody Bill and his men watched dumbfounded as she caught both lines dangling from the pulley, and swung through the air in a circular arc. She landed right behind Bloody Bill with the grace of a cat. Before he could piece together what had happened, Irene whipped the line around Bill's throat and pushed him over the railing. She gave a wink to his men as she grasped the other end of the tow-line when it zipped by, sending her skyrocketing to the deck above while Bloody Bill plummeted, acting as her counterweight.

She pulled her derringer the moment she touched down on the loading dock. Bill's men scrambled over themselves as they struggled to pull their leader back to the observation deck. It was unlikely the makeshift hanging would do much damage to the reincarnated Bill. He had already been killed once, which made accomplishing it again something of a difficult feat. No matter—his men would still have to pull him up and cut him loose, which gave Irene precious minutes to make good on her escape.

She ran through the stacked crates that made the loading dock a maze. All she had to do was make her way to the other side of the ship, where the smaller gyrocraft were stored. If she managed to get there without further detection, then there would be nothing stopping her escape.

A heavy metal crash filled the air, and the entire vessel shuddered. Irene allowed herself a smirk. Planting the dynamite in the munitions had acted as a suitable diversion for her true intentions: sabotaging one of the four rotor-blades that kept the *Conqueror* afloat. It wasn't enough to sink the vessel right away, but it would ensure that Robur would have to give up on his next target and return to the staging grounds immediately for repair.

It was then she heard a shuffling from behind, followed by an unnatural grunt. Irene turned and nearly dropped her derringer. An enormous form sat uneasily in an iron cage that was barely big enough to hold it. The thing turned its head to look at her with the saddest eyes she'd ever seen. Irene had seen such creatures before, although never in this part of the world. It was dressed as man, but there was no mistaking it...

It was a gorilla.

"Reeves. *Reeves...*"

Bass Reeves snapped awake, pulling the revolver from its holster beneath his bedroll. Mordecai stood over him, his Navy Colt already in hand.

"What's going on?" Reeves asked.

"This is gonna sound crazy, but somethin' just fell outta the sky..."

"What?"

"Dunno what it was. There was this sound... buzz like a honeybee, but louder. I woke up and saw it fallin' right from the clouds. It was big. 'Bout the size of a covered wagon." Mordecai nodded east. "Looked like it hit the ground a few miles that way."

Reeves looked over to where Mordecai gestured. It was dark, the only sights that were visible too soft and hazy to make out by the glow of the moon. Reeves pulled himself up, felt his skin prickle in the night air. It wasn't just the temperature. It was the tingle he got every time someone was about to draw on him, or when someone snuck up on his campsite without announcing themselves...

They'd seen it for themselves earlier in the day, with their own two eyes. The blackened husk on the ground that once was a small town named Sweetwater. They hadn't caught up with the gang Devil Bob Canyon rode with, but they were following their trail. Upon seeing the desolation at Sweetwater, Reeves felt the tingle in the back of his head. No gang could annihilate an entire town in such a fashion, even if they numbered over a hundred riders. Dark forces were at work, plotting sinister ends... He felt like he was walking in a fog, seeing shadows and not getting a grasp on what they truly were; like seeing a ship on the horizon flying the Jolly Roger, only to get closer and discover it wasn't a ship at all, but rather the head of a giant sea monster.

"Better go check it out," Reeves said.

Mordecai and Reeves found a strange metal craft bent against the Earth when they rode upon the scene moments later. Wisps of smoke drifted upwards as a strange *whir-and-click* sound emanated from the thing, roughly the size of a rowboat. A pair of leather seats were placed back-to-back in the center, between a pair of odd-looking handlebars. A series of rotor-blades spun listlessly on either side of the craft, two large ones at the back and a pair of smaller ones beneath the fronts, eerily continuing in some mechanical fashion. As they approached, one snapped loose, embedded itself in the dirt near the men, causing their horses to whinny and nearly throw Mordecai and Reeves from their saddles.

"What the hell you reckon that is?" Mordecai asked, after calming his horse.

"Somethin' I'm inclined to stay back a few paces of..."

"An excellent idea, gentlemen," another voice called out from behind. Mordecai and Reeves spun around to find the barrels of three firearms trained upon them—a woman holding a repeating rifle, and a hulking silhouette a few paces behind her with a pair of especially large revolvers.

"Now," the woman said, as calmly as if she were a schoolmarm giving instruction, "if the two of you would kindly dismount, my companion and I are in need of transportation."

Mordecai shot a look at Reeves, his hand crawling over his Navy Colt. Reeves shook his head. "We don't want any trouble. Ma'am. But you can't have our horses..."

"I'm sorry, gentlemen, but I'm afraid time is of the essence. I must get a wire to the Agency office in Chicago immediately, and if I have to shoot the two of you to do as such, then so be it."

"Chicago?" Reeves asked, raising his eyebrow. "You a Pinkerton?"

"I am."

"Bass Reeves, U.S. Marshals," Reeves said, hopping down from his horse. "This here's Mordecai Jefferson, a bounty hunter in my employ. We're on the trail of a gang that's been wreaking havoc in these parts. Every town they ride through seems to be wiped clean off the land it was built on."

This gave the woman pause. "It's not the gang that's responsible. Not totally; they're just the scouting party. Robbing and looting; taking care of all the business that can be dealt with by land..."

"By land..." Reeves narrowed his eyes, confused. "What does that mean?"

The woman lowered her rifle. "It means that we should probably cease pointing firearms at each other, as we are on the same side. My name is Irene Adler."

Mordecai looked to the hulking figure, who kept both guns trained on himself and Reeves. "Tell that to your friend," he said.

Irene nodded to the silhouette behind her. Slowly, the revolvers went back into their holsters. Elongated arms touched the ground, and the brute swung over closer by its knuckles. Now able to see the thing in full, Reeves and Mordecai had the breath sucked right out of them.

Mordecai was the first to speak: "That feller needs a shave."

"Is that what I think it is?" Reeves asked.

"He is, although he's not an 'it.' His name is O'Neil, and I owe him my life."

O'Neil touched the brim of his cap to both men. Both stared slack-jawed at the oddly human gesture. There was no mistaking it: he was a gorilla, but he was dressed and had the manner of a man.

"He can't speak," Irene continued, "but he can read and write. He's quite gifted, actually. Superb penmanship."

Reeves looked back and forth between the fallen craft and the unlikely pair now facing him. "Just what the hell is going on here?"

"Nothing short of the end of the world," Irene said.

"What do you mean, ten-to-twelve hours?"

Robur was in a fury, so angry that his shouts came with flakes of spittle. Bloody Bill Anderson kept his distance—he'd already gained his captain's ire by letting the girl escape... with the beast that had earlier tried to ambush them in tow, at that. He was more than happy to see that anger redirected at the engineer currently in Robur's sights.

"You have to understand, Sir," the engineer said, unable to lift his eyes from the ground, "the damage was quite extensive..."

"You have *four hours*," Robur said, biting his words off at the end. "Make them count."

Robur called Bloody Bill's name as he spun and marched away, not bothering to pause and let his lieutenant catch up. Robur's feet clapped against the archway built into the canyon, towards his office. The sounds of hammers and smiths filled the valley, working nonstop throughout the day and night. They had established a crude base of operations there once enough capital had been raised (thanks mainly to Bloody Bill's raids on the surrounding towns), and construction of the fleet was well underway.

Bloody Bill didn't mind the noise. He was glad to be back on solid ground again. It wasn't natural, being up in the clouds like that. But, of course, there was little that was natural about Bloody Bill himself these days. The most unsettling thing was that he could *remember* dying before—the crack of gunfire and the rending of his flesh by lead balls. And then... nothing. When they brought him back, it was like waking up from a deep sleep. Hands kept pulling him up from the blackness, back into the fire and the light and the noise, when all he really wanted to do was stay asleep. But now it looked like he would never fall into that sleep again. He didn't bleed no matter how many bullets or blades tore into his flesh, and he found he could even go without eating or drinking, if he so desired. Sometimes he wondered if he could ever find that sleep again, and if he would in fact prefer that to his current circumstances...

All of which is to say that, these days, Bloody Bill was grateful for any chance to keep his feet on the ground.

"Collect your men," Robur said, stirring Bill from his musings. "I want them ready to go as soon as the ship is repaired..."

Bloody Bill perked up. The best cure for a glum mood was a call to action.

"Where you want us to ride next?"

"Ride?" Robur finally stopped, turned to look Bloody Bill in the face. "Oh no... you'll be coming with us on the *Conqueror*. The time for secrecy is at its end. Now we announce ourselves to the world..."

"That's... quite a story."

"You don't believe me?" Irene asked.

"Not saying that," Reeves said. "It's just a lot to take in."

Which was an understatement. Strange enough that he was sitting across from a gorilla that could operate a firearm; now he was supposed to believe said gorilla had escaped with this woman from an *aircraft* double the size of two man-of-war battleships. But the proof was right there, staring him in the face—the craft the pair escaped on was in shambles not even ten feet from where they sat.

"He's got how many others?"

"Only one that's operational. But he's building *twenty* others, each with its own host of smaller craft. With a force that size, there will be no stopping him—he could topple the governments of the world in days."

Reeves rubbed at his mustache, trying to make it all fit. The very act of picturing it in his mind was like trying to force a square rod in a round hole—it just wouldn't fit, no matter which angle you attacked it from. He looked over at Mordecai, who had his flask out. He shook it over his mouth, trying to get the last drops from the empty container.

"You seem to be taking all this in stride," Reeves said to Mordecai.

Mordecai screwed the lid back on his flask. "Seen a thing or two in my time," he said, putting his flask away. "Giant ships what sail on the air ain't gonna be enough to rankle me."

"It's enough to rankle me. And then some..." Reeves retrieved his hat and lifted himself from the ground. "If what you say is true, then we don't have time to dawdle."

Irene did the same, dusting off her skirts. "I quite agree. If we can get to the nearest town, then perhaps I can send a wire in time..."

Reeves shook his head. "Even if you get word to the Pinkertons, it'll be days before they mobilize. We don't have that kinda time..."

"What other option is there?" Irene asked. "The four of us can't take Robur on our own..."

"Maybe not. But maybe we won't need to." Reeves went over to his horse, and carefully undid the straps to one of his saddlebags. "At least, not directly."

"What does that mean?" Irene asked.

Reeves opened the saddlebag to let the group see its contents. Irene's eyes went wide.

"What the hell," Mordecai said. "I never figured on dying of old age, anyhow."

Robur found it increasingly harder to concentrate as the hours of the night wore into the morning. The *Conqueror* would not be ready for air until sunrise, and its captain was restless. He had virtually given up on a regular sleeping habit, and was down to two hours of sleep for every forty-eight hours. Much of this could be attributed to his recent discovery of cocaine. The "seven-percent solution" seemed to work for a certain famed Baker Street detective, and Robur could not argue with the results: when there was work to be done, it could be done in record time. His mind could make lightning-fast connections, discover and compute the solutions to problems in a flurry of blistering activity.

But it caused him considerable trouble in the odd moments of down time. Robur had taken to giving himself regular injections, even when there was no work to be done. As a result, he was constantly restless—like a machine with no "off" switch, the gears turned over and over, relentless and unceasing. He stood from his desk and went to the window behind him. Below his command station office in the valley shipyard, workers labored to bring his grand designs to life. The very first fleet of airships the world had ever seen, and they were all under his command. The world would soon be his, as well, and yet... there was an emptiness. During his most intense bouts of fevered highs, he saw himself drawing a saber and running out into the shipyard, cutting everyone down where they stood, frozen in their slow, ponderous lives. Lumbering objects in his path, preventing him from getting to where he was going and achieving true greatness...

That was the trouble: no one could *keep up*.

He stood at his perch, willing the sun to rise on the distant horizon. Like a good soldier, it did his bidding.

O'Neil shifted his position for at least the third time in the last thirty minutes. The ragged Texas landscape sent shockwaves rolling through his stubby knees, crouched beneath a blanket in the back of the covered wagon they had "confiscated" from a snake-oil salesman on the trail. It was all according to the man Reeves' plan—which, as far as O'Neil could tell, was largely made up as they went. O'Neil didn't like their chances, but Reeves was a U.S. Marshall of some repute, so he went along with it. O'Neil had his own reason for tagging along, anyway—the massacre at Sweetwater could not stand. Those responsible must be brought to justice. That, and he had grown fond of the woman Irene in the short time they had spent together. He didn't want to see her harmed.

All of a sudden, the wagon pulled to a halt. Voices carried through the canvas:

"What is this?"

"Parts and maintenance delivery," the man Mordecai replied.

O'Neil couldn't say he thought much of him—bounty hunters like that were responsible for the profession's undesirable reputation.

"I hadn't heard of any delivery..." the other voice said.

"Well, you're more than welcome to check with your foreman," Mordecai said, "but this was requested special by the captain. Don't think he'll take kindly to any delay..."

"OK," the voice said. "But we've still gotta check your cargo."

"Go on, then."

Footsteps scraped the gravel outside. O'Neil heard the canvas covering of the wagon peel back, boots clacking against the floorboards as the sentry stepped inside. O'Neil held his breath, let his body go loose beneath the blanket. Even a single twitch would be enough to give everything away. A minute passed—the sentry was taking his sweet time looking over the wagon's interior. Mordecai offered encouragement: "*Grandma was slow, but she was old...*"

"All right, all right," the sentry said.

The wagon bounced as he jumped out, and began moving again as Mordecai led the horses on. A short while later, it came to a stop once more. Mordecai dismounted the driver's seat and stepped in back.

"The coast is clear," Mordecai said. "For now, anyway."

O'Neil threw the stuffy blanket off, happy to taste fresh air again. He and Mordecai maneuvered over to the three barrels lined up in the corner. The first lid came off. Irene stood up from inside, dusting herself off.

"I'll be happy to *never* do that again," she said, giving an appreciative nod as O'Neil helped her climb out.

Mordecai got the second lid open. Reeves popped up, rolled his shoulders as he stood upright again.

"Way you steer a wagon, Jefferson, it's a miracle our cargo didn't blow us all to Kingdom Come..."

"I think I'd rather be judged by the Almighty than go through what we're about to pull off," Mordecai said.

O'Neil peeked through the canvas flap—the wagon was staged in a cavern filled with wooden crates. The sounds of metal striking metal and men shouting filled the valley. There had to have been several hundred men in the makeshift shipyard... more people than he had ever been around in his entire life. His hair prickled, and he let the flap fall back into place. He instinctively put a hand to one of the revolvers at his belt. The gesture normally gave him some measure of comfort. It didn't work this time.

Reeves went to the third barrel and threw off the lid. He dug in the straw until he found what he was looking for. Gingerly, he pulled out his saddlebag and opened it, revealing the bright red sticks of dynamite therein.

He retrieved a rolled-up fuse from a side pocket, and smiled at the other three. "All right, troublemakers," he said, "let's make some trouble."

"*Get on, you ornery cuss!*"

Bloody Bill Anderson tugged at the reins, but the horse reared back with a high-pitched *whinny*. Bill cursed again, yanked the reins forward in a tug-of-war match. He was strong as an ox these days, and managed to drag the horse to the foot of the loading ramp to the *Conqueror*, the iron shoes on its hooves screeching against the metal grate flooring...

The horse bucked back, began kicking its hind legs in every direction it could muster. Its hoof caught a worker straight to the head, knocking the man off his feet. Bloody Bill gave slack to the reins, and the horse backed off the loading ramp. It gave a defiant huff, but otherwise remained calm—so long as it was on solid ground.

Others rushed over to the kicked worker. Bill expected him to be dead, but to his surprise, they managed to get him back on his feet. His armor-plated welding helmet had a dent the size of Kentucky in it, but the worker was otherwise unhurt. Bloody Bill sighed, handed the reins to one of his men.

"Put 'em back in the stables."

His man hesitated. "Captain said he wanted the horses, too..."

"So tell him to get down here and drag their asses onboard hisself."

With that, Bloody Bill marched off. He stuck a wad of chaw into his cheek and spat the first excess into the canyon below. He looked over the *Conqueror,* docked in the staging area at the valley's peak. Engineers swung down on tow cables, welding and hammering and risking life-and-limb as they rushed to finish repairs to Robur's ship. He spat again. Much as he wanted to shoot the thing earlier, he was inclined to agree with the stubborn horse: man wasn't meant to be in the clouds.

Just then, movement caught Bill's attention. In the valley below he saw something moving. A figure flitted from platform to platform, unseen by the workers toiling away on Robur's airships, deftly trailing some kind of rope or wire behind it. Bloody Bill knelt down at the canyon's ledge to get a better look: it was a man. Bill thought it might have been an Indian at first, due to the way he was dressed, but closer inspection revealed him to be a white man.

In one hand he held a lengthy fuse; in the other, a bundle of dynamite.

Irene and O'Neil crouched in the wagon, counting down the minutes until Reeves and Mordecai had finished setting the dynamite. It was maddening, but it was the way it had to be—Irene was previously the only woman in Robur's employ, and as a result was very well known amongst the men (much to her chagrin), and O'Neil wasn't exactly the type that could blend in easily with a crowd.

Thus, the majority of the work was left to the U.S. Marshal and his partner of questionable morality. Irene couldn't say she was surprised; although the logic was sound, she once more found herself waiting on the men in her life.

O'Neil seemed to notice her disposition. He produced a pad of paper and a pencil, began writing with his stubby fingers. Irene watched in disbelief—even though she had seen him do so before, the sight was still astonishing.

He held up the pad for her to read: *Taking them a long time.*

"Setting up enough explosives to destroy the shipyard is going to take longer than they anticipated," Irene said. "You could almost set your watch to it, how often men will overestimate their abilities."

O'Neil wrote again on his pad: *Don't trust Mordecai.*

"No, I can't say I'm fond of him, either. But Marshal Reeves seems an honorable man, and if he sees fit to trust him, then that's good enough for me."

O'Neil remained unconvinced. He held up his pad again: *Maybe we should check? Just in case?*

Irene sighed, straightening her skirts as she stood. "I suppose it wouldn't hurt to pop out for a second and give a quick look-around..."

She peeled back the canvas door just enough to peek through. Satisfied that no one was in earshot, she snuck out of the wagon and went to the entrance of the cavern. Nothing appeared out of the ordinary: workers toiled away at the skeletons of airships, the valley filled with sparks and steam. She looked up to the landing platform, and that was when she saw it...

"Oh god," Irene let out in a gasp. O'Neil jumped out of the wagon just in time to see for himself: Mordecai stood on the edge of the landing platform, talking with the scarred man O'Neil had encountered previously. Bass Reeves was marched in front of them by a pair of guards; his hands were cuffed behind his back.

Mordecai nodded, and they took Reeves away.

"Who are you?"

"Land surveyor," Bass Reeves said. "I'm afraid you're in violation of several codes..."

Robur frowned as he circled around him, studying him intently. He paused at the window of his cabin, onboard the *Conqueror*. The rising sun poured in behind him, silhouetting him against the horizon outside. He looked like a giant, towering over the orange-hued landscape beneath him. Reeves couldn't say that he was terribly impressed.

"He's a U.S. Marshal," Mordecai said. He stood at the door with Bloody Bill and two other of the guards. Reeves shot him a glare, to which Mordecai only returned a self-satisfied smirk.

Robur addressed Bloody Bill: "They were planting dynamite?"

Bill nodded. "Enough to blow the whole shipyard. This'n' turned on his mate soon as we put a gun on 'im."

Robur wheeled back to Mordecai. "And why should I trust a man whose loyalty is so easily bought?"

"Keep makin' better offers than the competition, and I'm your huckleberry," Mordecai said with a grin. "Plus, you won't be able to find the others without me..."

"What others?"

"A big, hairy fella, and a woman."

Robur and Bloody Bill exchanged glances.

"*You bastard drunk son of a bitch...*" Reeves started.

"That's quite enough," Robur interjected. He studied Mordecai for a moment. "Very well, Mr. Jefferson... consider yourself hired."

He nodded at the guards, who returned Mordecai's weaponry. Reeves made a promise to himself that he would kill Mordecai Jefferson if it was the last thing he would ever do. Even if all he had to hand was a ladies' umbrella, he would find a way.

"Escort our Marshal friend to the prisoners' hold," Robur said, gesturing for the party to leave his cabin. "And when you find Ms. Adler... *bring her to me.*"

O'Neil peered around the stacked iron girders, piled one on top of another like logs in a cabin. Irene was hiding behind another pile just ahead. Satisfied that the coast was clear, she motioned for him. Awkwardly, he hobbled over, feeling vulnerable and exposed. He was never comfortable amongst large groups of people. He wasn't comfortable around people in general, if he was being honest—even the people he liked, like the town of Sweetwater, or Irene herself. When you had experienced the depths of human cruelty that O'Neil had been subjected to, it made you naturally suspicious of everyone. He always tried to see the best in those around him, and more often than not was disappointed... much as their current predicament would attest.

"There," Irene whispered, pointing to the platform ahead. A tow cable led to the other side, where the *Conqueror* was staged. "That's the best shot we have of crossing the shipyard undetected. If we can shimmy along to the other side, we'll be right there at the loading platform."

O'Neil retrieved his pad and pencil: *What then? Only three now, and no dynamite.*

"We'll have to escape and regroup; get word to the Pinkertons. It may be too late, but we have little choice now." She slung her repeating rifle over her shoulders. "Anyway, we can't worry about that; our primary objective is freeing Marshal Reeves. Come on," she said, tiptoeing her way to the tow cable.

O'Neil sighed, then nodded. He remained unconvinced, but he followed after her, all the same.

Irene slid down and grasped the line with both hands. She lifted one leg high and managed to hook an ankle around the line—O'Neil looked away to keep his modesty. Irene pushed off from the ground completely, bringing her other leg up and hooking her ankles together over the line. Taking a moment to get her balance, she began to shimmy along the tow cable, bobbing up and down like an upside-down caterpillar. O'Neil followed in her stead, feeling quite natural as his hands and feet gripped the line and worked end-over-end along the cable. They dangled nearly thirty feet in the air, silently crossing over the shipyard as workers toiled beneath them.

When they reached the point of no return, Irene felt something wet and slick. She paused to inspect her hand, saw that it was coated in a brown film of grease. Just then, her boots slipped on the cable; losing her grip, Irene plummeted towards the ground so very far below...

But just as soon as she felt the pull of gravity, she stopped just as suddenly; suspended in mid-air, almost as if she were floating. Irene looked up—O'Neil dangled from the cord by his hands, holding Irene aloft by gripping her by the corset with his foot.

As O'Neil struggled to lift Irene back to the tow cable, a worker passed by directly underneath, carrying a bundle of rebar under his arm. O'Neil and Irene collectively held their breath as the worker paused, rearranging the bundle of rebar to get a better hold. The repeating rifle's strap slipped from Irene's shoulders, began to fall right at the spot where the worker stood...

Irene got a grip on it before it fell out of reach. But just as she took hold of the rifle once more, one of her boots came loose, and plopped right on the floor in front of the worker. He looked at it curiously for a moment, before raising his head and seeing the sight directly above him. His jaw hit the floor, and he dropped the bundle of rebar in a *clang* that must have reverberated through the entire valley.

"So much for the element of surprise," Irene said.

The worker began shouting, pointing up at the strange display for all to see. The other workers stopped what they were doing, began running and shouting themselves. O'Neil pulled Irene up to his shoulders and continued across the tow cable in great, swinging arcs.

"*O'Neil,*" Irene said, gesturing below them. Armed sentries were now rushing their way, brandishing firearms. One of them fired off a shot—O'Neil felt an angry hornet buzz past his rear. More gunshots followed, the angry hornets now a full-on swarm...

Dangling from the line, O'Neil swung his feet up to his holsters and drew both six-guns.

"You can shoot like that?" Irene asked.

O'Neil looked up at her and winked. He cocked the six-guns with the thumbs of his feet and began firing down below. Irene sat up on his shoulders and pumped the lever on her rifle, joined him in firing volley after volley. O'Neil continued swinging along the tow cable, and the two of them rained death from above...

"When you're done locking him up, I got a special job for you," Bloody Bill said to Mordecai. "*Don't* bother the captain; come straight to me."

Mordecai nodded, clapped his boots together and gave a mock salute. "Aye-aye, Sir."

Bloody Bill shook his head in exasperation, then left the prisoners' hold. Mordecai laughed to himself, and opened the bars to the closest cell on the block.

The black-gloved sentries shoved Reeves in violently. Mordecai leaned in the doorway, looking smug. "Boy, oh boy," he said, "I bet I could fry up an egg on that face a' yours right about now, way you're lookin' at me..."

"Why don't you come in here and give it a try?"

Mordecai only laughed in response.

"Why'd you do it, huh?" Reeves asked. "I mean, I always knew you were a low-down, dirty dog, but even then, I never thought of you as a man who'd go against his word..."

"Only skin I worry 'bout's my own, Marshal," Mordecai said. "You oughtta know that by now." Mordecai put a hand to the tomahawk hanging from his belt. "I like to gamble, sure, but in the end, I always back the winning horse..."

In a flash, Mordecai wheeled around and whacked one of the sentries upside the head with the blunted edge of his tomahawk. In the same motion, he drew his revolver and stuck it in the face of the other. The sentry froze, his hand on his gunbelt.

"Take that hand away," Mordecai told him. He did as he was told, and Mordecai cracked him in the head with the butt of his revolver.

He retrieved the keys, and undid the cuffs behind Reeves' back. Reeves rubbed at his wrists. The two men stared each other down.

"You wanna hit me, go ahead and get it over with."

Reeves strongly considered it, but waved him off. "So I'm the winning horse, huh?"

"You saw that captain," Mordecai said. "He may have the firepower for now, but he's headed for a noose, sooner or later."

"Your loyalty is touching," Reeves said, lifting one of the sentries by the shoulders and pulling him into the empty cell. "Why tell 'em about O'Neil and Ms. Adler?"

"Only way I could figure out of the predicament without catchin' a bullet," Mordecai said, grabbing the other sentry and dragging him in. "'Sides, I figure they'd be so preoccupied with catchin' them, it'd give us a chance to get away."

"I'm sure *they* appreciate that." Reeves leaned over one of the sentries and took the gun from out of his belt. It was a broom-handled Mauser pistol—Robur certainly didn't skimp on cost. Reeves stuck it in his belt, closed the cell door and locked the unconscious sentries within. "So now what?" he asked Mordecai.

"You're good at improvising... I'm sure you'll think a' something."

Just then, a series of gunshots filled the valley outside. Mordecai and Reeves looked at each other, then rushed out of the prisoners' hold. As they made their way through the hall below-decks, a large port window shattered in front of them. O'Neil and Irene came crashing through, rolled on the floor to a stop directly in front of Mordecai and Reeves.

"Howdy," Mordecai said.

Still sprawled on the ground, Irene and O'Neil immediately turned their guns on Mordecai, who raised his hands slowly.

Reeves stepped in the way. "Much as I'm inclined to let you shoot him, we're gonna need all the help we can get..."

"The last we saw, he was leading you away in handcuffs," Irene said.

"We done kissed and made up," Mordecai replied.

Reeves offered his hand and helped Irene stand. "Mr. Jefferson has his own peculiar way, but he's back on our side. For now." Reeves shot Mordecai a glance. Mordecai only smirked.

"How glad I am to hear it," Irene said. "But O'Neil and I seem to have stepped in something of a mess ourselves..."

Gunshots pelted the airship's hull outside, began whizzing through the open window. The party ran further down the hall—O'Neil smashed open the first door they came to, and everyone piled in. It was an officer's quarters, currently unoccupied. All four took the moment to catch their breath.

"Not gonna be long 'til we have the whole of Robur's army up our ass," Mordecai said.

"I'm fresh out of ideas," Reeves replied. "They found all the dynamite we placed, and we got nothing else to hand..."

Irene paused, thinking. "Perhaps not," she said.

"What do you mean?"

"Well, we are standing in a warship," she said. "If it can level whole towns, then surely it can do the same for a shipyard..."

All four exchanged glances. Mordecai grinned.

Alarm bells sounded throughout the valley. Robur's black-gloved security force barked orders at everyone within earshot... everyone, be they soldier, shipman or steelworker, was ordered to take up arms and find the intruders. It was rumored that there were only a handful of them, but Robur wanted no chances taken—he wouldn't allow even the slightest odds that an interloper could escape and reveal his secrets to the world at large. And his men would carry out his orders without question; any of them who were caught fleeing were shot on sight, allowing his rule over his mini-kingdom to be as ironclad as his airship.

Everyone was tasked with finding the interlopers... except the small crew in the helmsman's station. Repairs to the *Conqueror* where now complete, and Robur was eager to take to the air once the present matter had been dealt with. The helmsman, his navigator and the engineer-on-duty were the only members of Robur's force specifically ordered *not* to join in on the search for the interlopers... and that was precisely how said party of interlopers were able to easily subdue and capture the station with little incident.

Mordecai finished tying the last concussed crewmember in the corner of the room. He relieved them of their Mauser pistols. "You really know how to fly this thing?"

"Well enough," Irene said, taking position at the steering column. "We should have enough time for two full sweeps of the yard. Two volleys of canonshot... you think you can manage that?"

"All that, and we'll be back in time for breakfast," Reeves said.

"After the last volley, I'll set course for the ship to crash into the valley, and meet you at the escape craft platform." She turned to look Reeves in the eye, doubtful. "We won't have much time... maybe only minutes."

"We'll make it," he said, trying to convince himself as much as her.

Mordecai went to the door and checked the hall outside. "You sure you'll be okay on your own? Once the ship starts movin', this'll be the first place they swarm to..."

"The door latches from the inside; I'll manage. Besides, it will take all three of you to work the canons."

Reeves nodded. "Let's get to it, then." He slapped Mordecai and O'Neil on the shoulders, and the three made their way to the door.

O'Neil paused. He shared a glance with Irene. "Good luck," she said.

The gorilla gave her the slightest of nods, then left with Mordecai and Reeves.

Robur watched the tiny people scuttle to-and-fro from his cabin window. They were no bigger than ants from his vantage point, scurrying about their mounds and hills like terrified children. They should be afraid... barely a handful of intruders had caused him much headache on what should have been his day of triumph. It was the woman's doing, of course. It was that more than anything that infuriated him—she, unlike so many others, was actually able to keep up. He didn't have to repeat himself to her, or bother with explanations. She did as she was told and made no mistakes. And then she betrayed his trust... It was an offence that could not stand.

Suddenly, the *Conqueror*'s rotor-blades started spinning. Robur paused... *he didn't give the order to take off.* The ship lurched forward and up—cables snapped as it rose from the landing platform and swung through the air, heading straight for the shipyard and the row of airships undergoing construction...

Robur frowned. It was *her*... he knew it, could feel it in his gut. He strapped on his belt, which held both sword and pistol. He moved to leave the cabin, but stopped, reconsidering. Robur went to his collection of gramophone discs and made a selection. He laid it in the player and let the needle fall on the disc. The horns placed all around the *Conqueror* thundered to life, blaring Wagner's "Ride of the Valkyries" through the valley.

It was a most appropriate choice, if Robur didn't say so himself.

"All right, men: we're only gonna get one shot at this..."

Bass Reeves gripped the lanyards to two cannons, one in each hand. O'Neil and Mordecai both did the same on the starboard side—eight cannons each lined either side on the deck of the *Conqueror*. Music had started playing, loud enough to fill the entire valley. It felt like an ill-omen to Reeves, a sign that something was deeply wrong, but there was no turning back now. They were so close to being done; the task of bringing Robur down for good was now finally in reach...

Steering the ship below-decks, Irene was bearing the ship down on the yard below; on cue, she swooped down and to the left, exposing the cannons on the starboard side to the ground below. The partially-built airships came in range, lined up neatly in a row; almost as if they were arranged for target practice...

"Now!" Reeves cried, and pulled the lanyards to his cannons in quick succession. O'Neil and Mordecai did the same: the *Conqueror* shuddered as plumes of fire and white smoke ejected from its side. The airship skeletons beneath erupted, sending bent steel and flaming detritus flying in all directions. Irene brought the ship up again, and hooked in the air...

"All right," Reeves yelled to the others, "let's finish 'em off..."

The three ran over to the port side, but where stopped by the crack of gunfire. A bullet ricocheted off the cannon's hull before Reeves could take hold of its lanyard—all three turned to see Bloody Bill Anderson on deck, with smoking revolver in hand. Nearly thirty of his men lined up behind him, all armed with rifles, shotguns and various pistols. “Hate to interrupt a party what I ain’t been invited to,” he said, “but I’m afraid the party’s over now.”

“I’ll distract ’em,” Mordecai said. He pulled his Navy Colt and tomahawk, and leapt into the crowd with a yell...

The *Conqueror* jerked in the air as the first volley of cannons went off. Irene held steady to the steering column; the ship creaked as she brought it back on-course, lifting it up to swoop down again for the second volley. It was a remarkable feat of engineering, able to turn its massive weight on a dime. She would give Robur credit for that much, at least...

The pounding at the door continued; a veritable army of Robur’s men shouted and threw themselves at the locked door, but it held firm. All Irene had to do was the steer the ship in another sweeping arc and complete the destruction of the shipyard. Beyond that, she didn’t know what the future held for her... she didn’t know if she would even *have* a future.

She managed to turn the ship around in a complete arc, placing the port side cannons in range to finish off what the starboard side began; hoping against hope that O’Neil, Reeves and Mordecai had enough time to get into position again...

Suddenly, the pounding against the door stopped. Irene halted as she heard what sounded like a faint sizzle. A muffled voice called out on the other side of the door: “*Fire in the hole!*”

She had only a second to get out of the way as the door blew off its hinges in an earsplitting boom...

Bullets bounced off the cannon in front of him as O’Neil knelt behind it, reloading his six-shooters. The cannon was barely big enough to provide cover for his large frame, but it was all he could manage to do as all hell broke loose on deck of the *Conqueror*...

Ahead of him, Reeves did the same, taking the odd opportunity to break cover and fire into the crowd whenever he got the chance. Mordecai was still in the midst of their attackers—having expended all three of his revolvers, he went to work with only a knife and tomahawk. Covered in blood from head-to-toe, it was hard to tell whether it was Mordecai’s or his enemies’...

The three of them had managed to whittle down their numbers, but the force was still overwhelming. O’Neil looked below—the shipyard was almost in range again. He rapped a six-shooter against the metal of the cannon, getting Reeves’ attention.

Reeves nodded, motioned for O’Neil to provide covering fire while he let loose the first of the cannons. The gorilla popped up from behind cover and let loose with his modified six-shooters—the blast from each was so big it was enough to knock a normal man right off his feet. Reeves got into position at the first two cannons, taking both lanyards in hand while O'Neil's six-shooters boomed...

Right as he was about to pull the lanyards, the port-side exploded in a hail of gun-fire. O'Neil and Reeves were forced to leap away as the cannons were summarily torn apart, the shells exploding from within their own barrels. O'Neil and Reeves gathered themselves in time to look up, and both stared unbelievingly at what was bearing down on them...

Robur flew a two-man gyrocraft, with another following directly behind. At the back of each, a gunner was positioned, wielding a gas-powered Gatling gun to devastating effect. Bullets washed over the deck, annihilating everything in sight; several of Bloody Bill's men were caught in the crossfire. O'Neil and Reeves returned fire, but the deft gyrocraft were too quick for their bullets.

Robur and the other swept over them, hooked in the air to make another attack run. O'Neil and Reeves looked at each other for the briefest of seconds, helpless... there was nothing they could do. They were outmatched and outgunned in every conceivable way. All they could manage to do was dive for cover as the gyrocraft pelted the deck again with another devastating blast from their heavy guns.

But, as the flyers passed by, something most unexpected occurred: Mordecai leapt from the deck, caught the blade of his tomahawk on the landing skis of Robur's gyrocraft as it swooped over the deck of the *Conqueror*. O'Neil and Reeves watched in disbelief as he swung wildly from the craft, carrying him up and over the side of the airship...

The men rushed the helmsman's station as soon as the door was blown open. Smoke and dust filled the air, blotting their vision; they cautiously edged their way inside, rifles up and at the ready...

Two shots cracked from above—the first two in the station each dropped with a thud. Irene swung down from the ceiling; upside-down, she took aim with two Mauser pistols and made quick work of the rest of the guard. She unhooked her knees from the rail in the ceiling above and flipped to her feet, again taking aim with the Mausers—no one was left standing.

Irene dropped the guns and went back to the steering column in time to bring the *Conqueror* down for the second cannon volley... except, nothing happened. The airship sailed over the remaining ships in the yard harmlessly, with nary a thing dropped on them.

She went to the periscope at the rear of the room, connected to the deck above. Peering through it, she saw what looked like hell itself: bodies stacked upon one another, the deck holed like a piece of Swiss cheese. O'Neil and Marshal Reeves were pinned down by Bloody Bill and his remaining men, and damned Robur was flying the combat gyrocraft overhead, turning his guns on friend and foe alike... She turned the periscope over to the port-side, felt her heart sink—all the cannons where destroyed, now rendered totally useless.

Irene leaned back from the periscope, frozen with indecision. What was she going to do now? The shipyard was already burning, but enough remained of the in-progress airships to continue construction once the fires were put out. There was only one option now, Irene realized with cold determination. She retrieved a rifle from one of the fallen men, and went back to the steering column. She steered the ship upwards again, in preparation to bring it down for another attack run. The last run the *Conqueror* would ever make...

Having gained the appropriate altitude, she set course for the shipyard below. She slid the rifle into the wheel, locking it into place. It would be precious minutes until the *Conqueror* would come crashing down on all that Robur had built, rendering it little more than ash and rubble.

She left the helmsman's station, praying there would be enough time...

Everything was spiraling out of control so fast, Reeves barely had time to process it...

The *Conqueror* was rising into the sky once more—Reeves had no way of knowing whether it was Irene's doing or not. Separated on opposite sides of the deck, he and O'Neil took potshots at the other flyers as they passed by, but were ultimately forced into cover again by the barrage from their gas-powered Gatling guns. Even worse, they could do nothing as they watched Mordecai dangle from Robur's gyrocraft, swaying perilously like a snake that had latched its teeth into a vulture as it flew away...

"Well, well, well," a voice called out from behind. Reeves turned in time to see a figure emerge from the fire and the smoke...

"Bass Reeves, the slave turned lawman," Bloody Bill continued, showing his teeth in a yellow grin. Reeves didn't give him a chance. He flicked his Mauser up and pulled the trigger. The pistol clicked; it was empty.

Bloody Bill drew a machete from a scabbard at his side. "Want you to know, boy: I'm gonna enjoy this."

Reeves threw away the Mauser, cracked his knuckles. "Not half as much as me..."

Bloody Bill lifted his machete. Reeves had nothing but his hands.

Robur yanked the controls violently back-and-forth. The gyrocraft rocked from side to side in a dizzying whirl of motion. He looked below and frowned. The intruder was still clinging to the skis, hanging on with the zeal of an unwanted tick.

He maneuvered the controls again—the gyrocraft plummeted in a diving spiral. It was an extreme response, but Robur had little choice. He had already given up the *Conqueror*—better to lose one ship than the entire fleet. The damage already dealt was extensive, but not disastrous. Robur could still turn the tide of this day to his advantage, still rebuild what was left, even if he had to destroy his own flagship to do so... It was infuriating, but Robur decided to focus that fury to complete the task at hand. It was only four intruders... more insects in his way, considerably deft flies in need of swatting.

He brought the craft out of the spin and leveled out once more, sure this time that he would finally be rid of his hanger-on. Gunshots cracked from the rear—Robur turned behind him just in time to see the man wrestling with his rear gunner over a pistol. They rolled to the very back of the craft, dangerously close to the rotor blades. Robur saw the events mere milliseconds before they happened: the man kicked his gunner up into the spinning blades. The gunner's head came off cleanly, spinning away into the distance like a child's rubber ball...

Robur locked the controls in place to continue flying straight, and drew his pistol. He had come to understand a universal truth that never ceased to prove itself to him at every turn: *if you wanted something done right, you had to do it yourself.*

He spun and took aim, but was caught off-guard when the intruder drew a knife and threw it straight at him. The pistol leaped from Robur's hand, fell away into the abyss. No matter—as a gentleman, Robur preferred combat by sword, anyway.

He drew his saber, and lunged at his would-be marauder. The man was armed only with a Native American tomahawk, and although he had little in the way of style or form, his sheer fearlessness kept Robur from dealing the killing stroke.

Tiring of the sport, Robur decided to end the duel in the simplest manner available to him: he kicked the man square in the chest, sending him plummeting to the burning earth below...

O'Neil grunted, hoisted himself up further on the support beam. The four rotor-blades that kept the *Conqueror* aloft were stabilized by additional beams—a complex framework of steel girders that allowed the rotor-blades to shift direction without fear of toppling over. O'Neil was almost at the summit of the supports, his fur being whipped around by the massive wind created by the spinning blades as if he were caught in a hurricane. He had to reach the summit, grab hold of one of the cables that held the supports together...

The situation had devolved into a veritable mess. Watching helplessly as Mordecai dangled from Robur's gyrocraft, O'Neil knew he had to do something to help. It was true that O'Neil held little love for the man, but they were still partners—pards on the trail together—and you didn't leave a trail-mate behind.

With a final grunt, O'Neil reached the summit. He had only a moment to get his bearings. The gyrocrafts were fast approaching; O'Neil's timing would have to be exact. He gripped one of the support cables in his rough-skinned palm, and put the barrel of his six-shooter against the iron cord. He waited for the nearest gyrocraft to be in reach, and then pulled the trigger.

The cable snapped with a metallic whip, and O'Neil went swinging out over the open air. The gyrocraft flew by right underneath as his path reached the end of its pendular arc—he let go of the cable and landed directly in the center of the craft. The gyrocraft bobbed wildly at the added weight; O'Neil gripped the sides to prevent tumbling over. The gyrocraft soon steadied, and the pilot and gunner took notice of their new passenger. They froze at the sheer sight of him at first, but soon drew their pistols... O'Neil merely swiped his massive arms in a circular arc, knocking both men free of the craft and sending them careening to ground below.

That left O'Neil on his own, hurtling through the air at a dizzying speed on a foreign craft. He crawled to the pilot's seat, wrapped his enormous hands around the twin control handles. O'Neil had watched Irene operate a similar craft when they made their previous escape... he figured he could manage it well enough.

He tried shifting the controls forward, and found himself rapidly descending. Pulling back brought the gyrocraft back into elevation. He lowered the left control, and the gyrocraft hooked left. Having more or less the gist of it, he steered the craft toward Robur's, which was higher up, just ahead of him. Mordecai had managed to pull himself onto the gyrocraft, and now, amazingly, was dueling with Robur as it flew. Robur got the better of him, though, and shot him off the craft with a single kick...

O'Neil yanked back on the controls, lifting his craft up to where Mordecai was falling. He was rocketing towards him, set to pass overhead and get chewed up by the gyrocraft's rotors...

But O'Neil lifted a hand from the controls, grabbed Mordecai by his belt just as he zipped by overhead. He set him down in the craft behind him. Mordecai pulled himself up and caught his breath. He considered O'Neil in the pilot seat for a moment. "Still not the craziest thing I've seen," he muttered.

Ahead of them, Robur regained control of his gyrocraft. Mordecai turned to look behind him, and saw the gas-powered Gatling gun on a rotating platform. Mordecai got up and grabbed hold of it, quickly familiarizing himself with how it moved and where the trigger was.

"Hey," he called out to O'Neil, "get us closer to the bastard!"

O'Neil turned and saw Mordecai at the Gatling gun. He gave a quick thumbs up, swung the controls to steer them in Robur's direction. Mordecai whipped the gun towards Robur's craft, lined up his shot as best as he knew how. He depressed the trigger, and the gun went wild—Mordecai almost shot up their own craft as he regained control of it. By the time he got the Gatling gun lined up again, Robur had seen their craft on his tail. He began to swerve his craft all through the sky—try as he might, Mordecai's bullets couldn't catch up with Robur.

Mordecai tried a different tact: he pulled the Gatling gun way ahead of Robur's craft, leading his shot the way you would for a running animal in the distance. Anticipating Robur's flight-path, he depressed the trigger again, unleashing another stream of bullets. This time the barrage hit home—the rotor-blades on Robur's craft were destroyed. His gyrocraft went into a tailspin, spun right into the thick of the flaming wreckage of the shipyard.

Mordecai let go of the Gatling gun, and slumped down on the platform. He called out to O'Neil: "I sure hope you know how to get us down from this thing..."

O'Neil hoped he would, as well.

Reeves lost count of how many blows he landed on Bloody Bill during their melee. Haymakers that would have laid out normal men seemed to do little against his scarred combatant. Reeves had felt the bite of Bill's machete during the fight, but otherwise managed to avoid serious injury thus far. He didn't think he'd be able to keep it that way for much longer; already fatigue was setting in and making him sloppy...

In desperation, Reeves brought a knee up into Bloody Bill's crotch. It was a dirty move, but when it came to life and death... well, you could be dirty or you could be dead.

It seemed to produce the desired effect—while Bill was otherwise incapacitated, Reeves grabbed his wrist, forced his own machete right into his scarred chest.

Bill stumbled back a few paces, looked down at the machete like it was a splinter in his thumb. He looked back up at Reeves and, with a grin, plucked the machete right out of his chest.

"Gonna take a whole lot more than that, boy..."

Reeves stumbled into something as he backed away... it was a cannon, blown out of its perch by the gyrocraft earlier. Except this one was still intact—with its barrel pointed right at where Bill was standing.

"How 'bout this?" Reeves said, grabbing the lanyard at the cannon's end. Bloody Bill's yellow grin suddenly disappeared. Reeves yanked the lanyard, and the cannon jumped.

Bloody Bill Anderson was swept right off the deck of the *Conqueror*, went sailing into the air as he was carried away by the cannonball. As he watched Bloody Bill drift into a speck on the horizon, Reeves felt something behind him. He turned to see Irene, dirty and rundown and with her skirts all in tatters, but otherwise unharmed. They said nothing as they watched Bill ride the cannonball for several miles, before finally hitting the ground and exploding.

"You think he survived that?" Reeves asked.

"If he did, he's going to feel it in the morning."

Reeves smiled. "I can't believe we pulled it off..."

"Don't get cocky yet," Irene replied. "I've set the course for the *Conqueror* to crash into what remains of the shipyard."

Reeves didn't say anything in response. The two of them ran along the deck to the escape crafts—a store of gyrocrafts staged just below the main deck, accessible by ladder. Neither Reeves nor Irene bothered with the rungs, instead sliding down by the sides. Irene showed Reeves where to sit in the escape craft, then quickly unlatched the bindings holding it in place. She jumped in the pilot's seat and started the rotor-blades, as the ground below reached up, looking like a massive boulder bearing down on them, crushing all in its inescapable path...

They lifted off from the *Conqueror*, unsteadily. Irene pulled the control handles back as far as they could go to carry them as high as possible. Reeves looked behind in time to see the bow of *Conqueror* bend as it crashed into solid ground. A rending, metallic shriek filled the valley as the mighty airship collapsed on itself, then went up in an awesome column of flame. The flames expanded ever outward, getting closer and threatening to overwhelm their tiny escape craft. Reeves felt the heat on his face, as if he'd been locked in a stove with no hope of escape. Irene continued climbing, fighting for every inch the craft would allow...

The flames singed the rotor-blades in back before dissipating into the air, leaving behind a cloud of smoke through which nothing could be seen.

Irene set down the escape craft, the landing skis scraping along the dirt before coming to a halt. Reeves climbed out of the passenger seat, thought to himself that he was never more thankful to be on solid ground.

"Fancy meeting you here..."

Reeves and Irene turned to see Mordecai and O'Neil stumble away from a wilted gyrocraft. "You managed a better landing than that 'n'," Mordecai said, nodding at O'Neil. The gorilla snorted, looked away.

All four turned to look at the valley behind them. A wall of black smoke stretched high into the air, giving the otherwise clear blue sky the appearance of an overcast, cloudy day. Already they saw masses of people gathered together, survivors escaping into the surrounding landscape.

"Is it over?" Mordecai asked.

"It is for now," Irene replied. "Although I suspect the future will hold both wonders and terrors to make the likes of this pale in comparison."

"I sure hope I'm not around to see it," Reeves said.

They watched the valley smolder in the distance for some time. Finally, O'Neil broke away. He held out his hand to Reeves, who promptly shook it. "You're a fine lawman, O'Neil," he told him. "I'm glad we had you."

"You make for fine bounty hunter, too," Mordecai said. "You ever wanna partner up, look me up sometime." O'Neil grunted, gave Mordecai no further acknowledgment.

He approached Irene, swallowing a lump in his throat.

"I suppose this is it, then?"

O'Neil nodded, finding it hard to look her in the eye. "You're the best I've known," Irene said, holding out her hand, "human or otherwise."

He took her small hand in his, dwarfed in comparison, and gave it a gentle kiss. With that, he hobbled away, disappearing behind a rocky outcropping. They saw nothing more of him.

"What a sad, strange, beautiful creature," Irene said.

"What about you?" Reeves asked of Irene. "Back to the Pinkertons?"

"I think my time as someone else's employee has come to its natural conclusion," Irene said. "On to another life now, I suppose. Perhaps I'll travel across the Atlantic, and visit old friends..."

She climbed aboard the escape craft, and strapped herself into the pilot's seat.

"Can I offer either of you gentlemen a ride?"

"Much appreciated, Ms. Adler, but if it's all the same to you: I think I'd rather keep my feet on the *ground* from this point on."

"I go where he goes," Mordecai said, "seein' as he owes me money."

"Very well." Irene started the rotor blades, retrieved a leather skullcap and a pair of goggles beneath the seat. "Perhaps we shall all cross paths again."

She lifted up from the ground, and flew into the horizon. Mordecai and Reeves gave a final wave, and watched her until she was sucked up by the hot, wavy air at the edge of the world.

"That enough to earn me my thirty-two hunnerd?" Mordecai asked.

"How 'bout I buy you a drink, instead?"

Mordecai shook his head. "*Figures...*"

Epilogue

The last of the survivors of Robur's airship-yard evacuated just as the sun was setting. They had gone through the wreckage, salvaging what they could; hoping to have something to show for the months they'd spent toiling away at the behest of a madman. They counted their lucky blessings, and promptly got the hell out of there.

It was when they had all gone and the valley grew silent and still that a mound shuddered in the desolated landscape. From out of the rubble and piles of ash, a figure rose. He brushed himself off, and looked over the smoldering ruin. Years upon years of work, and it had been lain to rubble in a single afternoon.

But no matter. For all that he had lost today, it was little more than a minor setback. A nuisance... another challenge that, given time, he would master like all the rest. Like he did before, like he would do again until the world recognized him for what he was: a conqueror.

He would rebuild from this. From these ashes, Robur would build a Terror the likes the world had never seen...

In this story, Matthew Dennion has chosen to tackle one of our favorite characters of all time, Erik, the Phantom of the Opera, in his true form and not the diluted doppelganger that appeared in the eponymous musical. For such a popular figure, we have had relatively few stories featuring Gaston Leroux's immortal creation, but we will recommend to our readers Kim Newman's "Angels of Music" sequence (in Vols. 2 & 4), Rick Lai's "The Tomb of the Veiled Prophet" (in Vol. 12), and our own "His Father's Eyes," published as a bonus story in our translation of the original novel...

Matthew Dennion: *Doctor's Note*

Journal of Dr. Abraham Van Helsing, London, December 1st, 1878

Today was the first day of the inaugural physicians' conference at the prestigious Royal College of London. The size and diversity of the conference is truly astounding. Later, Professor James Moriarty will be giving a lecture on the possibility of meteors and asteroids bringing unknown diseases from space to Earth. I shudder to think of space presenting us with dangers as we already have more than enough of them to deal with here on Earth.

The next day, Doctor Henry Jekyll, a brilliant young man whom I briefly met in school as I was finishing off my doctorate, is scheduled to be giving a lecture on brain chemistry. This is a field in which I am extremely interested. I am looking forward to attending his talk and learning what this brilliant man has discovered. There are numerous lectures being held on nearly every field of interest to the medical community. I doubt that I shall have time to attend every one of them.

In addition to the knowledge and insight I hope to gain from the conference, I was also fortunate to find a friendly face in the crowd in the form of young Doctor John H. Watson. He was a student of mine last year and recently graduated as a surgeon himself. I was sad to hear that, after the conference, he planned to join the military as a field medic. John is both intelligent and brave. It concerned me that he would place his life in such danger. However, I must also consider the perils that I often face myself. The horrors that John will soon face on the battlefield seem tame in comparison to the creatures that I find myself hunting.

In truth, aside from the conference drawing me to London, there have been several murders which have occurred in the city where bodies have been found drained of blood. While one should never jump to conclusions, this is a clear sign of the presence of vampires in the city. It was these reports, as much as the medical conference, that have brought me here.

Knowing my expertise in blood-borne diseases, John asked me about these exsanguinated bodies. He said there rumors about a circus that had come to town just as the bodies started to appear. He went on to indicate that there was a much lauded sideshow of freaks that was part of that circus, and the people of London felt as if some of the ghoulish characters in that freakshow may somehow be responsible for these deaths.

I reminded him that, as doctors, we, of all people, should understand that the performers in such sideshows are most likely humans afflicted with rare and horrible medical conditions. They deserve our understanding and compassion more than our suspicions. While I do believe this to be the case with most traveling performers, I would be remiss if I did not admit that I had come across the forces of evil using a traveling show as a means to enter towns, take the lives they needed, and then move on.

It was only a few years ago that I came across Cooger & Dark's Pandemonium Shadow Show. I had originally thought it to be a band of vampires. They may well have been, but they were also different from any vampires that I had encountered before. While I was able to drive them away from the town it had preyed upon, I was unable to slay the enigmatic Mr. Dark, or any of his followers. I believe that particular carnival may have fled to America, but at the current time, I am unable to say for sure.

Knowing John's curious nature, as well as his attraction to mystery and danger, I offered to accompany him to that circus after the day's lectures. He quickly agreed. Tonight's actions shall serve several ends: first, I shall get to spend time with a friend; second, I shall either discover a lair of vampires, or at the very least, help a group of unfortunate people who have found a way to make a living off their misfortunes.

I shall go prepared for the worst and, should I find a nest of vampires, I shall return the following day and deal with them under the protection of the sun.

December 2nd, 1878

The trip that John and I had made to the circus was certainly enlightening. As I had suspected, there were people there with numerous congenital anomalies. As we walked through the fairground, we had a wonderful discussion about my work in pathogens and their relations to the various deformities afflicting the performers.

Of particular note was an acrobat and knife-thrower who sat behind bars. He appeared to be just under twenty years-old, but his age was difficult to determine due to the truly horrific appearance of his face.

While the notion that the killings may have been carried out by one of the performers went against my initial instinct, I had to admit that this boy's face did bear some resemblance to the disturbing faces I had seen on numerous vampires just as they were about to feed.

Furthermore, the boy's skill with throwing knives as well as the agility and strength he displayed during his performance seemed almost superhuman, which added to my suspicions that he may indeed be a vampire. In order to test this theory, I momentarily turned away from his cage and checked a small mirror I carry with me at all times, in order to determine if an individual is a vampire or not.

I tuned my back to the cage and angled the mirror so that I could see the performer. To my relief, I was able to see his reflection and concluded that his appearance was simply an unfortunate deformity and his skills natural talents.

As I turned around, I noticed a tall man with dark hair and a lithe blonde woman standing in front of the performer's cage—two persons whom I had not seen in my mirror!

A quick double check in the mirror confirmed that these two did not cast a reflection.

I approached the cage where John was still watching the performance when I heard the woman refer to the man as "Angelus." Of course, I had heard of the vampire Angelus and his sire, Darla. Their savagery was second only to the Vampire Lord Dracula himself.

I heard Darla comment that the performer was not one of them.

I was intrigued that the vampires had also thought the acrobat was one of them. I found myself staring at them when Angelus turned and looked at me. Luckily, I was saved when John asked me if there was any chance that the performer's blood could have caused his deformity. His question allowed me to subtly shift my attention back to him and speak about blood types. and how mixing different types could cause genetic defects.

The rest of the night, we made our way around the circus. I did my best to keep the vampires in my sight, while at the same time avoiding their detection.

After following them for roughly an hour, I saw the horrific couple enter a hotel on the outskirts of the fairground. It seemed as if they were not part of the circus, but were following it so that the murders they committed could be linked to the circus, diverting suspicions away from themselves.

With my suspicions confirmed and their nest located, I was ready to act the next day.

December 3rd, 1878

Today's events turned out to be much more interesting and enlightening than I could ever have possibly imagined.

After breakfast, I met John once more and we attended the lecture of Doctor Jekyll. His research was truly groundbreaking. He hypothesized that by altering the brain's chemistry, he could remove the evil urges that all men harbor.

Many of the doctors there scoffed at the idea. Sadly, many in my profession are closed-minded when it comes to anything outside of what has already been established. I, however, was intrigued by Jekyll's findings, which, combined with my own research, could potentially lead to a cure for vampirism.

As curious as I was to engage in a conversation with him after the lecture, I had to excuse myself from John's presence to address the threat posed by Angelus and Darla. Knowing of their savagery, I had my doubts as to whether I could slay them, even with the aid of daylight.

I returned to my room and was preparing my arsenal when I suddenly saw the deformed acrobat from the circus standing in my room. He introduced himself as Erik. When I asked him how he had found me, and entered my room so quietly, he replied that he had been trained as an assassin, so these were easy tasks for him.

His skills had also allowed him to overhear my conversation with John the day before, and he had come to ask if I could possibly help him with his deformity. I told him that I might, although I could make no promises, to which he replied that he would be unable to pay for my services.

This presented a unique opportunity. Erik was clearly far more skilled than most humans. I told him that I was planning to slay a nest of vampires. To my surprise, he took the revelation of the existence of vampires without much surprise. I offered him the opportunity to join me in this mission as payment for my services.

Erik agreed to assist me, even though I made sure to explain to him the dangers involved. He reasoned that, if I died, I would be of no help to him. He also observed that, if these vampires were following the circus, they represented a threat to him and his fellow performers; so he felt he had more than a vested interest in seeing them destroyed.

Bringing Erik with me turned out to be much more fortuitous than I would have thought. In addition to Angelus and Darla, there were six other vampires in the nest. Erik fought them all with a skill and ferocity that rivaled that of the vampires. He slew three of them himself and nearly managed to slay Angelus, before Darla got the better of me and offered to trade my life for her lover's.

Erik agreed and the two vampires escaped into the London underground. Despite losing them, Erik and I had slain the rest of the nest and thus freed the circus from their curse.

Erik escorted me back to my room and I asked him if he could return after I had a few hours rest, at which point I would start researching his condition.

December 4th, 1878

I was unable to find any traces of Angelus and Darla. Despite my failure, today was another amazing day in terms of my work as a doctor.

Erik's blood helped to confirm my hypothesis on different blood types and their possible effects on a fetus. It seems that his condition is due in part to his blood type being so different from that of his mother that her body's natural defenses attacked his when he was still in her womb; that, at least partially, caused his deformity.

However, while this information can be helpful in preventing such afflictions in future pregnancies, I doubted it would be of much use to him now.

Since one form of blood type had attacked Erik as a fetus, there was a chance that the infusion of a different blood type might help to lessen the severity of his deformities by directing his body to heal the worst of them. But I am skeptical that this will be the case.

Despite my feelings, I gave Erik my word that I would try my blood transfusion process on him. I will document the treatments and ask John to review my work to make sure my findings are as free from bias as possible.

December 8th ,1878

After several days of treatments via blood transfusion, the effects on Erik's afflictions have been minimal at best. It seems that, no matter how much blood I infuse into him, his body produces more of the wrong blood type and negates any positive effects arising from the transfusion. John's review has confirmed that this is indeed the case.

I think that, to prevent his body from continuing to produce that wrong blood type, we may need to change something in his brain—but this is a matter far beyond my field of expertise.

While Erik was frustrated by our lack of progress, I have informed him that my findings will help to revolutionize blood transfusions and save countless lives. As this altruistic concept seemed to him Erik no happiness, I suggested that Doctor Jekyll's work in altering brain chemistry may be able to produce the necessary adjustments that we seek.

I have agreed to introduce him to Jekyll and share my work with him in the hope that he can find a successful treatment where I could not.

December 10th, 1878

Today, I said goodbye to John as he was required to report to his new post with the military. I told him I would miss his company and wished him the best of luck.

After seeing him off on his train, I went with Erik to meet Doctor Jekyll. It is such a shame that he must wear a mask when traveling through the city, but I understand the pain he would suffer as onlookers would be repulsed by him, or scoff at his deformity.

Fortunately, Doctor Jekyll was fascinated by Erik's case and eager to work with him. I presented him with my current research on blood transfusions and my findings. He believed he might be able to change Erik's brain chemistry and thus change the type of blood that organ is directing his body to produce.

As much as I would like to stay and see if Doctor Jekyll's efforts are successful, I must continue my work in the battle against evil. While Angelus continues to elude me, I have become aware of a being known as Akasha. I have read about this creature being alive since the times of ancient Egypt. If my suspicions are true, she may be the oldest vampire in the world.

I thanked Erik for his help and wished him well. I offered him the opportunity of joining me in my mission after he completed his treatments, regardless of the outcome. He replied that he was tiring of the circus, but his true love was music, and he felt that his pursuit of that would be his only path to fulfillment and happiness.

I hope Erik's association with Doctor Jekyll will benefit them both and lead them to unlocking secrets which will help make the world a better place.

Journal of Doctor Henry Jekyll, London, December 10th, 1878

It seems as if fortune has smiled upon me! The esteemed Doctor Abraham Van Helsing has brought his research to me, as well as a fascinating subject with which to experiment on. The subject in question is a circus performer known as Erik. According to Van Helsing's research, he had a significantly different blood type from his mother which caused her body to attack his when he was still *in utero*, thus causing extreme deformities.

Van Helsing has hypothesized that Erik's afflictions may be remedied to some extent if his blood type was to change to one closer to his mother's. But the issue which he faces was that Erik's brain would instruct his body to produce the same wrong blood type, thus counteracting Van Helsing's treatment.

This presents an excellent opportunity for me to study my hypothesis that good and evil are not mere moral constructs but actual physical manifestations caused by the release of certain chemicals in the brain.

Thus the chemicals in Erik's brain which caused his unique blood type triggered his mother's reaction to him, her body detecting "evil" within the fetus and not only attacking it out of self defense, but also seeking to make the child physically deformed so that his outer appearance reflected the "evil" inside of him. Having a child born deformed would serve as natural repellent to most humans and, as a natural reaction, he would either be left alone to die, or if he grew into adulthood, would be shunned by the rest of humanity. Either way, the deformity is an outward expression of his inner "evil," working as a deterrent and also greatly reducing his chances of reproducing, and thus preventing his "evil" from spreading.

If I am able to isolate the chemicals responsible for this in Erik's brain and either make them inert or remove them, this could change humanity forever. I am skeptical as to whether Erik's physical deformities will lessen as a result, but that ultimately does not matter. If I am able to isolate what is causing the "evil" in this man's mind, and purge it, I can do the same for every human on the planet. I can expunge hatred and crime across the world. In fact, his deformity would no longer isolate from the rest of humanity as men would simply accept him as he is. Tomorrow, I shall start my psychological examination of Erik and look for evidence to support my hypothesis.

December 11th, 1878

The psychological evaluation of Erik has given more credence to my theory. The subject has revealed to me that his skill sets include music and assassination. Could there be something more conflicted in a man? One aspect of his brain has a propensity to create music—an act which brings joy and happiness to all. I had Erik play his violin and sing for me, and he is nothing short of a musical prodigy. In fact, his skill is so great that I have agreed to accept payment for my services in the form of him playing for me every night. I am sure this skill comes from the part of his brain which releases the chemicals that move him to be a good person.

Erik's other skill is killing people. He has confided in me that he has ended numerous lives in his travels. Some of these murders were at least partially justified in that he killed a person who represented a physical threat to himself or others. In other cases, they were not as justified as he murdered people who mocked or scorned him.

Today, I subjected Erik to the painful process of extracting samples of spinal fluid, blood, and even putting a syringe through his abnormally thick skull to extract samples of brain chemicals while he performs various acts. While most patients would have screamed violently during the process, he remained silent. He remarked the the pain caused by the extractions was nothing compared to what he felt every day of his life.

I took samples during a control session while he was simply staring at a wall; then when he was playing his music; and then I had him kill several lab rats. I will review what chemicals are present in all three samples. In addition to the samples, I also took photographs of Erik as during all three sessions to review his appearance as he carried out these actions.

December 14th, 1878

For the past several days, I have been studying Erik's samples. My findings have been astonishing, to say the least. When he played his music, I discovered a chemical in his brain, blood, and spinal fluid that I am calling the "Angel

Substance." This particular chemical seems to confirm my theory that it is the chemistry of our brains that drive us to be good people. Additionally, the photographs I took of us as he played his violin when compared to the control photo seemed to show that both of us appeared more attractive when listening to his music.

I also found a chemical that I am currently calling the "Hidden Substance," as it seems to appear when Erik is engaging in evil actions. I decided on the name as it's a side of ourselves we want to keep hidden from others. When reviewing the photographs of Erik killing the rats, it is undeniable that we both appear more ugly than we had during either the control test or the music one.

These findings seem to support the notion that these chemicals can cause physical changes in people's appearance. We each seem to have a good version and an evil version of ourselves, and these two versions are revealed by varying degrees based on the amounts of Angel Substance or Hidden Substance produced by our brains.

I took samples of my own blood and, now that I know what to look for, I was able to find much smaller traces of both chemicals in my own blood. While Erik's count of the Angel Substance was about double mine, the amount of Hidden Substance was more than five times the amount in my blood. This, along with his mother's attacks when he was still in her womb, likely accounts for his deformity. He has a disproportionate amount of Hidden Substance in his system, and thus his physical appearance is affected by it.

I, on the other hand, have levels nowhere near that of Erik. I seem to have a much higher count of Angel Substance than I do of Hidden Substance. This would explain why I am a doctor whose passion in life is healing people and relieving suffering, while having little to no evil intentions toward anyone else.

I shall now determine if the production of the Hidden Substance can be overridden by the application of increased doses of the Angel Substance, or removed in some other fashion.

December 17th, 1878

My studies have revealed that increased doses of the Angel Substance are not able to counteract the effects of the Hidden Substance. Erik has subjected himself to multiple extractions of the chemical from his skull, spine, and bloodstream, and even when three times the amount of Angel Substance is applied to a sample of the Hidden Substance, both continue to exist. This would support Doctor Van Helsing's findings. The production of varied blood types and chemical cannot simply be overridden by the application of different strains from those which the hosts produces. The body needs to stop producing the original type in order for a new type to take its place.

Erik was dejected by these findings, as well as by the fact that his circus is moving to Paris, which will mean that he will no longer be here as I conduct my research.

I was able to offer him some hope. I suggested that, when he arrives in Paris, he should remove himself away from human society and focus exclusively on his music rather than his skills as an assassin or knife thrower. Taking these steps will also increase the amount of Angel Substance produced by his brain while reducing the amount of Hidden Substance.

I also suggested to Erik that a possible course of treatment might not be to try and shut down the area of his brain that produces the Hidden Substance, but to overwhelm it and burn it off. Using his samples, I believe I can find the correct chemical reaction to initiate the production of Hidden Substance in a human brain. It is my hypothesis that I can cause that area of the brain to break down from overuse just as any muscle or tendon would.

I would not use Erik for a first experiment since his brain already produces a large amount of Hidden Substance, without producing a proportionate amount of Angel Substance. Doing this could result in the creation of an insane homicidal maniac.

Rather, I shall test this on myself, as I produce hardly any Hidden Substance and a disproportionate amount of Angel Substance. I suspect that, with minimal increases in negative urges, which I should easily be able to control, and slight physical side effects, I can force the area of my brain which produces the Hidden Substance to destroy itself. Once I have perfected the process and doses, I promised Erik to go to Paris and cure him of his evil.

As Erik is in hiding, and I named the chemical I discovered the Hidden Substance, I have decided to call this experiment "Project Hyde." (The misspelling is my having some fun with the chemical's distortion of people's brains.) It is my ardent belief that, within a few years, I shall purge myself of evil, then use Erik as an example of how evil can be purged from anyone, before taking my findings to the world at large and finally ending evil in man forever.

Brian Gallagher has put the adventures of Marie Nizet's Captain Vampire, the indomitable Boris Liatoukine, (now available in a collected form as The Return of Captain Vampire*) behind him. He embarks here on a new sequence, featuring Gustave Le Rouge's criminal mastermind and mad surgeon, Doctor Cornelius Kramm, leader of the now-defunct cartel of the Red Hand. The adventures of the aptly named "Sculptor of Human Flesh," penned in 1912-13, were translated by Brian Stableford and released by BCP as a trilogy: 978-1-61227-243-6, -244-3 and -245-0. They were followed by a sequel written by Stableford, published in Volume 10. Brian Gallagher now picks up the torch...*

Brian Gallagher: *The Doctor of Sarajevo*

Sarajevo, 28 June 1914

Countess Sophie Chotek was relieved. The assassination attempt on her husband, Archduke Franz Ferdinand, had failed. A grenade thrown at them earlier had clattered over the roof of their car and damaged the vehicle behind them, causing casualties.

Her husband had a premonition of trouble, and it came true. He was thinking of creating a new province within the Austro-Hungarian Empire, encompassing Croatia-Slavonia, Dalmatia and Bosnia-Herzegovina, with the city of Zagreb likely being its capital. She remembered him discussing it with her. His ideas not gone down well in Serbia and with various radicals, and this attempt on his life had clearly been a response to it. Still, they managed to get to City Hall for a speech by the mayor, in which her husband interrupted with a sarcastic remark about his welcome to the city. She was proud that he later gave a speech in which he thanked the people of the city for the failure of the assassination attempt.

They were now on their way, by car, to the hospital to see the casualties. They were accompanied by Oscar Potiorek, Governor of Bosnia-Herzegovina. Suddenly, she heard him exclaim:

"This is the wrong way! We are supposed to take the Appel Quay!"

She sensed danger immediately and saw a man on the street, with a pistol aimed right at them. She heard two shots ring out. She felt pain in her stomach. She turned and saw blood ooze from her husband's neck. She fell sideways, her head coming to rest on the Archduke's knees. The last thing she heard was the heir to throne pleading with her not to die, for the sake of their children.

The Serb assassin was tackled to the ground by the crowd that had come to see the Archduke. The gendarmerie took charge of him. He was delighted. He was sure that he had just assassinated the man who would have prevented the union of Slav lands under the control of Belgrade by carrying through reforms.

It was unfortunate that so many people in these lands—including those who had restrained him—were not convinced of this, preferring the Empire over union with Serbia. Only a few Croats and Muslims were radicalized. *They did not know what was good for them*, he thought.

The gendarmerie had his pistol—a 9mm Browning, supplied by the Serbian Black Hand organization. They had trained him to shoot in the Topčider forest, in Serbia. He was grateful, the training had worked well. Now, he would face a trial. He cared only for his cause, and soon everyone would know his name: Gavrilo Princip.

Berne, Switzerland, August 1914

Doctor Cornelius Kramm warily regarded the man who had summoned him to what was referred to as the British Envoy Extraordinary and Minister Plenipotentiary to the Swiss Confederation at 50 Thunstrasse. This Percy Phelps was clearly not interested in a medical consultation with the man now known as "Doctor Malbrough." At least, not on medical matters.

"Perhaps I had better come to the point, Doctor Kramm," Phelps said. "His Majesty's Government would like to employ you to obtain a certain item from the General Philippovich barracks in Sarajevo. You would be well compensated,"

Doctor Cornelius responded, deciding to affect ignorance of his name.

"I fear you are mistaken; there is no Dr. Kramm at my practice. I, Doctor Malbrough, am the sole practitioner there, along with my staff. And we certainly do not work as couriers—if that is what you are asking. However, we do some facial surgery," he waved gently at Phelps's face, "and certainly, I think I could help you in that respect."

Phelps was affronted. How dare this man—a criminal—be so insulting to him? He would put on his cross face and put this damnable fellow in his place.

"Now, look here. You are the criminal known as Cornelius Kramm, one of the former leaders of the Red Hand organization. After its destruction, you fled to Australia where you worked as Doctor Malbrough, before leaving to set up a branch of your practice here in Europe, which is a front for your criminal-for-hire activities."

Phelps sat back, most satisfied.

Doctor Cornelius said nothing, leaving an awkward pause.

"You were recommended to us by your fellow criminal, Professor Moriarty, Doctor Kramm," an exasperated Phelps continued. "But we can make life difficult if you do not cooperate."

Doctor Cornelius was pleased. Not by the threat, but by how easily he had drawn the man out. Now he knew that the British were not entirely trustworthy, but also that they were serious about their offer. He also knew that he was not in a position to antagonize them in any serious way. He put his hands up in a placatory gesture.

"My dear Mr. Phelps, you don't expect me to admit to such things, do you? It is clear you are well informed, and your mentioning my colleague, Professor Moriarty, gives me great confidence. Please, give me further details about your proposal."

"As I have said," replied Phelps, placated, "we are in need of a certain liquid, for scientific purposes, you understand."

Indeed, Doctor Cornelius did. This was something of military value that the British did not want their Austro-Hungarian foes to retain.

"A phial of this liquid is kept securely in the General Philippovich barracks in Sarajevo," Phelps continued. "It is well guarded in a special section. We want you to steal it, and hand it over to our agent who will verify it is real. This will be done in Sarajevo. At that point, you will be paid £20,000 into your Swiss bank account."

"Hmm. Yes, it can be done," responded the Doctor. "I have one question, however. You clearly know me. Therefore, you must be aware that one of your countrymen, Lord Burydan, is an enemy of mine. I can't imagine he would approve of your hiring me."

"We know all about that," replied Phelps, waving that away. "The good news is that, on the declaration of hostilities, Lord Burydan swiftly enlisted and is an infantry Major—he was in the army previously. He's in France. He will not get in your way, Doctor Kramm."

"Good," said the Doctor, nodding. "Before we discuss further details, firstly I am usually referred to as 'Doctor Cornelius.' In my specialized field, people seem to prefer my Christian name. It's become something of a trademark, shall we say. Secondly, there is the matter of my compensation. Your offer is derisory to be frank..."

They eventually came to an agreement and Doctor Cornelius left. Phelps was pleased with the result. Certainly, the Doctor had upped the fee somewhat, but it would be worth it. With Professor Moriarty refusing the job—the unpatriotic swine!—this sinister doctor was the only option. Physically, the Doctor had looked thin, indeed almost emaciated—did he not eat? However, if he was successful, Allied possession of this liquid would be the last part of a weapon that would end this war before it had barely begun.

Evidenzbureau[1] *facility, Vienna, September 1914*

"My dear Countess, how wonderful it is to see you," said the man who headed this particular *Evidenzbureau* department. "I have a new mission for you. I have made some preparations."

Countess Irina Petrovski sat opposite him. She was unimpressed by his tone. "Your Serene Highness Prince Wilhelm, please remember that I do not work for you," she said. "I carry out some of your missions for the good of Poland and the Empire."

The Prince realized that he had been presumptuous. "Of course, I do recognize your independence," he rushed to add. "However, this is a mission of great importance; one that could decide the outcome of the war. Please, you may call me Prince Wilhelm."

The Countess nodded and gestured for him to continue.

"We are concerned over the General Philippovich barracks in Sarajevo. It has been reported to us that questions are being asked about them and, in particular, their security. These questions are being asked at all levels of society, not merely the lower classes. This is of concern to us. We would like to find out who is behind them."

"Surely," the Countess replied, "that is the sort of thing that happens in war? Why do these particular barracks concern you so?"

"The barracks have a special significance. There are a number of special items kept there that could be of great value to our enemies. We are giving thought to moving them elsewhere, but for all we know, that would tip the advantage the other side. We want to find out who in Sarajevo is making inquiries before any decision is made on relocation.

"Discreet inquiries on the ground have produced no results and we can hardly arrest leading members of society or pull them in for interrogation—that could cause any number of problems. Essentially, we would like you to visit Sarajevo and mix with the higher echelons of society and find out what is going on. Naturally, we will provide appropriate recompense. I know you would prefer to be operating against the Russians at the moment, but believe me, you will be serving the war effort better in Sarajevo."

"Very well," said the Countess, nodding. "It would be interesting to see Sarajevo at the very least. Certainly, I would wish to pray at the Catholic Cathedral there for the soul of Archduke Ferdinand, a man who promised much for the Empire when he took over. I will leave at once."

"Excellent!" exclaimed the Prince. "You remind me of a fine woman I once knew..." he looked wistfully out of a window.

---

[1] The Habsburg Empire's military intelligence service. Formed in 1850, it was the world's first such organization.

The Countess felt weary suddenly. Surely, he was not going to bore her with the tale of Irene Adler once again? She had come across the woman and considered her a bit dull. How she had managed to confound the famous Sherlock Holmes was beyond her. It amused the Countess that this Adler had caused the Prince any problem at all—a woman in his past that he thought could trouble his ludicrous claim to be the King of Bohemia. Well, Emperor Franz Joseph, the actual King of Bohemia—amongst much else—dealt with the "Grand Duke" most firmly. He was fortunate that the Emperor had given him this job with the title of Prince. The Adler thing was meaningless in the end.

To the Countess's great relief, the Prince reverted back to the mission.

"We must make arrangements. We have already set up a social occasion for you to attend..."

After the Countess had left, an aide came into the office.

"The Countess has accepted the mission. She will soon be leaving for Sarajevo," the Prince told him.

The aide, a young army officer, responded, "Your Serene Highness, I understand that the Countess has done many services for the Empire."

The Prince bade him to sit. "Yes," he replied. "As you know, this department deals with matter of an unusual scientific nature. The Countess is well suited to such things. She was involved in an incident on the Trans-Siberian Express in 1906 in which a creature from beyond our world was running amok."

The officer looked startled.

"Ah, I see, you have not been fully briefed. I will see to it that you will be. Since that incident, the Countess has had a number of adventures, following the mysterious death of her husband. She is motivated by Polish patriotism. She wishes to see the parts of her homeland ruled by Russia liberated and unified with our Galicia within the Empire. There is heavy fighting there with the Russians at the moment.

"She was born in Galicia, and thus is our citizen, and married the Count Petrovski, who was resident in the Polish lands occupied by Russia." Here, the Prince paused. "You have been with us for only a couple of weeks? Seconded from the 96th Karlovac Infantry Regiment?"

"Yes, sir" the aide replied.

"Ah!" said the Prince with a pleased look. "I must tell you all about another remarkable woman, one named Irene Adler..."

September 1914, Sarajevo

Doctor Cornelius was most satisfied. In only a few weeks of opening his new practice in Sarajevo, he had attracted some wealthy clients from the city, Croats, Muslims and Serbs, and the rest of Bosnia-Herzegovina, and beyond. He recalled with amusement one dignitary's comment:

"How good of you to set up here, Doctor Malbrough, in order to promote our city after the assassination."

The "sculptor of human flesh" cackled. What a naive fool that man was! He had even referred some customers to him. And it was not long before some of them were revealed to not have the money to pay for his services...

One such person now knocked on the door of the practice. The Doctor let him in, and they went silently to his consulting room, where they sat down.

"Now, Baron von Kuffner," said the Doctor, what have you for me?"

Baron von Kuffner, a thin tall man in his fifties, looked nervous as he answered:

"What is this information for, Doctor? We are at war... The information you seek could be used by my Emperor's enemies."

Doctor Cornelius drew breath. "That his hardly your concern," he replied. "I have completely healed those scars on your face, and you failed to pay me, due to your unfortunate debts. If you prefer, I could simply start proceedings to recover my fee, which would disgrace you. No doubt, someone will offer you a pistol and a bottle of whisky..." Then, he added menacingly, "Perhaps me."

Baron Von Kuffner there and then that told him everything he had gleaned from his contacts in the General. It was good information, but not enough.

"I need more, Baron," said Doctor Cornelius.

The Baron looked concerned. "That is all I know. What else can I do?"

"I advise you to think harder."

The Doctor beckoned to someone, seemingly behind him. Suddenly there was a knife at the Baron's neck. He had not even realized that there was anyone else in the room. So he did as instructed and said:

"There is a reception in three days' time, being held by the mayor in honor of the military. There will be some officers there. I could perhaps talk to them?"

The Doctor waved the man with the knife away.

"More than talk. You will gain the precise location of the item I want. And passwords. And you will help me to make their acquaintance."

The Countess was pleased with the reception at City Hall, known as Vijećnica. Ostensibly, it was being held to honor the Austro-Hungarian armed forces. In reality, it was an opportunity to observe those who had been asking questions about the General Philippovich barracks. Aside from the military officers, the elite of the Sarajevo society was there: civic dignitaries, members of the local cultural societies, and leading members of the religious communities of the city. There was a small orchestra playing *Die Bosniaken Kommen*[2] always popular with the troops. She had received many admiring looks from men interested in this elegantly dressed, auburn-haired, beautiful woman.

---

[2] *The Bosniaks are Coming*, a military march composed in 1895 by Austrian composer Eduard Wagnes.

She turned respectfully to the man she was with.

"Your Excellency, I must thank you again for your hospitality,"

"It is my pleasure. The Emperor himself wrote to me. I understand that your work is of importance. I am of course also pleased that you have attended church, and your grasp of my language is impressive."

The Countess was pleased that she had his favor. This was the Catholic Archbishop of Vrhbosna[3], the Croat Josip Stadler. She was staying at an apartment arranged for by the Church. Her cover was that of a journalist writing for a Catholic newspaper—being a Countess gave her work a certain celebrity value. It was an invaluable cover for much of her work. And the Archbishop, who had dabbled in politics with his own Croatian political party, was well known as being loyal to Vienna.

"Yes, I know a number of languages. The example of our multi-lingual Emperor is a great example. It certainly helps with my article on the Church here. I was very impressed by your Sacred Heart Cathedral. I felt at great peace praying there."

"I am pleased to hear it," the Archbishop said.

He looked over to a small group of men. There was Baron von Kuffner, talking to two military officers.

"Countess," he said, "I believe one of the gentlemen you wish to meet, Baron Von Kuffner, is in discussion with two military officers. Should I introduce you?"

The Archbishop was aware that the Countess had a special mission, although he was unaware of the precise details.

"Yes, now would be an excellent time," replied the Countess.

Baron Von Kuffner was one of those identified by the secret police as having asked indiscreet questions.

The Archbishop guided her toward the group. The two officers were members of the Bosnian-Herzegovinian infantry, in dress uniform complete with cutlasses. The Archbishop made the introductions, then moved away, to let the Countess do her work.

"I'm sorry to interrupt your conversation, but I was curious to meet some of our gallant soldiers, and yourself Baron—I have heard so many good things about you."

"You flatter me, Countess," the Baron replied. "I wholeheartedly support our soldiers; I only wish I could fight alongside them. I am a reserve officer, but despite my protestations, due to an old liver complaint, the doctors will not let me return to active duty."

---

[3] The Roman Catholic diocese of a large part of Bosnia-Herzegovina, including Sarajevo.

"How devastating for you," the Countess replied, knowing full well that her information was that it was *his* protestations over his 'liver complaint' that had prevented his return to the military.

"Yes, however, I do give the troops some moral support!" the Baron said. "Now, I must take my leave to pay my respects to the Mayor, but I shall see you gentlemen later."

"Well..." said the Countess.

She was not used to someone just walking off from her. Clearly, there was something wrong with him. Not least as he walked straight past Mayor Čurčic.

"We shall not be leaving you, Countess!" exclaimed the young officer who had been introduced to her as Lieutenant Novotný.

"I should hope not," she replied with a winning smile. "He clearly is more impressed by you two than me. Are you seeing him again later?"

"Yes," responded the other officer, a Captain Hodžić. "He is very interested in discussing the war and politics. He has invited us both to an excellent establishment in the city where we can discuss such matters further."

"Over drinks no doubt?" teased the Countess.

They all laughed. However, she was concerned. She had no doubt now that the Baron was a little too interested in the personnel from the General Philippovich barracks. A number of officers had been briefed about anyone asking questions, but some had not, including these two. However, it would be important to see what happened next. They were not likely to believe her if she told them of her true purpose, and to brief them now may tip off the Baron or anyone working with him, if they were being observant, which she was wise enough to assume.

She continued to talk animatedly with the officers about her work on her article. However, she managed to slip word to a waiter—in reality a member of the secret police branch of the local gendarmerie—about what to do next.

The evening wore on, with a few dignitaries starting to leave. The Countess had met many people, and many more were keen to meet her.

"What was the situation here after the assassination?" she asked Mayor Čurčic.

The Mayor was well acquainted with what had happened.

"There was great anger," he replied. "Regrettably, there were some attacks on the Serbs and their property. The Croats and Muslims are loyal to the monarchy, and there was some over-reaction. However, we have taken action against Serb organizations."

"The Archduke was a great man, with views on reforming the monarchy that would have benefited the people of the Empire, including my own," she observed. "Now we have a war. Belgrade must be held fully to account. It is unfortunate that this man Princip is too young to be hung."

Čurčic nodded. He had heard that the Countess was a woman with firm views. Like many, he found her highly intriguing. She was a woman who seemed not to recognize any second place to men, and appeared to lead a highly adventurous lifestyle.

One of the staff came up to the Countess and said something. The Mayor recognized the man—a member of the local secret police. He had been informed that they would be here, but knew not why; however, it seemed that the Countess was somehow involved. Before he could say anything, she turned back to him and said:

"My dear Mayor, I fear I must take my leave. However, I hope we shall meet again before I depart this city."

And before he could respond, she was heading to the exit.

The gendarme who had spoken to her earlier, was waiting at the exit of hall.

"Countess, the two officers are leaving with the Baron," he said. "We must move swiftly. We shall follow and report back to you."

"No Inspector Lovrić," replied the Countess, "I shall come with you."

The Inspector could see that she brooked no argument; he was also mindful of his superior's order to do whatever she asked. They left swiftly.

Outside, the Countess and Inspector Lovrić were met by another member of the secret police, Sergeant Ahmić. He simply pointed at the spot where the two officers were walking with Baron von Kuffner on the Appel Quay, by the Miljacka river.

The Countess and the officers had little choice but to follow. A horse and cart came up from behind and stopped by the three men. The two officers suddenly reacted as if they had been hit by something.

'Halt! Gendarmerie!" shouted the Inspector.

A shot rang out. Baron von Kuffner collapsed. Two men from the cart leaped out and bundled the now groggy officers in.

The Countess and the gendarmes dashed forward, but the cart was already moving off.

The driver was Doctor Cornelius. He put his gun back within the coat. Von Kuffner had been followed and was now a liability. It was much easier to simply kill him. He had shot the two officers with drugged darts. The Doctor was wearing a hat and some bandages around his face, in order to prevent anyone from recognizing him. He had wanted to make sure that he was present at this vital moment in the plan.

The Countess motioned to the gendarmerie and they followed her to her vehicle—a yellow roadster. She jumped into the driving seat, with the secret policemen getting in behind her. She drove off, headlights glaring in the night, and, within seconds, was behind her quarry.

Another horse and cart rolled up to the body of the Baron, men from the cart picked it up and rode away, much to the puzzlement of onlookers.

In her car, the Countess exclaimed:

"Prepare to fire, officers! I have no doubt that they're about to attack us!"

She was not wrong, as two thugs appeared from under the coverings of the cart. Before they could fire on the car, however, a metal slab slammed up from under the hood, covering the windscreen, with only a small slot for visibility.

The Countess prayed that the bullets would not get through the slots. The two gendarmes behind her were standing up, trying to fire over her, but not getting their aim due to the constant movement of the vehicle and the bullets firing back at them. The thugs fired at the car, but the bullets simply bounced off. Even the wheels seemed impervious.

Both vehicles ceased firing at each other; a momentary stalemate with the Countess only yards away, but unable to overtake, her car being vulnerable on the sides.

One of the thugs informed Doctor Cornelius of the situation. He nodded. He saw that they were approaching a fork in the road. He unhooked the horses and ensured they went along the other road, with the cart barreling along the Appel Quay straight ahead.

The Countess did not know what had happened, but she sensed victory. Then, suddenly, the cart somehow accelerated away, going a faster pace than her own vehicle. The covering of the cart flew back onto the road. The Countess stopped her car just in time before it hit it.

She and the gendarmes watched what seemed to be a moving platform with wheels, with sheets of metal moving up to enclose the riders, turning off onto another road and disappearing.

The Countess was less than pleased.

"Why didn't they throw out the covering at us in the first place?" Inspector Lovrić said.

The Countess glared at him, but then softened.

"Yes, yes. a good question, Inspector. Our foes have advanced cars, but it appears perhaps not much in the way of common sense? To your headquarters! The city must be searched."

Doctor Cornelius's vehicle disappeared into a small warehouse, with his hired hands laughing and slapping him on the back.

"Well done, boss!" they were saying in their broken German.

The Doctor did not appreciate such familiarity. There was a time—when he was one of the Lords of the Red Hand—when they would have paid for that. However, the Red Hand, once one of the world's foremost criminal organizations, had effectively been destroyed by a group of French adventurers and that lunatic Briton, Lord Burydan. He still employed a few Red Hand people, such as these local louts, but he could hardly lord it over them.

They were laughing and getting out a bottle of the local drink, Rakia. They seemed to have enjoyed themselves. He had not. He felt annoyance at having to be so directly involved, when previously he could have had top quality people to do the job. And he was aware of his lack of experience in more physical matters.

He should have had a couple of grenades on hand to throw at their pursuers… He had to learn things fast.

"Enough of the drink. Disguise the vehicle, and then we go to my surgery."

They quickly did as they were told, disguising the vehicle—which the Doctor had made at great cost in better times—as a cart again, along with horses. They left from another exit. If anyone had seen their strange vehicle enter, they would not likely see the horse and cart leave.

The surgery was not far away. They arrived there before the gendarmerie started searching the streets. In the night, however, there was not much the gendarmerie could do. They did receive a report of something that looked like a car enter a warehouse, but when they looked during the daylight hours, they found nothing.

The Countess awoke. She had gone to sleep at 3 a.m., by which point it was clear to her that her quarries had got away.

It was now 7 a.m. She was tired, but she would find some time to catch-up on her sleep later. She bathed and dressed. Her attire was highly fashionable, but probably not the best for running around. However, she had little intention of dressing in a functional way that may attract attention. And anyway, she was a Countess—she would always dress in a manner appropriate to her station.

She looked in the mirror. How her life and changed over the past eight years! Coming across that creature from another world on the Trans-Siberian Express had changed her outlook on life. It was clear that ungodly, demonic forces really did exist. They had to be fought—she could not stand idly by. On that occasion, others had taken the lead in defeating the creature. She would not be doing that again. Further, she felt that a more active role in freeing Polish lands from Russian control would be better than hoping for the best.

Her husband, the Count, had a different view—even employing a deranged Russian monk as a spiritual adviser, strangely believing this would help in currying favor with the Tsar. The monk had died on that train, and the Countess, having found him repugnant, was less than grieved. Interestingly, she had heard that the current Tsarina was causing concern with a similar character she had around her. *That will not end well*, she thought. Her husband, of course, had forbade her newfound assertive activities. The argument had ended with his unfortunate death in 1910. She still missed him, occasionally, despite his appalling arrogance.

There was a knock on the door. It was Ljubica, the maid provided to her by Archbishop Stadler.

"Countess, there is a gendarme waiting for you."

She went into the front room, beckoning the maid to come with her. It was Inspector Lovrić.

"Good morning, Countess. I have urgent news about Lieutenant Novotný and Captain Hodžić."

"Good morning Inspector," the Countess said, never forgetting to be polite, "Have they been found?"

"In a manner of speaking, Countess. They reported for duty at the barracks this morning, insisting that nothing untoward happened to them last night."

At the General Philippovich barracks, the Countess was received by the officer in charge, a General Auersperg, in his office. As head of the barracks, he himself had been at the reception the night before, and, consequently, had spent the night awake, being kept informed of the search for his two missing officers.

"Countess, thanks to you, I have had no sleep last night. My officers have told me that they spent most of the night at an establishment, no doubt drinking, with Baron von Kuffner. The establishment, the *Crvena Ruka*, has corroborated this. They even let them sleep there for a few hours."

The Countess was puzzled, but did not show it. She had already been told this by Inspector Lovrić. There would be an explanation at some point, but right now, she needed more information.

"General, both myself and the gendarmes with me not only saw your men bundled in a cart, but Baron von Kuffner shot dead."

"As you know, there is some corroboration for what you say," replied the General. "There were witnesses to your chase, and some blood was indeed found where you claimed the body was, but the Baron is alive and well. You no doubt would wish to see the officers for yourselves?"

"Of course," she said.

The General nodded to an aide, who left the room. He returned shortly, with the two officers. They saluted smartly to the General, ignoring the Countess.

"Please tell the Countess where you were last night?" General Auersperg ordered.

Captain Hodžić relayed to the Countess what she had already heard. She looked to Lieutenant Novotný.

"And you confirm this?"

He nodded.

"Please, do confirm it in words."

"Yes, Countess, what the Captain said is the truth. We spent the evening discussing the war and politics and slept at the *Crvena Ruka*. We had permission for the entire evening, so there was no need to return to the barracks prior to when we had to report."

The Countess nodded.

"Your voices sound different, gentlemen," she observed.

The General laughed.

"A good night's drink would do that! Look at them, not a bit of being worse for wear! A credit to the Emperor!"

The men all laughed. The General then said:

"I trust you are now satisfied Countess? Clearly you were mistaken."

The Countess stood up and smiled at the General.

"Thank you, General. I am neither satisfied, nor was I mistaken. I shall take my leave now."

The General had heard of the Countess's assertive manner. Given that he was under orders to cooperate, he thought it best not to antagonize her. He motioned to his aide. They made their polite farewells, and the aide took the Countess out of the room.

"Infernal woman," the General said after she had left. "Now, back to work, the pair of you," he laughed.

Lieutenant Novotný and Captain Hodžić saluted and left. They indeed had work to be doing.

The Countess drove to the main gendarmerie station. Many of the locals took an interest in her car as she drove past—and the fact that a woman was driving it.

As she was arriving, Baron Von Kuffner was leaving. She was stunned—it really was him! The Baron simply looked at her and walked on. She met Sergeant Ahmić at the entrance.

"Make sure that he is followed," she instructed.

"That has already been done," he responded.

Inside, in a side office, the Countess heard to Inspector Lovrić's report.

"We spoke to the Baron; he came to us of his own accord, claiming to have heard that he had been 'killed' last night. It certainly was him, yet we all saw him shot last night. Could we somehow have been mistaken?"

"All three of us, Inspector?" said the Countess. "No, that is not possible. I believe there is some other force at work here. I do not believe that he has come back from the dead, but I certainly believe we may in the presence of something perhaps not part of normal experience. I have had experience of such things."

"What could that be?" asked the Inspector.

"I do not know yet, but I have little doubt matters will become clear soon. I have no doubt that the officers are not quite what they seem. There may well be a threat to the barracks by our enemies. I will attempt to get them quietly removed from duty for a short time. I must contact Vienna."

In the General Philippovich barracks, Captain Hodžić approached a particular locked room, with a heavy steel door. It was a small area dug below the barracks themselves. Outside the door, a bored Sergeant sat at a desk. He longed to get to the front, to partake in the war. The Serbs had committed a terrible act, and they should be duly punished for it. His wife, whilst sympathetic, did wonder if he was too enthusiastic, fearing that he might not come back. He told her it would be a great honor for her if indeed he did die in the service of the Empire. She seemed less impressed than before. There were times he could not understand her. He was jolted out of his thoughts when an officer approached. He leapt to attention.

"Just doing a routine check of the secure area," said the Captain.

"Yes, sir. Please sign in first," replied the Sergeant.

The Captain signed and the Sergeant opened the door for him. He looked around the room. There were a number of items around, many of which seemed damaged or incomprehensible. Next to him was a glass cabinet with what appeared to be something he had seen used to unblock drains—a burnt metallic rod with a cup on the end. The label was German, but he recognized something in his own language—something from far away? Perhaps the military had secret plumbing methods?

He shook his head and looked for what he came for. He found it soon enough. A simple metal phial labeled *Fulgurator explosive fluid.* However, it was locked in a glass cabinet.

He was ready for that. He took out a pick from his pocket, and, within a few moments, had unlocked the cabinet. He carefully took out the phial—he could feel the liquid moving in it—and carefully put it in his tunic. It made a slight bulge, but he did not think it would be noticed. He was entirely correct.

"All in order, Sir?" asked the Sergeant.

"Indeed so, Sergeant."

The Captain signed the book and left. The Sergeant looked after him. *That was a quick inspection,* he thought. And was his voice different? No matter, such is the way of officers.

A short time later, the two officers found themselves at Doctor Cornelius's surgery. The Doctor himself was there, along with another man whom the officers did not recognize.

"We have what you want," said Captain Hodžić.

He handed over the phial to the Doctor. The surgeon looked at it, and then turned to the man next to him.

"Well, then, Monsieur Hart, I trust this will satisfy you?"

"Let us see first," the man replied in French-accented German.

Hart moved to some apparatus on a nearby bench, clearly set up for chemical usage. Whilst he began his test, Doctor Cornelius spoke to the officers. Hodžić told him what he had seen written on the cabinet. The Doctor pondered this. Part of a superweapon? He could, of course, eliminate this Hart and keep the phial. But what use would it be without the rest of the weapon? And did he really want the British—and, it seemed, the French—as his enemies just now? No; it was much easier and profitable to take their money. In his current position, he could not do much else.

"You two," he said to the officers. "Go up the stairs to the operating table. I will now restore your natural features. And I will see to it that the real officers are let onto the streets shortly. They have been drugged and will remember nothing. They will be disorientated, but it will no doubt be assumed they had too much to drink at lunchtime as they had last night. There will be questions, but not as many as two officers really going missing."

Hart looked up and came over at that.

"How is it that you perform such surgery? That you can replicate men's faces so exactly?"

"Come now, Monsieur Hart," the Doctor replied. "You surely do not wish me to divulge my trade secrets?"

Trade secrets, Doctor Cornelius thought, *that had such an origin that even Mr. Hart with his apparent knowledge of superweapons would have difficulty believing.*

"You killed Baron von Kuffner and replaced him. What are you going to do about that?"

"Oh, his corpse shall be found in the Miljacka river. I have his body in my other facility, encased in ice to slow decay. One of my forgers has already written a suicide note, it has been sent to the Baron's solicitor. Of course, the gendarmerie will be puzzled as to why he did not simply kill himself at home, but the fact of the man's debts will override any concerns. At least for the moment. We only need a day or two to complete matters and be on our way. Doctor Malbrough will be returning to Berne very soon. By the time the Austrians, including their agent, this Countess Petrovski, put anything together, it will be much too late."

Hart nodded. He turned back to his apparatus. Whatever he was doing, it was ready. He took out a piece of paper and put it into a small glass beaker of liquid which had been heated to boiling, but had now simmered down. The paper was black.

"You've earned your money, Doctor Cornelius," he said. "This is what we have been after."

The Doctor performed a small bow. One of his minions came in and whispered something to him. His face, never particularly joyful, hardened.

"It seems the gendarmerie have arrested someone from the *Crvena Ruka*, a barman. He works for me, one of my Red Hand operatives. I don't know how they know of his past, but we must move fast. He may not last under interrogation."

Doctor Cornelius noted that Hart had clearly not realized that *Crvena Ruka* meant "Red Hand" in the local language. Some fool had called the pub that name in the past, and he and the other Lords of the Red Hand had not objected, it being a matter for the lower levels of the organization. Technically, he still owned it, but the details were suitably murky to prevent his identification. Nonetheless, this was not a good development.

At the gendarmerie station, Inspector Lovrić had just informed the Countess of the new developments. The two army officers had been followed to the surgery of one Doctor Malbrough.

"I have heard of this Doctor Malbrough," said the Countess. "He is said to perform surgical facial miracles—for a price. I understand he is originally from Australia. Could he be working for the British?"

"It's possible," replied Lovrić. "He's been considered above suspicion, due to his wealthy friends here. However, given the situation, I think we could certainly enter his premises to perform a check and see what the officers are doing there.

"We also did some checks on the staff of the *Crvena Ruka* as requested. One of them had emigrated to America, but returned recently to Sarajevo, and became a barman. Our files contain an American police report sent to us a few years ago. It was suspected that he was a member of the Red Hand, a criminal organization. We have him in custody."

The Countess realized the implications. One of the Red Hand's so-called "Lords" was Doctor Cornelius Kramm, another surgeon with miraculous skills. As for *Crvena Ruka*… She knew what that name meant.

"What does he say?"

"So far, he's corroborated the drinking story of Baron von Kuffner," the Inspector replied.

"Perhaps," suggested the Countess, "you could be more... persuasive? Within reason."

"Of course," replied the Inspector. "I was about to do so anyway. I will also ask Sergeant Ahmić to assemble some men to visit the surgery of this Doctor Malbrough. My gendarmes who followed the officers are already keeping watch there."

The Countess considered driving immediately to the surgery. However, there would only be the surveillance officers there, and who knew what would await them there.

Shortly, Sergeant Ahmić assembled a team of gendarmes outside the station. Inspector Lovrić came out and went over to the Countess, who was standing by her car. She noticed some flecks of blood on his uniform.

"It did not take very long for the barman to start talking," the Inspector said. "He has confirmed that he was told to corroborate the officers' story. They did not spend the night at the *Crvena Ruka*. He was given his orders by a longtime Red Hand agent in this city, despite the fact that the Red Hand has long been dormant.

"Another thing. General Auersperg has called to report that Hodžić and Novotný have been found in some kind of intoxicated state outside of the barracks. He thinks they are drunk, but their medical officer believes they may have been drugged. My men have not seen them leave the surgery."

"That's because the men inside are imposters," said the Countess. "Using whatever unholy means, this Malbrough, who is likely Doctor Cornelius Kramm himself, changed the features of two of his lackeys. For what reason, however? Hold your men for a moment, I would like to talk to the General myself."

They went back inside station, and the Inspector called the General. Having gotten him on the line, he handed over the telephone to the Countess.

"My dear General," she said in her most charming fashion, "I need your help. I am aware of the functions of the General Philippovich barracks; however, I was wondering if there was anything else that, perhaps, is not publicly known?"

She paused for a moment while he replied. When she spoke to him, her tone hardened.

"Yes, General, I know all about military security and that I am a civilian. However, I should remind you that I operate on the authority from the Emperor himself. Anything withheld from me is being withheld from him."

The General became more co-operative.

"I see, General. You have a vault of precious and obscure items, including weapon components… And would either Captain Hodžić or Lieutenant Novotný have access to it? The Captain does? And did he visit yesterday? You don't know? Please find out at once, and, more importantly, please check the contents of the vault. I see no reason that this should take you longer than fifteen minutes, so call me back. And remember, this task is being performed at the Emperor's behest. Goodbye."

She put the receiver down.

It took the General ten minutes to call back. Lovrić answered and handed the phone to the Countess.

"A phial, containing a liquid for some kind of powerful cannon? Missing? And Captain Hodžić did visit the vault yesterday? What? You say it is useless without the other components? French, you say? Like our enemies on the battlefield, who may very well have all those components already? I fail to be reassured, General, and I doubt the Emperor will be. Let us hope I can retrieve it for you."

She put the phone down.

"To the surgery, at once," she said.

Surreptitiously, the Countess and her gendarmerie colleagues—all wearing civilian clothing—entered the establishment next door to the surgery, a hat shop. The Countess was impressed; the secret police had managed to establish themselves discreetly behind a screen, whilst the shop conducted its affairs, thus not giving rise to any suspicions from the surgery. However, she was a little concerned at being seen to disappear behind this screen with some men. A female shop assistant came over.

"Would madam and her colleagues wish to see our forthcoming catalogue?"

The Countess bowed her head, and, led by the shop assistant, they disappeared behind the screen.

"Thank you, Kata," said the Inspector.

The Countess was further impressed; some kind of listening device had been set up, with two gendarmes intently listening on earphones. One of them quickly relayed the situation:

"Doctor Malbrough has been talking to a Frenchman; unfortunately, we have only just set up, and missed what was said earlier. They are talking about leaving Sarajevo, in ways to avoid the gendarmerie."

He went back to his earphone.

"The Frenchman has just referred to the Doctor as Doctor Cornelius," he added.

"We must intervene. Now!" said the Countess, pointing next door.

Inspector Lovrić motioned to Sergeant Ahmić and the men ran out. They smashed through the surgery door, glass flying everywhere, cutting some of them. One of the officers took a bit of glass into his eye; he gave a cry and halted his charge, blocking his colleagues' way.

In that moment, Doctor Cornelius grabbed Hart and shoved him towards the back of the premises, waving a gun at the gendarmes. Whilst moving back, he hit a switch underneath a small table.

Lovrić held a gun towards the two men. He barked an order:

"Stay where you are, or I will shoot you both down."

Doctor Cornelius pointed a gun directly at Hart's head.

"Officers, you really do not wish to be responsible for the death of this Swiss diplomat, do you? I assure you it will be portrayed as an act of gendarmerie blundering," he said. "And, given your recent failure regarding the Archduke, this would not look good for any of you, would it now?"

Inspector Lovrić looked uncertain. This man was unfamiliar. If he was a diplomat, he was not one that he had met.

Hart swiftly played his role.

"Please," he said in French, "I am just a diplomat. I am visiting this man to discuss some surgery on my face. He is highly regarded. I know nothing of what is happening, let alone why he has a gun to my head. Please do as he says. And be assured that I will assist in having him be struck off whatever medical register he is on. His behavior is most unethical, and your Emperor shall hear about all of this. I am very well connected."

Doctor Cornelius groaned inwardly. Hart was overdoing it. He swiftly shoved the Frenchman forward. It was best not to let these gendarmes have time to think or allow more theatrics from Hart.

The Inspector waved his men back. Doctor Cornelius pulled Hart onto the street, one arm around his neck, the other with a pistol aimed straight at his head. On the street, there were a few bystanders, a number of whom backed off when they saw the gun.

A strange vehicle appeared on the road, rolling up to outside the surgery—the same one that had previously been disguised as a horse and cart.

But also standing in the street was the Countess. She, too, had a pistol, aimed squarely at the two men. The vehicle door was just a couple of feet away, but her pistol prevented any further movement towards it.

"I am a Swiss diplomat…" started Hart.

"Please refrain from relaying any such nonsense to me," ordered the Countess. "I really do not believe you, not least because I am on excellent terms with Swiss diplomacy and I have no idea who you are—except that you are in league with Doctor Cornelius Kramm here. It would be regrettable if the Doctor shot you, given that we need to interrogate you both, but the retrieval of that phial is my primary concern. Shoot him, by all means, Doctor Cornelius. I will then shoot you, and I will have the phial. I could also just shoot you both anyway."

Doctor Cornelius considered his options. Was the Countess bluffing? He had come across formidable women before… and given she was already pointing a gun at him, he had to assume she meant what she said. Surrender would mean death. He was too notorious. Even if he were not to end up in America, from where he had fled after the destruction of the Red Hand, his crimes on the Continent alone would warrant his execution. No, he would use Hart as a shield and get in his vehicle—that was still his best chance. If Hart got killed, at least he would have the phial to hand over to his clients. He'd worry about explaining Hart's death later.

One of the bystanders was a man named Amar, who had been watching the proceedings. He had worked for the Red Hand for some time, and indeed enjoyed being a henchman. It was something he was good at. He had no time for politics, let alone working for radical groups. The Red Hand paid so much better—or rather Doctor Cornelius did—and the organization's demise had been a real loss to him. He was on his way to the surgery, having been told he may be needed. Now, he was in a quandary. Given where he was, the Doctor had to have seen him. If Amar shot the Countess, as his employer would no doubt wish, he would be executed for that. But if he did not, then what would happen if Doctor Cornelius escaped? He would certainly sign his death warrant if he did nothing—or worse. There had been rumors of foul experiments conducted on those who had failed the Doctor before. He decided upon a compromise.

A shot rang out. There was screaming, and the Countess, momentarily startled, looked behind her. In that moment, Doctor Cornelius and Hart bundled into the vehicle. The Doctor started it up and they drove away.

Three men had wrestled Amar to the ground. He had simply fired in the air, with his gun held low in an effort to conceal where the shot had come from. Regrettably for him, some of the bystanders had seen this and wrestled him to the ground. Now the gendarmerie had him, but he was pleased with himself. A spell in prison, perhaps, given that he had not participated in Doctor Cornelius's murder of the Baron, but a fate certainly better than the noose, or he Doctor's vengeance. Indeed, as the Doctor had escaped, he could look forward to some reward later. What he did not realize was that the Doctor was somewhat occupied with the Countess and her pistol and had not noticed Amar at all.

"A planned diversion, in case of emergencies. My people are well prepared," said the Doctor to his passenger.

"Indeed," said an impressed Hart.

Doctor Cornelius had no idea whatsoever where that shot had come from, but it was good to give the impression that he was behind it. It would help with his business image, now that the Doctor Malbrough identity was finished. He decided to emphasize his planning.

"And of course, the driver here… I was able to alert him to come to us immediately. I plan for every contingency."

Hart looked even more impressed.

"Doctor Cornelius, can this vehicle get us to the coast?"

"Yes, despite the terrain, we can get there within two hours—providing the authorities don't get organized enough to intercept us."

"If I had access to some telegraph equipment, I could arrange for us to be picked up. there any such facilities on our route? I am ignorant of this country."

Doctor Cornelius smiled. He moved over to a locker by his side and opened it.

"I trust this technology is sufficient?" he said.

Inside was a telegraph machine.

The Countess was furious, but there was no time for recrimination. She dashed over to her car and drove in pursuit, not even waiting for the Inspector who was busy with the man with the gun.

Inspector Lovrić saw her drive off and turned to Sergeant Ahmić.

"We need to the get word out. We have to stop that vehicle."

The Countess was in pursuit. Within minutes, both vehicles were out of the city. She was concerned. What if Doctor Cornelius simply decided to stop? She was by herself with only one gun. His vehicle seemed to cope well with the roads, as did hers, but she was not armored like the machine she was pursuing. Her car was something remarkable, British in origin. Her own private mechanics often had difficulty in understanding its advanced functions. Nicknamed "Elizabeth," she had been a gift from her friends, the British scientists Professor Saxton and Doctor Wells, in gratitude for her help during an incident in London in 1912. That was before the war. They were on opposite sides now, thanks to a terrorist with a gun. She hoped that the gendarmerie would be able to determine where they were going. She glanced at her compass and a map. They seemed to be heading roughly West.

After an hour of pursuit, they came near the town of Županjac. A barrage of fire came from nowhere, hitting the Doctor's vehicle. The Countess could see some soldiers, but they flashed by—they had only small arms. It seems that Inspector Lovrić had indeed got the word out. The bullets were ineffective, but it seemed that they knew where the vehicle was going. When it stopped, the Countess would not be alone, at least not for long.

Later, she could see where they were going. They were now in Dalmatia, heading straight for the coast, north of the city of Šibenik.

In his vehicle, Doctor Cornelius looked out of a slit at the back.

"The Countess is still in pursuit. Perhaps we should have stopped and dealt with her, but that may have slowed us down. When we get to the coast, it will be a different matter. I trust your friends will be waiting for us, Mr. Hart? And that I shall be escorted to safety, along with my driver, of course."

He cared nothing for the driver; but hiring might be difficult if word got out that he abandoned his hirelings.

"You will be looked after, Doctor Cornelius. You have, after all, given us the key to victory in this war. One thing that I am curious about. This 'Red Hand' that you used to lead. It was criminal, but it sounds political?"

Doctor Cornelius was slightly surprised by the question. No doubt Hart was fishing for any details that may be of use to him and his masters.

"Not remotely," he replied. "In fact, my late brother Fritz and I did consider calling it 'Spectre,' but Mr. Marx had already used that word, so we thought better of it."

Hart nodded. "Pity, it has a ring to it."

The Countess could see that that the Doctor's vehicle was slowing down. Ahead was the blue of the Adriatic Sea, shimmering in the Sun.

The vehicle slowed down, coming to halt near a cove. The Countess could see some gendarmes nearby. They waved to her and ran to the vehicle. *They must have come from Šibenik*, the Countess thought. One of the gendarmes came over to her. He spoke in broken German.

"Please, Countess, stay back. These men are dangerous. Let us arrest them."

"I am well aware of that," she snapped back. "Very well. Are there more of you? These villains may well have accomplices waiting here."

"Not that we have seen," the officer replied.

He could have been no more than twenty. The Countess softened.

"Nevertheless, please be cautious," she said. "I am grateful for your concern for my safety."

He gave a shy smile and went back to his four colleagues standing around the vehicle. They were banging on it, demanding the occupants come out.

The Countess decided to be patient. It did look like they had captured Doctor Cornelius and this Frenchman called Hart. She had her pistol at the ready, in any event. She looked at Elizabeth, marveling at how the wheels were somehow intact after such a chase.

Suddenly, out of nowhere, came machine gun fire. The five gendarmes collapsed, dead.

From behind some trees came a group of Royal Navy sailors—she recognized the uniforms. Two were carrying a Maxim machine gun. She looked around. There were two men behind her with rifles aimed at her. She dropped her pistol, to their relief. Their apparent leader, a large man, dressed in a civilian tweed suit exclaimed loudly, in English, flexing his fingers:

"Always good to get one hands dirty!"

It was clear that he was the one who had done the firing. He pointed over to the Countess.

"Countess, would you be so kind as to join us?"

He pointed directly at her with a pistol. She looked at the bodies of the young gendarmes, including the one who had spoken to her. He had almost certainly saved her life; the machine gun fire had been indiscriminate. No offer of surrender had been made.

"Who are you?" she asked.

"One moment, Countess," their leader replied.

He turned to the Doctor's vehicle and slammed his palm on it twice.

"Come out! All is safe!"

The door of the vehicle opened, and Hart came out, followed by Doctor Cornelius and his driver. The Doctor stood and stared at the man who had told him to come out.

"Yes, Doctor Cornelius, it is I!"

The leader swung round to the Countess.

"I am Lord Burydan, at your service. I am in command of this operation."

He turned back and looked at the Doctor again. The Countess considered his turning his back on her more than rude. The Doctor looked at Lord Burydan. This man, along with his allies, was responsible for the destruction of the Red Hand. It was because of him that he had to fake his death, first going to Australia, and then to Berne.

"Yes, Doctor Cornelius," said Lord Burydan. "You have been unknowingly working for me. Ironic is it not? It disgusts me, of course, to use a vile criminal such as you. However, this is war, and my role in the Secret Service means that scum such as yourself have to be used. However, you are long overdue for execution for your many crimes against innocents."

"I have done as you asked; I expect safe passage and payment," said the Doctor calmly.

“Safe passage? Of course, we shall not turn you over to the Hun here…” he gestured to the Countess, “but I see no reason why we can’t drop you off at an American diplomatic station on our travels.”

The Countess spoke, annoyed by this vulgar Lord.

“If you mean by ‘Hun’ that I am German, might I point out that I am both Polish and a citizen of Austria-Hungary.”

Lord Burydan sneered at her. “That makes you Hun,” he said.

The Countess remained impassive.

Hart intervened. “Lord Burydan, whatever you think of this man, he was instrumental in getting us what we need to win this war within weeks—even days perhaps. We must ensure his safety and payment.”

“Very well,” Burydan said, with no enthusiasm. “Now, we must leave. Other policemen are no doubt on their way, along with soldiers. You, Countess, will come with us. I have no idea how much you know, but I certainly do not want the Hun to know it.”

“At least, not yet,” said Hart.

“I refuse,” she responded. “How dare you kidnap a woman! And was it necessary to murder these men? You had a machine gun, you could have asked for their surrender.”

“I know you pursued our agents from Sarajevo in that car,” he pointed at Elizabeth, “...and I know of your reputation as an adventurer. A fine occupation for a man, but not for a woman. As for these dead men, this is war.”

“One moment,” said Doctor Cornelius. He entered his vehicle, and then emerged. “It will explode when someone enters.”

“But a child could enter it!” exclaimed the Countess.

He smiled at her and gestured to Lord Burydan. “This is war.”

Lord Burydan simply nodded.

They moved down towards a cove. There was what appeared to be a fishing boat. The Countess realized it was some kind of camouflaged motorboat. They would no doubt be heading out to a larger vessel.

A few minutes into the sea, and a large explosion took place on the coast.

“It seems your vehicle was found, Doctor!” exclaimed Lord Burydan.

The Doctor looked satisfied. It was unfortunate that the vehicle was destroyed, but he did not want its advanced technology, built by engineers who were rumored to have shared some of Captain Nemo’s mechanical secrets, falling into the hand of the Habsburg Empire. He had paid good money for its construction; he would simply do so again after he got paid.

The Countess was assessing Lord Burydan. She knew of his role in destroying the Red Hand. He, too, was an adventurer, and she had heard he had signed up to fight with his old army regiment—clearly an invention to cover for his Secret Service activities. He was right about Doctor Cornelius, of course. However, his manner and his relish in killing those poor men was disturbing. She had noticed the sailors around him appeared to regard him warily. This did not seem to be fear, but rather uncertainty, as if they did not know what he might do next.

She looked at the Adriatic coast moving further into the distance. A thought came to her. She was not being restrained. She stood up and jumped off the boat into the water. She dived underneath, then surfaced. Her dress restricted her moves, and potentially could be dangerous, but she managed to get her shoes off. Then she heard shots.

"Get back in!" Lord Burydan bellowed.

She swam back. One of the sailors helped her on board.

"What were you thinking, Miss?" the sailor asked. "There was no way you could escape."

The Countess knew that. Escape, however, had not been her intention.

An hour or so later, the boat rendezvoused with what looked like a medium-sized cargo vessel, with an American flag. The Countess knew better, and when she got aboard, she could see that it was crewed by men in British naval uniforms. Presumably, there was a strong chance of capture this close to the coast, and the men did not wish to be shot as spies.

"What is to be done with me, Lord Burydan?" asked the Countess, mustering as much dignity as she could in her drenched state.

"Frankly, I think we should take you to London to stand trial as a spy. There is word that such people will end up being executed at the Tower of London."

"Lord Burydan, I can hardly be considered a spy. Might I remind you that I have operated on the territory of my Emperor and have been brought aboard against my will. If anyone is a spy to be executed, it is you, as you were not wearing a uniform when you murdered those gendarmes."

Lord Burydan looked infuriated. Hart quickly intervened.

"We can use her. A witness. We complete our operation and release her to tell the story. Having gained the last component of our weapon from one of their own barracks, it will be a further, devastating psychological blow. She will confirm what we will make public."

Lord Burydan beamed. "An excellent idea. I love the devious French mind! To the bridge!"

Hart gently indicated to the Countess to follow him. He was concerned for her; from what he knew of her, she was an honorable foe. Although he was pleased that his plan would also have a strategic effect.

Doctor Cornelius observed all this silently. He knew well that Lord Burydan had a violent, sadistic streak, at odds with his public image. Once, this Lord had thrown two Red Hand operatives into the sea to be eaten by alligators; yet, the men had been defeated and posed no threat. He would have to be cautious, especially as the Countess had raised the man's ire.

Lord Burydan and Hart led the Doctor and the Countess to the Bridge. There, the ship's commanding officer Captain Huntly looked at her and was horrified.

"This woman is dripping wet, Lord Burydan. She must be given dry garments—although we only have naval clothes."

Lord Burydan looked irritated. "I intend to explain our plans to the Countess!"

"I really must insist, Lord Burydan."

Captain Huntly had orders to follow the commands of this arrogant Lord, but this treatment of a woman was most intolerable.

The Countess raised her hand. "Thank you, Captain. Let us not annoy Lord Burydan. And I am most curious to hear his plans."

Lord Burydan beamed again. "You have heard of the French inventor, Thomas Roch?"

The Countess nodded. "The French weapons designer?"

The Lord nodded. "Yes. He had designed a superweapon, known as the Fulgurator. In an incident in which Monsieur Hart here was closely involved, he was working for some pirate or the other. This weapon could destroy warships at will, just like that," he clicked his fingers for emphasis. "He, and his pirate friends, ended up dead, along with a British submarine which was lost with all hands. Hart here, having actually been with Roch during that time, has been in charge of a French effort to reconstruct that weapon. We British had some information as to where a crucial element was being kept. Somehow or the other, the Hun—my apologies, the Austrian or whatever kind of Hun—had this fluid in Sarajevo. They were at a loss as to how to use it, given they had no knowledge of how to construct the Fulgurator. Now, we have it and intend to use it."

"Against warships?"

"Oh, no, Countess. Roch had underestimated his own skill. We think we can destroy towns. And we intend to do so today. Our target is Pula. We intend to wipe it off the face of the Earth. My superiors consider it would be uncivilized to destroy Vienna or Berlin, but Pula is less of problem."

The Countess was horrified. Was this possible? Pula was the major naval base for the Austro-Hungarian Navy, with warships and submarines stationed there. It would be a major defeat for the Empire.

"You say the whole city would be destroyed? Including civilians? Women and children? Those are crimes of war, to which you will be held accountable."

"Accountable by whom, Countess? I intend to see Berlin and Vienna destroyed. Why wait for negotiation or surrender? The British and French empires are to use this weapon—as we see fit. We shall conquer all those who look at us the wrong way."

At this point there was a feeling of unease throughout the bridge.

Hart spoke. "Our mission is solely to attack Pula. Berlin and Vienna are not on the agenda. Our orders are clear. In fact, I shall be adjusting the machine to limit the damage to Pula."

"Of course," Lord Burydan replied. "I merely wished to impress our power on the Countess."

"Now that you have, I would like to get into some dry clothes," the Countess said.

Captain Huntly ordered a rating to take her to his cabin and to provide her with whatever dry clothes he could find. He did not like Lord Burydan. The use of his ship as a spy boar was dangerous. A submarine would have been better, but Lord Burydan had insisted otherwise. He may have been right; patrols had left them alone. Risky, nonetheless.

The Countess looked around her as she was taken to the Captain's quarters. This was why she had jumped into the sea; it would mean having to be taken somewhere for dry clothing—a possibility for action. They passed an open door, with a man on telegraph duties. They came to the Captain's quarters.

"Stay inside, Miss" the sailor said, letting her in. He closed the door. "Charlie!" he shouted to someone. "Get some clothes for the posh foreign bird, mate!"

Posh foreign bird? thought the Countess. *These British!*

She hitched her dress up and removed a small pouch from a garter on her leg. She was pleased to see it was still there, given her dip in the sea, and even more to see that it was indeed waterproof as she had been told. Inside, were a number of small items, but it was the three small needles that were of importance.

A couple of minutes later, there was a knock on the door. She opened it and gratefully took the clothes from the sailor. Closing the door, she changed into what was a naval rating's fatigues. Naturally, it did not fit. However, it was at least more practical than her dress. There was not much she could do with her hair, but she put it up, and placed the three needles—very carefully—in it. She opened the door.

"I am ready. Please take me back to the bridge"

"I thought the Captain intended for you to stay here?"

"No, he did not."

The rating looked uncertain. This posh foreign bird could be right for all he knew. Worst that could happen was a bollocking—those were survivable.

He nodded toward the corridor and she got out and walked down. She stopped at the telegraph room, still open. She went in.

"What's in here?" she asked the operator.

She took a needle out of hair and pricked the radio operator on his hand. He was too surprised to stop her and simply gave a small cry and withdraw his hand sharply.

"Miss," said the rating, putting his hand firmly on her upper arm.

Swiftly she took another needle from her hair and scratched his hand.

After a few moments, both men were groggy. She grabbed the rating and pulled him into the cramped room, propping him by the wall. She awkwardly leaned over the telegraph operator and started sending information. It was fortunate that she had invested in being trained in such equipment within the commercial sector; even more fortunate that the *Evidenzbureau* had provided with the information needed to contact them.

She sent the message and left the communications room. The two sailors were still groggy and unable to move. That would not last long. She walked down the corridor; she thought it best to get off the vessel, fast. She would take her chances in the sea, but only if no one saw her jump in, which would be difficult.

A rating appeared entered the corridor ahead of her, with another behind him. She acted first.

"What kind of ship is this? I have been left by myself in a cabin without any guard to attend to me. Take me at once to your Captain!"

The startled ratings took her not to the bridge, but the bow. There was a strange contraption, looking like a large cannon, but with a box at the base of it with dials on it. A map of Europe with latitude and longitude was nearby, along with a large compass. Hart was looking over it, along with Lord Burydan. The Captain was also there. To the side, watching carefully, was Doctor Cornelius.

"Ah, Countess," said Lord Burydan. "You are just in time. The co-ordinates are set. No sense in hanging around. We merely have to point this thing in the right direction and press a button. And then… Farewell, Pula!"

At sea, all military vessels had received a message from Pula. The *Evidenzbureau* had acted swiftly with the Countess's information.

Captain Jelačić of the U-Boat U-48 looked through his periscope. He could see the vessel mentioned in his orders, with a neutral American flag on it. He hoped his superior officers had gotten this right.

"Prepare torpedoes," he ordered.

"Must we be so close to Pula, Lord Burydan?" asked Captain Huntly. "If this weapon has a long range as you claim, can we not fire this weapon from much further. We may be disguised but we are somewhat exposed."

"No, Captain," replied Lord Burydan. "The first test of the weapon is best done at close quarters to ensure a direct hit. More importantly, I believe some kind of massive cloud may be seen. Have you forgotten why we have a photographer?" he pointed to a rating with camera apparatus.

This man is endangering us all, thought Captain Huntly. As soon as Lord Burydan fired his weapon, he would order the ship to move at speed to safer waters. As far as he was concerned, he would interpret his having to obey this man's orders as having come to end with the attack on Pula.

The Countess knew she had to stall for time.

"Lord Burydan, surely attacking some land nearby would send the correct message?" she said. "Is there any need for such loss of life?"

Lord Burydan looked at her as if she were mad. He went over to the controls, pushing Hart aside.

"Total and immediate victory is what is required," he exclaimed. "No negotiation. Unconditional surrender. The end of your empire, which our diplomacy aimed at encircling for years, is one of our war objectives. And we will certainly deal with the Kaiser at the same time."

He turned a dial.

"You've turned up the power!" said Hart. "That will obliterate Pula entirely!"

"Quite so. And then, I will fire at Vienna and Berlin. Within minutes, the war will be over, our enemies in ruins. Who will worry about the Hun then? They will not come back from defeat. Britain and France will rule the world, as is our right."

"Are you mad? Those are not our orders!"

"They effectively are. Our masters gave operational control to me did they not? I will interpret that as I wish." He pointed at the map of Europe. "Thanks to you, I know very well how to use the Fulgurator." He took his pistol out of his holster. "And no-one will interfere."

Doctor Cornelius certainly was not going to; he was thinking of potential bases of operations that were not likely to blown up by this madman. He watched as Lord Burydan moved to the controls.

The Countess took out her last needle and lunged at Lord Burydan. He smashed her across the face with his pistol and she fell back onto the ground. She had just saved Pula.

At that moment, a huge explosion ripped through the ship, as torpedoes from the U-48 hit their mark.

The Fulgurator shifted and fell off the platform. Lord Burydan wildly hit a switch on it. A bright bolt of light soared upwards into the air. Within moments, there was explosion high in the air, with a blinding flash visible on the coast, disorientating the crew even further. The Countess had done her job. Lord Burydan was scrambling for his pistol, only to find it in the hands of the Countess. Captain Huntly had already barked orders to abandon ship.

"Abandon ship, gentlemen," said the Countess to Hart and Lord Burydan.

She pointed at them with the pistol. She had to ensure that they did not take any part of the Fulgurator with them. The Captain was busy supervising the men towards boarding the motorboat that they had used to bring the Countess and the others to the ship.

Hart moved away, but Lord Burydan lunged at the Countess. She fired at his chest, but the lurching ship meant that she hit him in the shoulder. He fell away. She pointed at the pistol again at Hart.

"*Au revoir*, Monsieur Hart," she said.

"*Au revoir*, Countess," he replied, and headed towards the lifeboat.

He considered getting the ratings to come back with rifles, but he did not fancy their chances.

Coming out of a doorway, was the rating and telegraph operator she had poisoned, recovering but still groggy.

"Captain!" she shouted.

Captain Huntly turned and saw her pointing at the men.

"They need help," she cried.

He and a rating rushed over and grabbed the men and took them away to the lifeboats. Men would die on this ship; but she was glad that the ones she had drugged were heading to safety, rather than dying without a chance. Flames came out of the doorway they had used; a fire had started and taken hold. There was a rifle on the deck. She picked it up. She turned, only to see Doctor Cornelius attempting to take the phial from the Fulgurator. Even now, he tried to seek advantage.

Perhaps an extra payment for saving at least this, he thought.

The Countess fired in the air. The Doctor got the message. He moved away. There was no time to retrieve any parts of the weapon. And she did want to live. She fired some rapid shots into the machine. A bullet hit the phial, and its mysterious liquid splattered all over the deck.

"Join your paymasters, Doctor Cornelius."

It occurred to her that perhaps she should kill him. He deserved death, but only by legal process. More importantly, when the time came, she was unsure she could explain to God why she killed a man in cold blood.

Lord Burydan had gotten back to his feet. The pain of the shot had deranged him more than he already was. The ship was lurching to port, and the platform holding the fulgurator slammed to the side of the boat; the weapon flew off the boat and into the sea.

"Farewell, Lord Burydan!" the Countess cried.

She jumped over the side. Lord Burydan heard her, but he was not facing her; he was staring at where the Fulgurator had gone over the side. Doctor Cornelius saw a chance. He grabbed him from behind and shoved him into the burning corridor, seeing him fall to the floor.

Captain Huntly staggered back on the bow.

"It is only us left on board, Captain," said the Doctor. "The woman has jumped, and we can do nothing for those souls in the fire. Lord Burydan went in there, looking for survivors… I fear he is lost."

But at that very moment, Lord Burydan came out of the door, aflame. He was clawing at this face.

The Captain rushed over to him and pushed him overboard. Doctor Cornelius was already in the water. He saw the Countess swimming away, avoiding the motorboat. Flames were blasting out of the doorways. There was no more he could do. He jumped into the water, grabbed Lord Burydan—as Doctor Cornelius had not bothered—and swam to the motorboat. Once on board, it moved off at speed.

The Countess swam hard. She wanted to avoid any possibility of being taken down by the swell the ship would make when it headed to the bottom. She saw a U-boat surface. Men appeared on its conning tower. She did not want to be taken for a British sailor. She cried out in German:

"Help! I am Countess Irina Petrovski!"

Captain Jelačić saw her through her binoculars.

"We were told to look out for that woman; she is on our side. Pick her up!"

He could see the British motorboat heading away. He contacted Pula. His orders were clear: bring the woman back to Pula, other units would pick up the British.

Weeks later, Doctor Cornelius was back in Berne. Not in his office, of course. His cover had been blown, and the Swiss gendarmerie were taking the place apart. Swiss neutrality was irrelevant; it was his criminal activities in their country they were interested in. Instead, he was in a comfortable house, amusing himself with the international press. *The Sculptor of Human Flesh Lives!* screamed one tabloid headline. Somehow, the British eluded the Austro-Hungarian navy and had reached a submarine vessel of their own.

Due to his exposure in Sarajevo, he had been driven underground. But he had prepared for such eventualities. The money the French and British had paid him was substantial. And Lord Burydan was hideously scarred, a wreck of a man now. That also amused him. It was revenge for his role in destroying the Red Hand. He would now plan his next move. This war had, so far, been very profitable indeed.

In Vienna, Countess Irina Petrovski was at the Hofburg palace. She was receiving the Military Order of Maria Theresa from the elderly Habsburg Emperor, Franz Joseph. She was bursting with pride, and was in a good mood, despite news of things going badly in Galicia against the Russians. She believed the Russians would be fought back. She had been complemented on her beauty, but she was more pleased with the praise for her bravery. Any problems about her being woman—and not formally in the military—were set aside. She was happy that the gendarmes from Sarajevo were at the ceremony; given the June assassination, this success would help their reputation.

The Emperor gave her the medal.

"Thank you, my child. You have done well."

He said it in Polish, which for the Countess was a great sign. The heir presumptive, Charles, was present. He had expressed a wish to listen to her ideas on Poland. She was delighted. Perhaps Franz Ferdinand's thinking on reform would still see light. But first, there was a war to be won.

As mentioned earlier, Martin Gately who has built a corpus of stories featuring Gaston Leroux's journalist sleuth, Joseph Rouletabille (now available in a collected form as The New Exploits of Joseph Rouletabille*), has decided to embark on a new sequence as well, this one starring Jules Verne's Robur. But unlike Nathan Cabaniss, we are invited to behold the "birth" of Robur in this first in a series of stories focusing on the adventures of "Young Robur," detailing who he was, where he came from, and how he became the future misanthropic "Master of the World" that Verne depicted in his books....*

Martin Gately: *The Woodlanders in the Desert*

Arizona Territory, 1866

Thy dawn O Master of the World, thy dawn;
The hour the lilies open on the lawn,
The hour the grey wings pass beyond the mountains,
The hour of silence, when we hear the fountains.
James Elroy Flecker

Isn't it interesting that all the right and admirable views Robur held made him a misfit and a villain in his own time?
David Frankham, August 2020
(Phil Evans in the 1961 movie adaptation of *Master of the World*)[4]

Deputy Sheriff Thaddeus Frycollin spurred his horse down the slope and found himself enveloped in the pall of red desert dust kicked up by his mount's hooves. There were two bad *hombres* out there somewhere, and he wasn't sure if the dust cloud was going to make it more difficult to draw a bead on him, or if he was just magnificently drawing attention to himself. Either way, it was obvious McKay and Stine had left the trail and were in hiding places somewhere amongst the boulders down below. Actually, neither of these bank robbers were particularly good shots, and he'd probably have to wait until he was almost upon them before they attempted an ambush.

The field of boulders before him was a veritable labyrinth. Each huge rock was between ten and twelve feet high, and some were as wide as sixteen feet. Frycollin dismounted and wrapped the reins almost ritualistically around a small weather-bleached tree stump. Had she a mind to do so, his horse, Betsy, could've

[4] Quote provided specifically by Mr. Frankham for this story and used with permission.

dragged the stump and wandered off, but she wouldn't—she was far too well trained. He removed his Colt Navy 1851 with shoulder stock from his saddle holster and started moving forward, ready to shoot from the hip.

The golden sun continued to shine down from a turquoise sky. Through a gap in the regiment of boulders, Frycollin thought he saw a town or a village way to the north in shadowed hills, but it could only be a trick of the light. Nevertheless, it had looked like uncanny stucco buildings clustered around a church tower. Yet, he knew that there were no settlements this far into the desert...

There was a sudden prismatic haze, as if the sun was being reflected off of a body or water, or a host of mirrors, and the mirage disappeared completely. Well, almost completely... From high up where the church tower had been, there was still a scintilla of bouncing light, and it gave him the unaccountable feeling he was being observed. Whatever it was, he resolved to ignore it. This was not the time for distractions. There happened to be two desperate fugitives concealed somewhere in these rocks, and the thing they were desperate to do was get the drop on him.

"Don't move, you black bastard," rasped McKay.

Frycollin felt the barrel of the man's LeMat revolver press into his back just south of his right kidney.

The shambling bulk of Elias Stine hove into view around a boulder off to the left. He was covering Frycollin with what looked to be a cheap Sharps carbine. The bank robbers obviously hadn't stopped anywhere long enough to use the proceeds of their last haul to buy decent weapons. These days, most anyone with any class had switched to a Winchester.

"Where's the rest of the posse?" demanded McKay.

"They left the trail about a quarter of a mile back, they'll be in positions of concealment all around you by now," lied Frycollin.

Naturally, he had come after this pair alone.

"Positions of concealment! Listen to 'im talk," mocked Stine, as he strode forward and nonchalantly relieved the Deputy of his Colt Navy.

"Looks like we got ourselves a hostage," said McKay.

"Have we?" questioned Stine. "Do you really think they'll care if we threaten to kill one o' his kind?"

"Oh, they'll care, believe me," reassured Frycollin.

"I wasn't talkin' tuh you, boy," said Stine, as he struck Frycollin a hard blow across the mouth with the butt of his carbine.

It was a blow he could easily have tolerated without any sort of reaction, but he needed an excuse to drop to his knees and this provided it. Practiced sleight of hand meant the derringer he always carried tucked into his boot was now cupped in his hand, and neither of the two men had seen it. They had been too busy looking at him rather theatrically wiping the blood from his mouth. The one thing he hadn't anticipated was he'd have one of them in front of him, the other behind, and that they would maintain these positions. It wasn't going to be easy.

The execution of the shot aimed at Stine's knee went pretty well. The man actually looked around to see where the bullet had come from, as if he had been sniped at by someone else from Frycollin's fictional posse.

Frycollin could see the gleaming white of exposed kneecap bone through the hole in the fabric—at least for a second—then blood started to flow and be absorbed by the material of his pants, like ink on a blotter.

Stine dropped onto his backside, whimpering and cursing. The Sharps carbine abandoned as he cradled his shattered knee. The shot at McKay did not go so well, however. Frycollin rolled and ducked as if he too were trying to avoid shots from the imaginary sniper. Coming out of the roll he fired the derringer's second and final round at McKay's head. But the bank robber had glimpsed the tiny pistol in the lawman's had and reflexively jerked his head away in a whipping action, so the bullet only creased his temple. He staggered away, firing blindly with both his own revolver and Frycollin's.

Frycollin felt his collar bone shatter as the bullet struck it. Infuriatingly, the round had come from his Colt Navy. He hurled the derringer at McKay with his good arm, and leaped to his feet as best he could as the bank robber retreated around to the far side of the boulder.

The fight seemed to have gone out of Stine, but this did not prevent Frycollin from kicking him hard in the head to take him out of the picture completely. He grabbed from the sun-baked ground the cheap and nasty Sharps carbine; he was going to have to use it one-handed.

Grimacing somewhat from the pain of his injury, the lawman looked down at his shirt to see the denim was turning to a deep, purplish crimson as it soaked up his blood. His tin star—that normally impressive mark of his trade—was now mounted on a nausea inducing field of red. He wondered now how much latitude of action he would have until he passed out from loss of blood. And he wondered at the hubris of undertaking this endeavor without companions.

McKay would either return back round the huge, wind weathered boulder the same way he had departed, or circle all the way round it. In any event, it would be best for Frycollin if he backed off. And in doing so, he became aware for the first time of a figure standing atop the boulder.

A lad of perhaps eighteen or nineteen, well-built, muscular, with a head that was perhaps just a little overlarge, or overly spheroid—giving the impression it must be rather overstuffed with brains—stood there. Yet, there was something about the set of his handsome features, the sweep of his brow, which suggested the strength and tenacity of a young bull. Here was the personification of the Zodiac's Taurus; a minotaur, but in entirely human form.

Inexplicably, the boy was carrying a small golden crossbow, and its bolt was connected by a slender copper wire to a brass cylinder worn by the youth on his back like a hiking pack. Had the boy's initial silhouette not been so very different in appearance to McKay's, Frycollin might have loosed a shot at him. As it was, the boy was merely a massive distraction, even more so as he put an index finger to his lips to request silence, lest the Deputy give his position away.

McKay was suddenly in sight, with pistols blazing. As he fired, the youth shot his crossbow with great accuracy, hitting the bandit in the back of the shoulder. Immediately, he yelped in pain, dropped his weapons, and commenced to jig around like some possessed scarecrow before collapsing on the ground, still twitching.

Frycollin had been hit mid-thigh by one of McKay's shots. His only concern now was to prevent himself from bleeding to death. He removed his neckerchief and tried to apply it as a tourniquet, but his strength was starting to fail him.

The youth jumped effortlessly down from the rock and started to assist him.

"I saw you from the church tower with my telescope," explained the boy. "You looked like you could use a modicum of assistance…"

Frycollin grimaced and ground his teeth as the tourniquet was tightened to the maximum possible extent.

"I thought I saw some kind of small town with a mission church in the heat haze yonder, but I reasoned it was just a mirage," said the lawman.

"The Woodlanders' Haven is no ordinary town," said the boy. "It can only be seen at certain times of day or when the sun is right… but the important thing is to get you there right away for medical treatment. We have a very experienced nurse."

The youth shouldered his crossbow and gently lifted up Frycollin like he was no weight at all, then commenced as if to walk to the town.

"No, no," said Frycollin. "First of all, get my Colt Navy pistol from over there; second, my horse is still around here someplace. Bring him here and put me in the saddle and it will be easier for both of us.

Equally gently, Frycollin was set back down while the boy picked up the two fallen revolvers.

"Which one is it?" he queried.

"Don't think I ever met a boy in the Arizona Territory who didn't know what a Colt Navy looked like," smiled Frycollin through the pain. "Mine is the one fitted with a shoulder stock."

"We aren't allowed any weapons in my community," said the boy. "This electric crossbow is my own invention and I'd impose on you to keep its existence to yourself. You'll see I have to stash it in a concealed locker just outside the town limits."

The boy looked casually down at the fallen form of Stine.

"You know this one is dead?" said the boy.

He was right. One of McKay's wild shots had struck his partner under the chin, creating a ragged exit hole decorated with spongy brain matter on the crown of his scalp.

"No loss," stated Frycollin, flatly. "He brutalized a woman customer in one bank he robbed, and shot a teller in another."

"The other one will be unconscious for around twelve hours. I'll have to sling him across the rear end of your horse. Grand Pater Platanus will decide what is to be done with him," grinned the youth.

"There's only one thing to be done with him. I need to take him back to the Territorial capital to stand trial," said Frycollin, with just a touch of incredulity edging into his voice.

But the handsome boy only laughed sardonically.

"You have exceeded the limits of your jurisdiction, deputy sheriff."

Frycollin started to drift into unconsciousness; he had suffered two gunshot injuries in quick succession. He awoke very briefly when the boy poured water from a canteen into his mouth. Then, later, he occasionally stirred if his horse, which the boy was leading by the reins on foot, stumbled slightly.

Frycollin was still slumped over the neck of his horse when he next came round. The boy was crouched at the base of a low hillock, apparently concealing his forbidden crossbow inside a cylindrical hole with a small, hinged, camouflaged door.

The landscape had become bewildering. They were picking their way through a forest of tall mirrors, some oddly curved, bent back on themselves, others just large and rectangular. There were also tall sheets of plain glass, bigger than the department store windows he had seen back east. Both mirrors and glass were supported by carefully constructed wooden frames. Some skilled carpenter had been at work here. It seemed that the purpose of it all was to deceive the eye—to keep from sight this Woodlanders' Haven by means of a Pepper's Ghost-style illusion perpetrated on a colossal, almost industrial, scale.

They moved beyond the arrangement of mirrors and, suddenly, the little town—really only a village—became plainly visible. Beautiful whitewashed stucco houses, modest but well-kept villas with elaborate gardens, and overlooking it all the tall campanile of a mission church. Yet, none of this should be here. Frycollin knew there were no settlements this far into the desert. Everybody knew it. Had they built this place entirely in secret? But, how? Why? The buildings of the little town started to spin. Frycollin lapsed back into oblivion.

Frycollin could feel how professionally his shoulder had been bandaged from the second he awoke. The bandages were wound around so tightly it gave a feeling of compression and immobility that was oddly comforting. He could also feel he was heavily loaded with tincture of laudanum. His left leg was propped up on pillows and equally tightly bandaged. The drug had produced a characteristic floating sensation, accompanied by a carefree semi-drunkenness. He'd been given it once before, when he'd been stabbed in Carson City, and he still recalled the crashing headache and lethargy that had ensued when the doctor had stopped administering it.

Sun streamed through the stained-glass windows of the infirmary, dappling the white stucco walls with patches of lime, mauve and rose. It was an infirmary in which he was the only patient. The staff were minimal. Virtually all of his needs were met by the formidable Sister Avellana, or her novice Sister Myrtle. His questions tended to be evaded. He could not determine what religious order, if any, these women belonged to. Christian iconography featured heavily in the décor, yet it was not the typical Catholic statuary one usually saw in the South West. He could not precisely place it, but he wondered if it was Greek Orthodox or Russian. He'd briefly been inside a Greek church during his time in Philadelphia.

There wasn't much more to say about the infirmary staff: Sister Myrtle was as quiet as a mouse. He was certain of one thing: Sister Avellana had learnt her healing craft far away in some field hospital in war time; everything about her efficiency and skill signaled it. Oh, perhaps one more thing: neither of them spoke English with any discernible accent. Not a trace of a regional inflection and certainly nothing resembling a foreign accent. Where, then, had they come from? No answers of any kind were forthcoming.

The boy, whom he now knew to be called Robur, brought him peaches from the orchard to aid his recovery. Robur told him, once he was well enough, that he would soon have an audience with Grand Pater Platanus, the divinely appointed leader of the Woodlanders.

Frycollin asked after McKay, but could not get a straight answer from either Robur or the nurses. McKay was subject to confinement. And that was all. One time, he had been awoken in the night by the sound of a man begging for mercy. Had the voice been McKay's? He couldn't be sure, for sometimes it seemed to be mixed with animal calls, as if from some far-off menagerie. Would a Christian community scourge and punish a criminal? Maybe they would. But while they kept him full of laudanum, he had difficulty thinking coherently about any subject.

Something he did realize: in his haste to get medical attention, he had forgotten all about recovering the proceeds of the bank robbery. There was a horse wandering out there in the desert with nearly $20,000 in its saddle bags. Had it succumbed to the heat? Found its lonely way back to town? Or joined a herd of wild mustangs? He wasn't going to find out laying here. He had to get word back his superiors, but all his requests to Sister Avellana were met with an evasive indifference. He was not to concern himself with anything other than his recovery.

What seemed to be about a week later, Sister Myrtle introduced him to his wheeled invalid chair, and eased him gently into it. Each morning he was pushed out onto the balcony overlooking the peach orchard. The fresh air and sunshine did cheer him somewhat, and eased his misgivings about this strange and inexplicable community. It was tranquil and relaxing here. And he was certainly getting better. They were easing off gradually on the laudanum. He could feel the tightness of the stitches in his leg and shoulder, sore and lumpy. Perhaps he didn't sleep as well now, but he was glad to be free of the grip of the drug.

One afternoon, he was dozing fitfully after a long morning out on the balcony—it was perhaps a couple of hours since Sister Myrtle had helped him back into his bed.—when he was awakened by the most delicious aroma he had ever smelled. It was so intensely spicy that he was immediately salivating. It was emanating from the large communal kitchens which lay beyond the boundary of the orchard. Usually, the food he was served was a little unimaginative and bland. It seemed as if tonight, he was going to be offered a superb *chili con carne*.

Suddenly, he felt ravenous, and his belly grumbled audibly at the prospect of having to wait another few hours for something substantial to eat. Then there were the sounds of a fiesta commencing: a hubbub of people and lively guitar music. But it was a party to which he had not been invited. Nevertheless, he wanted to see what was happening. He was pretty confident that he could make it out of bed and into the invalid chair, and then wheel it safely onto the balcony.

He swung both his legs over the side of the bed, and then eased down until his feet touched the floor. A jolt of pain erupted in his thigh, and he felt the stitches under stress. But they held, and he realized it would be just as difficult to get fully back into bed now as to lower himself into the wheeled chair. Without thinking, he attempted to use his left arm to bear some of the weight, and the pain was shocking. He gritted his teeth and continued, much relieved when the chair was taking all of his weight.

He tried to propel himself towards the balcony, but nothing much happened. The chair moved about half an inch. How had he gotten so weak? He pushed again and ignored the sickening grinding in his shoulder. With the renewed effort, he started to gather momentum, and the invalid chair began to creep quietly across the marble-tiled floor. His stamina saw him through and the chair came to rest about six inches from the balcony wall. Fortunately, the chair was well oiled and neither of the nurses emerged from the nursing station to make any kind of investigation.

Frycollin looked down into the peach orchard, and very nearly guffawed with amusement when he saw what was in progress. A crowd that must surely have represented all of the young people of Woodlanders' Haven had gathered to watch two young men eat. The two sat at a trestle table with large white bowls in front of them. By the side of the table was what could almost have been described as a witches' cauldron; but in it was not any kind of potion. This was the place from which the extraordinary aroma had originated!

One of the young men was Robur; the other he did not know, He was a corpulent looking youth with an untidy mass of straw-colored hair. Presiding over these proceedings was a mustachioed man of Gallic appearance dressed in the tall hat and whites of a top restaurant chef. Over the thrum of guitar music in the background, Frycollin could just about make out what was being intoned by the chef. It confirmed what he had already surmised: this was a good, old fashioned chili eating contest.

"Robur! Carpinus!" shouted the chef, brandishing his serving ladle for maximum effect. "You will each be served one full ladle of chili at a time. Once you have eaten it, you will be served another. There will be no water… There will be no leaving the table once the competition has commenced. Whoever eats the most chili wins. If you consume the entire cauldron, more is being prepared in the kitchens."

Suddenly, Robur looked straight up at Frycollin's balcony.

"Wait, Topage!" implored Robur. "I want to bring my friend down to the contest..."

And with that, Robur leapt up and took off like a hare in the direction of the infirmary.

Within moments, a grinning Robur was carrying Frycollin bodily down the stairs with great gentleness and ease. And a chair was brought out almost as if the deputy sheriff was going to be the third contestant.

"Hey! Do I get to eat some of this stuff?" asked the deputy sheriff.

There was a general murmuring of laughter from the good-tempered crowd.

"Just try a very little," said the chef, Topage. "You will find it very hot, *mon ami*."

Half a ladle was deposited into a small white crockery bowl for Frycollin's consumption. He spooned some into his mouth with gusto. He decided immediately it could not have felt so very different had he put volcanic magma onto his tongue. Yes, there was the texture of high quality, beautifully cooked mince, of beans, tomatoes, and perhaps even finely chopped mushrooms, but this was all overpowered to the nth degree by chili heat so powerful that it created the sensation that the interior of his mouth was being stabbed by tiny unseen daggers. He swallowed the stuff down just to get it away from his tongue, and prepared to let loose a string of invective from his wide vocabulary of curse words that he would never have usually used in polite company. But his throat was so sore now that he could articulate nothing more than a froggy croak.

Topage removed the lid from a bottle of cold beer and handed it to Frycollin.

"This will wash some of the sting away," said the chef. "Anyway, it works better than water, or milk."

Frycollin took a long swig then paused to glance at the label. A professionally printed bottle label proclaimed this to be *Woodlanders' Haven Beer*, with an illustration of the stucco village below the wording. It all seemed highly incongruous.

"Let the battle commence!" said Robur, resuming his seat.

Carpinus merely nodded and looked impatient. The crowd forgot their mirth at Frycollin's discomfort and settled down to watch the contest. The lawman merely sat there, wishing he could pack his entire mouth with mountain snow until the pain abated.

To begin with, the contest seemed fairly even. Robur filled his mouth with the super-hot food as if it was merely coal being stoked into a boiler. He was irresistible, indefatigable... He actually seemed to be enjoying himself. And Carpinus was a worthy opponent. His capacious gut absorbed ladle after ladle. Frycollin could not help but imagine their innards—each young man gradually transforming his stomach into a fiery representation of Dante's Inferno.

After perhaps six ladles full, the competition began to slow. Great beads of perspiration broke out on the forehead of Carpinus, then his cheeks turned a deep and ruddy scarlet. He began to ruminate on the chili like a cow, chewing it over and over. At this point, Robur pulled ahead, finishing a ladle and gesturing to Topage for another. But Carpinus refused to quit. He forced more of the stuff into his gullet as his eyes began to stream uncontrollably.

Robur ate like a machine, but even he was starting to look flushed. He was now perhaps three ladles ahead. The other young people of the Haven chanted Robur's name as if he was some athletic hero rounding the corner at the end of the race. Carpinus called for another ladle, but as the food plopped down into his bowl, he thought the better of it. His complexion had shifted from ruddy to greenish, and with undue haste, he got up and ran from the table, displaying a speed one would not necessarily have associated with his overweight form.

The crowd laughed at the boy's sudden departure, but with good humor rather than malice. Topage declared Robur to be the undisputed winner, and Frycollin slapped him hard on the back to congratulate him.

"My good man," began Frycollin, "your digestion would be thought first class, even in an ostrich!"

And Robur laughed heartily at this, for it was surely the most unusual, and yet the sincerest compliment he had ever received.

"Then that shall always be my proudest boast," said Robur. "But it is an unusual turn of phrase. Why compare me to an ostrich rather than any other animal?"

"Well, only from personal experience, after I escaped slavery, I spent a little time in Philadelphia, and in the zoological gardens there, they used to keep an ostrich. The crowd would throw large inedible objects for it to eat so they could see its neck bulge after it swallowed them. I saw it successfully eat a baseball once. The keepers caused a ruckus when somebody threw a soccer ball into its enclosure one time—not sure why, it would've been too big for its beak anyways…"

They chatted a little while longer until a furious Sister Avellana came down to retrieve Frycollin and broke up the party. Not wanting to receive a tongue-lashing, Robur melted away into the crowd just seconds after the nurse's arrival.

Then Sister Avellana drafted Topage into carrying Frycollin back up to the infirmary. The lawman had anticipated some sort of punishment or reprimand, but there was none. The invalid chair was put back by the side of the bed exactly where it had been, and he was given an instruction not too exert himself, coupled with a surprisingly large dose of the orally administered laudanum. The result was that he slept a deep and largely dreamless sleep until the drug wore off in the middle of the night.

He returned to consciousness as suddenly as a released cork bobbing up to break the surface meniscus of water. He could see a little portion of the night sky through the glass of the balcony door, and the firmament was a sickly green with a shimmering curtain-like shape billowing constantly across it. Yes, he recalled it now. There has been reports in the *Tucson Tribune* that the Northern Lights were being seen an unprecedentedly long way south this year. He'd imagined they'd be something faint and rather dilute. But, in fact, it hurt his eyes a little to look at the phenomenon. He rolled over and did his best to get back to sleep.

The day came when Sister Avellana told Frycollin he would have an audience with Grand Pater Platanus that afternoon. They obviously thought he was substantially on the road to recovery. It was true, he could stand for short periods and was starting now to walk with crutches. He'd had regular visits from Robur, and the girl who seemed to be his sweetheart—Artemisia—but he could not get any sense out of either of them as to when he might be allowed to leave the Haven and be escorted back to Prescott, the Territory capital. It also still seemed impossible to convince them to send word to the Sheriff's office that he was alive, but recuperating. He had given up asking where McKay was.

He could not help but wonder if McKay had already had an "audience" with the Grand Pater and parlayed his way to a release. Frycollin was not a particularly religious man; he had seen, in his early life, too many devout men who were dripping with cruelty, and he did not trust the reasoning of the overly religious. McKay's crimes were not something that could be unilaterally forgiven by the religious leader of this strange community. And forgiveness itself was a fool's game. What could be more delightful to any miscreant than the possibility of being easily forgiven with no expectation he should reform? Breaking rocks at the Yavapai County Jail for a couple of decades was both what McKay deserved and what he would get if Frycollin had any say in it.

It was a quiet and somber Robur who arrived to wheel Frycollin along the link corridor between the infirmary and the Grand Pater's Council Chamber. At the arched doorway entrance to the chamber was a sight which caused the lawman's heart to momentarily jump: a gaggle of white robed and hooded figures that looked like they belonged at a Klan meeting.

As they got closer, Frycollin realized these were ecclesiastical robes, and the faces beneath the hoods were bandaged tightly with fresh white bandages; the same was true of the hands. Yet, he had never seen these people being treated in the infirmary, though that had to be Sister Avellana's trademark bandaging.

The bandaged people parted before Robur and Frycollin, and they were admitted to the rather beautiful and tranquil council chamber. Light flooded in through the stained-glass windows making a haphazard pastel mosaic of hues on the white stucco walls. The chamber was a circular auditorium of empty rosewood seats. Only one man was present, another figure in white, but devoid of bandages.

As they neared him, Frycollin saw Grand Pater Platanus was a man perhaps nearing seventy. Tall and upright, he might've stepped out of a children's storybook of Bible tales, cast from the very template of an Old Testament patriarch, with the jutting square-cut beard, the fiery eyes beneath a worry-creased brow. He held in his hand a stout wooden staff which had the look of a weapon rather than an aid to walking, and his robes were richly embroidered across the front with the design of a tree in full leaf. The patriarch stood next to a small table. Something was on the table, but covered with a green cloth. He looked a little like he was waiting for their arrival so he could perform a parlor magic trick.

"Good afternoon, Deputy Sheriff Frycollin," said Grand Pater Platanus. "I have much been looking forward to this meeting."

But the man's tone and words were mismatched. His voice was hesitant and lacking in warmth. Frycollin gained the immediate impression this was actually an appointment the Grand Pater had been putting off, and wished he didn't have to trouble himself with.

"So have I," said Frycollin, forcing a smile. "I've been wanting to ask you when Robur here will be able to head over to Prescott to let my superiors know I'm still alive. He can borrow my horse if he needs to."

Frycollin looked over his shoulder at Robur, who was nodding and grinning enthusiastically.

"That is a highly generous offer, but this is a strict religious community, and its members must be sealed off from the temptations of the outside world," said Platanus.

"Well, Prescott has its problems, but it's not exactly Sodom and Gomorrah rolled into one. The boy could spend a day or two there without undue peril to his soul," assured Frycollin.

"That is not your decision to make, Deputy Sheriff," said Platanus. "I have a particularly duty towards the young people of Woodlanders' Haven, many of whom have never traveled beyond the forest of mirrors which preserves our privacy. They are innocents. And innocents they must remain."

"I take it that, when I am fully recovered, you won't hinder my departure?" asked Frycollin.

"Of course not. You'll merely be required to make a solemn religious vow not to reveal the location of this community," said Platanus.

"I'm not exactly a religious man," said Frycollin.

"Then perhaps we have problem, or at least a conundrum for you," said Platanus. "The sooner you discover how to rekindle your religious faith, the sooner you will have your liberty."

"That's not fair!" interjected Robur. "I only brought Frycollin here because he needed medical attention. He is a man of the law and man of honor; we should trust him, not compel him to make vows. If Professor Oxalis were here…"

Suddenly, Platanus' voice was like thunder.

"But Oxalis is not here. Just as Lucifer was cast down from Heaven, so Oxalis was driven out into the wilderness when he fell so far from the high values of this community and sought to defy the laws of God," he bellowed.

"Without the genius of Oxalis, you would not even have your forest of mirrors…" said Robur, before suddenly falling silent with his eyes downcast, his capacity to defy his leader all but exhausted.

"I need to check on my prisoner, the bank robber, McKay," explained Frycollin. "Where are you keeping him?"

"He is being kept in a very safe place," said Platanus. "However, he is no longer your prisoner, but rather mine. Until I have effected a total rehabilitation of his criminal tendencies, he will remain here. The brothers and sisters of the Eschar will be his special guardians, watching over him day and night. There are no banks here for him to rob, and we have very little of monetary value."

"Who are the Eschar?" asked Frycollin.

Platanus relaxed at this question, and suddenly looked less cagey, but Frycollin didn't trust him. It felt like he was questioning an unwilling witness.

"Many years ago, this community was located in the forests of California—the woodland our name suggests—until one summer, our compound found itself in the path of a devastating forest fire. Through the Power of Christ and the skill of Sister Avellana we prevailed. None died in the conflagration, but some were so badly burned that I declared their survival to be a miracle. I vowed then that we would not suffer so again. I led us here, and whatever happens to us in this place, at least we will not suffer such agonies again," said Platanus. "The Eschar are my most loyal supporters, some might say fanatical—their sins burned away by the fire. They are the purest of us all. You will have seen some of their number just outside this chamber."

Frycollin looked again at Robur, wanting some sign of confirmation that this represented the true origins of this strange community. The youth gave the slightest nod of his head. It was true as far as Robur knew, though it all happened when he was only a small child.

"Move back to God quickly, Mr. Frycollin," said Platanus. "Since your arrival here, the green sickness of the Heavens has increased and increased. Every night, it is brighter. God is dissatisfied with your presence here."

"You're darn right," shot back Frycollin. "He's angry you haven't released me. If you let me go now, I'm sure the Good Lord will move the Aurora Borealis back to where only polar bears and Eskimos can see it."

Platanus ignored the jibe and instead lifted the cloth on the small table at his side to reveal Frycollin's Colt Navy.

"Robur, since you were his apprentice, fire up Oxalis' forge and melt down this weapon," said Platanus. "It has no place here, and has already polluted our tranquility for too long."

Robur took the pistol from his leader and tucked it into the capacious pocket of his robe. Frycollin had no intention of protesting; it all would have been a waste of breath. He would work on Robur once they were out of this chamber. It would take all of his powers of persuasion, and possibly a little blackmail into the bargain, but he could not be expected to make his way across this territory unarmed.

With the audience ended, albeit not really to the satisfaction of either party, Robur wheeled Frycollin out of the chamber and back towards the infirmary.

"I need that pistol, Robur," said Frycollin with some force. "Don't be tossing it into any furnace."

"How can I disobey him?" said Robur. "He is one of the greatest holy men ever to have lived, and I am just a boy. If only Professor Oxalis were here.. He was the only one who could ever reason with the Grand Pater, or get him to change his mind. But, that is all behind us now. Oxalis has been cast out into the desert like some Judas Goat. For me, it is akin to a bereavement. I have learned nothing of science and engineering since he left, and my education is not complete. The Grand Pater sees no purpose to science, he'd rather we all just studied scripture…"

"How did this falling out between Platanus and Oxalis arise anyway?" asked Frycollin.

"It was simple enough," explained Robur. "Oxalis wanted to build a flying machine to allow him to soar up into the Heavens."

Normally, Frycollin was a man who could easily think of a witty riposte or remark, but on this occasion, words failed him. His jaw hung rather slackly and his eyebrows raised up towards those very same Heavens Robur had just mentioned. The only thought he could muster was: *is this actually an insane asylum?*

It was almost two weeks later when Frycollin found Robur moping in the peach orchard. The lawman was now just using a single crutch; in fact, he could've probably done without it completely—albeit he still had a painful limp—but he did not want to reveal that to the Eschar, who often seemed to be observing him, doubtless on the orders of Platanus.

Frycollin guessed that Robur was still mourning the death of his formal education, but in that he was completely wrong.

"It is Artemisia," proclaimed Robur. "She no longer wishes to be my love. She has thrown me over for another."

"Why, the girl must be some kind of fool," sympathized Frycollin, as best he could.

"Precisely," agreed Robur. "Who could be more handsome and accomplished than I?"

"Perhaps she's looking for someone a little more modest," said Frycollin, stifling a chuckle.

"I feel an intention forming to get away from here, even if only for a few weeks, to clear my head and find Oxalis," said Robur.

"Hold your horses a minute… find Oxalis? Surely, he could be anywhere by now. You might never locate him," reasoned Frycollin.

"Sometimes he comes back, close enough to send flashes on his heliograph. So maybe he's just a few miles away. He left me a heliograph and a codebook when he suspected he was going to be cast out. But the Eschar found them in one of their searches and confiscated them. And if the Eschar ever saw the signals, they wouldn't let me leave the compound for days, or even weeks."

"I'm a man-tracker, my friend," said Frycollin. "If he's come that close, then I'll be able to follow his trail back to wherever his new base of operations is."

"And are you well enough now for such an expedition?" asked Robur.

"Getting stronger every day," grinned Frycollin, as he theatrically—and temporarily—cast away his crutch before seeking demonstrate his current faltering mode of walking.

"Say, what was he signaling to you anyway?" asked Frycollin.

"Well, my memory is good, but without the codebook, I was only getting fragments. A couple of words which kept repeating were 'hop' and 'ant,' I think. I couldn't really make head nor tail of it," confessed Robur.

And so, the secret enterprise of leaving the Haven was entered into by the boy and the man. All of their preparations had to be clandestine, and there seemed to be only one person who enjoyed Robur's complete confidence. This was Topage, the *cordon bleu* chef who had somehow become head of catering and provisions for this all but self-sufficient community. Equally, he was trusted by Platanus, and allowed to arrange hunting expeditions and travel to town to obtain the things which could not be grown in the community's extensive and artificially irrigated kitchen gardens.

Therefore, it was Topage who secretly prepared two horses for them at the Haven stables, having previously filled the saddlebags with rations and the canteens with the sweet water of the aquifer well.

It was dawn as Frycollin and Robur prepared to leave, and the chef embraced the boy, kissing him farewell on both cheeks in the Gallic fashion. Robur reassured Topage that he would be careful and not away for long, the evidence for this being that he could not exist for an extended period without the Frenchman's cooking.

After having picked their way through the forest of mirrors, they paused while Robur retrieved his electric crossbow from its camouflaged hiding place. Frycollin felt a little ashamed that he had originally planned to blackmail the young man for help in escaping the Haven by threatening to reveal that the boy had possession of this forbidden weapon. He was glad it hadn't come to that. And his heart would not have allowed to him carry out the threat anyway.

He looked down at his Colt Navy, which he had awkwardly wedged into his saddle holster. He was now without a gun belt and the ammunition it carried. He only had the rounds loaded in the revolver's cylinder. He had no idea what happened to his Derringer. He drew some comfort from the fact that he was wearing his star on his shirt, and that he had on his black Stetson.

Robur, who normally shunned any form of headgear, had been persuaded to wear a wide-brimmed gardener's hat just to keep the desert sun off. He gestured in a vaguely southerly direction when asked where he had last seen heliograph signals from Oxalis, and the quest began.

Grand Pater Platanus had reasserted control over himself now, after a long period of prayer which had culminated in a direct communion with God verging on theophany.

He had initially been very angry with Robur, but had now accepted that the unworldly young man had fallen under the influence of the irreligious outsider, Frycollin. He had, of course, already forgiven Robur. But that did not mean that he could allow him to live. There was only one way to deal with this, and it was likely to means death for all concerned. And that included the blasphemous traitor, Oxalis. God had shown it all to him ever so clearly.

He could see the flow of future events: Robur and Frycollin peregrinating across the wasteland, before finally stumbling on the scientist's squalid lair. Then a journey to Prescott, where a posse would be formed to investigate the Haven with a view to finding McKay so that he could be put on trial. Then, on some pretext, Platanus would find himself deposed by the authorities, and Oxalis would be installed in his place. The primacy of Christianity would also be lost, and science would be raised up as a higher god with Oxalis as its new Messiah. Yes, it was all very clear!

Grand Pater Platanus reached the bottom of the staircase, arriving at the lower levels of the Haven, where only he and the Eschar were permitted. He stopped at the strange cell where McKay was incarcerated; strange because it really only had three walls, the third being a linen screen onto which a perpetual magic lantern phantasmagoria show was being projected. There were visions of Hell, there were visions of Heaven, and each was accompanied by either extraordinary pain or ineffable pleasure, both either inflicted or delivered by the Eschar.

McKay's mind had snapped weeks ago, though perhaps even stranger, it had not been the phantasmagoria or the pleasure/torture that had accomplished this. It had been the bandaged folk whispering into his ear the Old Testament verses of the Ten Commandments, over and over again for perhaps twenty hours a day, until their voices were brittle croaks. Nothing of his original personality existed now. He had been fully indoctrinated in the ways and history of the Woodlanders. He was a fanatic. He loved Platanus. He wept with joy when the Grand Pater entered his cell and unchained him from his torture couch. McKay wondered what he had done to earn such high favor, and the answer was: he had not done anything, *yet.*

Platanus led his new acolyte to a spiral staircase which led even deeper into the bowels of the Haven. Eventually, they walked out along a wooden gantry above a collection of cages, tanks and various other enclosures. This was Oxalis' menagerie. He had collected unusual animals from all over the world in his youth. It would be more correct to say that these were the *remnants* of his menagerie. Some of the animals had perished in the fire in California, though some had escaped into the forests, including a breeding pair of manlike apes Oxalis had captured in Tibet. Sometimes, Platanus wondered what happened to those apes, and if they had managed to adapt and thrive...

They reached the end of the gantry, and Platanus pointed down at a massive glass tank of sand. One of the Eschar was down there using some kind of winch to lower a small metal cage from high overhead down onto the sand. McKay saw what was in the cage and it made his skin crawl. A mass of large rats were clambering all over each other and fighting to get out. As soon as the cage touched the sand, a catch sprang open and the rats were released. It was almost ten feet from the sand to the top of the glass enclosure, so there was no way they could leap out. Within seconds, the sand began to ripple, and nearly a dozen sinuous, scarlet, eel-like worms the size of pythons erupted from beneath it and hunted down the rats, consuming them with a single gulp. Some of the rats were stunned with a crackling electric shock emitted by the worms before being eaten.

"My former friend and the co-founder of this community, Oxalis, discovered these creatures in a cave system in Derbyshire, Central England," said Platanus. "They had been there for centuries. A knight had brought the egg cases of their progenitors back from the Barbary Crusade. And when this warrior needed to impress the local citizenry, he would capture one and overfeed it until it grew to a bloated gargantuan size, then slay it in front of an audience to convince them he had killed a dragon. In fact, at this rather smaller scale, they are more agile and dangerous."

"Could they kill a man?" asked McKay.

"Easily, my friend. And therein lies the rub. Oxalis and I had many disagreements, but one thing we always agreed on was our profound pacifism. Although this community needs defending, we could never form an army and expect our adherents to take the life of another. But Oxalis found a way to control these creatures, and shape them into our proxy army. What he never expected was for them to be used against him."

McKay looked back at the eel-worms' high sided enclosure and noticed, for the first time, the sealed off glass cylinder which ran from the tank and terminated at the sandstone wall. Was this a means by which the creatures could be released to the outside world?

"Come, I have a special task I need to explain to you," said Platanus.

Robur surveyed the base of the cliff face carefully with his telescope. The trail had led them here over the course of several days, but now it had petered out on the rocky ground in the shadow of the cliff.

He tracked upwards. There was a wrecked and abandoned pueblo about half way up the cliff. The steps up leading to it had fallen into ruin and collapsed, giving it an almost surreally inaccessible look.

He angled the telescope back downwards and that moved it laterally to the right. Frycollin had insisted that this was bandit territory, and so they could not discount the possibility that they were following the trail of an outlaw rather than that of the Professor.

Robur continued to scan along the ground at the foot of the cliff, looking for any sign of an outlaw camp. At length, he saw a ragged cleft in the rocks. It looked to be the way into a cave. But what he saw coming out of the cave made him blink to clear his vision, and then doubt his own reason before passing the telescope quickly to Frycollin.

"Take a look at this, I must be dreaming…"

Frycollin put the telescope to his eye, and Robur directed his view down to the cleft. After a few moments of scanning, he finally saw it. It looked like a sculpture or the Natural History Museum's model of a giant ant, about five and half to six feet long, and a dull red in color.

Just as the lawman was wondering who had placed it there, it reared up onto two of its back legs, and stood in a bipedal, humanlike fashion. Then Frycollin realized that the ant-creature was "wearing" tatters of cloth on its abdomen and thorax, as if garbed in rudimentary clothing, and even jewelry in the form of gold metal armlets. More worryingly, the thing had picked up from the ground a long wooden spear and assumed an aspect similar to that of a soldier in a sentry box.

Frycollin handed back the telescope to Robur.

"If there's a nest of those things, and they've captured your Professor Oxalis, then Heaven help him. I've only got five rounds. I could only kill a handful of them."

Robur looked down at the ant-soldier through the telescope.

"My friend, you must not kill any of them. They are obviously intelligent. If necessary, we must reason with them. I cannot countenance the deliberate taking of life due to my pacifist principles," said Robur.

Robur continued watching the cleft and its guardian and was taken by surprise when an Indian warrior, dressed in typical white smock and pants of this region emerged immediately behind the ant guard. He anticipated a conflict between the Indian and the ant creature, but he was quite wrong. They were, in fact, on the friendliest possible terms. But within moments, it became obvious that the Indian had spotted them.

Robur hurriedly passed the telescope back to Frycollin so he could see the Indian man before he retreated back into the interior of the cave.

"That's a Hopi," said Frycollin. "He's not a hostile, and sure as eggs are eggs, he'll speak English. Let's get down there and make ourselves known."

They went back for their horses and then led them down towards the wrecked pueblo and the cave entrance.

They were perhaps only twenty yards away when the Hopi and another figure—a bespectacled man in his sixties, sporting a leather workman's apron and protective goggles perched high on his forehead—emerged from the cave.

Frycollin saw that Robur was now weeping uncontrollably. They had found Oxalis!

Then the lawman and the young man entered a world they could not have dreamed existed. Professor Oxalis took them inside the cavern to an underground pueblo, where the Hopi and their legendary allies, the insect-like Anu Sinom, had lived in collaborative tranquility for millennia.

As they went deeper into the tunnels beneath the cliffs, Oxalis explained that he had held a lifelong belief that, behind every legend, was a kernel of truth. His knowledge of the Hopi Ant People stories had been a factor settling on this locale for the new Woodlanders' Haven.

Frycollin hoped he did not cause offence to the ant people when he retied his neckerchief over his nose and mouth. The odor of formic acid was almost overpowering to him in these lower levels, though it did not seem to bother Robur, who was still giddy with excitement at being reunited with his mentor.

Down and down the party continued to go. During his months here, Oxalis had rigged up electrically-powered incandescent globes strung on the walls on insulated wires. As they passed the cyst-like dwellings of the Anu Sinom, the people came out holding their young, since it was still a novelty for the insect folk to see non-Hopi humans.

Oxalis told them he was taking them to see Makya, the leader of the Hopi. Finally, the spiral ramp they had been following started to level out, and Frycollin was surprised to see that the air was suddenly fresher. Then, he saw the reason why as they passed beneath a cluster of ventilation shaft "chimneys" such as one might find in an old mine workings. He could just glimpse oval patches of the powdered sapphire sky, far above.

Finally, they came to the rather grand residence of Makya and his wife, Humeata, where they received a cordial greeting from the couple and their Anu Sinom friend, Naki, a female personage of high importance among the Ant People. Sitting on woven metallic rugs, they were served the gelatinous honey tea enjoyed by Hopi and Anu Sinom alike, and of which Oxalis had become something of a connoisseur.

"How are your parents, Robur?" asked Oxalis.

"Still living anonymously within the cadre of the Eschar," stated Robur. "They do not acknowledge me, let alone show any sign of love. More than ever, the Eschar have become a kind of fanatical religious police enforcing the will of Platanus."

"I am sorry to hear that," said Oxalis. "Although I suspected the presence of a hidden tribe of Hopi and the Ant People when we first relocated here, I was hesitant to forge links with them while I was still a member of the Woodlanders' community."

"Why was that?" asked Frycollin.

"Because I knew that it would stir up Platanus' evangelical zeal," replied Oxalis. "He would have deployed the Eschar to convert the Hopi to his own inflexible brand of Christianity, and demanded they sever their links with the Anu Sinom. His beliefs do not allow for intelligent non-human creatures with souls."

"Oxalis has told me how this Platanus would have come here to impose a false belief system upon us and seek to get us to relinquish the truth of our origins," said Makya. "Our allegiance with who you call the Ant People dates back to a time when they saved my people from starvation. They first allowed us to share their nest and food millennia ago and have taught us much."

Frycollin turned to Naki.

"Then the Anu Sinom are the original inhabitants of this land," said Frycollin. "Here before the Hopi, here when the world was new…"

Naki's antennae resonated like tuning forks until a buzzing simulacrum of human speech started to emanate.

"Not exactly," said Naki. "We came from… somewhere else."

"You've noticed the greenish curtain of energy hanging over the desert at night?" asked Oxalis.

"Of course! The newspapers are saying it is the most southerly manifestation of the aurora borealis ever recorded, or according to Platanus, it's a sign that God is displeased with me," smiled Frycollin.

Oxalis gave a hollow bark of laughter.

"Well, it is neither of those things. According to the ancient Anunkai Tablets of the Anu Sinom, it is the doorway through which they first swarmed to this world. It appears regularly throughout their history. It is the means by which they propagate themselves to whatever worlds there are. But something has gone wrong for them here. They no longer breed so prodigiously; their numbers have dwindled away… Their females are born without wings, and so are unable to pass through the curtain and establish new nests."

Naki's antennae vibrated excitedly.

"That is why we were so interested in Professor Oxalis' experiments to duplicate flight," buzzed Naki.

Oxalis nodded.

"Here, away from the disapproving eye of Platanus, I have brought my work to a natural fruition, beyond the flying models Robur once helped me to design and build. I now have a full-scale prototype assembled in the one the nest's ventilation chimneys."

"Let me see it right now!" demanded, Robur, as he leaped to his feet.

"My dear boy, could we at least finish our tea?" asked Oxalis.

Frycollin had imagined that the flying machine would be some contraption of wooden wings and baling wire, adorned with homemade gasbags, or some fancy variation on the reconnaissance balloons he had seen during the war. His mind was reeling at the sight of the unearthly-looking vehicle Oxalis had put together with the assistance of the Hopi craftsmen and the Anu Sinom.

It stood on the rock floor of the ventilation shaft like a monstrous silver artillery shell; though its proportions were somewhat slimmer than those of a typical shell. In the cabin at the front there was just barely room for three men: a steersman, a navigator and an engineer. Perhaps most remarkably, the craft was an ornithopter, but with its great metal wings folded closely to its sides, as if it were some titanic prehistoric avian.

"This, gentlemen, is the *Storm Petrel*," said Oxalis. "It is the first of its kind. Yet, it is also merely the first iteration of aero-vehicle. There are many ways to fly, and with the assistance of my apprentice, Robur, I shall discover them all."

"When do we launch it?" asked Robur, impatiently.

"First, you must learn to fly it," said Oxalis. "I have created a duplicate of the steering and control mechanisms to allow me to teach any volunteers who accompany me the principles of aviation while safely on the ground."

Frycollin continued to look the craft up and down.

"Well, I'll tell you one thing, Prof," he began, "I'm sure not leaving *terra firma* in that thing."

Robur spent most of the next week learning about the *Storm Petrel*'s systems, and practicing on duplicate steering controls, upon which Oxalis declared him to be a natural.

Frycollin was alarmed to hear that the *Storm Petrel* was to be launched out of the chimney using a controlled build-up of heated gas collected from thermal vents deep below the nest—effectively shot like a bullet out of a gun. It all sounded both hare-brained and dangerous. And while the lawman could care less if Oxalis killed himself, he did not see why Robur had to be involved and risk his life.

Robur, of course, would rather have died than miss a chance to be one of the first humans to experience powered flight. Frycollin was impatient to leave the nest and get back to Prescott, but he did not see how he could do so in good conscience when he had not taken every possible opportunity to talk Robur out of this foolhardy venture.

Frycollin and Robur were allocated the same billet, a cozy little whitewashed cave that was partitioned off into various "rooms." It was nicely appointed with furnishing that would not have been out of place in some rancher's hacienda. Frycollin worked on Robur, talking to him long into the night seeking to dissuade him from being in the aero-vehicle when it launched; telling him the endeavor was suicidal.

It was on the day when the *Storm Petrel* was due to launch that the Anu Sinom guards dragged McKay before Oxalis, Frycollin and Naki. He was in a sorry state, and looked like he had been wandering on foot for days. He claimed to have escaped the Woodlanders' Haven on a horse, but it had broken its leg. Into the bargain, he'd lost his hat, and appeared to have a nasty case of sunstroke. Not surprisingly, McKay had initially thought he was delirious when he first encountered the Anu Sinom.

Oxalis was rather more sympathetic than Frycollin, and arranged for the invigorating honey tea to be served to the bank robber after he had been placed on a couch in his own apartment. To Frycollin, the man looked dehydrated; yet, he was carrying what looked to be two full canteens which he seemed unwilling to take off or relinquish. The canteens' carrying straps were crossed over his chest like bandoliers, with a canteen at each of his hips. It was suspicious; there were no waterholes nearby. But then, Frycollin found everything about McKay to be suspicious.

Oxalis poured McKay a glass of honey tea, and took a position beside him on the couch, applying a sweet smelling propolis balm to the man's terrible sunburn. McKay took a swig of tea and declared the concoction to not be as refreshing as water, and clumsily unscrewed the top of one of his canteens, resulting in some of the liquid inside being dashed over the front of Oxalis' apron and shirt. Frycollin leaped forward with alarm.

"What is that? Has he splashed vitriol on you?" shouted Frycollin.

"Relax, my friend. It's just common or garden water," said Oxalis.

"Sure, that's right," agreed McKay. "Just water." And to prove it, he took a long draught of the liquid.

The bank robber was left with an Anu Sinom guard. Frycollin, Oxalis and Naki headed to the ventilation chimney where Robur was making the final preparations for the launch of the *Storm Petrel*. Hopi craftsmen had released the valves, and now super-heated steam was building up in the chamber beneath the aerovehicle.

"As soon as you and Robur have safely landed, I'll head off with McKay to Prescott," announced Frycollin.

"Ah, I think you may misunderstand, Mr. Frycollin," smiled Oxalis. "When the *Storm Petrel* intercepts the energy curtain, I expect we will be flung into another realm completely. Perhaps the home of the Anu Sinom, or possibly somewhere completely different. Either way, we'll be leaving Arizona far behind."

"You're just as crazy as Platanus," judged Frycollin.

Oxalis laughed. "Yes, but in a completely different way. His madness comes from blind faith, whereas mine is born of an insatiable desire for knowledge."

Naki's antennae suddenly buzzed and whirred. She was receiving a message from elsewhere in the nest. "Something terrible has happened. We must return to your quarters at once," she said.

Robur was just climbing down the ladder from the *Storm Petrel*'s cabin as Naki said this, so they all ran together up the spiral slope back towards Oxalis' cavern apartment.

The Anu Sinom guard had beaten out the flames as best he could. The blackened form of McKay still lay on the scorched couch. And Frycollin was astonished to see he was still alive.

"He poured liquid from one of his containers over himself, and set himself on fire," said the guard.

"He immolated himself? But why?" asked Robur.

"Because my mission and my martyrdom are now complete," the words issued from McKay's charred meat lips. "They are coming for you, Oxalis, and there is no escape. This hive of devils and sinners will soon be purged from the

Earth. But I am free. My burns elevate me to a place among the Eschar. In death, I will sit at the right hand of God."

There was a rattle in McKay's throat, then his head lolled. He was dead.

"His mind was twisted by Platanus and the Eschar," said Oxalis sorrowfully.

"Is someone or something really coming to destroy the nest?" asked Frycollin, as he checked the chamber of his Colt Navy.

"No… He couldn't have… Yes… It makes sense now. In one canteen, one of my chemical attractants; in the other, a flammable liquid. We must move quickly, or none of us will survive this day. Platanus has released the fully adult form of the worms I found in Stonerich cavern. Now I wish I had slashed my knife through their egg cases, stamped their larvae under the heel of my boot. I have brought doom on us all," wept Oxalis.

"Worms? You're kidding me?" questioned Frycollin.

"There's no time. These things crawl twice as fast as a horse can run. They spit acid like a cobra spits venom; they generate a lethal electric charge like the knifefish of the Orinoco. They are the ultimate proof that this is a fallen Creation, or that there is no God. For nothing with any good in it would ever have brought them into existence."

Naki's antennae vibrated again. "The surface and entrance guards are overcome. The worms are too swift for the Hopi and my warriors. Makya himself has fallen," she said.

"Then tell all your people, both Hopi and Anu Sinom, to fall back to the lowest possible levels and seal them inside," begged Oxalis.

"The order is given," buzzed Naki.

"I am contaminated with the pheromone attractant," said Oxalis, looking down at the stains on his shirt and apron. "If I leave in the *Storm Petrel*, perhaps the worms will abandon the attack."

"Then let's get you to it," said Frycollin, already starting to drag the Professor back towards the spiral slopeway, with Robur close behind.

As they made their way down, Frycollin could smell a new scent in the nest, over and above the formic acid and cooking fire smoke to which he was now acclimatized—something caustic and alien which stung the eyes. It was the stench of the worms spraying their acid.

They reached the end of the slopeway, and the glistening form of the *Storm Petrel* was now in view. But, horrifyingly, between the trio and the aero-craft was one of the Stonerich Cavern worms, like some eyeless, bulbous scarlet python. Its wedge-shaped head lifted from the rock floor and tasted the air. The glands on either side of its jaw pulsed as it prepared to launch a stream of acid at Oxalis. Then came the salvo of echoing shots from Frycollin's weapon—and it took every round he had to kill it.

Robur did not need to be told; he was already sprinting past the worm's reflexively twitching body on the way to the *Storm Petrel*'s ladder. Frycollin looked back at Oxalis, and a warning shout died in his throat before he could give it. Another worm was hurtling down the spiral slope at high speed and was almost upon him. It lashed at Oxalis with its tail delivering a lethal azure charge of static which caused the inventor to drop rigidly to the floor.

From the control cabin door, Robur emitted a wild howl of grief, and then, every fiber of his intellect reasserted some semblance of control over him. His mentor would have been proud.

"C'mon, Frycollin. We must launch now!"

"I can't go up in that thing. I'll find another way out."

The worm slithered closer to the lawman, and he backed away.

"There's no time, the launch gas is at maximum pressure now, and if you stay in here when I take off, you'll be incinerated. Besides, I do not want to do this alone," pleaded Robur.

That was the convincer. He was just a boy, alone and mourning. He'd lost the only real father he'd ever known. Frycollin made a dash for the ladder.

Then it all happened so quickly. There was the roar of the exploding gases, followed by the nausea of acceleration. Frycollin looked out of the porthole. He could see a town far below, too small to be Prescott—maybe it was Rock Ridge?

Robur wrestled with the heavy controls, shifting them to horizontal flight, and setting the aero-craft's wings in motion. They vibrated, rather than flapped. Through the front window they could see the shape of the green curtain of energy, albeit faint in the sunlight. It really did have the aspect of a doorway. They were heading straight for it.

Scientific curiosity must be contagious, because Frycollin found himself really wanting to know what was going to happen next.

Lately, Travis Hiltz has delighted us with pirate yarns, a genre which, despite the success of the Pirates of the Caribbean *franchise, has not seen much of a revival... except under Travis' pen! So here is another stellar cast of adventurers cruising the legendary Seven Seas...*

Travis Hiltz: *These are the Voyages...*

1607

The beach was white sand, idyllic; a light breeze ruffled the sea. A long boat had been dragged up, its bow resting on the beach, the stern in the water.

A Moorish sailor, barefoot, clad in a loose linen shirt and knee breeches, lazed in the sun, enjoying the light duty of guarding the boat, while the rest of the landing party trudged inland. He contemplated doing some fishing, but it sounded like too much effort.

"Yusuf ! Yusuf-ben-Moktar!"

The sailor sat up quickly, at the sound of his name, blinking in the sunlight and wondering if he was in trouble.

There were several more shouts and then two men came bursting out of the forest. One wore a tattered soldier's uniform, but it was the uniform of an army that would not exist for several centuries. The other was an older, white-haired gentleman, dressed in a black suit of Edwardian cut and style.

"Yusuf! Get the boat in the water!"

The soldier held one of the older man's arms, helping to propel him along. The duo stumbled frantically down the beach, pursued by what appeared to be a swarm of crawling insects.

Yusuf paused, confused, as the ants seemed to be brandishing swords and were dressed in long coats.

"They're people," he shouted. "Tiny people!"

"Yes, we know!" the older man shouted back. "Push off!"

Their tumbling in was the final push the boat required, and Yusuf quickly clambered aboard, as they drifted away from the beach. The tiny army skidded to a halt, shaking their weapons and fists with angry impotence.

While the older man in black settled on a bench, the soldier gave the sailor a hand vigorously rowing. The white-haired man fished within his coat pockets, pulling out a colored handkerchief and mopping his brow.

"Well, that could have gone better."

The soldier nodded his agreement, peering out at the crystal blue water.

Outside the bay sat a grey, weathered hulk of a frigate. It bore its years with a proud, weary acceptance.

Quickly approaching were two trim vessels of war. In keeping with the army that had pursed the party, the ships resembled children's toys.

As the older man watched the minuscule war ships' attempt to cut off their escape, the flap on his front breast pocket opened and a tiny figure climbed out, perching on his shoulder, to get a clear view.

"My countrymen are a stubborn lot!" he shouted, to be heard over the sound of the waves and the voices of the others in the boat.

Everyone huddled down in the boat, as the small warships began to fire upon them.

Yusuf-ben-Moktar struggled to turn the boat, and the wave caused by the oars threatened to capsize the warships.

The boat made its escape, soon reaching the larger ship, the *Rose Hawk*, while the tiny warships fired pellet-sized cannon balls and shouted in anger. Rope ladders came over the side, and sailors scrambled down, to aid the boats' occupants, and then to secure the boat, before they could sail out of the bay.

The scholar and the soldier leaned on the rail, catching their breath, as well as watching the distant enemy ships.

"That was a wash," the soldier grumbled.

"I feel I bear some share of blame," the tiny swordsman standing on the rail said. "It did not occur to me to warn you that cutting your sandwiches triangularly is a capital crime in Lilliput."

"Yes, yes," the older man muttered, sitting perching on a nearby barrel. "Your assistance was much appreciated."

This trio, appearing so out of place amongst this crew of seventeenth century mariners, were not native to this time period. The gentleman, dressed in Edwardian black, was the eccentric time traveler known as Doctor Omega. His uniformed companion was Lieutenant Marcel Renard, a French soldier from the first world war. Perched upon his shoulder was the Chevalier Shelfin Bundt Arbornoth, a minor noble from the Court of the king of Lilliput. His innate, moral sense and longing for adventure had caused him to side with the travelers over his own people.

A sailor came shuffling up to the trio.

"Captain wishes a word," he said.

Doctor Omega nodded and, leaning heavily on his cane, made his way along the deck.

Private Renard was part of a company of WWI soldiers who had, through the unknowing use of a makeshift time machine, been sent hurtling back to 13th century Spain. After months of carousing and misadventures, most of these "timeslip troopers" had returned to their proper time.

There were, however, complications, and a few had been left behind, while others had been scattered through history during the trip home. Doctor Omega, and his fellow time traveling savant, Professor Helvetius, had been working to correct this situation.

Several of Doctor Omega's traveling companions were working to stabilize the fabric of history, while his handyman, Fred, had been dropped off in 1914 to collect the pieces of the troublesome time machine. Doctor Omega had embarked on a mission to collect that last few, lost soldiers. It had proven to be more difficult and bothersome then he'd imagined.

They entered the captain's cabin, a cluttered collection of charts, clothing and knickknacks accumulated during a lifetime spent traversing the seas.

Doctor Omega sank gratefully into a well-cushioned hanging chair and awaited the captain's attention shifting from the chart table to his guests.

Sir Oliver Tressilian, also known as Sakr-el-Babr ("the Hawk of the Seas") was a tall man, tanned from years spent sailing off the Barbary coast, broad at the shoulder, slender at the hip, with hair black as midnight, a black beard, and eyes as fathomless as the sea he navigated.

He tucked his quill back in the ink pot, rubbed at his upper lip, and then glanced up, expectantly at the unusual trio.

"So," he said, with a haughty smile. "Went well, did it?"

Doctor Omega merely harrumphed in reply.

Renard's shoulder twitched and he leaned his head over. He then nodded, stepped forward and held out his arm. Shelfin scurried down, and once standing on the captain's desk, made a leg and presented his sword.

"My service to your fine vessel!" he announced, dramatically.

Sir Oliver gaped for a moment, before regaining his composure and replying with a nod.

"Welcome aboard, Monsieur. I hope you do not mind bunking with these gentlemen," he replied. "Perhaps Renard would be kind enough to show you your new quarters, whilst I have a word with the Doctor?"

The French soldier took the hint and he and the tiny swordsman left.

Doctor Omega leaned on his cane, wearily willing to let the Captain speak first.

"While you were away, your ghost returned," the buccaneer said, sternly.

"She is neither 'mine,' nor a 'ghost,'" Doctor Omega replied, irritably, implying this was a continuation of a disagreement that had been revisited throughout the voyage.

"What is she then?"

"Lotte is… complicated. Did she speak to anyone?"

"Startled the man on the forecastle, so he nearly toppled over the side," Sir Oliver continued. "Then pestered several, others asking if they wanted to play…"

"Yes, yes, but did she pass along a message?" the older man grumbled.

"Of course," the bearded corsair nodded. "After she frightens my crew, she always does. She said, 'my father is coming.'"

Doctor Omega sat back and tapped thoughtfully with a crooked finger at his sharp chin.

"Curious."

"Is that meant to imply good news or ill?"

"If Lotte's father plans to join our quest, he would be a most formable ally," Omega nodded, thoughtfully. "I am curious as to how he would manage to rendezvous with your ship, however…"

"While we are speaking of our travels…"

Sir Oliver leaned forward and drew out a length of parchment from a compartment. He unrolled a map and began weighting down the corners with bits of bric-a-brac from his desk.

"Would you care to share what our next destination might be?"

Doctor Omega leaned over to the map, fishing a pince-nez out of his coat pocket as well as a metal protractor and several scraps of paper. He then spent several minutes, consulting his notes and the map intently. Finally, he took off his pince-nez and used it to point at two spots on the map.

"Here," he said, decisively. "And… here."

The Captain peered at the map for several minutes before looking up at the time traveler.

"That's empty ocean. Both spots."

Omega frowned, took the stub of a pencil from his pocket. With a stern gesture, he marked the two spots.

"One of the islands tends to vigorously avoid any attempt to map it," he said, returning to his chair. "The other is ringed by high cliffs, making it inaccessible to all but the most intrepid explorers."

"You will, of course, have a list of 'conditions' for exploring them, as you did with Lilliput and… what was the other island… Paradise? The one inhabited only by maidens…?"

"Are you indulging in some kind of monkey business, Captain?" Doctor Omega asked. "Or is this a serious objection to our arrangement?"

"No, not at all!" Sir Oliver smiled, sitting back. "I want only two things in this world: enough coin to pay my way and to indulge my longing for what's beyond the horizon, and you have supplied both, amply! Your ways are… odd, to be honest, and knowing you have secrets teases at my mind, but I feel more than content with entering in your employ, Doctor!"

Doctor Omega frowned at the haughty mariner. He'd had a choice of buccaneers, and had picked the 'Seahawk' because he appeared to be the most honorable of a morally challenged lot.

"The first island will be difficult to approach, for it is prone to be surrounded by storms and other strange phenomena," he explained. "The second is rocky, but easily arrived at. In both instances, only Private Renard and I shall be going ashore."

"Of course," Sir Oliver said with a gallant gesture. "I well understand, you not wishing to have any of the crew wandering about the Nameless Isle!"

"How did you know that?" Omega asked, accusingly.

"I'd be a poor sailor, if I hadn't heard a few stories about the strange island '*with the warmest, brightest light one has ever felt*'," the Captain responded.

The two men locked gazes, and Doctor Omega paused, unsure how to proceed. He knew the reputation of Sir Oliver Tressilian as a generally trustworthy adventurer, but any man can be tempted, and the secret of the Nameless Isle was rumored to be enough to tempt the noblest of souls.

"My pardon, the jest was in poor taste," Sir Oliver said, with a rueful grin. "I read the name off one of your scraps of paper. I saw it jotted down. It drew my interest, along with the many exotic dishes served at that place, Lee Ho Fook's."

Remembering that the list of islands to be investigated was written on a takeout menu from the eatery in question, Doctor Omega relaxed slightly. He was unsure of the Captain's intentions, and so settled on a disapproving frown.

"Hummph! Well, if you're done being amusing, I believe I will go rest. How soon do you think we will arrive, at either island?"

Appearing contrite, the pirate leaned forward, tapping at his chin thoughtfully.

"The Nameless Isle should be reached in a matter of days," He said, all business. "Weather holds and your stay there isn't too long, I'd say another seven days to Caspak."

"Satisfactory," Doctor Omega muttered, rising slowly to his feet and hobbling away.

The days passed, the stories of Lilliput and a further sighting of the "ghost girl," along with more mundane chores, kept the crew occupied, until their arrival at the Nameless Isle.

Shelfin was assigned several of the cabin boys to convey him about the ship, as the novelty of being a mode of transportation soon lost its appeal to Private Renard. Never having served in the Lilliputian navy, the tiny swordsman was fascinated with the ship and all aspects of the voyage.

The sea grew wine dark and choppy.

There was no cry of 'Land Ho!', as no one was sure that any land existed with the dense bank of fog the ship approached. Only the fog's lack of movement hinted at anything solid within its mass.

"You still wish to follow your course of action?" Sir Oliver asked, concernedly studying the tempest-tossed water. All joviality had faded from his tone, now that they were within sight of their destination. "At least, someone more skilled at handling a boat...?"

Both Doctor Omega and the French soldier frowned, but for different reasons.

"No," the savant replied. "This is a delicate matter. If you'd please."

Sir Oliver and Omega shared another glance, and then the Captain simply nodded.

Soon, Doctor Omega and Renard were bobbing along. The French soldier was determined to prove his boating skills to the Captain.

The waters surged and it was a struggle to keep the boat on course. It felt to the time-displaced soldier that the water was actively pushing them away from the fog bank and its mysterious contents.

"Pull the oars in," Doctor Omega instructed from the front of the boat.

"What?" Renard protested. "We can't!"

"Do as you're asked!" the older man snapped, glancing over his shoulder.

He then returned his gaze back to the swirling mist, sitting patiently huddled in his traveling cloak. The French soldier, frowning skeptically, pulled in the oars, and sat, anxiously gripping the sides of the rocking boat.

The sea pushed them deeper into the fog, and, in the distance, they could hear breakers, the sound of waves striking land. Unsure how inviting or safe that land was, Renard felt no sense of relief. For all he knew, they were about to be dashed against the rocks. He held tight, bracing for what he was sure was the inevitable crash.

The sea and fog moved about them, like a living thing. Renard could swear, he could see shapes… forms, moving about the boat: almost human, but not quite or maybe more than human, perhaps guiding the boat along. He found himself transfixed, staring into the storm, trying to catch a solid glimpse of their airy entourage, all thoughts of his peril melting away.

He almost fell off his seat when the boat came to a sudden halt, upon a gravelly beach.

As if a switch had been hit, clouds rolled back and the sun shown down.

The two men climbed out of the boat. Renard shaded his eyes with his hand and peered about nervously. Doctor Omega trudged up the beach.

A figure stood, on a slight rise, where the sand met the straggling grass that marked its border.

An older man, clad in the plain robes and skullcap of a hermit scholar. His beard was white as the sand and tumbled down to his chest. Thin, bony hands clutched his wooden staff, as he surveyed the two new arrivals. He made no movement to join them, patiently waiting for the equally aged time traveler to reach him.

"Omega," he said simply.

"Your Grace," Doctor Omega replied, with a respectful nod of his head.

"You are being polite. You seek a favor?"

"I seek, merely the answer to a question," Doctor Omega said. "I hope to locate some soldiers, lost not just on the seas, but in time."

"Ah," the other man said. "That would explain matters. My... servants had come to me, concerned over some ripples in the ether..." He nodded to himself. "So, to answer your question: no, I have had no visitors to my island."

"Well, then..."

"But I am expecting some," the old duke continued. "And your presence and the presence of your vessel are not part of my plans for receiving them..."

He allowed his next command to float in the air between them.

"Yes, I see." Doctor Omega said, with a frown. "We shall be on our way. My best wishes to you and your daughter."

He turned and began to trudge back to his boat.

"Omega."

The time traveler stopped and looked back at Duke Prospero.

"There is a tempest brewing. I shall keep it at bay, as long as time allows, in order that you may reach calmer seas"

"Most appreciated."

The two men exchanged smiles, dry and knowing, before parting.

"Was he of any help?" Renard asked, when Doctor Omega reached the boat.

"Some," the older man said, with a thoughtful nod. "Let us be on our way. We can talk back at the ship."

Once off the beach and into the water, Renard found their return journey much easier than their arrival. The small, weathered boat, glided across the sea and while the fog still hung heavily, it seemed not to impede or confuses their progress.

Days passed, not uneventfully, as they sailed.

It was with a certain relief when they came in sight of the island of Caspak.

Grumbling accompanied the announcement that only the white-haired Doctor and Renard would be going ashore.

The island was a rugged, uninviting lump. The boat scraped across the rocks, as Renard hauled it ashore.

Feeling the weight of his travels, Doctor Omega hobbled up the beach, his eyes intently studying the rocky ground, until he spotted the faint traces of a path.

Renard caught up with him where the beach morphed into equally rocky hills.

"What're we looking for?" he asked, glancing around.

"Traces of your friends," Doctor Omega replied, absently.

He peered about, then stopped, and poked at something on the ground with his cane. Renard kneeled down and plucked it from the dirt.

"It's a button," Renard muttered, holding it against his own uniform jacket. "A uniform button."

Tucking it in his pocket, Renard walked quickly up the path. Doctor Omega struggled to keep up. The landscape remained rocky. This section of the island seemed made of jagged rock and barren hills.

Renard, wandered along, until he spotted a cave.

"Hello…!" he called, tentative, yet hopefully.

He ducked to enter it, his eyes struggling to make out shapes in the darkened chamber.

When finally, Doctor Omega caught up to him, Renard was standing, his gaze locked on what looked to be a pile of rag and bones on the cave floor. The bones were two skeletons and the rags were the remains of their World War One era military uniforms. Scattered about the two skeletons were gold nuggets and gems that sparkled in the faint sunlight.

"Ah," Doctor Omega said, fanning himself with his free hand. "I feared as much. My condolences. Any thought to who they were?"

Renard shook his head, as he kneeled down to examine the remains.

"Might be Duranton," he muttered. "He was tall… and greedy. The other, I dunno…"

He shrugged, resigned. He dusted off his hands, his eyes on the bones. He then took notice of the treasure scattered about.

"Paying Captain Tressilian won't be an issue."

He moved to pick up a coin, but was stopped by Omega pressing the tip of the cane against the coin.

"No," he said, simply. "The treasures of Caspak are not a gift, it is a burden. It is not for us. We found what we came for."

He waved vaguely at the two skeletons. The French soldier nodded, and began gathering up the remains of his comrades.

Back on the beach, they fished out a length of tattered sailcloth from the bottom of the boat and bundled up the skeletons. Doctor Omega sat, leaning on his cane, while Renard kneeled on the rocky beach, tying up the makeshift shroud.

He stood up and shifted the bundle into the boat.

"Um…Doctor…?" he said, peering out at the ocean, while he reached out to tap the older man's arm.

"Yes? What is it?" Doctor Omega asked, wearily, before following his companion's gaze. "Ah!"

There was a ripple in the water, and then a man came striding up out of the surf. He was impressively tall, seven feet if he was an inch, his wide brimmed, peaked hat adding another foot to his height. His ash-colored hair touched his collar, and his beard extended down his chest. His soaked garments and boots were tattered and travel-worn. There was a satchel slung over one shoulder and he held a staff nearly as long, as he was tall.

Renard gaped as the bearded man, shaking the water from his hair and beard, while he strolled over to the boat.

"Omega," he said simply, upon spotting the time traveler. "Walk with me."

With an effort, the Doctor got to his feet and the two strolled along the beach, leaving Renard to sit on the edge of the boat, shaking his head in bafflement.

The journey back to the *Rose Hawk* was silent and subdued. Doctor Omega, brusquely explained that the bearded wanderer, whose name was Isaac, had agreed to join them on their mission, but would be making his own way to the ship.

Captain Tressilian was at the rail to greet them. His attempt at a joyous welcome was cut short upon spotting the grim bundle they returned with.

He performed a brief last rites over the bones and had them stowed in the ship's surgeon's quarters.

"So, you have found some of your wayward soldiers," he said, as he and Doctor Omega strolled about the deck.

"Yes, and I fear we will find the remainder in a similar state," the older scientist mused. "We may have reached an end to our quest. Unless something occurs to change matters..."

His morose pondering were interrupted by shouts from the crew.

The Captain, the Doctor and the soldier joined the crew by the anchor-side rail. They were gathered in a rough semi-circle, leaving space for the ghost.

Lotte was the translucent image of a young girl, her dress and hair plain. She danced about the deck in impatient joy, much to the sailor's distress.

"Ah," Doctor Omega nodded in understanding. "I forgot to mention..."

Several of the sailors by the rail shouted and pointed over the side.

Emerging from the water, Isaac Laquedem pulled himself up the coarse anchor rope. He reached the rail.

"Permission to come aboard, Captain?" he asked, blandly.

"Um...granted," Sir Oliver nodded.

Isaac swung a long leg over, and, nodding his greeting to the crew, walked down the deck. As he passed Doctor Omega, he reached into the battered satchel that hung at his hip, and took out a tightly wound scroll, which he handed to the Doctor. He then strolled the length of the ship, his ghostly child following happily along.

Several of the sailors crossed themselves or muttered a prayer under their breath. All eyes were on the Captain and Doctor Omega.

"I... uh... believe there is room for him to bunk with the crew," The corsair muttered, keeping his tone dignified, while his eyes stayed fixed on the new passenger.

"Isaac requires no hammock," Omega explained. "Just be aware that he must… will always be walking. He will attempt to stay out of the crew's way and requires that they do the same."

He then tapped the Captain with his newly acquired scroll, and nodded his head in the direction of his cabin. They were soon joined by Renard and the minuscule swordsman.

Shelfin paced the Captain's table, studying the maps as he walked across them.

"May I ask what occurred on Caspak?" Sir Oliver asked, having regained some of his composure, settled in his chair and a full goblet in his hand. "No treasure, but several passengers, who… er… leave me at a loss for words."

The others all turned in the direction of Doctor Omega. He had unrolled the scroll and was intently reading it, oblivious to his companions' attention.

After several moments, he put down the scroll and took up his tea cup and sipped contemplatively.

"Well?" Renard asked, finally breaking the tense silence. "What does it say?"

"Hmmm, what…?" Omega said, startled from his thoughts. "Oh, yes, it's a message from another time traveler, like myself, an English acquaintance. Apparently, he was contacted by Helvetius and has passed along the results of his own inquiries. It gives us two more islands to search: two very promising, if concerning, locations…"

He passed the scroll to the Captain, who intently studied the navigational instructions.

He put the paper down, frowning.

"Yes, the first is desolate," He nodded. "The second is yet another of your islands that exist where none should be."

The span between islands was no less hazardous or fantastic. There were days spent trapped in a strange sargasso with an even stranger occupant. There was matching wits and swords with pirates: upon the water; pursued by the Dread Pirate Roberts; upon land, a supply run threatened by the equally dreaded Captain Mephisto.

The Rose Hawk plowed the seas, its rigging tight, as all available sail was unfurled. The crew's enthusiasm could be chalked up to their eagerness to make landfall in the hopes that any and all of their unusual passengers would be disembarking.

Isaac's constant walking proved unnerving; the sound of his footfalls, heard, day and night, lead to whispers that he was everything from some unholy golem, to a cursed sorcerer, to his being the fabled Wandering Jew. Any anxiety he caused was slightly offset by his mild, nonthreatening nature and willingness to help with the ship's chores.

He was well suited as a courier to all parts of the ship, as well as exhibiting a strength that was staggering, when he put his hand to weighing the anchor or helping with the rigging. He was often joined on his constant walking by his spectral daughter, as well as Omega and Sir Shelfin; the latter perching upon his shoulder or residing in a pocket.

They soon came in sight of the island of Borgabunda: a lush wooded peninsula.

"If nothing else," Captain Tressilian remarked, as they observed it from the wheel deck. "A good chance to replenish supplies. Yusuf, assemble a few men to join us."

"Us?" Doctor Omega inquired, pointedly.

"Yes, none of your solitary explorations this time. I can make out movement in the trees. Whether beasts, natives or your lost soldiers, you'll have an escort."

"I don't see anything," Renard muttered, peering through a telescope.

"I have a keen eye, Monsieur Renard," Sir Oliver replied, jauntily. "Will tall Isaac be joining us, or will he be making his own way?"

"I believe he'd like some ground under his feet," Doctor Omega said, "and so, will most likely decline taking one of the boats."

The party soon reached the blunt, rocky beach. A guard was left on the boats, and the group soon split: the Captain and his men going in search of helpful landmarks, as well as water and something to fill the ship's larder, while Doctor Omega, Lieutenant Renard and Sir Shelfin walked up the narrow beach, searching for some sign of their time-lost quarry.

The Lilliputian chose to walk for a bit, as he was unlikely to get lost on the empty stretch of beach.

"I don't see any sign of people," Renard muttered, shading his eyes with his hand as he peered about. "No buildings, no farming… not even footprints or a trail…!"

"Calm down," Doctor Omega said, patting him on the arm. "We have just arrived. Enjoy the walk."

"I've found something!" Sir Shelfin yelled, struggling to be heard over the surf.

"It's a footprint!" Renard said, kneeling down. "A hoof print! That must mean people!"

"Or it might just mean horses," Doctor Omega grumbled. "Start using your head! The Traveler's note referenced some time eddies, but nothing specific..."

Chastened, Renard walked along the beach, occasionally, parting the foliage to peer deeper into the woods. Aside from a few more hoof prints, they saw no other sign of habitation. Shelfin rode in Doctor Omegas' coat pocket, while the soldier trailed along, dejectedly.

Soon, Isaac came walking out of the ocean and fell in step with them, wringing out his clothes and beard while he walked.

"No luck?" he asked, quietly.

Renard, holding the wanderers' staff for him, while he dealt with his sopping garments, merely shook his head.

"There must be something here," the bearded man said. "Otherwise, why send us…?"

"The Doctor said something about 'time eddies', whatever those are. Maybe my friends aren't the only time travelers…?"

He glanced at the other man. Isaac chuckled dryly.

"I travel through time the traditional way: one day at a time. I leave the other sort to you and Omega. Your fellow soldiers may not be here, but there is… something. I can smell it on the wind."

They walked, soon losing sight of the ship. The solitude soon weighed heavy, causing the entire quartet to cast questioning glances at the least noise. As the sun crept closer to the horizon, the shadows grew longer and brought more feeling of unease.

"Something *is* out there," Renard muttered, under his breath. "I can feel it."

Isaac merely nodded and took his staff back. Renard moved closer to Doctor Omega, keeping one hand on the butt of his pistol.

"We should start heading back to the boat," he said, in a conversational tone, meant for both his companion and whoever might be watching them. "The Captain will be missing us."

"Yes, yes," Doctor Omega replied. "I'm sure he will, but I'm more interested in who is following us."

Oblivious to his friends' concern, the time traveler walked up to the edge of the forest and poked at the nearest bush with his cane.

"Come now, enough of this skulking. Introduce yourself."

The result was not quite what he had hoped for, as the shrubbery erupted with a half dozen, feral creatures. They were shorter than men, ape-like in stance. They had chalk-colored skin, weak chins, and over-sized red-veined eyes. Flaxen hair covered their heads and ran down their backs. They were clad in scraps of rough cloth and bore rudimentary weapons, mostly just sticks.

Isaac stepped in, swinging his staff. He mowed the creatures down as if they were wheat before a scythe.

"Morlocks?" Doctor Omega breathed. "They're Morlocks! How did they get… Oh, Helvetius, you are an idiot!"

"What? What's that?" Renard asked, brandishing his gun, and trying to draw a bead on the attackers.

Isaac seemed in no need of help, so he just stayed on guard. He was prepared to defend the Doctor, if any Morlocks got past the tall man's staff.

Shelfin leapt out of Doctor Omega's pocket, shimmied down his pant leg, raced across the beach, and promptly stabbed the nearest Morlock in the foot.

"Take that, foul miscreant!" he shouted in triumph.

The Morlock hopped about, cradling his injured foot, making himself an easy target, for Isaac's staff.

The creatures were soon routed, two laying sprawled and unconscious on the beach, the rest escaping into the trees.

"Flee, you poltroons!" Shelfin bellowed. "Or taste my blade once more!"

"Well fought, sir," Isaac said, scooping up the tiny swordsman.

He then turned and walked back down the beach. Renard, took Doctor Omega by the arm and steered him along. Unsure if their attackers were gone , he kept his gun in hand.

"What were those... Morlocks, you said?" He asked, keeping one eye on the trees. "Where do I know them from?"

"Hmmm?" Doctor Omega asked, absently. "What? Oh, yes, of course. Helvetius' harebrained attempt to return your comrades home and deal with the damage they caused to the time stream. You, as well as a tribe of Morlocks, were scooped up... Terrible mess... And it would seem that a portion of both parties ended up scattered about... Would explain the time eddies...!"

"I remember that... Sort of," Renard muttered. "Feels like a dream... There was a girl there and some explorer fellow..."

"Yes, yes," Doctor Omega nodded. "You were traveling from the past to the present, and I believe the Morlocks were traveling from far in your future to the past... Never did find out what that was about.... Anyway, the two groups collided and it caused no end of temporal disruptions."

"So, they don't belong here either?" Renard asked. "Should we be gathering them up, as well? Hate to think of anyone, even those repulsive buggers, being stranded."

"No, no," Doctor Omega replied, in absent thought. "I think they are fine right where they are. This explains a bit. I always thought the Yahoos were a lost tribe of Neanderthals, but the answer might be even more intriguing... Helvetius might have known what he was doing, after all... makes a pleasant change..!"

"You lost me quite a ways back," Renard said. "But, once we are safe on the ship, with a mug full of grog, you can explain it to me all over again."

Back at the beach, Captain Tressilian and the sailors were waiting, looking a bit the worse for wear.

"Ah, you encountered the Morlocks too?" Renard said, looking them over.

"A rather unpleasant group of... I have no idea what they were," the Captain replied, perched on the edge of the boat while he attended to a leg wound. "And then, we were almost trampled by some horses!"

"Houyhhnhnms!" Doctor Omega said, brightening. "Well, that confirms my theory!"

"I am so glad someone is enjoying this excursion," Sir Oliver scowled, as he tore a strip from his vest to bind his leg.

"Apparently, the good Doctor has solved some great mystery," Renard explained.

"So, any luck finding your friends?" the Captain asked,

Renard shook his head.

"Well, then, onward!" he exclaimed, clapping him on the shoulder.

A week later saw them reaching, their next destination, a fog shrouded island that existed on no map that Sir Oliver could find.

The ship was at anchor, its captain and passengers at the rail, studying the massive fog bank that enshrouded it, listening to distant waves break upon an unseen shore.

"Well, there it is," Sir Oliver said. "I think, hard to tell, even by my keen eye."

"It's there," Doctor Omega said, studying a small device he took from his pocket. "Strong traces of artron energy, as well as some curious traces of radiation… Best make this a short visit."

"I will join you there," Isaac said, stepping over the rail and dropping into the water.

"I'd prefer a boat, myself," Renard remarked.

"I too," the Captain said. "Mister Pitt, see to the boats, if you please."

The trip across was rough. The waves were fierce and once in the bay they encountered a maze of rocky shapes poking up from the sea floor, like talons.

The beach was strewn with shale and stones. There was a steep incline to a sandy area and then dense jungle and imposing mountains.

"Chilly," Doctor Omega said, huddling into his cloak.

Renard nodded and blew into his cupped hands.

"Drag the boats up," Sir Oliver instructed. "Yusuf, you and Mister Pitt, see about gathering some fire wood. What now, Doctor?"

"Up, that way, I believe," Doctor Omega said, consulting his device, and then gesturing towards the mountains.

"I cannot say I like the looks of this place," The bearded corsair said. "There is something… wrong about it. Can't quite put my finger on what…"

"Walk cautiously," Isaac advised, after he had walked out of the surf, wrung out his beard, and joined the search party on the beach.

"There are footprints!" Renard announced, and then pointed up the beach. "And that looks like the remains of a fire!"

"Seems we've reached our destination," Doctor Omega said. "I do agree, those hills look forbidding. Let's begin our search along the beach."

The party soon scattered, Sir Oliver directing his men. Isaac continued to trudge, alone, down the beach.

No matter which direction, everyone kept an eye on the distant hills, as an echoing noise was carried on the wind down to them. It was the cries of some beast that none of them could readily identify.

Soon, Doctor Omega, Renard and Sir Shelfin were left alone, save for the sailor left to guard the boats, contemplating their search plan.

"Which way?" the Lieutenant asked.

Doctor Omega ignored him, holding out his scanner.

"These readings are… odd," he muttered.

Still talking to himself, he began walking away from the beach and into the undergrowth.

"Um…?" Renard said, before scooping up his Lilliputian companion and jogging after the time traveler. He caught up with Doctor Omega just in time to get whipped across the face with a branch.

"Could you be a bit more careful?" he sputtered indignantly, as he spit out leaves, only to nearly collide with the white-haired scientist.

Doctor Omega was standing in the middle of the narrow path with his arms raised. Poking out of the surrounding foliage were a half dozen rifle barrels.

"What the hell…?" Renard muttered.

"Marcel?" A voice from the jungle asked. "Is that you?"

"Monoclard?"

"Put your guns down, you idiots! It's Lieutenant Renard! Marcel!"

A crowd of soldiers came scrambling out of the jungle, crowding the narrow path.

Their uniforms were the same as Renard's, though very worn at the knees and elbows. Several sported makeshift bandages and slings. They looked dirty and thoroughly bedraggled.

While Renard shook hands, slapped shoulders and attempted to explain the situation, Doctor Omega stayed to the side, frowning at his scanner.

Shelfin, perched on Renard's shoulder, clung desperately to the fabric of the uniform tunic, to keep from being flung off.

"How did you find us?" Monoclard asked.

"It was a bit of a trip," Renard replied. "Um… It's difficult to explain."

"Did you bring any bread?" Cipriani, a fellow with a scraggily mustache asked.

"How'd you get past the dragons?"

"I'm sorry… The what?" soldier, savant and Lilliputian asked as one.

"Dragons?" Doctor Omega asked, raising his voice to be heard above the din. "What do you mean by dragons? Not all at once! You, with the bandages on your head, speak up?"

"They… uh… they're huge beasts… like big toads or lizards!"

"You mean, dinosaurs?" Renard asked, wide-eyed. "But, they're all dead!"

"There have been exceptions," Doctor Omega said, casually. "But best if we continued this conversation away from here."

He and Renard helped the soldiers gather their meager supplies and aided those whose wounds kept them from being very mobile.

They soon reached the beach and the long boats.

"Pitt, go find the Captain," Renard said, as they helped his comrades into the boats.

The sailor jogged off down the beach, while the others anxiously scanned their surroundings.

"Dinosaurs!" Renard breathed, a bit awestruck, despite all the wonders he'd already witnessed. "Just out there, in the hills!"

"In the hills?" one portly soldier scoffed. "They are the hills!"

To emphasize the point, there was another distant growl and the hills seemed to tremble.

"Earthquake?" Doctor Omega asked, faintly.

"No," Monoclard said, shaking his head. "*It*'s waking up."

With that, the nearest hill opened its eyes.

The creature was huge: long as the locomotive that had originally taken the soldiers to the front, and standing three stories-tall at the shoulder. It was brown with yellow, stubby tusks, and a long, knobby tail. Its back was a spiked carapace.

The creature stomped forward on four legs, lazy from its nap and possibly in search of breakfast.

"Judging by the serrated teeth, not a herbivore," Doctor Omega said. "Curious, as it resembles an ankylosaurus."

"This is not a university lecture hall," Renard pointed out. "We need to get away! Even if *that* doesn't try to eat us, we could still be trampled!"

The soldiers nodded along in vigorous agreement.

"What?" Doctor Omega asked, distractedly. "Yes, yes, of course. Not to worry, it isn't paying the least bit of attention to us."

It was a sound plan—at least until Captain Tressilian and his party came around the curve of the beach, saw the huge beast, and immediately started firing at it with their muskets.

The bullets were no more than insect bites to such a creature, yet enough to get its attention. The enormous long snout turned and beady eyes took in the tiny, scurrying forms. With a snort that shook the trees, it lumbered towards the beach.

"Oh, dear," Doctor Omega said.

The soldiers and sailors used slightly less delicate language. Most of them rushed to the boats, while a couple reloaded and continued to fire.

"What is that thing?" Sir Oliver asked.

He had drawn his cutlass, but it hung loosely at his side, as he had realized its pointlessness.

"No time for explanations," Renard said, addressing Doctor Omega rather than the Captain. "To the ship!"

"That beast could easily chase us back to the *Rose Hawk*," Sir Oliver said, with grim practicality. "Take your foundlings in one boat. We will hold it off, and then follow after."

"They can't do this," Renard said, grabbing Doctor Omega's arm. "Even if we give them our army rifles, that thing will kill them. It's idiocy!"

"I hate to intrude!" Shelfin shouted, from Renard's shoulder, "but, if we lead the beast back to the ship, we could all end up stranded here!"

"I will keep the creature occupied," Isaac said, as he walked past them. "Get everyone away. This is no place for men."

They began to protest, but Doctor Omega silenced them with a glare and a gesture, before following after the tall immortal.

"Are you sure about this?" he asked, eyeing the steadily approaching behemoth.

"You know well that I am invulnerable to any and all earthly threats," Isaac said, a touch sadly.

"Yes, but I am not entirely convinced the inhabitants of this island are of an earthly nature."

"Well then, that should make it interesting," Isaac replied, with a small, sardonic smile. "Till we meet again, Omega."

Doctor Omega stood, watching Isaac Laquedem walk off. He nodded to himself and returned to the boats.

"Well?" the Captain asked.

"Isaac will deal with that thing and give us the time we need to set sail or whatever term you use." he explained. "Once we're away from this island, we should be fine. Well, don't just stand there!"

Soon, the two boats were loaded and the men frantically worked the oars, intently and worriedly, watching the lone figure striding determinedly towards the angry monster.

Back on the beach, Isaac spared the boats a glance and then turned his focus back to the enormous creature. Even at seven foot-tall, he had to crane his neck upwards, as it drew closer.

"Yes, this should be interesting," he said, tucking his hat into his satchel and adjusting his grip on his staff.

Back on the ship, the men scattered. The sailors frantically prepared for departure, while Renard found space for his comrades in the hull.

Sir Shelfin leapt from the soldier to Doctor Omega's shoulder and the odd duo stood at the rail, gazing at the dwindling island, listening to the distant sounds of combat.

By nightfall, the *Rose Hawk* was far from the island and on its way to rendezvous with Professor Helvetius on Villings Island. The white-haired time traveler was seated in a rickety deck chair, allowing himself to nod off, now that his task was near completion. A heavy, tattered volume, full of his scribbles concerning the journey, lay in his lap.

“Aren’t you chilly out here?” a voice asked.

“Hmmm? What? No,” Omega replied, blinking away his sleepiness. “The sea breeze is quite refreshing… Ah, it’s you.”

The ghostly form of young Lotte stood at his side.

“And what have you been up to, young lady? Not pestering the crew?”

“No, I just wanted to pass along a message. My father has left the island of monsters.”

“None the worse for wear, I hope?” asked the Doctor.

“He wanted me to tell you, his day of rest is approaching and so he won’t be rejoining you. He spotted an island that he thought he would pass the day on.”

“He has more than earned it. What of you? Playing messenger and frightening sailors is no way for a young lady to spend her time.”

The petite specter shrugged.

“Well, I myself have some leisure time,” Doctor Omega smiled, sitting up. “Fancy a game of checkers?”

After a long spell, Randy Lofficier returns with a new adventure of the Phantom Angel, the Sleeping Beauty of legend awakened in modern times by Doc Ardan in "The Reluctant Princess" (Volume 4). Since then, the intrepid Briar Rose has appeared in Randy's "The English Gentleman's Ball" (Vol. 5) and "The Spear of Destiny" (Vol. 6), and guest-starred in Emmanuel Gorlier's "Una Voce Poco Fa" (in Night of the Nyctalope*). In this story, Madame L'Ange steps into the 21st century, working alongside the much harassed Captain Berthaud from the remarkable Canal-Plus TV series* Engrenages *(*Spiral *in English)....*

Randy Lofficier: *The Phantom Angel and the Dwarves of Death*

Paris, Today

"Bonjour, Madame L'Ange," said Captain Laure Berthaud, as she entered my office. "I hope you can spare me a few minutes of your time. Inspector Guillaume Martin Paumier suggested I come to see you."

"What can I do for you, Captain?" I asked.

"We have a delicate problem and I'm hoping you can help us."

"Me?"

"Yes, Madame. You see, I know a little about you and your..., er, people."

"I'm sure I don't know what you mean, Captain."

I was once called Briar Rose and I lived the life of a princess. There were certainly many who envied that, but for me, it wasn't enough. I saw the long years of embroidery, fancy dress balls and meaningless conversations stretching ahead of me and I wept. I knew deep inside that there had to be something more.

So, when a wise woman (some would call her a witch) offered me an escape of sorts, I took it.

Her enchantment sent me to sleep for 500 years.

A brave explorer awoke me with a kiss and, at first, I was furious; I had a selfish desire to remain apart from the world.

But Doctor Francis Ardan explained that much had changed during my slumber and I decided to embrace this brave new world.

He was right; things were different and mostly better. Of course, there was still much injustice and many unhappy souls. I realized, however, that these things could provide me with what I had sought: a purpose for my life.

My attempts at helping others earned me a nickname. I was mysterious and brave, and young journalist Joseph Rouletabille dubbed me "The Phantom Angel." I liked it and quickly decided that I would prefer to be called Angel forever more. Or, rather, when I'm being just "me," I tell people my name is Rose L'Ange.

I was able to use the services of a top legal team, thanks to the Ardans' fortune, and through a lot of research, we learned that I was sole heir to my own vast fortune, courtesy of my ancestors. That gave me the freedom to live a new life of independence, while at the same time using my resources to help others in need. And, there were plenty of those! I used some of that money to buy a *hotel particulier* in the Marais district of Paris, and opened a private investigations agency on the ground floor: *L'Agence d'Investigations & Recherches L'Ange* was born.

When I first awoke, it was the 1920s. The world was still recovering from a devastating world war. It was all new and modern for me and I had much to learn. I used more of my money to get an education and become comfortable in this new world that was so different from the one I had known. I was able to appear and disappear in society in a way that made it less suspicious for someone like me, who never seemed to age; changing my "circle" frequently enough that no one noticed. No one nowadays remembers me as the ace vigilante from the 1920s.

Just as I was getting comfortable in this new era, Europe descended into a new world war, proving that the last one had not been "the war to end all wars," as people at the time had believed. My home in Paris was confiscated by the evil that was the Nazis and I fled the city to join in the Resistance as best I could. I even had an adventure or two with Leo Saint-Clair, also known as the Nyctalope. Those were not good years. But even in the darkest of times, eventually there is a light. The forces of "good" were allied and able to defeat the evil. At least for a time.

But I wasn't the only one from the enchanted realms that some might call "fairy tales" to have problems in these modern times. While we all shared one, major benefit, long life, we also had the burdens and problems that had followed us from our pasts. The petty hatreds, family feuds, rivalries, etc., were still with us. And these often made life complicated and unpleasant. Not everyone had the skills to free themselves of these things, and instead they turned to me.

Once the world was back on its feet, the problems of the little people were again in the forefront. I regained my Parisian residence and the clients came back.

The post war years passed. France and modern society was rebuilt. We had new tragedies, new enemies, but, at least, no more world wars. It was possible to live in this world and not fear too much, if one was careful. The marvels that came to be outshone the "magic" of my previous era in many ways. After all, who needed magic when they could turn to computers and iPhones for anything they desired.

And, that brings me to today, and the unexpected visit of Captain Laure Berthaud of the 2nd Division of the *Police Judiciaire*, or DPJ, a worthy branch of French Law Enforcement! I knew of Captain Berthaud from reading of her exploits (and disasters) in the press, but I had never expected that I would be on her radar.

Berthaud was a small woman, but she looked tough. She wore jeans and a sweater, with an old, worn leather jacket that looked almost as if it was part of her. Her hair was shoulder-length, dirty blond, pulled back loosely in a clip, but with rebellious strands escaping; it was clear the captain wasn't interested in her appearance anymore than I was interested in my own. Her brown eyes were intelligent and penetrating, and although she looked like someone who never got enough sleep, you could see that she missed very little. I could tell I was going to like her, despite my concerns.

"Come on, Madame L'Ange. You can't believe that your, er, 'special' circumstances have gone unnoticed by everyone?" she continued.

I looked at Berthaud, unsure of how I should respond. I don't like to lie, but I also am very hesitant to discuss the lives of those of us who live a parallel existence to the mundane world. Finally, I made up my mind.

"All right, Captain Berthaud. So you know about me. I still don't see what I can do for you. After all, the police don't need a modest private investigator like me to do their job."

Berthaud stared at me for a second, looking exasperated.

"The problem, Madame L'Ange, is that the people of your community don't trust us. I need someone with an *entrée* into your world who can ask questions that they won't answer for me. And, to be honest, I feel a bit uncomfortable dealing with fey beings from stories I read as a kid. It makes me feel like the world I know is spinning out of control."

"We're mostly the same as you, Captain. We live our lives, fall in love, and have our problems, all the same as in the mundane world. We've just been doing those things for a lot longer than you have! Now, tell me what's going on."

Berthaud sighed.

"Do you know the Nain Brothers? The seven dwarves who have a jewelry business a few streets over?"

I knew them well. They had been diamond miners in the Black Forest back in the Old Days. In today's world, they sold diamonds of unclear provenance to their mundane customers, but to those in the know, they sold a wide selection of magically enhanced stones. The magic stones had a variety of properties and while most of them were relatively harmless, there were a few that could be dangerous in the wrong hands. I gestured that Berthaud should continue.

"There was a heist in their shop yesterday. It turned ugly and Quee, the youngest one, was killed. His brothers are not taking it well. They're pretty sure the whole thing was orchestrated by the Dragon Tong from the 13th Arrondissement. Word is that they're getting ready to go to war. Clearly, we want to avoid that, and I was hoping you could help me talk them down."

Poor Berthaud was getting herself involved in quite a mess. There was something about the Dragon Tong that she didn't know.

"Are you sure you want to get in the middle of this, Captain? It's going to be messy."

"That's my job. I've dealt with the Tongs before."

"Not the Dragons, you haven't. Because, they *are* you know."

"They are what?"

"Dragons."

"Yes. They're called the Dragons. I know."

"No. They're not just *called* the Dragons, they *are* dragons! Real ones. Sure, they look human now, but that's because they have glamours they can use to disguise themselves. Those guys are real, honest-to-goodness fire-breathing dragons. They've evolved to be a little smaller than the Great Old Ones of the past, and that helps the glamour to work so they can fit in normal places without too much trouble. But get them riled up and they'll shoot fire out of their faces before you can draw your pistol."

Berthaud looked at me with her eyes opened wide.

"You have got to be shitting me!" she shouted.

I looked at her sadly and shook my head.

"Welcome to our world, Captain Berthaud," I said, then laughed.

I just couldn't help it.

We walked out into the crowded streets of the Marais. I loved this old Paris neighborhood. It was a heady blend of old world and modern hipsters, with Jewish grocery stores and delicatessens standing side-by-side with expensive boutiques and American-style burger joints. There were smells of fresh-baked bread and imported teas and coffees, voices chattering loudly in French, Yiddish, English, and every other language. It felt alive and wonderful.

I breathed it all in joyfully as we walked down the Rue de Turenne until we turned onto the Rue Saint-Claude, where the Nain Brothers had their shop, *La Pierre Enchantée*. The place was a mess; broken glass was everywhere and there was blood next to a series of small, numbered, yellow stands that clearly indicated where a body had once been located.

Berthaud went up to one of her colleagues, who she introduced to me as "Gilou." His gruff manner indicated he wasn't particularly happy to see me there. I ignored him and, instead focused on the small men huddling together in a relatively quiet corner of the shop. These were the six remaining Nain Brothers. They were Blick, Flick, Glick, Snick, Plick and Whick. Blick was the eldest and was clearly the head of the family.

Blick was seething. Dwarves are no pushovers despite being some of the smaller members of our fey society. Their years of manual labor had made them strong and hard. They didn't suffer fools and believed in hard work and being left to live their lives in peace. The heist and murder had shaken them; they clearly were distraught at the loss of their youngest, weakest brother, Quee.

Blick nodded when he saw me and I went over to have a talk.

"I'm sorry about Quee," I started.

"The poor kid," said Blick, rather ignoring the fact that the "kid" was something over 700 years-old. "He was harmless. They didn't have to kill him. He would have given them what they wanted eventually."

"And what would that be, Blick?" I asked.

The dwarf tried to be cagey with me, hemming and hawing rather than answering me directly. Finally, he gave in:

"It was a mind control stone. The possessor could use it to control anyone and force them to carry out anything he wanted. It's powerful and could be turned to dark ends in the wrong hands. I don't know why the Dragons wanted it, but it can't be because they're up to anything good."

"Doesn't sound like the kind of thing Dragons would normally be interested in, Blick."

"Maybe not, Angel; but they were and now our little brother is dead. They won't get away with it. We have plenty of powerful stones left that we can use against them. They'll be sorry they ever set foot in our Arrondissement!"

Berthaud had been silently listening to our exchange and now gave me a look indicating her displeasure at the way the conversation was going. It was clear she wanted me to nip this in the bud!

I wanted to stop any escalation as well. It wouldn't be good for anyone in our community for this kind of turf war to erupt. Not only would others be forced to take sides, but we all risked exposure to the world at large should things get out of hand. Our survival in the modern world depended on us all living with a certain amount of discretion.

"Listen, Blick," I said. "Don't do anything hasty. This could blow up in all our faces. I know you're angry and grieving, but why don't you leave things with me and Captain Berthaud? We'll try to find out exactly what happened, and we'll make sure that whoever it was who killed Quee sees the inside of a prison cell. You know that our kind don't do well in captivity. That will be a worse punishment than starting a war where a lot of innocents might get hurt."

Blick wasn't pleased. He turned to consult with his brothers. I could hear them whispering furiously back and forth. They occasionally turned to stare at me and Berthaud, but I couldn't tell what they were thinking when they did it. Finally, Blick came back to talk to me.

"OK, Angel. We'll give you a week. If at the end of it you don't come back with a remedy that satisfies us, we're going to take things into our own hands. We'll have justice—or war."

I agreed. What choice did I have? My investigative skills, as well as my ability to negotiate with deadly, fire-breathing dragons were going to be challenged for sure.

I turned back to Berthaud and said:

"Captain, we're going to have to find a way to solve this quickly if you don't want a bloody, magical war on your hands. The Nains aren't happy, but they'll give us some time before they try anything on their own. Do you mind if I have a look around the crime scene?"

"Knock yourself out, Madame L'Ange. The forensics people have already been through it, and if there was anything here, they'd have found it."

"There may be things that regular human eyes wouldn't notice, Captain. Sometimes you can be blinded and see only what you expect to see."

"Humph!" she said, shrugging in mild annoyance.

I knew what I was hoping to find. If it had really been the Dragons who had committed this outrage, there would be telltale clues. As I walked around the room, I concentrated on the cracks and crevices in the ancient hardwood floorboards. They could be a treasure trove of information. After circling around the room, I saw it: something shiny and golden glittering in a small crack in the parquet flooring. I bent down to look at it more closely and made a sound in surprise.

"What is it?" asked Berthaud.

I stood up.

"It's a golden hair. And that means the Dragons either weren't involved, or else someone else was here as well."

"How do you know, Madame?"

"Think about it, Captain. Dragons, even highly evolved ones, don't have hair; they have scales!"

I didn't know who else might have been involved, but there was only one way we were going to find out. We needed to talk to the Tong as soon as possible.

Berthaud and I left the *Pierre Enchantée* and stood on the sidewalk as we decided on how to proceed.

"Captain, the Dragons are going to be very hesitant talk to us. I'm not sure they'll be willing to tell us anything unless we can make it worth their while."

"I don't care whether they're real dragons or not, Madame L'Ange, they're still French residents and they have to obey the law. If they want to go to jail, I'm perfectly happy to put them there if they don't cooperate."

I didn't argue with Berthaud. I was pretty sure she'd never seen what dragon fire could do to the inside of a police station, and I knew she wouldn't believe me if I told her. I merely shrugged. If I'd learned anything in the almost hundred years I'd lived in this brave new world, it was that you can't make people believe things that fall outside of their personal experience. The Captain would just have to learn on her own.

She offered to drive us to the Dragons' lair and I agreed.

As always, Parisian traffic was brutal. I was sorry I hadn't asked Blick if he didn't have a stone that could have just transported us to the 13th Arrondissement without the need to spend 45 minutes in Berthaud's filthy grey Clio. I swear, she must practically live in the thing! It smelled of stale cigarettes and unwashed socks. There were items on the floor that I preferred not to look at too closely. Some things are better left unexamined.

By the time we got to the Place d'Italie, I'd decided I'd take the Metro to get back home rather than ride in Berthaud's trash heap again.

We drove inside the 13th Arrondissement towards the Rue de Tolbiac. Parking was a misery, but the Captain pulled up on a sidewalk and got out. Obviously she wasn't worried about getting a parking ticket. We walked to the Dragons' lair, which was a small warehouse located next to a Chinese restaurant, The Imperial Dragon. The smells of Chinese food reminded me that it was lunchtime, but food would have to wait a bit longer.

A very large "man" blocked the door to the lair. He was slightly Asian in appearance, but not of any recognizable ethnicity. If you knew what to look for, you could occasionally see the "glamour" that hid his true appearance shift a small bit, allowing something clearly not human to peek through.

"We're here to see Druk," I said, very politely.

"Who's asking?" the Dragon replied.

Berthaud flashed her ID and the guard reluctantly moved aside to let us in.

Inside the warehouse, it was dark. We could make out shapes in the smoky haze that permeated the air. Dragons' breath is notorious for giving off a pungent, smoky scent that isn't unpleasant, but also makes it pretty hard for humans to breathe without coughing a fair amount.

A powerful figure moved towards us in the darkness; it was all I could do to keep myself from jumping back in fear. But it wouldn't do to show the Dragons that we were afraid of them; they would take it as a sign of weakness and we'd never get what we wanted from them.

With a voice that was somewhere between a rumble and a hiss, the creature spoke:

"I'm Druk," he said. "What do you want with me?"

Berthaud impressed me; she didn't seem at all fazed to be talking to a 1000-year-old dragon in human guise.

"I'm Captain Berthaud of the 2nd DPJ." She held up her ID again. "We're here to talk to you about the incident at *La Pierre Enchantée* that left Quee Nain dead."

"Nothing to do with me, Captain," replied Druk with a rumble.

"You're wrong, Druk," Berthaud responded. "Blick Nain has pinned it on you. According to him, some of your men were heard threatening the Nains. You know we'll eventually find some evidence to prove you were involved."

"We are dragons; we have no need of their silly stones. Yes, some of our younger members display occasionally the foolish bravado of youth, but nothing more. We had no reason to want any of the Nains dead."

"Unless you can give me an alternative suspect, I'll have no choice but to book you for questioning."

Druk seemed to be smoking a bit, and it wasn't coming from a cigarette. He turned his penetrating gaze on me.

"You have a certain reputation, Madame L'Ange. Surely you will not allow this mundane person to threaten me like this!"

"Sorry, Druk. She's in charge here; I'm only around to provide introductions. But I'm happy to help if you're willing to meet me halfway. I don't want to see our kind dragged into court anymore than you do. Give me something I can use to get to the bottom of things."

I felt his eyes burning into me and could almost see the gears turning in his brain as he thought.

"Very well. I can tell you this much: the whispers have it that there is royalty involved. One who is losing control within his own house and seeks to take it back. Not all broken curses finish by having a happily ever after!"

Druk's words sparked something in my memory. I knew that I was not the only one from our community to have been reluctant to accept the life laid out for me by accidents of birth and tradition.

Berthaud interrupted:

"What kind of crap is that? Is that from a fortune cookie? I want real answers!"

"It's OK, Captain," I told her. "I think I know where we should be looking. We're going to need to take your 'trusty steed' again, though."

I shuddered at the thought of again sitting in her filthy Clio.

This time, I had the Captain drive us to the 16th Arrondissement where we stopped in front of a building of "standing" on the Avenue Mozart. I was rich, but living here would have given me pause before laying out what a Hotel Particulier with view on the Bois de Boulogne on one side and the Eiffel Tower on the other must have cost.

We went up to the door where a liveried footman stood guard. He looked down his nose at us in the way that only those who serve the aristocracy can manage; making you almost forget that they, themselves, are servants and not the boss!

"We're here to see Prince Fortunato," I said.

Berthaud held up her ID. I was starting to be impressed by how much that little document managed to accomplish so quickly.

"His Highness is not receiving," responded the footman, haughtily.

"Look here, *mon mec*," the Captain replied. "If you don't let us in now, I'll have a warrant in ten minutes and we'll be arresting everyone on the premises before you can slam the door closed again."

With poor grace, the footman moved aside to allow us entrance.

Even for me, the inside of this place was at the same time elegant and creepy as hell. There were what looked like living arms holding candelabra out of the walls! I thought I saw a human-sized teapot turn into a room, but I'm sure I was mistaken!

We were led by a butler into a salon that looked as if it hadn't changed in several hundred years, and were asked to wait.

After a few minutes, Belle walked into the room. I had known her for a long time, of course, but I must admit that I was shocked when I saw her. She looked drawn and tired.

"Hello, Belle," I said. "This is Captain Berthaud from the 2nd DPJ. We need to talk with your husband. Are you well?"

She smiled wanly at me and merely nodded her head briefly. Her eyes did not light up with the smile on her lips.

"We all make do, Angel. Surely, you remember?"

Before I could say more, Prince Fortunato strode into the room. He was tall and powerful with piercing golden eyes and a head full of golden yellow hair. When he appeared, he caused everyone in his path to catch their breath.

"I understand you would like to speak with me," he said. He bowed to me and the Captain. "I am at your service, Mesdames."

Despite his polite demeanor, it was clear he was wary. I looked at his golden hair. Without a forensic examination, I couldn't be sure, but it looked very much like the hair I had found at *La Pierre Enchantée*.

"Prince Fortunato," began Berthaud, "perhaps you'd care to tell us what you were doing in the Marais early this morning?"

"My dear Captain, I have no idea to what you refer. There is nothing that would call me to such a place."

I stepped in.

"Look, Fortunato. You can't pull that 'princely' stuff on me! I've known you for a long time. You may play the great man here, but you hang out at the Dragons' Lair with the hoi polloi more than anyone else. I've heard you've racked up quite a tab there. Cough up the truth! Why did you want that stone and why did you kill poor Quee?"

"Those Dwarves! What a waste of space they are! They should have been honored that I'd grace their ridiculous little shop with my presence! I asked them for a small favor and was treated with disrespect. How did they expect me to respond? If I let that Quee creature get away with it, everyone else would have felt free to treat me the same. Of course, I punished him for his insolence, then took what I wanted!"

"A mind control stone? Why would you need something like that? You're rich and powerful, you don't need extra magic, surely?"

"Look around you, Briar Rose! Look at this world in which we find ourselves. Aristocrats like me are no longer revered. Foreign heathens dare to ask us for the repayment of trifling debts of no real importance. Even in our own households our wives and servants treat us with ill-disguised disdain! I won't have it! Belle must remember her place! The mind stone will make sure that everything is restored to its rightful place."

I looked at Belle. She had tears welling up in her eyes and she cowered. So, that was it. Fortunato couldn't stand the way the world had changed. He expected her to remain the timid, cowed, creature she had once been. He could no longer control her by brute force and was turning to magic instead. The death of an innocent was not too heavy a price to pay for him to enforce his will.

Plus, in his day, royalty rarely paid their debts to money-lenders; it was easier to persecute or exile them when the tab had grown too heavy. His crime not only punished poor Quee, but put the Dragons in the frame as well, wiping out his debt instantly.

Berthaud pulled a set of handcuffs out of her jacket.

"Prince Fortunato, I'm arresting you for the murder of Quee Nain!"

Before she could cuff him, though, the Prince turned and started to run out of the room.

I ran after him and tackled him to the ground. He tried to throw me off, but as he was struggling to stand, one of the candelabra arms on the wall suddenly bashed him on the head!

The teapot that I actually *had* seen turning into a different room, came out of a doorway. She spoke:

"It's not just Belle whom he wanted to control! It's all of us! He doesn't seem to realize that in this new world, we all have rights. We would have been happy to keep working for him, but with salaries and vacations like everyone else. No wonder the aristocracy has almost disappeared. They no longer belong in our society!"

Berthaud and I marched him out of his palatial home and called a wagon to take him to the Conciergerie, where Inspector Paumier's *Brigade des Maléfices* keeps special cells for members of the Faerie and other "special" guests.

Later, I found out that, to keep things out of the papers, Judge Roban, the Magistrate charged with the case, had contacted Sâr Dubnotal, and Fortunato had been flown to that private island of his, at the other end of the world.

As for Belle, she sold her Avenue Mozart mansion to Shah Zaman of Samarkand and moved into a nice *pied-à-terre* on the Île Saint-Louis.

These things are generally better kept within our community after all…

Nigel Malcolm's near futuristic dystopian saga about a world where the forces of fascism appear to have overtaken Europe began with "Tomorrow Belongs to the Nyctalope" (Vol. 14) and continued with "Enemies of the People" (Vol. 15) and "Useful Idiot" (Vol. 16). This fourth and final chapter brings it to a smashing conclusion...

Nigel Malcolm: *The Revolution Begins Tonight*

The near future.

"Has this place changed much since you were here before, Leo?"

The question brought Saint-Clair back to the present.

"Not really. The greenery is possibly yellower than it was," he replied. "You could tell that I've been here before?"

Sexton Blake chuckled.

"Observation and conjecture really, rather than deduction." he replied. "There is a look in your eyes of, well, not exactly nostalgia, but certainly reminiscence. You have been here before, but not so recently as to recognize the newer buildings. You probably came here decades ago, but you might have been here more than a century ago."

Leo Saint-Clair looked at Blake, and fought off the temptation to think that he was actually telepathic. His friend would probably just say that the deduction was a simple one.

"Do you remember Yves Marecourt?" Saint-Clair asked.

Blake surveyed the mountains of the Pyrenees, and tried to remember.

"The mathematician?"

"Yes. When he was a young boy, he was kidnapped and was kept somewhere not far from here. Gno Mitang and I eventually rescued him." said Saint-Clair.

Blake listened to this, and looked around at the rugged surroundings, squinting.

"I recall that he had a troubled childhood. But he had great strength of character. And he was a mathematical genius, which probably helped him." The Englishman looked at his watch. "Anyway, we have just over an hour before President Schasch makes her broadcast, and our cabin is just up there. We'd better get ready."

With his blazer slung over one shoulder, and a rucksack held in his other hand, Blake trudged off up the track to the chrome colored cabin ahead.

"Right." said Leo, in response.

He took one last look around at the mountains. It had been a very different time back then. And a very different part of his life.

"And so it begins." he said, to himself. Following Blake, he added, "And so it ends" before clearing his mind and composing what he wanted to say in the speech he was going to give very shortly.

Denis Borel walked slowly around the nearly-stripped room. His highly polished leather shoes stepping on the dusty floor.

"I've been here many times before," he said, nominally to either Fred or the Doctor. "It's the Louvre."

Fred was a few feet behind him.

"Yes, and it's a great deal less crowded than when I last came here," he said.

Borel looked round at the hulking strongman, eyebrows raised.

"Yes. Denis," said Fred. "I have been to the Louvre Gallery in Paris. We're not all country bumpkins up in Marbeuf!"

"I didn't mean to suggest that you were," said Borel, quickly. "After all, we've been to ancient Mars, and the Shoulder of Orion, it is nothing to consider a trip to Louvre."

Fred continued to look around.

"I do remember there being more paintings and sculptures when I was here last," he said.

"Yes, same here. The dust on the floor suggests that the treasures that used to be here have been taken away. Either they were confiscated, or plundered." Borel rubbed his chin. "This is definitely after our time, but how far in the future are we?"

"Well, let's hope that they've taken away all that dreadful violin music too," said Fred.

Borel looked at him, appalled, but saw Fred grinning at him, playfully. The handyman was winding up the musician. It prompted Borel, partly as a speculation, and partly as a way to answer back at his traveling companion:

"There is the possibility that this is an age of Philistines."

"Not likely, my boy. The age of Philistines was from the twelfth century B.C.E. to the sixth century B.C.E., in Canaan, not 21st century Paris," admonished Doctor Omega, as he stepped out of his space-time craft, the *Cosmos*. He looked around at the room. "Oh dear, dear, they don't seem to appreciate art much round here, do they?"

He walked over and joined them, near the room's archway entrance.

"So this is Paris in the 21st century. What happened to leave this place abandoned.?" asked Fred.

"Nothing my instruments can show. No environmental factors. What indeed, hmm? Let's explore and find out."

Borel was looking out of the rooms' entrance.

"Er, Doctor, Fred, we're not alone here," he said, nervously.

Both the Doctor and Fred looked over, and saw a hard-faced looking young woman dressed in combat fatigues holding a rifle at them.

Omega stepped forward slowly, taking command of the situation.

"Bonjour, Mademoiselle. We come in peace."

"Who are you?" she demanded. "Are you from SNIF? The police?"

"No. We are merely three travelers. Explorers," replied Doctor Omega.

The woman looked fiercely suspicious.

"Explorers? In France?" she said, incredulous.

"We happened to, er, arrive here." replied the Doctor, choosing his words carefully.

"How did you get here?" she snapped.

"We, er, landed here."

"How?"

"Our vehicle landed here. In this museum," he answered. His voice was beginning to display an attempt to hide how flustered he was beginning to feel.

"Landed here? I don't believe you! How many of you are there?"

"Just the three of us. Please, Mademoiselle, if you don't believe me, step into this room and see for yourself."

The woman primed her riffle, and pointed it at Fred. The burly man stiffened a little, but reacted better to the situation than he would have, thought Borel.

She stepped cautiously into the room, and saw the *Cosmos* standing in the corner.

"That craft there," said Doctor Omega. "The one shaped like a massive bullet. That is how we arrived here. We materialize and dematerialize."

Fred looked at the Doctor, but Omega faintly shook his head. Borel realized that Fred had seen an opportunity to disarm the woman while she was distracted by the *Cosmos*, but the Doctor had told him not to.

The woman took a few steps back and looked at the three of them.

"Your clothes. Where are you from?"

"We come from all over, my dear." said Omega. "I am Doctor Omega, a scientist and traveler. This is Denis Borel, a musician and a recorder of my little expeditions. The gentleman you are pointing your gun at is Fred. He is very handy and well-respected in Normandy, so please put the gun down and tell us who *you* are."

She lowered the rifle, and seemed to relax a bit.

"I'm Ségolène." she said. "I'm part of the Judex Resistance Movement!"

The Doctor put his hands on his lapels. He also seemed to relax. Maybe a bit too much.

"Judex, eh? What's that old lunatic up to, hmm?"

Immediately, Ségolène pointed the gun back at him, anger on her face.

The Doctor instinctively raised his hands. The other two stiffened.

"I mean; I do know Judex. I've met him on several occasions. Hence my overfamiliarity," he laughed somewhat nervously.

"Met him? When did you meet him?"

"In several different '*whens,*' my dear. You are probably aware that he has been around for a long time."

"He died a few weeks ago," replied Ségolène, bitterly.

The Doctor was shocked.

"Oh, dear. Things really have gone wrong, haven't they? How did this happen, pray?"

Ségolène cautiously lowered her gun again, as she started speaking.

"His corpse was found in the street. It was all over the news. His corpse, stripped of his outfit, as Schasch gloated and reveled in it. His naked body was mounted on a pole on the Champs-Élysées. His hat, cape and mask are mounted in a glass case in Schasch's office. But while he may be dead, his name and legacy live on. We, the resistance, are Judex. And one day, we will mount Schasch's corpse on a pole in the Champ-Elysées, while Judex will get a full, proper state funeral with full honors."

The Doctor tried to be consoling.

"Yes, quite."

Denis Borel finally dared to speak up.

"Pardon me, Mademoiselle, but who is this 'Schasch'?"

Ségolène gave him a confused look. Then she laughed the dry hacking laugh of someone who has found nothing amusing for a very long time. The smile on her face seemed unnatural.

"You really aren't from around here, are you?" she said, making Borel feel a little embarrassed. "Schasch is the President of France, and has been for the last nine years. There haven't been elections for the past five. Or fair trials, freedom to move from one region to another, and all our standards of living have gone downhill rapidly. Yet, if anyone complains about it too publicly, they immediately disappear, never to return. Who is Schasch? You're lucky you don't know who she is! So, are you with us? Or are you going to travel on?"

Omega looked around at Fred and Denis. Then he spoke unilaterally on behalf of all three of them.

"We are with you, Ségolène. We will do all that we can to help you overthrow this tyrannical ruler!"

Denis and Fred exchanged a glance between them, a glance that shared a common experience of their travels with Doctor Omega. A glance that said:

We are off again on another terrifying adventure.

Within an hour, the newcomers had gotten accepted into the Judex Movement's group. Though many of the twenty people in it were initially suspicious that the newcomers might be infiltrators working for SNIF, their anachronistic clothes and sheer out-of-placeness made their claims to be time travelers convincing. In this crazy world of Judex fighting crime over decades, Fantômas committing crime for decades, three benevolent time travelers materializing with the skills to help them during their time of need made perfect sense.

Doctor Omega, Denis Borel and Fred all noticed how this resistance group had taken pride in keeping the below street level rooms in this abandoned building clean. The surfaces were dusted, the floor was swept, and sleeping mats and sleeping bags were rolled up neatly and stored in the corner.

A TV, with some wireless hardware connected to it—mismatched but new—was hanging on the far wall.

"We're expecting a national broadcast from Schasch any moment," Ségolène said to the three travelers as the rebels gathered around the TV.

President Schasch resettled herself at her desk. There were bookshelves full of books behind her. Some of her advisors had warned against showing a display of books. It gave off an aura of intellectualism, and they had spent time trying to foster a sense of distrust in that, although other advisors had suggested that it would be alright. Many of the books could be identified as authored by prominent eugenicists, Holocaust deniers, and Hitler apologists. The people would respect a strong leader who knew her own mind.

Out of the corner of her eye, she could see herself on a monitor. In front of her was an autocue, with a hastily written speech put together in response to the economic crash and the exposure of financial scandals, all of which were now under investigation by the police in many countries around the world. And many of those scandals implicated the French government and close associates of Schasch herself.

Adjacent to her, and just across the room, was one of those close associates. He stood there, framed by the doorway, regarding her with a fixed, stony stare that made her stiffen. He was an old man, but not old in a frail or kindly way. He seemed old in a way that suggested he was something ancient and primeval, as if he was an evil from the dawn of time. And yet, he also seemed ageless, as though he had always been old and would remain so until the end of time.

Colonel Bozzo-Corona would always be around, as well as his Black Coats, BlackSpear Holdings—all those many criminal spokes to his hub of evil.

Schasch knew that if she couldn't put out the fire of this worldwide scandal, then she would have to answer to him. The Colonel was powerful enough to replace her. It did not matter that she was the President, or that she was virtually unassailable by any other political opponents, most of whom were either dead or in prison. The Colonel could have her executed and replaced with a chimpanzee if he felt like it, probably with just the snap of his fingers. She almost believed he could even do it all on live TV and still not face any repercussions.

Then she got a grip of herself. She couldn't serve him if she were so paralyzed with fear. As the TV director counted her down, she just gave the Colonel a polite nod, and mentally blocked out everything except the autocue.

The light on the camera came on.

"Mesdames et Messieurs, I am speaking to you because France faces a new challenge. A few days ago, some mysterious hackers, who do not have France's best interests at heart, caused the stock exchange to crash, and exposed alleged financial impropriety. Well, let me be absolutely clear: none of our patriotic French corporatists have done anything wrong. Our valiant businessmen who work so hard to provide you with jobs and money..."

The Judex movement in the gallery basement collectively gasped as the image of Schasch's grim face froze and square blocks on the screen transformed into the face of a new person—a familiar figure...

"Hello," said Leo Saint-Clair. "Some of you might know me as the Nyctalope. I have been away from our country for a while, and returned only recently. I am horrified by what I find. France—my beloved France—is now an authoritarian state where those who disagree with the current régime are ruthlessly imprisoned or executed. This is not liberty. The majority of you must now see that President Schasch and her government have played on your fears and concerns for their own advantage. Living in fear is not liberty. A country where those who are different, who do not fit a narrow definition of what it means to be French, are despised and hated is not fraternity. My friends, the regime of President Schasch claims to be patriotic, but it goes against those eternal values for which we all stand. So, my fellow countrymen, I—and some friends of mine—plan to overthrow this tyranny. Please, join us—join us in the toppling of this authoritarian, intolerant and corrupt regime. Then let's restore a truly democratic government, led by an elected president. Thank you."

The screen went blank. The Judex Movement cheered louder than was wise. Ségolène and Doctor Omega both gestured at them frantically to be quiet.

In the Elysée Palace, Schasch sat there, stunned. Speechless. Not knowing how to react to a challenge for the first time in years. Then, she became aware of the assorted advisors, ministers, technicians, and various underlings in the room. All silent, bracing themselves for her reaction.

Sexton Blake disconnected the camera and switched off his customized laptop. Saint-Clair sighed to himself. That speech was a bit too florid, he thought.

"There's no going back now," he said.

"No," agreed Blake. "But we have planned for this. We must do our best, and let the chips fall as they may."

Saint-Clair stood up, and went to the window. Blake hastily packed away the laptop and the camera into his rucksack.

Within about five minutes, they had both left the cabin.

Schasch raged at the staff around her. They all stood looking sheepish, staring at the ground, hoping she wasn't going to rip them to pieces.

Then, she stormed out of the room. She wouldn't speak to any of the underlings in the corridor. She went directly into her private office.

"Computer, put me through to General Pichenet," she snapped.

Within a moment, her screen showed the image of Auguste Pichenet's still youthful face.

"General, did you see that hijack of my broadcast?" she asked, the anger still discernible in her voice.

"Yes, Madame President."

"Then, why didn't you stop it?" she shouted.

Pichenet, experienced in navigating the President's mood swings, was not surprised at the outburst.

"Well, Madame President, the Nyctalope is exceptionally good at this. After all, that's why we wanted to bring him back to work for SNIF a few months ago. We're doing what we can to hunt him down. His hack is being traced right now. One of my people…"

"What? You haven't you traced him yet? With the amount of money I've pumped into SNIF, you should have found him already! You should have already dispatched men to capture him!"

"SNIF is working on it as we speak," replied Pichenet.

"Well, try harder!"

Pichenet paused for a moment.

"I assure you that we are doing everything we can to track down the Nyctalope," he said, his voice calm and level—which only seemed to make Schasch angrier.

"Then bring him in! If you don't have him in custody by this time tomorrow, you will be lucky to patrol the streets in Marseille."

Schasch terminated the call abruptly, before Pichenet could respond to this hysterical threat. She sat there in silence for a moment, scowling at the blank screen. Then the screen came back to life, startling her.

It was Colonel Bozzo-Corona.

"You do realize that events are slipping away from our grasp?" he asked, as his dark eyes seem to stare into her soul.

Schasch immediately became nervous and servile. "Colonel," she stammered, "I have the situation under control. We were just, er, taken by surprise."

"How could you be taken by surprise? Did you really think that our enemies wouldn't try to bring us down? It's always an ongoing war, Schasch. You have to destroy all our opponents. Crush them completely. That is the only solution."

"Yes, Colonel."

Bozzo-Corona looked at her for a moment longer. It seemed like forever to Schasch. She was almost ready to believe that he could even manipulate time. Then, he spoke:

"See that this insurrection is quashed. Or I will see *you* quashed."

The video phone went dead.

Pichenet's head was buzzing. He had spent most of the last month thinking about his position, the role he played in this regime, and how to use it to bring it down. It had initially been a slow process. He used to think that what France needed was a strong leader who could return the country to its former greatness. But an offhand comment recently made by Choupette about mythical golden ages kept returning to his mind. Her confrontational questions about locking up protestors and ordering the captures or executions of dissidents had begun to make him realize that he had become a pawn in a brutal, tyrannical regime.

He could tell things were beginning to move fast. So he spent the next twenty minutes issuing orders to trace the signal sent by the Nyctalope, and sending out an alert to all SNIF personnel to be ready for a possible insurrection, but he did this mainly just to keep up appearances.

Oddly enough, he genuinely didn't know how many of his agents would oppose the upcoming revolution or support it. Pichenet knew some whom he was sure would support it. And he could make a very good guess as to who would oppose it. But it was impossible to know precise numbers. He just had to hope that most of them would remain loyal to him, rather than the government.

However, he did send Choupette, a.k.a. Hedwige Roche-Verger, his wife, to supervise the border patrol at the Menton checkpoint. He wanted her safely out of harm's way. Despite the curious looks she gave him as he gave her her assignment, she knew the situation—and him—better than most.

Una Persson was in a Parisian hypermarket. She was walking up and down the aisles, being careful not to bump into the crowd of shoppers there, or get lost into the frantic atmosphere around her. She had overheard a couple of gossipers talk about the President's broadcast. And now, this store was flooded with panic buyers crowding around the toilet paper. These situations brought out either the best or worst in people.

"Una. A pleasure to meet you again. Even under these circumstances."

She turned round to see a figure in a hoodie behind her. She recognized his voice.

"Meeting here is an enormous risk," she said.

He turned to face her directly and smiled. "I have disabled the CCTV camera." said Monsieur Zenith.

Una relaxed a bit more and smiled back at him.

"It's a pleasure to see you again too," she said. She glanced at the scenes around them. A small scuffle had broken out by one of the few shelves still stocked with pasta. "Especially after a few months in this place," she added.

"Indeed," replied Zenith, looking at the scene. "Though places like this do help us to appreciate some of the more opulent surrounding we normally find ourselves in."

"I'm not sure I would have described some of those places as opulent."

"Then, at least they are Bohemian. Not utilitarian like this."

Una got down to business. "Do you remember the Villa Fanferlot?"

"I can easily find it." said Zenith.

"We meet there tonight at seven o'clock."

"'We' being your charming self and Judex?"

"Yes. And hopefully one or two others."

"Seven it is," said Zenith, reaching out to take something from a shelf, only to see that it was empty. He shrugged. "I'd better take my basket full of nothing to the checkout. Until then, farewell."

The albino in a hoodie walked away as nonchalantly and inconspicuously as he could. Una wandered if she had ever seen Zenith as dressed down as this before, trying to be this inconspicuous. It made her chuckle.

In a rundown neighborhood in the northern section of Paris, an old, community-funded bus pulled up at a stop. Only Leo Saint-Clair and Sexton Blake got off.

They both stood there for a minute, watching the bus trundle off. Saint-Clair watched Blake analyzing the bus. It was twenty to thirty years-old, with bull bars fitted to the front, and steel mesh fitted over the windows. Blake would probably say that it had been neglected for decades, and now it was re-appropriated by a local community who wanted to make sure the repressed could still make it to work, and that old ladies could still go shopping safely, while the national government was more interested in national projects and grandstanding to the outside world. Though Blake would probably go much further and say something about the bus's history that would have been as thorough as if he had been there at the time to witness it.

"Let's go." said Saint-Clair, bringing Blake back to the task at hand.

He glanced around at the street. The lights should have been coming on by this time of the evening. Not that it would bother the Nyctalope, but he knew it meant some looters would be out, and that would be only one more problem to contend with.

He and Blake walked briskly down a nearby street, and approached the rundown Villa Fanferlot.

"In here," he said to Blake.

They walked up to the door. Saint-Clair pushed at it, but this time, it didn't open. It was locked, and the lock looked new. So, exchanging a glance with Blake, he rang the doorbell.

A moment later, it was opened by a tall figure in a hoodie—and a sense of humor.

"Give the password!" said Zenith.

Saint-Clair was uneasy, but Blake recognized Zenith immediately, from his voice.

"All these years, and your sense of humor still seems misplaced. Let us in, Zenith."

Zenith smiled as he recognized his best enemy.

"Blake! You old chestnut! So you're involved too!"

"May we come in?" asked Saint-Clair, irritably.

Zenith stepped back, and let the two into the house. They all walked into the drawing room. Blake observed Zenith's clothes.

"You seemed to have dressed down for the occasion," he said.

"I didn't want to get my suits ruined in the revolution," replied Zenith.

In contrast, Judex was standing on the opposite side of the room in a slouched hat and cape that seemed both new. Saint-Clair also observed that he seemed more rested and energized since the last time he'd seen him.

Standing nearby in a light-armored suit was Una Persson.

"Well, what a shame we aren't meeting under more pleasant circumstances. Leo, Sexton," she said.

"Hello." said Saint-Clair, smiling. "With any luck, those pleasant circumstances are on their way soon. Oh, before we go much further, Blake, you have something for Judex."

"Yes, indeed," said Blake, reaching into his blazer's inside pocket and producing an envelope. He handed it over to the dark-clad vigilante. "Yours, I believe. The deeds to a gold mine. We stopped over in New York en route to Spain and I was able to retrieve them during all the stock market confusion."

"I'm glad Sexton's on our side," said Mrs. Persson.

Judex looked inside the envelope, and flicked through the deeds.

"Thank you. I am indebted to you," he said, as he put them away in a pocket in his bodysuit. "That'll make things a lot easier, providing we survive the revolution," he added.

"Did you try any of the other ideas we discussed here a month ago?" asked Saint-Clair.

"I did assume a disguise and tried to convince Me. Karlsson to secure a court ruling to declare the National Emergency Act unlawful, but the Government's influence was too strong. She warned me to not even try it, and I would certainly have been arrested if I had carried on," reported Judex.

"So there is little choice," said Zenith. "We either assassinate, or we are assassinated."

Blake didn't like Zenith's tone. The albino adventurer sounded too much like he enjoyed the idea.

"Do you all want to assassinate President Schasch?" he asked the group.

"Sexton, what's wrong?" asked Una Persson.

Blake sighed and put his hands in his pockets. "I know we have to be realistic about what we can achieve. However, if we kill Schasch, it makes us as much of a murderer as she is," he said.

"Well, as you say, we have to be realists," said Zenith, a little defensively.

"And realistically, if we kill Schasch, we create a martyr to her cause," replied Blake, firmly.

Two opposite walls of Pichenet's classically decorated office were completely made of glass. The General stood there, hands behind his back, looking over Paris: its neon and searchlights; dots from spinner headlights moving along through the sky along designated air routes...

Then, he decided to get a report on the unfolding situation. They should have traced the Nyctalope's signal by now. He walked over and sat behind his imitation marble desk, and pressed the touchscreen on the vidphone.

It didn't work.

He tried again—and a couple more times. Then he decided to use his j-pad to contact the building's maintenance team. But just as he picked up the device, the vidphone suddenly came on. It was President Schasch.

Pichenet was startled.

"Madame President. You must excuse me, I seem to be having technical difficulties at the moment," he said, recovering his composure.

"No, I froze your account." said Schasch. "*All* your accounts. As of this moment, I have assumed direct control of SNIF, and I have found they know more about the rebels than you've let on."

Judex cut in to Blake and Zenith's argument.

"That is a risk we have to take," he said. "There are only five of us, and pockets of resistance fighters here and there around the capital and the country. We have no control over them, and no guarantee that that they can overpower the police or SNIF. We have to remove the President, key members of her government, and the heads of SNIF and the police. This is the only way we can bring this dictatorship down."

"Yes, yes, I admit that. However, it still makes us as bad as them. We stoop to their level," said Blake, realizing he was losing the argument, not because he was wrong, but because the circumstances and these people were against it.

"We do not have time for a moral discussion!" said Judex.

Blake thought he could sense something in Judex, beneath a bitter exterior, had died a long time ago. "Now, apart from me and Zenith, do the rest of you agree that we should assassinate Schasch and her collaborators?" Judex glanced around the room. "Una?"

"Yes," she replied, reluctantly.

Judex turned to the Nyctalope.

"Saint-Clair?"

The Nyctalope paused for a moment. He was about to answer when suddenly the field dampener on Judex's chest sparked and blew out. It caused him to jolt back slightly. The same happened to the field dampener on Una's bodysuit. At the same time, the rucksack on Blake's shoulder flashed and jolted him, causing him to instinctively throw the rucksack onto the floor.

"An E.M.P. gun!" said Judex. "Our electrical equipment in now useless."

"Leo, take a look out of the window for us," said Una.

Saint-Clair did as he was asked. He quickly strode over to the window overlooking the street out the front, and peered out through the shutters. Inside and outside the house was quite dark. The Nyctalope's night vision was perfect for this.

At once, he spotted a group of SNIF officers. One officer holding an E.M.P. gun was in front of them. He quickly ran out of the way of another officer, who had a massive weapon on his shoulder.

"SNIF! They've got a rocket launcher!" Saint-Clair shouted to the others, as he ran away from the window.

Outside Fanferlot Villa, the SNIF officer with the rocket launcher fired. Fanferlot Villa's front was immediately punched through. The shell exploded.

He fired a second shell. There was another explosion. The second floor collapsed. The building quickly became a fireball. All the dry wood and dust only fuelling the fire.

By the time the officer had fired the third and final shell, the villa was a burning wreck.

The troops all packed up and drove off, knowing that no one could have survived the inferno.

Pichenet's training kicked in. He maintained his cool and concealed his growing concern.

"Madame President, I..."

"Your enthusiasm for my regime has been waning for a while," said Schasch. "You've been working *with* the Nyctalope, not *against* him, haven't you."

"If you'll remember, the Nyctalope just disappeared on that night last month. I didn't..."

"You helped him escape!"

"I did not! He simply disappeared. You sent the Marchef to kill him, and later, the clean up team reported Saint-Clair missing."

"And that corpse of Judex! Did you really think I wouldn't have an autopsy done? After we used it for propaganda purposes, I had it examined. Apparently, he was a man in his fifties, with sclerosis of the liver, who died from pneumonia!"

The doors to Pichenet's office opened. Two officers walked in, both wearing flak jackets and helmets with digital cameras on them. They each pointed guns at Pichenet.

Pichenet looked at them. He was careful not to show any emotion at all, even though his heart rate was steadily increasing.

"Auguste Pichenet, you are a traitor," said Schasch. "You are hereby sentenced to death, sentence to be carried out immediately! Death to traitors!"

The vidphone went dead. She probably wanted to see his execution on national television, thought Pichenet, through the officers' digital cameras or the CCTV camera installed on his office wall. And it would be broadcast live on national TV, billboards, and projected onto the sides of tall buildings in towns and cities around France.

In the gallery basement, Borel and Fred watched as Doctor Omega, who had an accurate memory of the French President's official residence, painstakingly drew a map of the Elysée Palace on the wall, and explained it to Ségolène and her ragtag group. They were all arguing when someone pointed out that there was another national broadcast. They recognized the SNIF uniform worn by Pichenet, even though some of them didn't know who he was.

Pichenet didn't know if these two guards would be more loyal to him or the President. But he understood that if they didn't kill him, they, too, would be executed as traitors, and they would want to stay alive. They had families. He completely understood.

That was the way to try and gain some time. He might even be able to survive long enough to use the escape plan he had arranged a couple of weeks ago.

"You both know me." Pichenet said, addressing the two officers. "Jean-Philippe, you asked me to be your daughter's godfather. Olivia, we've worked together for years. Look me in the eyes and tell me you would kill me on behalf of this murderous president!"

They both stood there, the conflict showing in their eyes. Pichenet got up, and stepped around his desk.

"I can protect you both," he said, "I can see that neither of you come to any harm. Olivia, Jean-Philippe, when a state turns on its own people, it is never a good sign of a healthy country."

Then Olivia spoke.

"The Marchef will be here soon. Either we execute you, or he will see to it that we are all killed."

Pichenet put his hands out, palms forward in a placating way.

"The Marchef? The State's chief executioner? He won't just kill me. He'll kill both of you too. Your fates are sealed. Come with me. It is your only chance. *Our* only chance…"

Olivia's face was easy to read. Jean-Philippe less so, but Pichenet knew them both well enough to know that they were very conflicted. He had almost won them over.

Through the open doors, he could see the Marchef lumbering towards them. They were running out of time. The three of them could just about defeat him, hopefully.

"It's time to make your choice," Pichenet said to them, quietly.

Olivia opened her mouth to speak just as the Marchef clasped the back of her head, and the back of Jean-Philippe's head, in his enormous hands.

"No, don't!" shouted Pichenet.

The Marchef snapped both officers' necks. Pichenet was sickened by the crunch sound. His two friends flopped to the ground. Without even looking at them, the assassin walked towards Pichenet, who backed away.

The Marchef cracked a big grin. "Smile. You're on national TV," he said.

He cornered Pichenet, giving the general an unpleasant reminder of their last encounter, in this very room, a month ago.

As before, he grabbed Pichenet by the throat. As before, he lifted him off the ground and slammed him into the glass wall behind him. However, back then, he just had had to give this monster some information; concede to his greater power. This time, that wasn't an option.

Pichenet tried to grab the Marchef's hands and pull them away. Without success. The killer's fingers pressed into his target's throat harder than before.

At that moment, Pichenet's training kicked in. Against his own instincts, he let go of one hand. He reached down to his boot and pulled out a plastic dagger and thrust it into his opponent's eye.

The Marchef dropped Pichenet and staggered back. The general stumbled away from his foe's huge body. He was gasping in unearthly sounding breaths.

The assassin, meanwhile, laughed out of surprise. He pulled the knife out of his eye. Pichenet stared in amazement. A knife that long through the eye would have been enough to kill anyone. But the Marchef just seemed to remove it as if it were a bit of food stuck in his teeth. The killer waved the knife at Pichenet. They both knew where it was going next.

"You could have someone's eye out with that!" he shouted, in a rage.

Pichenet quickly reached into the boot on his left foot and pulled out a miniature gun. He emptied its maximum capacity of six bullets into his enemy's face. The Marchef reeled back a bit.

Pichenet, almost psychotic in his fury, took a running leap at the giant. He smashed the empty gun against the Marchef's head again and again, in a kill frenzy.

"Ha! How do… How do…" he tried to shout at his opponent, but his throat was still recovering from being choked. He was trying to say *How do YOU like it now?* while he was still struggling to breathe.

The Marchef finally sank onto the floor. His powerful arms were beginning to flail around, respond more desperately.

Eventually, the monster stopped moving. Pichenet, straddling the his chest, was staring open-mouthed in disbelief at what he'd just done.

He had felt humiliated by the Marchef's previous assault on him, and since then, he had spent more time that he cared to admit thinking about how he could have responded differently or better defended himself.

And now, he had wanted to kill the Marchef in a rage that he never even knew he possessed anymore—a rage over which he seemed to have no control, even after all his years of discipline and training. He didn't know if he should be more frightened of that than of the Marchef.

He began to become vaguely aware of a noise in the background. The alarm bell. He didn't even know how long it had been ringing.

With great effort, he prized his hands away from the lifeless giant's throat, clambered to his feet and hurried over to his desk, where his j-pad lay. On it was his escape plan, disguised as an app for a chess game simulation.

He pressed it with his blood-stained fingers. He didn't even know if his fingers were sticking out like that because they were broken, or because they'd lost their dexterity in the fight. The app worked anyway.

"Escape route!" he said into it. His voice still sounded hoarse, but at least he could talk again. Fortunately, the app recognized his voice.

Glancing through the door of his office and into the corridor outside, he saw several SNIF officers with automatic machine guns running towards him, ready to fire.

Pichenet flipped his desk over, so that its top was facing the officers, and he crouched down behind it.

"Please state the password," said the female voice on his j-pad, with surreal calmness.

"Langelot!" he responded, as his former subordinates opened fire at him.

Immediately, the office doors slid shut. They locked out his assailants before they got into the room. It would hold them off for a few precious moments.

They started banging on the door. Soon, they would be shooting at it.

Then, a device Pichenet had secretly attached to the glass wall whirred into action. It was an old piece of equipment, but a very useful one. It caused the glass to fracture into tiny crystals, leaving his office exposed to the outside world.

He looked round his office—his former office now, because he doubted he'd ever see it again.

The Marchef was still lying senseless on the floor, but somehow still seemed to be alive. There wasn't even a sign of where he'd been stabbed in the eye. He would probably soon make a complete recovery thanks to whatever demonic powers he had.

Pichenet also looked at the bodies of his two former officers and felt anguish and anger that they were dead.

Then, he realized that all this was perhaps still being broadcast to the nation. So he looked up at the CCTV. He didn't know if it had been cut off already, but while he had time, he thought he may as well give it a go.

"Overthrow this government!" he shouted up at the camera. "It is corrupt! It is evil!"

He glanced at the doors. He noticed that dents were beginning to appear. He glanced over at the open wall, and started getting worried that stage three of the escape plan hadn't happened yet.

But it did.

A black spinner, concealed on the rooftop for his personal use, and largely ignored by everyone at SNIF, floated down to just outside the former window, with its driver's door open, all just as pre-programmed. Pichenet caught a glimpse of the tarpaulin sheet it had been under until a minute ago, fluttering down to the streets below.

He went over to the opposite side of the room to the exposed wall and the spinner lined up. He took one last look at the Marchef, beginning to stir, and the door about to be ripped open. He then dashed across the room and took a flying leap into the spinner. He sat himself properly in the driver's seat and closed the door; the craft immediately drifted away from the building.

"Computer, upwards!" he commanded.

The spinner ascended and cruised off into the night just as the SNIF officers burst into the office.

In the basement of the Louvre, the members of the Judex resistance had watched all this on the TV, some of them open-mouthed, all of them astonished.

Some of the rebels began discussing amongst themselves how this national broadcast, of an incident that defied the Government, was still going out. No one could work out why the camera had been running all this time. Was it sympathetic anti-President TV technicians? Or was everyone there too shocked by the spectacle of General Pichenet overpowering the Marchef and giving that speech before making his spectacular exit? Or were they frantically trying to stop the broadcast, but couldn't because of a technical glitch? No one could understand it.

Doctor Omega was the first to snap out of the confusion and seize the initiative. He stood in front of the TV to address the group.

"That settles it. The revolution begins tonight!" he said, with his usual flair for drama.

The group remained silent for a moment, then murmurs began rustling through the crowd.

"How do you propose we get into the Elysée Palace?" asked Ségolène.

The Doctor seemed slightly taken off guard by this question. He frowned and rubbed his chin.

"Yes, hmm. Well, it looks like we will have to use the *Cosmos* after all," he said, reluctantly.

"But what if it fell into the wrong hands?" asked Borel.

"We will break into the Palace with the *Cosmos*, but then it needs to be brought back here," Omega responded, before adding: "By *you*, Monsieur Borel!"

The Doctor chuckled as Borel went white.

"By me? But I don't know how to…."

"Tut-tut! No need to panic, my boy. I'll show you how to operate the Fast Return switch," said Omega.

He took Borel by the arm and ushered him out of the room.

Villa Fanferlot was now a smoldering pile of rubble. In the middle of the road where it used to stand, amongst the potholes, there was a manhole cover. It moved, stiffly at first, but then it flung open. One by one, five shadows climbed out, looked around, and began walking toward the city center. Leo Saint-Clair first; followed by Judex, Mrs. Persson, Sexton Blake, and finally, Zenith.

The Nyctalope glanced about with his night-vision, double and triple-checking that no one was following them, even though it was obvious that any-one in the area would be either indoors or hurrying home in fear of the patrols.

There was something in the air; something he could sense about this city in which he had lived for over a century.

"Is something wrong?" asked Una Persson.

"Something feels… *different*. I can sense it. Like electricity. The city is alive in a way it rarely is."

"We should get on while we're presumed dead," said Blake.

"Agreed," replied Saint-Clair.

They all walked on, each of them looking around. Saint-Clair looked at Zenith, who had stood back for a moment. Then, the Albino seemed to walk more casually, as if he were on a stroll in the park.

Ahead of Leo, Blake started talking to Judex.

"Do you have access to a tablet or j-pad I could use?" he asked. "I need it to get us into BlackSpear Tower and open that safe."

Judex thought for a moment. "We can stop by a little hideout I have near-by," he replied.

"That would be very useful."

As the party walked towards the cluster of searchlights that signified Central Paris, they could make out the occasional neon light going dark. Some searchlight would break out of its regular sweeping pattern and move suddenly in a different motion. And there was the occasional flash of light. What was going on?...

Pichenet buckled up the seat belt. His fingers were doing what he wanted them to do now, so at least, they weren't broken. He should feel a bruise on his stomach from where he had landed awkwardly over the two front seats with the raised handbrake between them. He knew that, eventually, the adrenaline would stop pumping and he would really feel the bruises to his guts and throat tomorrow.

Looking at the controls, he discovered that there a couple of SNIF spinners had already been dispatched to chase him down.

He opened the glove compartment and pulled out a metal box with wires. He quickly attached it to the dashboard and switched it on. It was a force field generator that would make him more difficult to shoot down with any E.M.P. weapon. Pichenet had obtained it from SNIF's technical division. This model was a prototype that had been very effective in trials. He was on friendly terms with some of the staff there, and they had allowed him to take it home. This was about six months ago.

Pichenet then switched to manual control of the spinner, and dived down amongst the cluster of Central Paris skyscrapers, weaving around them to evade his pursuers.

In a deserted street, Saint-Clair and his friends made their way towards the increasing sound of noise.

A red spinner flew over some buildings ahead and nosedived. It was already on fire before it crashed into the road ahead, exploding into a fireball.

Judex was the first of the group to recover.

"Blake, Mrs. Persson and I can go this way," he said. "We're very close to my hideout. There, we can get what we need." He turned to the other two. "Good luck, Nyctalope. Good luck, Zenith."

Saint-Clair and Zenith both nodded their appreciation just as Judex, Una and Blake jogged across the road, giving the burning spinner a wide berth, and heading into another street.

Saint-Clair turned Zenith.

"Let's keep going. If we stay near the sides of these buildings, we'll be safer—from the crashing spinners, anyway." Then he added, "It almost makes me nostalgic when cars had wheels."

As they walked through the alleys, Zenith finally got to ask Saint-Clair:

"So you actually know a way *in*?"

The Nyctalope looked around carefully. "Yes. Secret passages, dating back to the time of the Third Republic."

Zenith was astonished. "All these years and I never knew!" he said. "That might have been useful on a couple of occasions."

"That's why it's a secret," replied Saint-Clair.

He saw some abandoned bicycles padlocked to a railing. "Could you unshackle two of those bikes for us?" he asked.

Zenith smiled. "Need you ask?"

He pulled out his sword and broke the chains with a couple of simple strokes, which chimed onto the ground.

They both mounted their bikes and began pedaling. As they cycled to the Elysée Palace through the deserted streets, aware that a battle was raging only a few blocks away, Saint-Clair was reminded of his last bike ride. It had been through the Zone. He reflected for a moment how he probably wouldn't be here now if it hadn't been for his mission into that strange place...

By now, ordinary people were attacking police officers and assaulting patrols. At SNIF HQ, officers attacked each other. There was no easy way to tell which side any uniformed person was really on—Schasch supporters or freedom fighters.

Up in his spinner, Pichenet knew this. He used his j-pad to activate a communication channel reserved to SNIF officers and their staff.

"Attention, all SNIF officers!" he broadcast as clearly as he could. "If you are with me and against Schasch, remove your belt sashes. Those not in uniform, tie a handkerchief around your necks. If you can, storm the Elysée Palace. Good luck."

He then repeated the message, before switching off the channel. The sash-wearers would have heard the same message, and would now be tracing the signal. So he decided to land the spinner, and abandon it, along with his j-pad.

As the spinner touched down in a boulevard, and the driver's door swung open, Pichenet quickly grabbed two more items from the glove compartment: a gun and the field dampener.

As he leaped out of the spinner, he saw a group of people fighting each other nearby. He decided to go over and help his side, whom he saw were already shedding their sashes.

He quickly cast off his own, and ran up to the fight, already aware that his muscles were aching.

Judex flew his customized spinner through the airspace of Central Paris. Swooping around various dogfights, only knowing for certain that the unmarked spinners were more likely to be the freedom fighters, he flew with meticulous skill, dodging and weaving through the chaos.

Una Persson sat in the passenger seat, while Blake huddled in the back. Both of them were holding on while the car jolted up, down, left, and right.

"It is beginning to feel as if I left my stomach back at the Villa," said Blake, tensely.

"Hold on!" said Judex.

The spinner swung around and they caught sight of the glass and steel BlackSpear Tower.

"You'd better brace yourselves," Judex added.

Una and Blake did as they were told, both terrified as the dark-clad vigilante slammed down the throttle and gained a frightening amount of speed towards the skyscraper, aiming at the window-sized wall on one particular floor of the building.

Judex pressed some buttons on the dashboard, which launched two missiles at the fiberglass wall. It cleared a way for the spinner to swoop into the room. It landed, shoving office desks and chairs out of its way.

The doors raised, and the three infiltrators climbed out. Judex and Mrs. Persson were both holding guns, while Blake was clutching a laptop computer.

They ran towards an area where there was a safe. Alarm bells were ringing.

Blake kneeled by the safe, and laid down the laptop and some extra wires. He stared at it for a moment, then lost his temper.

"Will somebody do something about that alarm!" he shouted.

Judex looked around, saw an alarm on the wall and fired his E.M.P. gun at it. It stopped immediately—at least on this floor—but it could still be heard in the distance.

"Thank you!" said Blake, before getting on with his task.

"It won't silence the gunfire, I'm afraid," noted Una Persson.

A few minutes later, private security guards burst into the room. They pulled out guns and started firing at the three intruders. Una and Judex took cover and returned fire.

Blake was able to finish, and opened the safe. Inside were a bundle of paper files, loose papers, and some memory sticks.

"Bingo!" he said.

They now had in their hands hard evidence of materials being used to keep some very prominent big business people and industrialists compliant and supportive of this regime.

Judex looked around at Blake from the overturned desk he was hiding behind, and nodded. There were no guards left—not alive, anyway.

Suddenly, the lights flickered. The building shook.

"That sounds ominous," said Una.

They could hear explosions from below—a series of bangs getting closer.

Outside the building, in the streets below, freedom fighters and Schasch loyalists had been battling. They became temporarily distracted by the sight of the BlackSpear Tower—a tall, thin structure—blow up floor by floor, in a chain reaction of explosions moving up the skyscraper, and lighting up the sky.

As the debris began raining down on the combatants below in a half-mile radius, the skeletal structure of the building was all that remained standing. But no one could tell for how long.

When news of the tower's destruction got to President Schasch herself, she immediately understood what it meant. She surprised her staff by calmly acknowledging the news and sending them away. Then, she pressed a few keys on her computer offhandedly, attempting to make contact with the Colonel, but knowing that she'd get no reply. He, and all his senior staff at BlackSpear, had already fled.

She reflected that he was like the prospector spivs who try on big, audacious schemes for money; but when it all falls apart and they face bankruptcy or jail, they just shrug it off and walk away, as if it were nothing. No bitterness, no grieving the end of a project, no feeling of chastisement or of needing to learn something from the experience. Just leave, and start another big, audacious scheme somewhere else. Whether Colonel Bozzo-Corona called it BlackSpear or anything else, he and his associates would rebuild their criminal empire and carry on as before.

"Rats deserting a sinking ship," Schasch muttered to the blank computer screen. "Bastards."

The Nyctalope stepped through the tunnel. He was holding Zenith's hand to guide him. With his night-vision, Saint-Clair could see ahead clearly. It was a properly constructed tunnel. The walls were laid with stone. He walked on confidently, only later realizing that Zenith had stumbled a couple of times. So he slowed down.

Eventually, Saint-Clair turned around and whispered to his companion:

"Just ahead of me are some steps. They will lead us up into the cellar of the palace."

"I see," replied Zenith, dryly.

Saint-Clair let go of his hand. "Are you ready?" he asked.

"One moment, please," replied Zenith, taking a few paces back, before unsheathing his sword very carefully.

"Be careful, Leo. I don't want to cut you with my sword. I have to trust you to stand back from it."

"It's alright, I can see it. I am a safe distance away."

"I'm ready."

"Right. Three, two, one…"

Saint-Clair slid open the door.

The cellar of the Elysée Palace was the same layout as he remembered, apart from a part of it that used to be open space, but was now bricked and plastered off. And the place had been redecorated.

Zenith was squinting hard, trying to get his eyes to adjust to the light.

"Where do we go from here?" he asked.

Before Saint-Clair could reply, three armed guards appeared and surrounded them, pointing guns and shouting at them to put down their weapons and face the wall.

Saint-Clair didn't have a weapon on him. He just stood there, taking his lead from Zenith, who seemed unnaturally calm.

"Please, gentlemen! Speak one at a time. And there's no need to shout," said the albino, waving his sword around as if he were gesturing at them with a newspaper.

Zenith seemed a little too calm and Saint-Clair began to wonder if the Albino didn't have a death wish. His casual manner was doing nothing to pacify the guards.

He was about to suggest to Zenith that they should do as the guards demanded when, just then, a wheezing, groaning sound filled the air. It came from the floor above and distracted everyone.

Saint-Clair knew that it meant that Doctor Omega had arrived on the scene. He'd been wondering when the eccentric time traveler would show up, ever since the Doctor had left him a note and a special undershirt at his flat a month ago.

But it was a useful distraction. Saint-Clair grabbed the end of the rifle pointed at him and rammed the butt into the guard's face. Zenith clearly had had the same idea and had started attacking the guards around him.

On the floor above, the *Cosmos* stood, squeezed into a corner of the Elysée Dining Room. The ship's door opened and nearly twenty Judex Resistance members filed out, ready to battle Schasch's guards.

Doctor Omega was the last person out of the *Cosmos*. He shut the door and slapped it twice to indicate the Borel to "drive on." The ship disappeared with the same sounds as when it had arrived. The Doctor watched it go.

"At least, I hope you've got the hang of it, Monsieur Borel," he murmured absently to himself.

Then a nearby gunshot and shouting brought him back to the present, and he scurried for cover. The battle had begun.

Schasch took a secret passage down to the basement. Down there, she stepped over a few dead bodies, and ran towards the Panic Room. On the way, she passed a few people lying injured on the floor, but didn't stop to help them. Why should she?

She used her thumb print on the special lock, and pulled open the reinforced door. Once inside, she pushed it firmly shut.

The lights and monitors, which were supposed to come on when sensors detected someone coming into the room, were already on.

Schasch turned around and saw Leo Saint-Clair standing on the other side of the room.

She quickly pulled out her pistol from her holster, but the Nyctalope bounded over quickly and grabbed her wrist. With a simple hand movement, he forced her to drop it.

"It is not a good idea to fire a gun inside a room like this, Madame President," he said.

She wrestled and railed against him, screaming and hissing, but Saint-Clair carried on restraining her arms until she eventually gave up. Then, he let her slump into the office chair by the monitors.

Eventually she spoke.

"Why?" she demanded. "Why have you done this? Surely, you, of all people, would hate the way things have become. How France has lost its way since the Second World War. All the migrants coming here, taking our jobs, taking our houses, and diluting our blood, polluting our culture... Isn't that why you joined forces with Vichy all those years ago?"

Saint-Clair shuddered at the reminder.

"I wanted to preserve what I thought of was our way of life," he said, angrily. "And I thought I could do that by siding with the brave Marshal who had led us to victory in Verdun—but I was wrong! And not only did I pay a heavy price for it, but so did my family, my friends—and ultimately, my country.

"Yes, France is different from what it used to be a hundred years ago, but it was different a hundred years before that, and it will be different again in a hundred years from now. I have seen France in the year 2103! Nothing stays in a fixed state forever. People will always migrate and mix. Yes, we all hate change, but change is an inevitable part of life."

He looked down at her squarely in the eyes.

"You want to know where the real France is? The real French values and culture? It's right here," he said, gesturing at his heart. "And it must be carried with compassion, kindness, and dignity. What you gave the French people is a parody of a past era, an era that didn't even exist then. I know this, because I've lived long enough through it all."

Saint-Clair could see the look of fear and desperation in her eyes. It occurred to him that they were always present in her eyes, to some extent.

"The people want… *need* a strong leader." The strain in her voice was all too obvious. "Why do you think they voted for me in the first place?"

"They need *better* leaders," replied Saint-Clair.

His response left only silence in the room. They could hear one of the monitors picking up distant gunshots.

Schasch suddenly reached into her boot and pulled out a small pistol.

Saint-Clair straightened up and raised his hands—more in weariness than surprise.

"Look at the screens," he said. "Your only option now is to surrender peacefully."

Schasch thrust the gun into Saint-Clair's face. He knew that she was capable of using it. They looked at each other in the eyes.

Then, quickly, before he could stop her, she pointed the gun under her own chin and pulled the trigger. Her body slumped onto the ground.

Saint-Clair just stood there, mesmerized by her corpse. He sighed. It was a nasty business. And this was a nasty way for it to end.

Stepping over her body as respectfully as he could, he walked over to the door and opened it.

He stepped out into a liberated France.

Saint-Clair walked up to the first floor, where he spotted the familiar figure of Doctor Omega. His jacket was slightly torn, and he was kneeling over the dead body of a young woman.

"This whole process is most upsetting," said the Doctor, who seemed to sense an ally coming up to him. "The regime is—was—nasty, and the manner of its downfall equally nasty..."

Saint-Clair helped him up from his crouched position, wondering why such an elderly man would even step into a battle zone like this. But he was certainly brave. Maybe, at his age, he had little left to fear.

The Doctor turned around to face him. He frowned, suggesting that he recognized the face, but was struggling for the name.

"It's Leo Saint-Clair," said the Nyctalope.

"Ah, yes, yes, of course."

"Who was she?" the Nyctalope asked, looking at the dead woman.

"I only knew her as Ségolène. She led the Resistance."

They both looked down at her for a moment. With the blank expression on her face, she seemed almost unnaturally young. Saint-Clair reflected that he and the Doctor were both unnaturally old. How unfair that they should survive while this young woman should die.

"Then she should have a full state funeral," he said. Then he decided to get back to more immediate matters. "Who's in charge now? Of the country, I mean."

On all the national TV channels, as well as on the streets of Paris, Lyon, Marseille, and all the other cities and towns, the blank screens that were still working all sprang back to life, broadcasting new images to the population.

Normally, it would have been an address by the president, or one of her top ministers. This time, it was a hare-eyed junior minister, whom nobody had heard of until now. A minister for trains.

"This is a public announcement," he said, in a high voice that almost sounded like it only recently had started breaking. "President Schasch is dead. Most of the senior ministers of the Government are dead, and the rest will soon be placed under arrest. I am now the Acting President..." The fear in his eyes seemed all the more obvious when he said that.

"As of now," he continued, "the Emergency Act is repealed. Political parties are no longer banned. Political prisoners are to be released immediately. Parliament is no longer in recess. There will be no more curfews. A Presidential election will take place in three months' time, and a Parliamentary election will be held one month after that. Please stop rioting and go home. Long live France."

The screens went blank. People in the streets quietly went away. Some helped the injured.

Meanwhile at the Elysée Palace, the Acting President looked up anxiously at the two figures either side of him.

"Was that alright?" he asked.

"That was fine," replied Zenith, looking along the length of his sword.

"Yes, absolutely!" said Fred.

About twenty minutes later, the *Cosmos* rematerialized and out stepped Una Persson, Judex, Sexton Blake, a rather relieved looking Denis Borel, and a chuckling Doctor Omega.

"You see, the trick is to materialize in the BlackSpear Tower *around* our friends here, at the precise time the building exploded," the Doctor explained. "And then instantly dematerialize with them before the explosions reached their floor of the building."

"Are you sure you aren't breaking any laws of time in the process?" asked Una Persson, hesitantly.

This seemed to quieten the Doctor for a moment, and he touched his chin thoughtfully. "Well, I suppose I did bend them a little," he said. "But the world needs all three of you!" he added, resolutely.

"I, for one, am grateful to have be rescued," said Blake.

Over the next few hours, there were lots of comings and goings in the Elysée Palace, which was basically an open house for the day. Doctor Omega, Borel and Fred departed swiftly in the *Cosmos*, not before the Doctor muttered something about having to get a special undershirt made for the Nyctalope.

Mrs. Persson said her goodbyes to Saint-Clair and Judex. She kissed them both. Judex seemed sad to see her go. She and Zenith left together.

Blake eventually said that there was a hotel in Paris that he usually stayed, and he wanted to see if it was "still there."

An interim government was put together. Over the next few days, ordinary citizens helped clear up the mess and rubble from the streets.

A few months later, free elections were held and a new French President and Parliament were installed. A new sense of hope and optimism took over from the grim sense that the new government would have to spend years undoing the damage done by the old regime; but at least, there was a sense that the country was moving in the right direction.

Auguste Pichenet stood in front of the bonfire he had made in his garden. Some police officers had come earlier and confiscated the SNIF computers and equipment. They would be searched through as part of a massive inquiry that would investigate the crimes and misdeeds of the Schasch regime. It would lead to prosecutions and imprisonment for some people, maybe even Pichenet himself.

It made him realize that those posters, pictures and commemorative plates that were still mounted on display in his home office had to be taken down, so now the room was almost barren.

He threw the remaining posters and pictures onto the bonfire. Many of these pieces of far right memorabilia had taken him years and lots of money to acquire. But now, he realized that they had lost the appeal they once had. He wasn't going to sell them, so he let it all burn.

He looked down at the pile of commemorative plates stacked up in a box. They would all end up at the bottom of the Seine later.

Only one last photograph remained. He held it in his hand. It was the famous one, the former pride of his collection—the picture of the Nyctalope in a Vichy uniform, standing side by side with Marshal Pétain.

Pichenet looked at it for a while. He thought about tearing it in half and keeping just the half with the Nyctalope—a man he had admired since childhood. But he knew that *this* was not how Saint-Clair would want to be remembered. After all, that's what these past few months had been about.

So he threw the photograph onto the fire, and watched it blacken and twist into ash.

In the underground parking lot beneath his apartment, Leo Saint-Clair packed his bags into the trunk of his spinner.

"Monsieur Saint-Clair!"

Leo looked across the lot, concealing his disappointment that someone had caught up with him before he could leave. Why was it more difficult to leave a liberated France as a free citizen than a Fascist one as a fugitive?

It was Auguste Pichenet.

"General," said Saint-Clair, "Of all the people I know, I should have expected you to find me before I go," he added, smiling politely.

"Not General, just plain Auguste now," said Pichenet.

"Well, I heard you gave evidence at the inquiry. I wouldn't be surprised if they bring you out of forced retirement to head a reformed SNIF—or whatever replaces it," said Saint-Clair.

"Maybe. There's a possibility that I might receive an official pardon."

"Join the club."

They stood in an awkward silence for a moment.

"So you're off now?" said Pichenet.

"Yes. Paris is quite… intense at the moment."

"Paris is *always* intense."

They both laughed.

"Where will you go?" asked Pichenet.

"I thought New Zealand," replied Saint-Clair. "It is one of the few places I haven't really seen much of. I may travel around some other places too."

Pichenet nodded. He had his hands in his jeans pockets. Saint-Clair had never seen him look so casual or so socially uncomfortable before. He normally exuded complete confidence.

"I just wanted to say sorry for putting you through some bad things," Pichenet said.

Saint-Clair paused for a moment as he thought about how to respond.

"That was part of your job. I bare you no ill will," he finally said.

"Even so," the former general responded. "And also, thank you. You may not have done it intentionally, but you prompted me to question myself. How I'd changed, and what I had been prepared to go along with. It'll teach me not to compromise so much in future."

"Well, it's a free country," said Saint-Clair, drily.

They shook hands and wished each other good luck. Then, Saint-Clair got into his spinner, started the engine, and drove out of the parking lot.

In the rear view mirror, he saw Pichenet put his hands back in his pockets and stroll off out of the nearest pedestrian exit—out into the sweet, Parisian spring morning.

Outside the underground lot, Saint-Clair took off, lifting the spinner higher and higher until he could see over most of the lower rooftops. As the vehicle swung around, he caught a glimpse of the SNIF tower, which looked almost untouched. Also the burnt out skeletal structure of BlackSpear Tower, though most of it had been carefully disassembled to make the structure safe. Soon, it would be removed entirely and construction work would begin on its replacement.

Saint-Clair reflected that there would have to be a lot of reconstruction over the next few years, and not just buildings. Maybe the next time he came to Paris, it would be different again. Hopefully, it would change for the better, but if not, he knew he would do something about it.

Rod McFadyen is Canadian, a long-time fan of the series turned author. This is his first contribution to Tales of the Shadowmen, *which features a clash that seems so obvious that one wonders why no one thought of writing it before...*

Rod McFadyen: *The World Will Belong To Me*

Paris, 1920

Paris was emerging from the horror of the Great War. Enforced rationing had ended and the city was starting to hum with the influx of foreign people and their money. Industry, construction, art and fashion all contributed to a growing vibrancy, an optimism that provided opportunity for those who wished to grasp it. Paris would even be hosting the Summer Olympics in a few years. A consortium of French businessmen, with the hearty encouragement of the French government, had organized a conference of international industrialists and financiers, to impress upon the world that Paris was open for business.

There was very little activity on the top floor of the Palace Hotel at that late hour of the night. A porter, holding a tray with a steaming hot pot of coffee, stood in front of the door of the most expensive suite in the hotel. He quickly looked down the hallway to ensure it was deserted. He put the tray down on a nearby table and took out a skeleton key, silently unlocking the door and then slipped inside.

Fantômas quietly closed the door behind him. He adjusted the moustache of his disguise once more, annoyed that it was again having difficulty staying in place. He stood in a softly-lit, stylish foyer that had draped French doors opening to a large living area on one side and another set opposite for the master bedroom and bathroom. The doors to the living room were open and a single lamp displayed the sumptuous furnishings in its dim light.

As expected, the doors to the bedroom were closed and the room was dark. It was currently occupied by American billionaire William Dorgan and his wife. He was here for the international conference and had spent the last two days meeting with representatives of the French Armed Forces and local heavy equipment manufacturers, eager to replenish France's armories. He'd made a fortune developing specialized weaponry for America, and his wife was happy to spend that fortune on expensive Parisian jewelry. That jewelry would be in a safe in the bedroom. Fantômas planned on emptying that safe, preferably without waking the Dorgans. Hopefully, the drugged coffee he'd brought up earlier would ensure that, but he was indifferent to the possibility that he might have to kill them.

He crept to the bedroom doors and opened them a crack to peer inside. He blinked at the unexpected scene, illuminated by the full moon appearing through the open balcony doors. He could make out a silhouetted figure by the side of the bed, dragging a large, curved knife across the throat of Mrs. Dorgan. Her husband lay unmoving beside her, moonlight displaying the blood-soaked bedsheets in front of him. The only sounds were the soft gurgles coming from the dying couple.

Fantômas burst into the room, drawing blades strapped beneath his sleeves. The figure sprang up and faced him, the bloodied knife in his hand.

"The jewelry is mine!" Fantômas spat out.

The man smiled, not at all intimidated. "Not here for jewels," he said in a thick Chinese accent. "I finish what I come for, but do not like witnesses."

He lunged forward aggressively, sweeping his knife in short, fast arcs before him, forcing Fantômas to back up a step. Then he unexpectedly shot out his foot, kicking Fantômas backwards into the foyer and shattering a large vase.

Fantômas quickly regained his feet as the man leaped into the foyer. He was Asian, with a nasty scar on his face that ran through one milky white eye, and dressed completely in black. Fantômas parried a thrust of the man's knife with his own blade. His other blade swept across the man's torso, cutting his shirt and leaving a shallow wound across his stomach. Fantômas then lowered his shoulder and barged into him, throwing him back against the French doors of the bedroom and shattering them.

So much for a quiet theft, he thought to himself.

The man grunted, glancing at his wound, but otherwise showing no discomfort on his face as he sprang to his feet and assumed a fighting stance once again. They circled each other cautiously, waiting for an opening.

They heard raised voices from the hallway and soon a pounding on the door. The crashing had obviously alerted someone.

"Some other time," the assassin said.

He sheathed his knife as he ran back into the bedroom and out onto the balcony. Fantômas followed. He was surprised to see the man dive off the balcony. He went to the edge and saw a line attached by a grappling hook to the railing and extending to the rooftop of the lower building across the street. The man was sliding down the line.

Fantômas debated cutting the line and letting the man fall to his death. His planned escape through the hotel was not viable now, so this was his best option to flee. He sheathed his knives and lifted his legs over the edge of the balcony railing. He yanked off the vest he wore as the porter and wrapped it around the line, grabbing on to both ends. He then leapt forward, sliding down the line to the rooftop.

The assassin reached the end of the line and dropped into a crouch onto the rooftop. He turned and saw Fantômas sliding down the line towards him. With a snarl, he whipped out his knife and slashed at the line. It went slack just as

Fantômas reached the edge of the roof. He rolled as he hit, unsheathing his blades again and coming up into a run to begin the chase.

He followed the assassin down the fire escape at the back of the building. Despite taking entire flights of steps in a couple of bounds, Fantômas did not gain on him. When the man reached the ground, he ran towards a car waiting at the curb of the side street, shouting in Chinese to a man leaning against the car, smoking a cigarette. They both leapt into the car and sped off just as Fantômas reached the spot. He watched, frustrated as the car disappeared into the night, but he was able to note the make and model of the car. There wasn't enough light to get the license plate.

His heart pounding from the exertion, he was now able to reflect on the night's events. Was the assassination an isolated incident, the result of a grudge against Dorgan? Or was it part of something bigger? If the former, Fantômas was indignant at being robbed of a lucrative score and vowed someone would pay. If the latter, he needed to be aware of what was in play and the stakes, and how they may affect his own plans.

He turned and walked off into the warm summer night.

Fantômas spent the next morning in his lair pouring over the research he'd compiled earlier on the conference. His finger absent-mindedly stroked the cheek of the green mask he typically wore when not in disguise, as he read and re-read the profiles and histories of the attendees. There were almost forty of them. He'd originally gathered the intelligence to determine which ones were targets to rob. Did any of them travel with large amounts of cash or gems? Did any of them have extravagant spending habits and were likely to purchase expensive items while in Paris?

He also scoured the newspapers of the past few days for any scraps of additional information. He noted that the murders of the Dorgans were not reported in any of the morning editions. He assumed that the police were suppressing the news for now to avoid public outrage.

He noted one story of interest. A British toxicologist, Dr. Bauerstein, also in Paris for the conference, had collapsed suddenly and died while walking through the lobby of his hotel the previous afternoon. The doctors ruled it a heart attack. However, Bauerstein was middle-aged and an amateur mountain climber. A heart attack, while not impossible, was unlikely. The medical signs of a heart attack could be disguised, given enough knowledge of poisons, or mistaken, if the verdict was declared by doctors eager to avoid scandal. It seemed a highly unusual coincidence to Fantômas. He did not like such coincidences.

He decided that someone was looking to disrupt the conference, or perhaps eliminate some business rivals. He dove into his research once more, looking for similarities between Dorgan and Bauerstein. Both recently made lucrative advancements in their respective fields. Dorgan's new weapons designs made ballistics much more accurate to calculate. Bauerstein's work with new chemical toxins had applications in many fields, from food to pharmaceuticals. If the advancements were the determining factor, who might benefit with their deaths? Who else might be targets?

Fantômas assigned members of his gang to watch over four potential candidates he identified as having been involved in similar scientific breakthroughs. They were to watch front and back doors of each hotel the candidates were staying, noting anything or anyone unusual, especially Asians in case that nationality was part of the pattern. He also had men stationed on the rooftops of the hotels as well. His experience the previous night demonstrated that doors were not the only means of access to a victim.

The men were instructed not to interfere. They were to let events play out and follow the assassins to their base. Fantômas did not want the pawns in this game; he wanted the king.

He was fully aware of the irony that he was assisting the police in finding a murderer.

Bec-de-Gaz stood on the other side of the ornate oak desk of Fantômas the next morning. He was one of the Apaches the evil mastermind assigned to watch the hotel of Gilbert Blythe, a Canadian inventor of several new metal alloys. Bec-de-Gaz was pale and agitated.

"Report!" Fantômas commanded.

The Apache nervously turned his cap in his hands. "You had me watching the roof of the Hôtel Majestic, where the Canadian was staying. I had a dark, cozy spot in the shadows of a ventilation shaft with a view of the entire roof. It was just after midnight when a man came up onto the rooftop through the locked stairway door, the same way I came. The moon was bright and I could make out he was Indian or Malaysian or something like that. I was perhaps three meters away from him, but he couldn't see me in the shadows. I didn't move at all, nor hardly breathed. He attached a rope to a post and tossed it over the side with the window of the Canadian's room, who was two floors down."

Bec-de-Gaz then shuddered. "He had a bag with him. He... he reached into it and pulled out a glass case with… *mon dieu…* I don't know what it was! It was some sort of insect, I think. It was a bright red. But the size! It was huge! It must have had a hundred legs! I've never seen anything like it before and I hope I never do again!" The cap in Bec-de-Gaz's hands turned faster.

"He tied himself to the rope and disappeared down to the window with the cage. I risked a peek over the side. He cracked open the window with a knife and opened the cage, letting the thing inside! After a few minutes, he blew on a strange whistle. The thing came back into the cage! I ducked back in the shadows before he… and it… came back up. I followed him and he led me to a small warehouse in the industrial section in Issy, by the river."

His report finished, Bec-de-Gaz exhaled with a sense of relief. Fantômas stared at him stoically for long moments, digesting his tale. He then stood up and motioned to the rest of the Apaches in attendance.

"Well done, Bec-de-Gaz. Show us this warehouse."

By noon, a small group of Apaches was staking out the warehouse from a hastily-rented room in a dilapidated boarding house across the street. The warehouse was a small wooden building with an entrance and a large delivery door in the front. In the rear, there was another delivery door with a small ramp that led to a dock on the river Seine. A rickety set of wooden stairs up the side of the building led to an external door on the second floor. That floor had windows that looked onto the street and was presumed to contain offices.

From the window of the boarding house, they noted all comings and goings during the day, as well as any movements in the second floor windows. Periodically, a gang member would saunter past the building, trying to glean additional information up close. Fantômas noted the car that fled from him two nights ago drive in through the delivery door and park there. It was impossible to tell for sure but as evening fell, it seemed that there was a total of perhaps seven or eight different occupants.

As he began formulating a plan, Fantômas thought back on the diverse ways the assassinations were carried out. He grudgingly admired them, as a reflection of the methods he himself might use. Clearly, the mastermind behind all this was worthy of respect and must be countered with extreme caution.

At 10 p.m. that night, two Apaches, pretending to be drunk, began to make a scene in front of the warehouse, shouting loudly and smashing wine bottles against the front of the building. Four other armed Apaches remained hidden in the shadows of the neighboring buildings, ready to spring out and join in the commotion when someone from the warehouse opened the door to investigate.

When the noise indicated someone had come out to see what was going on and a fight had broken out, Fantômas and two of the larger Apaches, armed with knives and pistols, quickly slipped from the nearby alley where they were hidden and scurried up the side stairs to pick the lock on the door. Inside, they saw a narrow hallway that ran the width of the warehouse to a stairwell on the other end. There were four closed doors, two on each side.

They took the first door on the left. One of the Apaches quietly and quickly opened it inward, moving to the left side, pistol raised, with the other Apache moving to the right and Fantômas stepping in the middle. It was filled with empty sleeping cots.

They followed the same routine with the door across from it, on the right side of the hallway. That room contained a small laboratory. A large table in the center of the room was filled with a microscope, Bunsen burner and various glassware and flasks containing numerous unmarked liquids. Another table against the wall had glass specimen cages, with strange insects and lizards, including the red multi-legged creature described by Bec-de-Gaz.

They burst through the third door, back on the left side. They immediately encountered three muscular, dark-skinned men wearing little more than loincloths with large knives hanging from their belts. Two were by the front windows looking down at the commotion in the street. The third was in the corner, tending to a large wok on a camping stove.

Even though taken by surprise, he reacted quickly and threw the wok filled with cooking oil at Fantômas and the Apaches. Fantômas shot him, ignoring the scalding oil. That gave a chance for the other two men to spring forward and they managed to knock the Apaches' pistols aside before they could be fired. The Apaches were soon engaged in close combat with them, hands struggling to reach for knives as they grappled. Not being able to get a clear shot at their assailants but seeing that his men were holding their own, Fantômas turned away and kicked open the last door across the hall, any opportunity of a quiet entrance shattered.

The scene in the last room before him was almost surreal. While the other rooms were relatively sparse, this room was filled with opulent furnishings and vases, exotic carpets and paintings, and a Chinese screen along one wall. Fantômas closed the door behind him, his pistol pointed at the sole occupant of the room.

The man was Chinese and dressed in rich blue silks. He was tall and lean. He looked elderly but moved with an almost feline grace as he burned papers in a brazier on a pedestal in the center of the room. His head was close-shaven and he wore a distinctive moustache. His eyes were an unnerving green, almost gleaming.

The man stared at Fantômas, taking in his dark suit, black gloves and blue mask. His face was expressionless.

"Who are you?" he asked in a voice that was deep and resonant.

"I am Fantômas."

The man nodded in acknowledgement. "I've heard rumors of your existence. I wondered if our paths might cross. I am Dr. Fu Manchu."

He continued to burn papers, seemingly oblivious to the pistol.

"And why have our paths crossed?" Fantômas asked. "Why are you in my city?"

"I am the avatar of the imminent ascendance of China," Fu Manchu said evenly. "The recent conflict signals the beginning of the decline of Western dominance. While you squabble over petty grievances and wallow in decadence, my country will rise to become the preeminent power on the planet. You say Paris is your city, but the world will belong to me."

"You can't be accused of thinking small," Fantômas smirked behind his mask.

Fu Manchu ignored the jibe. "Paris is not my regular base of operations, but the international conference provided convenient access to three individuals that I determined might provide technological advantages to my enemies. During this window of opportunity, I eliminated those advantages."

"It is good that you accomplished what you set out to do then, as I am closing any windows you may have—permanently!"

He stepped towards Fu Manchu, raising his pistol. Fu Manchu did not flinch.

Fantômas caught a sudden movement out of the corner of his eye. He turned just in time to see a sword swinging down to sever his hand. He managed to move backward in time to prevent the loss of his hand, but his pistol was shattered.

Fantômas jumped to the side, pulling out his blades from his sleeves. He recognized the wielder of the sword as the assassin with the milky white eye who killed the Dorgans. He had emerged from behind the Chinese screen. As they circled each other, a light of recognition appeared in the assassin's face.

"I know you, way you move, those blades. We fought in the hotel. Been looking forward to a rematch."

Fantômas was unable to properly engage with the assassin. The sword gave him too much reach. He would feint with the sword but pull back too quickly for Fantômas to close in for the kill without risk. He was playing with him. As they fought, he saw Fu Manchu move to the screen and disappear behind it. He could do nothing to stop him.

In desperation, Fantômas faked a lunge with his left blade and threw the right one when the assassin was distracted for that brief second. It plunged into the milky white eye. The dead assassin barely hit the floor before Fantômas ran to the screen and ripped it down. There was nothing there.

There was no door but, on closer examination, he noted a crease in the rug. He threw it aside to reveal a trapdoor hidden beneath. He flung it open to find a ladder leading a small room on the main floor of the warehouse. He could see an open door that led outside to the bank of the Seine. There must have been a boat there. Fu Manchu had escaped.

Fantômas jerked his head up to the shouts of "Fire!" He rushed out to the hallway. The facing room where his men were fighting was engulfed in flame, presumably from the camping stove that had been overturned. In the hallway, leaning against a wall, was a lone Apache, bleeding profusely from numerous cuts.

They made their way out by the side stairs they used to enter the warehouse. They joined the surviving Apaches as they fled the fire and made their way down the street. The entire warehouse was quickly engulfed.

Fantômas looked back, the dancing fire almost hypnotic in its allure. He was not sure what the police would find in the wreckage tomorrow. Remnants of the laboratory and its mysterious specimens. The bodies of the Asian henchmen. He only knew the wreckage would not contain the corpse of Dr. Fu Manchu.

He vowed that if the latter ever returned to Paris, he would correct that.

Christofer Nigro has embarked on a series of tales featuring Paul Féval, fils' *creation, Felifax the Tiger-Man (BCP, ISBN 978-1-932983-88-0), and his half-brother Felanthus, Chris' own creation. The arc began with "Eye of the Tiger-Man," (in* The Shadow of Judex*) and continued with "The Privilege of Adonis" (Vol. 10), "The Noble Freak" (Vol. 11), "Justice and the Beast" (Vol. 12), "Kindred Beasts" (Vol. 14), "The Anti-Adonis Alliance" (Vol. 15) and "Clash of the Jungle Lords" (Vol. 16). This is the latest installment...*

Christofer Nigro: *Wrath of the Cat People*

A few miles west of the Seonee jungle region, Madhya Pradesh, India, circa late 1937

Felanthus trudged through the verdant foliage of the Indian jungles with impressive speed. It was an unfamiliar place that he strangely felt at home within, as if he possessed an innate rapport with this environment and its many forms of fauna and flora. Most importantly, he knew this to be where his half-brother, the unquestioned lord of the jungles surrounding Benares known as Felifax the Tiger-Man, resided. Of course, Felanthus had considerably more feline in his morphology than his handsome, human-looking sibling, resembling a tiger much more than a man in his upper body. His mind was intelligent but not as fully developed as those who had more or complete human DNA, and reading maps was not his forte. Instead, he learned geography in a manner closer to how the non-sentient denizens of the animal kingdom did so, by roaming about and charting the landscape in their instinctual memory banks.

Hence, the man-tiger's current unfamiliarity with the topography of the vast Indian jungle resulted in a failure to realize how far he was from the portion of this green land that was Felifax's domain. Nevertheless, he had already (if all too briefly) met the sibling that showed him kindness and warrior camaraderie, and there he had committed his scent to memory. The track of Felifax was readily detected in various parts of the more southeasterly portions of the jungle the man-tiger sauntered through; however, no sign of the man behind the spoor could be found (little was the noble beast-man aware that his sibling had actually been in Paris searching for *him*, but had taken his quest back to India just a day previous).

However, during Felanthus's several days trek through the verdure of the Indian jungle, he had come across a much different scent. It was a heretofore unknown but irresistibly intriguing organic perfume. The scent was of a type that the man-tiger did not have a word for, but one which scientists would refer to as *pheromones.* It caused the orange-and-stripe-coated man-beast to momentarily defer from tracking his brother to move well into the Seonee region of the jungle to follow this new scent. When he finally located its source, Felanthus was utterly astounded… but pleasantly so.

Upon reaching a large section of shrubbery growing between two banyan trees, the man-tiger stood witness to a creature strangely similar to himself step from the shrouding greenery into plain view. This entity was likewise a chimera of human and feline traits but was unmistakably female in form. Her head was somewhat reminiscent of a puma—a type of big cat Felanthus had never come across and which was not native to either Great Britain or India—with pointed ears and greenish-yellow eyes possessing a vertical pupil that are both characteristic of cats.

Her body was quite humanoid in appearance and was only partially covered with rigid tawny-hued fur that was bereft of the stripes that decorated Felanthus's own full-body coat. Her hands were human-shaped with longer-than normal fingers that oddly possessed only four digits—but each of which were tipped with fierce-looking sharp talons.

As the female felinoid stepped out of the clearing and cautiously approached the man-tiger, he could make good observations about her physical morphology. Her hips were wide but basically contoured like that of a human female. In fact, her limbs and torso, while distinctly feminine, were well-toned and muscled like that of a female athlete who participated in the Olympics. The bottom half of her legs beneath the knees were bent like those of a cat, with elongated feet somehow reminiscent of a feline's extended back pads but possessing more human-looking toes equipped with sharp nails.

Also unlike Felanthus, she was not fully naked, but wore what appeared to be a tunic composed of surgical bandages below her bare shoulders and covering her abdomen, beneath which several small bumps were apparent that indicated she had several pairs of human breasts. A simple bluish cloth garment covered her lower extremities, where it could be seen that she had shapely buttocks resembling those of a human woman with no evidence of a tail.

Felanthus could scarcely ponder what he was seeing… and feeling. The sensation was strange but also oddly pleasurable as the puma-woman approached the man-tiger and reached one of her four-fingered, human-like hands out to him.

"Hullo," she said in a scratchy but clearly feminine voice—and in English, a language the man-beast was familiar with. "I am Aissa."

Felanthus found himself letting down his guard as he reached out with his paw-like but still dexterous five-digit hand and gently touched hers in response.

"I… am Felanthus," the man-tiger repeated in English with difficulty. "I… don't talk easy, because I… don't talk much. So… forgive, please. You… look like I look. How did you… come to be?"

Aissa cocked her cat-shaped head and squinted one of her yellow-green eyes. "I know good doctor. And another good doctor. One made me, and the other one… made me better. Will you come meet them?"

Felanthus moved his hand away from Aissa's softly touching fingers and released a light snarl. "The doctors… are men? Men… are bad to me. Bad! I not go meet!"

"Then," Aissa replied in a soft purring tone, "stay here with me for a bit?"

Felanthus seemed to calm again.

"Do you like me?" the puma-woman queried.

The man-tiger moved a few inches closer, looking upon Aissa's semi-hairy feminine form and sniffing the air around her again. "Yes. I… like you. I will… stay. Have another to find here… but I will stay… with you. For now."

Aissa appeared to form a smile as best her semi-feline jaws could manage. She then gently touched Felanthus's ochre-furred arm. This act seemed to please the cat-man in a manner he had never experienced before.

"Lay down here," the cat-woman said, pointing a clawed index finger at a nearby bed of shrubs. "With me."

Her scratchy voice issued forth in a smooth manner that had a soothing effect on the man-tiger. As did the prospect of what she suggested, representing a concept he seemed to understand, albeit on a purely primal level. But that was all it took for her to sell the idea to him.

Felanthus thus laid on the soft bed of vegetation with Aissa, and together they shared an experience that those in the human world often referred to as the "call of the wild." It was an experience the man-tiger would never forget.

For several hours. Prince Rama Tamerline, a.k.a., Felifax the Tiger-Man and his four compatriots—two of them human, and two entirely feline—trudged through the thick jungle undergrowth in search of Felanthus's spoor.

The former two companions were Mowgli, the fully human but formidable lord of the Indian jungle within the Seonee region; the second was the intrepid British hunter and former poacher called Matthew Challenger, grandson of the great explorer Professor George Challenger. The latter two accompanying the Tiger-Man were his trusted Bengal tigers, Rudra the man-eater and Durgane the crusher, the offspring of his original two faithful big cats to carry those names. All sauntered through the verdant woodlands attempting to detect any sign of Felanthus's whereabouts, and by this point were partially successful.

"I believe your brother to have come through this area," Mowgli said. "Those tracks we spotted were odd, like none of the peoples I have ever met during my lifetime here. And look at the way they seem to switch periodically from walking on two legs like a man to all four like other peoples who live fully wild."

"This bloke refers to animal species as 'peoples?'" Challenger noted aloud. "That is right queer, I say."

"Only because you lack equal respect for any of the jungle's many inhabitants who are not men," Mowgli snapped back with a sneering tone.

"Whatever you say, mate," the hunter replied while adjusting his olive green pith hat and checking his .50 caliber Mauser rifle. "We all have our ways and quirks, right?"

"Yes, you would know about that, wouldn't you, Challenger?" Felifax snipped at his ersatz brother-in-law.

"What was that, now?" Challenger said with a tone of chagrin. "Did you just insult me?"

"Only if a statement of truth and an insult can be one and the same," Felifax rejoined with a satisfied grin.

"Sod off," the hunter blurted in a harsh whisper.

Mowgli was unconcerned with the acerbic exchange as he suddenly stopped to examine another set of tracks. "It would seem your brother is not the only unusual one in this part of the jungle today, Rama."

Felifax did not bother to ask what his long-haired, well-muscled ally meant. The Hindu prince simply walked over and examined the same set of tracks while sniffing the air about the trail. His enhanced sense of olfaction was evident even in his full human state, and his ability to track a spoor was at least on par with both that of his fellow jungle lord and the highly trained and experienced white hunter at their side.

"You are right, friend Mowgli," the Tiger-Man concurred upon completing his own examination. "It would seem my brother is not the only cat-person out and about in this section of jungle."

"Seriously?" Challenger queried while walking up to conduct his own examination of the spoor. "Strewth, this is seriously bonkers! Mowgli, do you have animals in your neck of the woods that walk like men as well as think and 'talk' like them?"

"Only the monkeys at times," Mowgli answered. "And neither set of tracks belong to monkeys. They combine the look of two separate peoples from this land: men and cats. Rama says one of them belongs to his brother. But the other? I am as much in the fog about that as you."

"More than that," Challenger continued, "it looks here like one of these cat-chaps was actually tracking the other."

"Felanthus is the one being tracked," Felifax noted. "I am now more concerned for his safety than ever. If Mowgli is not familiar with the tracks of the other one, that means this cat-person is likewise an intruder to this region. We must make haste in finding my brother, and I pray to Shiva that we find him before anything of ill note can happen."

The three men continued their quest, this time more steadfast than before, with Rudra and Durgane close behind their footsteps.

After a few hours had passed, Felanthus opened his bright green eyes. Aissa still laid beside him, with one of her slightly twisted human arms wrapped around his hirsute torso in an affectionate manner. Both displayed a hybrid of human and bestial traits during their liaison, with affectionate post-coital snuggling being a clear example of the former. This was a rare occasion in his life where the man-tiger felt happy and at ease with the world around him. And one of the even rarer occasions where he was not lonely. He had experienced camaraderie with another beast-person in the recent past, but not only was it not to last, it could not match the pleasurable sort of connection offered by Aissa.

Moreover, this Indian jungle environment somehow felt more at home, more comfortable, than the non-tropical wooded area of the Bois de Boulogne back in Paris. And this despite the fact that Felanthus had arrived in this part of the world just a few days previous. If only his bond with the beautiful Aissa would last, and she could accompany him on his search for his brother, so she too could be welcomed into the family of Felifax as the man-tiger expected to be. However, his passionate euphoria caused him to forget about the matter of how the puma-woman came to be here and how she was created; the striped man-beast fully understood that hybrid beings such as himself did not occur in the world through natural means.

The failure of Felanthus to ask this question first and foremost, or to inquire further about the two doctors she mentioned, were to prove extremely costly.

No sooner did the cat-man purr in satisfaction over the embrace of his new paramour upon awakening than his keen sense of smell detected others in their midst. One of them was familiar, and extremely hated.

"See, *mon ami?* I told you Aissa would bring Felanthus into our grasp," uttered a deep voice with a strong French accent. "Or, rather, *back* into *my* grasp. Hah!"

Felanthus shot up into a crouched bipedal stance with his foreclaws extended. He snarled viciously at the sight before him.

The one who uttered that statement was an infamous member of the otherwise esteemed Tornada clan of surpassingly brilliant science prodigies. This Professor Tornada was one the man-tiger had met and fallen into the dark clutches of not once but *twice* in the past. The orange-furred beast-man would be damned and slaughtered many times over before he allowed that to happen again.

However, Tornada was not alone, for not only did he have two large snarling mastiff dogs on a double leash in hand, but beside him was another man, this one different from the men he saw in the company of the scientist before... along with three other individuals who were not *exactly* human. Such odds could not help but give momentary pause to even so powerful and fearless an entity as Felanthus.

"You…" the man-tiger snarled as he recognized Tornada from sight as well as scent.

"*Oui, mon ami,*" the bald and bearded bandana-wearing scientist replied with a vile grin, his head displaying its characteristic nervous tic like always. "Now you see the folly of having escaped from me before. I can always track one such as you, no matter where in the world you go. I recognized the reported sightings of you in Paris for what they were, and though you had left upon our arrival there, it was not difficult to trace the reports to the itinerary of the plane traveling to India which you had snuck aboard. And as it turned out, this was a part of India I had an interest in traveling to for quite a long time now, as did my *cher collègue* here."

Felanthus snarled once more at the scientist and the unfamiliar man standing beside him but was again given pause when this aroused the wrath of the two mastiffs under Tornada's control—which the scientist was barely able to hold back.

That other man was a large, well-built individual dressed in drab blue clothing, which provided a stark contrast to Tornada's immaculate white apparel with black necktie. The man seemed to be in late middle age or older despite his robust physique, with a mane of white hair and an equally lustrous white beard. He appeared oddly at ease both in the company of Tornada's entourage and facing the man-tiger himself.

As for the other three, they were all animals in human shape that appeared crafted from similar means as Aissa. One was another female, with a lithe form that matched the traits of a human and feline much like that of the puma-woman, but with splotches of blackish fur that revealed her feline side to be that of a panther. As for the other two, they were both males, one of which resembled a chimeric construction of man and leopard; while the other possessed a covering of brown shaggy hair, a very hefty build, and a bestial but still vaguely and hideously human countenance whose animal side was not immediately discernible.

"Now, before you bring this reunion to its logical violent conclusion, my dear Felanthus, where are my manners?" Tornada continued. "Allow me to introduce you to my good *compatriote* here. This is Doctor Moreau, a colleague of mine from back into our misbegotten youths, one who learned much of his impressive craft from my own work."

"Hah," Moreau scoffed. "I do not deny that I was… inspired by some of your techniques, Tornada. But let us not forget that you were the one who was so inspired by *my* work that you had actually taken on my identity and found an uncharted tropical island of your own where you set up shop and conducted experiments to fashion beast-men similar to mine using modified versions of my own methodology. Ouran and Lota here are examples of what you concocted in your own 'House of Pain' and look how much they resemble the Leopard-Man of my own creation who also stands beside us here.

"In fact, why not be honest to the point where you admit you even deliberately had a ship wrecked at sea so a man would make his way to your 'island of lost souls' much as Edward Prendick accidentally found his way to mine… all so you could mate him with Lota in a truly perverse duplication of my situation, which Wells wrote up in his book that was taken from Mr. Prendick's account. You so went out of your way to replicate my own experiments right down to the exact situation that you hired a former mercenary in imitation of my friend Montgomery and created a beast-man servant like my own loyal M'ling. You had also previously sculpted a female big cat into the form of a woman much as I did—though you constructed Lota out of a panther, not a puma, as was my Aissa.

"Moreover, so much did you duplicate my work and situation that when Mr. Edmund Parker and his fiancée Ruth escaped from your island, the story given to that sensationalist author Wylie resulted in his working it into a screenplay that Paramount turned into a picture show passing off your adventure as an 'adaptation' of Prendick's account of my situation—even changing certain names and modifying events to make them more closely resemble my own adventure. Of course, you did not expect Parker's fiancée and that silly captain to arrive, an event I did not have to deal with, so…"

"Oh, enough of that, Moreau!" Tornada exclaimed with a dismissive wave of his hand and another noticeable head tic. "*Oui,* I tried to replicate what you did down to the fine details just to demonstrate how my own improvements would produce better results than your own… and to maintain a bit of anonymity I needed at the time. My genetic manipulation of the cell plasm and the addition of the energies from that galvanic generator were marvelous additions to your crude vivisection methods! Note how Lota looked far more human than any of your own misbegotten creations!"

Felanthus cocked his head as his rage was joined by confusion over the seemingly petty argument being carried out by these two rivals in their shared vocation.

"Hah," Moreau scoffed once more. "The galvanic generator was inspired by the experiments of another colleague of ours, Doctor Pretorius! And let us not forget the further techniques you picked up from yet more colleagues you have worked with, including Doctor Cornelius Kramm and Sir Edmund Sexton—the latter being the apparent creator of this Felanthus creature using advanced gene splicing methods. Not to mention your further inspirations from Mengele's attempts to produce viable offspring between primates and humans via the natural way—which he was quite unsuccessful at until he received some help from Doctor. Sexton.

"Speaking of which, most of your creations looked no less 'misbegotten' than my own, including Ouran there. Lota may have initially looked more human than my poor Aissa, but she ultimately fell victim to the same partial reversion to the animal state that afflicted my own beast-men. And finally, let us not forget what happened to that previous body of yours when your foolish breaching of the Law I taught my own Beast-Men caused them to turn on you and vivisect you to pieces!"

"Yet I stand before you now whole," Tornada forcefully reminded Moreau, "courtesy of the cellular replication and consciousness transference processes I developed in tandem with that diminutive German geneticist. It helped me grow a few spare bodies of my own just in case unexpected factors like the arrival of Mr. Parker's fiancée threw my carefully calculated plans into disarray, and ensured that my consciousness would be transferred to it if a previous body happened to die.

"Allow me to further remind you how that was the same replication technique I used to create those non-living doppelgangers of yourself and Aissa to make it appear you and the puma lady had killed each other after she escaped from your House of Pain and you recklessly went out into the jungle in pursuit of her. All at the behest of Professor Moriarty's machinations, so I could have you secretly spirited away from your island when it became obvious your plans went hopelessly awry. And so your gifts could be provided to the British government while Moriarty was still affiliated with it, and even the Diogenes Club left him alone as a result. You would not have made it off that island intact, nor would have Aissa, without my intervention!"

"Boast all your enormous ego demands of you, Tornada," Moreau lamented. "Was it not my work that aided Her Majesty's government in thwarting that invasion? Did I not continue my work, now in Britain, in more impressive ways than ever? Did I not recreate one of my most formidable specimens, the Leopard-Man, to serve as both my personal bodyguard and as an homage to my earliest work?

"Why, your insistence on taking up my identity has already convinced one chronicler of my tale that I am psychotically detached from reality—not to mention short, rotund, and bald. Such depictions will doubtless be used by future chroniclers of my story as well. All courtesy of your egoistic indulgences in the work of others and identity hijacking!"

"Do get over yourself, Moreau!" the white-attired scientist spat back. "Was it not my work that not only put you in the position of owing me your assistance on this lucrative venture, but which also helped retard your further aging, as well as that of your precious Aissa? And how it helped mend the terrible injuries that my Lota and Ouran inflicted upon each other as a result of Parker's maneuverings? Luckily, their reported demise at the end of Wylie's recording of my story was misstated. Not only that, but..."

"Enough, you men!" Felanthus roared, his tolerance of the scientists' bickering having come to an end. "This Tornada... is bad! That means... his friend must be bad! I will rip you both apart!"

Before the man-tiger could make a move—and before Tornada could release his dogs or order Ouran the Beast-Man, Lota the Panther-Woman, and the apparently unnamed Leopard-Man to leap to his defense—his claws were stayed by Aissa's gentle hand.

"No, Felanthus," the puma-woman said. "The doctors are friends of mine, and Moreau is my master. They provide the Law we live by. They only want you to live with us. Don't you want to live with me?"

Felanthus was once again confused, but only momentarily. "If you are with… bad men, then you are bad too, Aissa! I can't feel special way for you anymore. You led them… to me! You turned out to be… bad, like last friend did!"

"Aissa, calm him!" Tornada ordered. "This area of jungle has truly unique animals in it. Their intelligence is said to match that of humans due to some strange mutation to the local fauna. Just imagine the specimens Moreau and I can create from the likes of them! They will already possess human intellect that will not require hypnotic means developed by Moreau to simulate and bring forth; their intelligence will not atrophy and revert back to pure bestial instinct over time like most of our other creations! We can create an entire civilization of Beast-Men from them, one that will eclipse the rule of ordinary man!"

"You mean… beast-men that will… serve your evil ways," Felanthus said. "You will use *them*, like you… used *me*. I won't allow! Even if I have to… fall before you!"

"Then unfortunately, *mon ami,* that is what you must do and will do," Tornada stated firmly. "If you do not join us of your own volition, where you can have Aissa for your own, then I will simply kill you and glean what information I can by vivisecting your putrid carcass."

"That is not necessary, Tornada!" Moreau insisted. "All we need do is teach him the Law! Make him respect it! We can build such an incredible society, but it must be constructed on orderly principles, not by force and the threat of murder!"

"Oh, do not be a hypocritical fool, Moreau," Tornada retorted. "Your Law for the Beast-Men was always predicated on the use of force, and the threat of your House of Pain. It was never as altruistic as you seem to think. It was all in the interest of sheer scientific discovery, which you rationalized as being part of some ethos for your own convenience. You are much more like me than you would care to admit, for I take no pretense to morality over the advancement of science!"

"You lie, Tornada!" Moreau insisted. "Ethics must always accompany science, even if they require a system of harsh realizations behind them!"

Tornada sniggered. "'Harsh realizations.' Listen to yourself, Moreau! And laugh along with me!"

"Felanthus…" Aissa said as she stood between the man-tiger and Tornada's barely-restrained pair of mastiffs. "Please come with me… with us. The doctors aren't bad. The pain when Moreau first created me… it was necessary to make me into this. I didn't understand at time. But now I do. Please try to understand with me."

"They tricked you!" Felanthus howled. "I will kill them... now!"

"No!" Tornada yelled as he let go of the leashes that held back his fiery-tempered mastiffs.

The two slavering hounds leapt at Felanthus with the clear intent to tear him to pieces. But the man-tiger was as capable of ripping apart an opponent as these dogs, even more so. The first 150-pound mastiff was met with powerful resistance when he attempted to take Felanthus to the ground. The hound had his bowels ripped out of its belly by a single crisscrossing swipe of both the man-tiger's claws. The other canine bit into Felanthus's left leg and nearly pulled him off his feet. He swiped at the hound and cut into the back of its neck, but those gashes failed to stop the animal's determined attack.

"Kill him!" Tornada screamed.

Before Moreau could decide on a course of action, including brandishing the firearm he had on his person, Aissa leapt on top of the attack dog.

"Leave him!" the puma-woman demanded as she used a combination of her teeth and claws to rip the dog's hide clear off its back.

The canine howled and whined in agony before falling still in a bloody skinned heap.

"Aissa, how dare you!" Tornada hollered. "You have broken the Law!"

"Only *your* Law, Tornada!" said Moreau. "The Law of convenient interpretation!"

"Shut up, you!" Tornada then turned to Aissa with his own firearm drawn. "You will die, you filthy animal! And you will get no resurrection this time!"

"Tornada, don't!" Moreau hollered but his colleague's quick trigger finger pumped two high-caliber bullets into Aissa's chest before the burly British scientist could wrest the weapon away.

The puma-woman screeched in pain as both lungs were perforated by the leaden projectiles. She then fell, only to find herself caught in Felanthus's furry arms before hitting the ground.

"Aissa! No!" the man-tiger bellowed. "I know now... you are not bad like them!"

"Felanthus... I'm so sorry..." was Aissa's final words as blood trickled from her cat-like maw and her yellowish-green eyes rolled back into her head.

Then, she was still. Felanthus had long ago learned to recognize the stench of death, and he howled his fury into the sky above him.

It was a loud, reverberating cacophony that was heard a half mile away by Felifax and his group.

"That was Felanthus!" the Tiger-Man shouted to his troop. "It came from that direction! Let us make haste, now!"

The Hindu jungle lord raced with great speed towards where the sound had emanated. Keeping good pace were Rudra and Durgane, with Mowgli close behind and Challenger falling far to the rear but still doing his athletic best to keep up.

"Wait up, will ya now?" the hunter yelled. "Bloody hell, I hate it when he does that!"

"Moreau, stop being a fool and put that gun away!" Tornada demanded as he and his long-time colleague held each other at bay with mutually drawn firearms.

"While you continue brandishing your own weapon at me?" Moreau retorted. "You must believe I am truly the fool you accuse me of being!"

"All these years of collaboration — however sporadic — and mutual exchange of ideas thrown away over a mere disagreement? You know better than this, *mon ami.*"

"Oh, this is over a matter of considerably greater magnitude than a simple disagreement, my esteemed colleague, and you are well aware of that!"

"Just as you are aware of what a sham your pretenses to moral superiority are, Moreau!"

"You kill Aissa!" Felanthus interjected into the argument. "I not wait… for one of you to kill other! I kill you both… with my own claws!"

However, before the man-tiger could charge his hated targets, the three Beast-Men displayed similar animalistic speed by leaping forward and intercepting his attack. Even the mighty Felanthus was no match for the combined counterforce of Ouran, Lota, and the Leopard-Man. The bestial trio swiftly sent the man-tiger back into a wide banyan tree, a move that stunned him into submission. The three bared their respective fangs and moved them closer to the ochre-furred man-beast's throat as they held him up against the dense bark of the tree.

"You not attack the master!" Ouran angrily him.

"Or *my* master too!" the Leopard-Man added.

"You are one of us!" Lota said in a manner noticeably more articulate than her male allies. "You should follow the Law!"

"Both men… only use you!" Felanthus replied. "The Law… only good for them! They treat you… as lesser! Tornada… killed Aissa! She one of you! And she meant much to me!"

"Aissa broke the Law!" Ouran shouted, his sharp incisors coming even closer to the restrained man-tiger's orange-furred throat. "And… she almost killed me before! She deserved fate!"

"The Law… is made by men *for* men!" Felanthus pleaded while struggling to no avail against his three assailants. "You have… no say! Are you… not men?"

"That is what the Law once said!" the Leopard-Man stated. "To make us be as men! But Tornada changed the Law that my master made. Now the Law says… we must serve and protect those who are *real* men!"

"Meaning… your masters only," the man-tiger said. "They use you against… other men. And kill you… when they need you no longer."

"Only if we break the Law!" Ouran shrieked as he slammed the man-tiger up against the tree again. "Like Aissa broke the Law!"

"The new, *better* Law!" Lota added.

"But *we* represent a higher Law in this jungle," came the deep voice of a man from directly behind them.

This particular voice was one that was likewise familiar to Felanthus, but in this case was true proverbial music to the man-tiger's pointed ears. It was the voice of his brother, Felifax.

"A much better Law," concurred Mowgli, "and one that will never allow the likes of those two men to use the peoples of Seonee like they intended! Their forms were given them by the Mother Spirit for a reason, and they will not have their bodies painfully sculpted to look like men!"

"No, they will not," the Tiger-Man further agreed. "They, like my flesh-rending companions Rudra and Durgane, shall remain in the form that the gods intended."

Felifax moved his hand in the direction to indicate the growling and hissing Bengals. Moreau and Tornada could not help but notice the big cats' backs were raised in a position indicating they were ready to tear into the opposition with all due prejudice at a moment's notice.

"*Mon Dieu!*" Tornada exclaimed as he turned his bandana-covered head to notice Felifax standing before him. "It is you! The Hindu tiger-prince who claims to be related to this Felanthus! I hoped that Gouroull, that creation of Frankenstein, had killed you in our previous encounter!"

"And I had hoped that *someone,* anyone, had killed you by now, Tornada," Felifax rejoined. "So, it would seem both of our hopes have come up short. Nevertheless, I am pleased to see you again, so I may kill you myself."

"And Moreau," Felifax continued, "it is fancy meeting you again as well. *Unfortunately* for you."

"Brother…!" Felanthus called out in a raspy peal of excitement.

"Yes, Felanthus," Felifax replied, "I have finally found you! And I brought help with me. So, you no longer face these odds alone!"

Moreau then took advantage of Tornada's distraction to grab his accomplice's gun wrist and push it down and away from any possible target. The bigger man's strength enabled him to quickly cause Tornada enough pain to force him to drop his firearm.

"That will be enough of *that* now!" Moreau said, lowering his own weapon.

"And I… have had enough of *you* today!" Tornada replied through the pain of his twisted arm… just before punching Moreau in the testes.

The larger man grabbed his pain-riddled genitals and collapsed to the ground, releasing his former ally in the process. “Tornada… you… dishonorable plebeian!”

“Ha ha! Never leave the family jewels undefended, Moreau!” Tornada proclaimed as he reached down to recover his firearm.

However, the bald-pated scientist did nothing more than scream in further pain as Felifax hurled his blade into his foe’s wrist. Tornada was so shocked by the sudden perforating wound that he fell backwards on top of Moreau. By that time, the white-haired scientist had recovered just enough from his throbbing testicles to wrap one of his brawny arms around his colleague’s throat, squeezing the air out of it and holding him immobile.

“You will… pay for your folly, Tornada!” Moreau decreed.

“Aaaggh! We will see who pays!” Tornada responded as he slammed the elbow of his good arm repeatedly into his captor’s rib cage. “Particularly since I always have a backup plan!”

Tornada forced his injured arm into one of his coat pockets to produce a silver-colored whistle. He then worked the object to his mouth and blew into it. No sound was heard by anyone present… but another duo of snarling and slavering mastiffs in a cage hidden within nearby forest greenery certainly did. The whistle also sent out a silent acoustic signal that caused the lock on that cage to pop open and drop to the ground. Both trained canines recognized this as their cue to run to their master’s vicinity and kill for him. The two mastiffs pushed the now unlocked cage door open and ran towards the direction of the ultrasonic sound at top speed.

“Damn you to Hell, Tornada!” Moreau hollered at the realization of what his colleague must have done while he struggled to hold him amidst the cascade of elbows to his sternum.

Within seconds, the barking and growling dogs rushed into the clearing, quickly picking out the standing opponents as the main threat. And no sooner did that occur than Felifax was moved to act.

“Rudra, Durgane—take those dogs! Mowgli, let us reduce the odds against Felanthus!”

All took heed of the command, even Mowgli, despite his being the proper king of this part of the jungle. The two Bengals engaged the ferocious mastiffs, and two brutal battles ensued as the four beasts rolled about on the verdant jungle ground. The outcome was never in doubt to Felifax, of course, but it did regrettably provide a distraction for the human element of their opposition.

In the meantime, the enraged Hindu prince’s eyes took on a cat-like appearance, the tan skin of his back and torso suddenly became mottled with darkish stripes, and his incisors enlarged — all indications that he had called upon the destruction goddess Black Kali to “activate” his tiger strands of DNA. Felifax had now truly become the Tiger-Man!

The now quasi-feral jungle lord waded into the Panther-Woman, knocking her clear off Felanthus's person. Mowgli slammed his skull into the Leopard-Man's diaphragm, knocking his felinoid foe back with the sudden evacuation of air from the cat-man's lungs.

This left the bestial Ouran alone with Felanthus, who had the power to resist the might of this single adversary. And resist the man-tiger did as he pushed at the shaggy man and knocked him on his spine. The beast-man quickly jumped back to his feet and charged at Felanthus, the muscles beneath his hirsute skin rippling like steel chords and his fang-like teeth bared and ready to pierce flesh.

"You break the Law!" Ouran hollered as he rushed at his enemy. "None escape the Law!"

"Shut… up!" was Felanthus's only reply as he stopped the beast-man's charge with a cruel slash across his monstrous visage. "Now face… true Law of Jungle!"

With that pronouncement made, Felanthus leapt on Ouran, and the two rolled about the vegetation as they pounded and tore at each other like the savage beasts they partially were.

Felifax's tan and now striped skin was cut in numerous places as Lota slashed and bit at him. Her strength was terrific, but the Tiger-Man could match it in his feral state. As the two grappled to a seeming stalemate, Felifax finally took advantage of the fact that he did not need to rely upon animalistic fury alone but could also make use of the great fighting skill he possessed. The jungle lord managed to tap into a portion of his human side to accomplish this.

When the Panther-Woman hissed and charged at him, her extended talons bent on ripping into his flesh again, Felifax stood ready in a wrestling stance. He ducked down as she lunged at him and used the inertia of her leap to hurl her over his head. The Tiger-Man heard an unsettling but welcome cracking sound as her back struck a large tree behind them. Lota fell to the ground and struggled to raise her head to hiss at her foe once more as if her only recourse was to strike him with the feline equivalent of expletives. She then slumped into unconsciousness.

The Leopard-Man proved to be tough opposition for Mowgli, but despite being fully human, the jungle lord of Seonee was himself a force to be reckoned with. His natural speed and agility enabled him to dodge several of the Leopard-Man's clumsy but powerful swings, and he managed to slice open the cat-man's tawny-colored right arm with a quick slash of the knife. Mowgli knew, however, that he needed to end this quickly or he may not live to see the evening.

"You break the Law!" the felinoid shouted as he ignored the blood spurting out the gash on his arm to prepare for another attack. "You are man, but not even real men may break the master's Law!"

"I determine the Law here and no one else!" Mowgli replied defiantly as he held his blood-drenched knife in anticipation of his foe's next attack.

The Leopard-Man snarled in fury at the blasphemy he heard and charged at the long-haired jungle lord. His wound had slowed him down, however, and Mowgli was able to evade the next blow with little difficulty. He retaliated with another slash of the blade, this time to the beast-man's gut. The big cat wearing the form of a man screeched in agony while grasping at his bleeding abdomen. Mowgli took full advantage by going on the offense and smashing into the creature with all his Olympic-level might, pushing him back hard against a tree.

The jungle lord then slammed the Leopard-Man's malformed skull against the bark and followed up with a wicked elbow to a section of the manimal's lower neck where he knew a sensitive nerve cluster should be located. Thankfully, this held true despite the creature's altered anatomy and the Leopard-Man fell to the ground as consciousness departed his bleeding body. Mowgli was thankful for this, as he truly pitied this being for what had been done to him against his will and hoped to find a way to help him rather than slay him.

Felanthus and Ouran continued to rip and tear at each other as their violent altercation lingered on. The shaggy beast-man focused on enforcing his master's Law, while the man-tiger used the loss of his precious Aissa as fuel for his rage. In the end, Ouran proved wanting in this battle as Felanthus drew sufficient blood to cause his foe to fall before he could do the same to the man-tiger.

"The Law… no one escapes the Law…" Ouran muttered before his battered and bloody form collapsed into silence.

"Your master's Law… has been broke," the victorious Felanthus said as he stood over his insensate foe with Ouran's blood dripping from his extended claws.

Rudra and Durgane then culminated their battle with the second duo of mastiffs, as one of the canines having its throat torn out and the other suffering its bowels being ripped from its stomach.

Next to these battles, Tornada finally managed to extricate himself from Moreau's strong choking grip with a particularly nasty elbow strike to the rib cage. Now freed, the white-garbed scientist rolled a few meters across the ground and recovered his gun.

"I will soon deal with you, Moreau," he said, "but the first bullets will be for that tiger-beast and those pompous jungle lords!"

Tornada pushed himself to his feet, aimed his firearm at the just victorious Felanthus, and a thunderous bang was heard at the discharge of gunpowder.

However, it was Tornada who fell to the ground with a gaping bullet hole in his upper chest area, not the man-tiger. Moreau looked in the direction of the blast to see Matt Challenger, who had finally caught up with the group, holding his rifle with a wisp of smoke wafting from its barrel.

"Much obliged that you blokes left one for me!" the hunter quipped to his allies as their respective battles reached a climax. "Considering I'm always the one late for the party."

"Damn all of this," Moreau said to himself as he procured Tornada's firearm.

The white-haired scientist fired several shots at Challenger, who managed to duck behind one of the trees in time. This was not surprising, since Moreau's intention was to drive the newcomer back, not kill him. With that done, the scientist grabbed the gravely wounded and barely conscious Tornada by the collar of his ivory-colored coat and dragged him across the ground into a cluster of nearby shrubbery as if he were a mere rag doll.

"Come along now, old friend," Moreau said while lugging him to cover. "We have business to settle if you should survive this… or find your way into another body you constructed for yourself."

Challenger peeked from behind the safety of the thick tree and called out to the rest of the group, all of whom had just defeated their corresponding opponents.

"Begging my pardon for disturbing all of you, but the big blighter just got up and made off with the sodding git I shot! Over there, in those shrubs! Let's go get 'em already!"

Before the group could descend on the fleeing scientists, their attention was drawn to a loud whirring sound that turned out to be from a small skycraft that was hidden in the nearby canopy of foliage. It had a dirigible-like fuselage about five meters long with a powerful motorized propeller attached to the top that allowed Moreau and the badly wounded Tornada to ascend over fifty meters in a few seconds and depart the area at great speed.

"Bloody hell," Challenger said. "Did you see that flying craft? That looked like British government issue, if you ask me."

"Something we need to look into," Felifax said, having relinquished control to his human side in time to witness the escape. "And you can rest assured I will."

Challenger then turned to see Felanthus gently cradling the corpse of Aissa in his formidable arms.

"Um, Rama, that one is ours, am I right?" he queried. "The one that's still alive, I mean."

"Yes, that is my brother," the Hindu jungle lord confirmed. "And it would seem he has suffered a painful loss by Tornada's hand. That must have been the cat-person that was tracking him. I would guess she was under the control of their twisted Law, but that did not stop her from securing my brother's heart."

"Ah well, at least I sent a lead one into his flaming chest before the big guy pulled out of here," the hunter mentioned. "That one I shot was the Tornada chap, right?"

"It was," Felifax validated just before turning to console his brother. "Felanthus… I am sorry for your loss, as it seems that cat-woman meant much to you in the short time you must have known her. But, for whatever this may be worth, I have finally found you. And I will now take you home to meet the rest of your family."

Felanthus lifted his cat-like head, where the three men standing before him noticed that the orange fur under his eyes was dampened down by moisture.

"It… worth a lot to me," the man-tiger said. "Thank you for… coming for me."

"No need to thank me," Felifax said as he ran over and warmly embraced his brother. "That is what family is for."

"Aw, hell," Challenger said to Mowgli, who sat aside stroking the fur of Rudra and Durgane. "Do you happen to have a hanky hidden somewhere in that loincloth, mate?"

"Much thanks for your help in ridding my land of those men and their evil plans for the peoples of Seonee, "Mowgli stated. "If ever you need my aid, you have only to ask."

"Oh, it was nothing at all, really" Challenger remarked.

"My thanks to you as well, Mowgli," Felifax said as he continued to console his brother. "And if ever you and the peoples of your land need us, know that we will be at your side as well."

Felifax and Mowgli then firmly shook hands as they prepared to return home to their respective families.

With John Peel, one never knows what to expect! From Biggles to Doc Ardan, Whitechapel to Pellucidar, Doctor Omega to Captain Nemo, his imagination truly knows no bounds. We certainly recommend his latest two BCP collections, Return to the Center of the Earth *and* Twenty Thousand Years Under the Sea, *to all those who may have missed some of his TOTS stories. In this new tale, John returns to the fantastic worlds of two of his favorite authors, Jules Verne and Edgar Wallace...*

John Peel: *The Child That Time Forgot*

1895

I am an engineer by trade, which has led me to many interesting places and varied tasks, none as significant, as fascinating, as frustrating and as fulfilling as when I was engaged to work on Standard Island. There can be few of you who have not heard of this self-propelling island, but for the benefit of those few, I shall briefly describe it.

Standard Island was the work of genius constructed by the Standard Island Company out of (where else?) California. The company was owned by millionaires. Millionaires? No, *hundreds* of millionaires; men who would consider a mere millionaire to be the closest thing to a pauper in their imaginations. Constructed of steel boxes, joined—one would imagine—unbreakably together, then covered with soil, trees, plants and, ultimately, buildings that would form Milliard City. Immense, powerful electrical engines turned immense screws so that the island could be powered and steered wherever it wished to go. And it wished to venture freely across the stretches of the Pacific Ocean. And on Standard Island and in its capital (and only) city of Milliard would live those self-same multi-millionaires and their immediate families. Joining them on this journey of vacation and exploration would be a host of workers and servants—of which I had been selected to be one.

Despite being an engineer, I was not involved in the construction of the island itself. My particular specialty was not in immense projects but in smaller, more intimate mechanisms, and it was for this that I was employed. While there would be a great deal for the inhabitants of Milliard City to see and enjoy merely in a months-long sea voyage, there would, inevitably, be days when boredom might encroach on the ordered lives of these extremely wealthy men and women—and boredom might lead to dissatisfaction, which would never be tolerated. These wealthy scions must be kept amused and entertained at all times! And so the island employed a Master of Entertainment, one Calistus Mumbar, and this Calistus Mumbar employed (among others) myself. I was tasked with helping to create diversions that would keep the owners and inhabitants of the island happy.

It was a challenging and fascinating opportunity for me. Mumbar was an amiable man to work for, if a trifle over-enthusiastic and something of a humbug. He claimed a relationship with P.T. Barnum, and, I confess, it was easy to see a resemblance between the two men. He demanded spectacles and delights to supply to his clients, and it was my job to supply such delights. Nothing was denied me, and I was encouraged to follow whatever pathways my imagination took me. And my salary was beyond exorbitant, so I had nothing to complain of. I was happy in my work.

As had been planned, Standard Island was launched with all due spectacle and pomp. I had a hand in designing the fireworks show that signaled the official start of the week-long festivities that marked our casting off from the Californian mainland where the... ship? City? Island? had been constructed. It worked perfectly; the two huge engines drove our vessel slowly and majestically away from sore and out past the Channel Islands and away from the American mainland—and all the while a vast party was underway. It was an amazing time. I partied a little myself, but with care, as I still had a great deal of work to do, both to justify my large salary and to keep the effervescent Mumbar happy.

Eventually, of course, even this party settled down and ended, and the inhabitants of Milliard City began to learn how to live from day to day on a floating island. Everything was novel, and even the most mundane of tasks would prove to need new ways of solving old problems. There was, however, no pathway to solving the largest problem the island had.

I've mentioned that the owners and inhabitants of the island were millionaires many times over. This did not mean, however, that they all thought alike or had the same aims in lives. This cannot be surprising, after all. Though some of these families had been born wealthy and had always been brought up in an environment where money was no object, others had earned their fortunes. We had amongst us steel magnates, stockbrokers, and newly-rich oilmen. Some were filled with fire and ambition, while others wished only to bask in what their money had accustomed them to expect out of life. Standard Island was divided into two for convenience—we had a Starboard Harbor and a Larboard Harbor, for example. This way, whichever side of the island would be closest to one of the more fixed islands we visited would have a harbor from which to venture or to which supply ships might dock. But aside from being administrated in two halves, the island was split into two camps. One group were staunch Protestants, and the other devout Catholics. One side had an impressive church and the other a majestic cathedral. And both sides had an equal say on the city's council.

And both sides had to be entertained by Calistus Mumbar, and—by extension—myself. The two sides were, of course, far too genteel to go to war with one another over matters, but if one side approved a plan, the other side would invariably find reasons to dislike it. And if one party praised and supported an idea, the other would poo-poo and denigrate it. This caused Calistus Mumbar distress, and whatever caused him distress led to my being inconvenienced. As a result, it wasn't long before my overgenerous salary and free working conditions began to look parsimonious and restricting. For example, though the island was large, there was still insufficient acreage for a horse racing track, and millionaires like to wager on such sports. So I proposed to build an electrical track, with mechanical horses on a small scale that could be run and that gamblers could bet upon. It should have been a perfect solution—but, alas, one side thought it marvelous and enthusiastically supported my plans. Naturally, then, the other held firmly to the belief that gambling was an abhorrent evil and in no way to be encouraged. (Somehow, though, the island's casino never seemed to lack from devotees from both parties…)

As there was nothing I could do about this problem, I simply sighed and worked on other ideas. At the same time, I had made the acquaintance of Commodore Simcoe, who was the Captain of the vessel that was Standard Island. As an engineer—and also as merely a man filled with curiosity!—I was intrigued by the mechanisms that enabled the island to exist and move, and with the Commodore's blessing, I was able to visit and study the island's lower regions, its engines and its steering mechanism. It was an elegant piece of engineering, and I was duly impressed.

I discovered that I was not alone in my researches. There was another student of the island, and a very pretty one at that. This was Cecile DuBois, a lovely and lively blonde lady from France. She was employed as a governess and tutor by the Tankerdon family—leaders of one of the two factions (the other being the Coverleys). Though originally from Normandy, she spoke fluent English, German and Italian, thus recommending her as a governess for the younger offspring of the family. And, like me, she found Standard Island fascinating, and was determined to understand all of its secrets. It is not at all surprising, therefore, that we joined forces in our explorations. It is even less surprising that I found myself falling in love with this enchanting and highly intelligent young lady.

Because of our interests, we were on hand when our strangest adventure commenced. We were conversing with Commodore Simcoe on the plans for the next port of call. We were still more than a week from—ah, but no; I shall not reveal our destination, for to do so might give away information that we later vowed never to reveal. I shall merely say that it was a small island chain of reputed beauty, at which Standard Island was planning to remain for a week or so before moving on. As I said, we were about ten days out from our target islands when the Commodore received a report from one of his staff. He briefly read it, and then scowled and read it again, more slowly.

"That's rather odd," he observed.

"What is, sir?" I asked. "If it's not a matter of secrecy, of course."

“No secrecy,” he replied. Then he chuckled. “In fact, something that might interest the both of you—students of the island that you are.” He waved the paper slightly. “We are experiencing slight turbulence that appears to be originating towards the east.”

Cecile furrowed her pretty brow. “But that would suggest we are approaching land,” she remarked. She gestured at the chart we had been examining. “And, yet, there is nothing indicated close by.”

“Yes, it does, and no, there isn’t.” He shook his head slightly. “It is… intriguing. Though I must admit that this section of the Pacific Ocean is not altogether thoroughly explored—we are off the major shipping lanes, after all, and any vessels that may have strayed this far out might simply have missed a solitary island. It is a vast ocean, after all.”

“Will we be investigating, then, Commodore?” I asked, hopefully. Exploring known islands was most enjoyable, but the thought of a hitherto-undiscovered land was most intriguing.

“Oh, yes,” agreed Cecile, eagerly.

He laughed, gruffly. “The decision is not mine,” he said, firmly. “The city council will have to approve any deviation from our planned course.” Seeing our disappointment with this remark, he smiled slightly. “Don’t be too worried—it is quite likely that there will be sufficient members who feel the way you do that this is a mystery worth looking into.”

That was encouraging, at least. We were in the tower of the observatory in Milliard City, and had a splendid view from here—or, at least, we would have had, if it had been daytime. In the darkness of the night, we have a magnificent view of the Milky Way and the stars of the Southern Hemisphere, but could see nothing nearer to our island that the stars. “Isn’t there a danger that we will pass it in the night?”

“I may not be able to make the decision to investigate on my own,” the Commodore replied, “but I can order the engines to be slowed, so that we will not have to backtrack if the council decides to take Standard Island closer to investigate.”

That was moderately reassuring. But I expressed my worries as I escorted Mademoiselle Cecile to her lodgings. We were both most intrigued by the idea of an unknown island. But Cecile was more optimistic than I.

“Whoever discovers a new island and marks its position will have the right to name it,” she pointed out. “And do you think there is not one millionaire on this island of ours who would not pay a small fortune for the honor of naming a new island in his own honor?”

Ah, she knew how to make me laugh! But how true it was, as we discovered the following morning. The council had approved our slight change of course to take a look at our mysterious companion in these seas, and the Commodore had executed their orders with alacrity. Then the two factions had returned to arguing about which of them would have the honor of naming the island. That would keep them happy for at least the rest of the day, if not the week.

Meanwhile, the Commodore was preparing one of the electric launches to take a small team to investigate the island. Both Cecile and I begged to be a part of the expedition, but the Commodore shook his head firmly. "There may be natives on the island," he said. "If so, we do not know their nature. Some of the islanders in these seas were cannibals until relatively recently, so we cannot take any chances. Colonel Stewart has appointed a band of his trained militia to be the first men ashore. Whether the council will allow any further exploration will depend entirely on their report." Then his severe face softened slightly. "If that is favorable, though, I promise you that you will be allowed to accompany the next expedition."

My dear friend and I were only slightly mollified by this assurance, because there was as yet no guarantee that there would ever be a second visit. Still, there was nothing we could do about the matter—though the idea of sneaking aboard the launch was broached by Cecile. I pointed out that there was nowhere for us to remain hidden even if we should somehow manage to slip aboard unobserved. Resigning ourselves to the reality of the situation, we resolved to remain in the observatory tower and to survey our approach to this hitherto unknown island.

We had expected to be able to utilize one of the telescopes to monitor our approach, but that proved impossible. Despite the fact that the skies were mostly clear and cloudless, as we approached the island conditions changed rapidly. The clouds closed in and a sea mist arose. Before we had even sighted the first glimpse of our target, it was impossible to see more than a few hundred yards. Commodore Simcoe, cautious as ever, slowed the engines and we were virtually simply drifting in to where the island was located. As sometimes happens in such conditions, though visibility was reduced to almost nothing, sounds appeared to be amplified. We could hear the mournful howl of the siren as the electric launch set off from the Larboard Harbor, though the virtually silent electrical engines were too faint to discern.

Standard Island came to a halt, as the engines were shut down, save for the occasional move necessary to keep us safely stationed offshore. The fog was thick and oppressive, and there was nothing to be seen. It was even impossible to be certain that there was even an island out there. The air was still, and the only sounds we could now hear were those of the daily activities accompanying life in Milliard City. Even though the fog crept across our streets, our wealthy inhabitants kept up their accustomed activities.

The long wait was almost physically painful. Both Cecile and I concentrated on hearing anything out of the ordinary—to see anything was physically impossible—but we were terribly frustrated. To be so close to a mystery and to be unable to take a step forward to solve it! What was the island like? Was it inhabited? Were there strange wild animals, and strange wild me? We knew that there was little likelihood of danger from wild animals, as no Pacific Island had any savage creatures larger or more vicious than some wild pigs. But the nature of human beings was unpredictable. How large was the island? Was it a lone point in the midst of a sea, or merely the first of a chain of similar islands? My delightful companion and I discussed such points for hours, but it was all sheer speculation, as we had no information for a firm foundation.

After what seemed to be an endless wait, the Commodore sent one of his men to alert us both that the launch was returning to its berth in Larboard Harbor, and that he expected an initial report shortly. His compliments, and would we care to join him to share in the intelligence thus to be provided? Would we! Wild horses (which did not, of course, exist!) would have failed to keep us out. Our messenger was hard-pressed to stay ahead of us as we rushed to the Commodore's reception room.

He looked worried, which was certainly not a good sign, and greeted us rather gruffly. "The launch has docked," he reported. "There were three men injured, one of them severely. He has been rushed to the medical officer."

"What happened?" I demanded.

"The lieutenant in charge is on his way here with his report," the Commodore replied. "Naturally, he wished to be sure his men were being treated properly before coming here. I expect him momentarily." And, indeed, it wasn't more than three minutes before the officer himself appeared and saluted the Commodore.

The main was in rather poor shape himself, for which he apologized, assuring Simcoe that the only reason he hadn't changed into a fresh uniform was that he felt his report was too urgent. He had clearly been through some shock and strain, as his clothing was quite filthy, and he himself was scratched badly in places. He had a thick bandage on his right arm that showed leakage from blood, but he assured us, when we expressed concern, that he would go for medical treatment as soon as he had alerted us.

The island, it seemed, was inhabited by a native species, but these natives were not the cause of his injuries. "We did not see their village at the first," he explained. "Due to the fog, we had bypassed it. We settled the launch close to a beach and a group of us went ashore. On land, the mist is far thinner, though it seemed to gather and pool in places. But we could see fairly clearly. We had landed beside a tangle of jungle, and in the distance we could see smoke. That informed us that there were people living there, but some miles from where we had landed. We decided to trek through the jungle so that we could observe them more closely.

"The shoreline near us consisted mostly of steep cliffs; anything larger than our launch would not have been able to make landfall. But there were pathways to the top of the cliffs, and so we climbed, leaving a small party to watch over the launch. And there we found…" He shuddered slightly. "Monsters. It is the only word that describes them: monsters!"

"Can you be more specific, lieutenant?" the Commodore asked.

The poor man groped for words. "They were like gigantic lizards, sir—crawling, and some standing upright. And all of them seeking victims to devour. They came after us as soon as we reached the heights of the cliffs. We used our rifles, but most of them barely seemed to notice the shots. I... ordered an immediate retreat, but they were so fast... Two of my men were badly injured, so I and two others kept up defensive fire while the mauled men were evacuated. Fortunately, those creatures are not adept at climbing, and couldn't follow us down the cliff-face. We were able to retreat, though most of us were injured to one degree or another." He shivered again at the memory. "We were fortunate that no one was killed." He looked earnestly from the Commodore to Cecile and myself. "There was no other choice to be made. For God's sake, sir—if you are a reasoning, caring man—do not let anyone else land in that hellish place. We should leave, now, and forget we ever found this accursed island."

The man had reached the limits of his strength and nerve. Sympathetically, Simcoe said: "Thank you for your report, lieutenant. I will be certain to pass it along to the council—along with your recommendation. Now, go and rest." The man nodded and half-stumbled his way out of the Commodore's office. Simcoe turned to face Cecile and myself. 'What do you make of that?"

"A brave man who has reached his limits," I replied promptly.

"But... monsters?"

Cecile frowned. "On the surface, it sounds difficult to believe," she opined. "But, clearly, those men were faced with something that they could not understand, nor cope with. Their injuries are frightful, though there is hope that they will all survive. Clearly, they met with something extraordinary." Then, in a softer voice, "Lizards..."

"You have an idea?" I asked her. I had become accustomed to her thinking processes and saw the signs that something had occurred to her.

"A wild and fantastic one, yes," she confessed. "This island is remote, and has been cut off from contact for who knows how long. In Australia, a similar state of isolation has resulted, as you know, in creatures that are quite unique to the island. Where in the rest of the world mammals evolved to mastery, in the Antipodes their place was taken by marsupials."

"You suggest that in this case of our mysterious island, that isolation has led reptiles to a state of dominance?" I asked her.

"Why not?" she argued. "It has happened before, in the age of the dinosaurs. Once such monsters ruled the entire world—is it so hard to believe that they might come rule a single, remote and isolated island?"

"Rule—or rule again," the Commodore muttered. "Perhaps here their dominion has never run out."

Cecile inclined her head. "Of course, I am merely speculating," she pointed out. "To be absolutely certain, I should have to see these creatures for myself."

"No!" both the Commodore and myself exclaimed immediately. I deferred to his authority, and he continued: "You have seen what such creatures have done to a well-armed party of professional soldiers. I would never agree to your risking your life for so little gain."

"The advancement of science is never a little gain," she argued. "If dinosaurs—or dinosaur-like creatures—exist here, then this would be an immensely significant moment for science. While I thank you both for your concern for my welfare, my life is insignificant when faced with such a possible advance!"

Fond as I was of her, I could not help but believe she had temporarily taken leave of her senses. "It hardly matters how little value you place on your life—a valuation I would vehemently disagree with, incidentally!—it is pointless to speculate. Once the council receives the report from the shore party, they will undoubtedly follow the lieutenant's recommendation and forbid anyone else from landing upon this island."

Needless to say, I could hardly have been more wrong. The Commodore presented his report to the council and, after some highly vocal discussion, they ordered him to prepare another party to take a second launch to the island!

I couldn't believe this, but Simcoe reluctantly confirmed it. "There is to be another expedition."

"But whyever would they agree to undertake such a foolish venture?" I cried.

"Because they are sporting gentlemen," the Commodore answered. "The Tankerdons and the Coverleys alike have hunted the most dangerous species on Earth. The prospect of going after species that have been unclaimed by any other hunters was more than they could bear to pass up."

"Did you not tell them that the weapons of the landing party were virtually useless against the monsters that inhabit the island?"

"I did. They pooh-poohed the issue, saying that they had elephant guns that would stop any creature that this world, this hellish place, might have bred. They actually appeared to find the thought that the creatures are almost impossible to kill to be a challenge, and an irresistible one at that."

"Then they are foolish, and may well be going to their deaths."

"They relish the thought."

"Then they are not foolish—they are insane!"

The Commodore sighed. "I cannot disagree with your assessment."

I glanced around, and saw that he and I were alone in his office. "Where is Mademoiselle DuBois?" I had been expecting her to comment, but she was nowhere to be seen. I discovered why a short while later, as I came across her hurrying down the street back to the observatory, her eyes gleaming and a broad smile upon her lovely face.

"My dear Roger," she said, clasping my hands in her own. "You have heard the news?"

"That Standard Island is governed by madmen? Yes."

She came to a halt, and regarded me with uncertainty. "You do not approve of this second visit to the island?"

"The party in the first one was mauled and barely escaped with their lives," I pointed out. "To risk further lives unnecessarily is foolish."

"I am to go with them," she said simply.

"You!" I stared at her in total shock. After a moment, I was able to regain use of my voice. "Surely you cannot intend to go blasting away at the creatures on this island!"

"Of course not!" she replied, indignantly. "How could you think such a thing of me? I go along to study them for science."

"But… you risk your life to do so!"

"Many people before me have done the same; can I do less?"

I stared at her in shock and horror. The thought of my dear, sweet, gentle Cecile on this island from the maws of Hell shook me to my core. "I forbid it!" I said—boldly and foolishly.

She scowled at me ferociously. "And who are you to forbid me anything?"

"One who values your life more than he values his own," I admitted.

That sufficed to melt the fierce frown upon her brows. "Dear Roger," she said, softly, her eyes sparkling. Then she pulled herself together. "But you cannot and will not forbid me this."

"In which case, I shall accompany you," I resolved. "If you perish, I shall perish with you."

"Oh, Roger, I am certain that neither of us will perish. We shall have several of the greatest game hunters in the world for our protection."

I confess, that thought did not reassure me as much as it seemed to do her. We had no assurances that their rifles—however effective they might be against elephants—could even penetrate the hides of the monsters of the island. But my dear Cecile was totally committed to what she saw as her duty to science, and I was committed to what I saw as my duty to her. But I was more than half convinced that both of us would end up as healthy servings on a monster's feast.

If anything, our mighty Nimrods were even more convinced of their abilities than Cecile was. Commodore Simcoe wished above all that he could accompany us on the second launch, but he reluctantly acquiesced to the view that he was engaged as the captain and navigator of Standard Island, and therefore had to remain behind. In his place, Colonel Stewart, as head of the militia, would be in strict command. Even the wealthiest of hunters had to agree to follow his instructions, and to abandon the hunt if he decided it was too dangerous.

The Commodore took me aside before we departed. "Have you ever used a firearm before?" he asked me. I confessed that I had never even held one. "Then there is no point in giving you an elephant gun," he decided. "You would be more dangerous to yourself and your companions with one." He handed me an automatic pistol. "This is likely to be ineffective against any larger creature, but it could prove useful in limited circumstances. Try not to shoot yourself in the foot with it."

I thanked him—more for his friendship and concern than for the gun—and reluctantly clambered aboard the launch. Cecile was ready and waiting, her eyes sparkling with excitement. Our contingency of hunters was already aboard and eager to be off, all of them carrying or wearing their massive weapons, and speaking eagerly to one another of their hopes and prayers for what they termed *Sport* and I considered to be immense folly. I could not (and still cannot) see why there is anything appealing about chasing and slaughtering animals that wish only to be left alone to live their lives.

The fog that had enshrouded the island earlier still clung to the sea about us. Visibility was low. The motors of the electric launch were virtually soundless, so our trip reminded me of the myths of the Island of the Dead. I almost expected strains of Rachmaninoff's icy music to accompany us. The hunters were huddled together, discussing the merits of their portable cannons, but as we progressed, even their voices softened and finally died out altogether. The only person immune to the chilling mood was Cecile, who seemed to be caught up in a feverish expectation of her forthcoming service to Science.

We could hear the lapping and soft crashing of waves upon a shore before we could discern anything in the gloom. Even though it was the forenoon, we could not make out the sun—merely a section of the fog that seemed lighter than the rest. We all strained our eyes and nerves as we attempted to catch a glimpse of something—anything!—in that all-encompassing mist. And then one of the sailors gave a cry and pointed. I could barely make out the spume on a wave as it fell on some as-yet unseen strand. And then the fogs seemed to part, falling away around us, and at last the island was visible.

Well, a portion of it, at the least. There was a short, rocky beach that led to an immense mass of a cliff that stretched in both directions as far as we could see. There appeared to be no path to ascend to the far-off summit, but a couple of the sailors had been on the first launch, and they were certain that there was a narrow pathway that wound up the cliff-face, and it only needed to be rediscovered. Though I furtively prayed that it should elude us, one of them gave a cry and pointed. As we drew closer, I could see that there did indeed appear to be a trail that led up that rocky wall. We might be able to ascend after all.

We were able to go ashore on the brief, rocky beach—I had to carry Cecile from the launch so that she would not get soaked; she had on a light dress since she had anticipated a climb, but for women "light" is a relative term, and included several layers of undergarments. Colonel Stewart then gave the order to ascend. Our party was led by two officers of the militia, followed by four soldiers, then the four hunters (two from each faction), then Cecile and myself, and then two more soldiers to guard the rear. The colonel would remain below with the remainder of the men in case a rescue party of any sort would be needed. Stewart made it quite clear that final authority over the group would be held by his lieutenant and not any of the millionaires. He cautioned us not to get separated, and then allowed us to proceed. I had hoped he might forbid Cecile to accompany us, but he made no such mention. Fingering the pistol in my pocket for comfort, I stayed with her on the pathway.

The climb was strenuous, but not overly difficult. The cliffs were, on average, about 300 feet tall, and I was careful not to glance backwards. I am not afraid of heights, but I am certainly wary of them, and these cliffs were quite sheer. It was impossible to discern anything at their summit until we achieved it, but at least the fog seemed to stay clinging to the surface of the sea, and as we rose, our vision became sharper. We appeared to be ascending out of the clouds and into much crisper, fresher air.

Though we could see nothing but rocks and the pathway we were following, we were not so limited in hearing. There were far off cries and other sounds that reminded me of the various tropical forests we had already visited on our trip, although I could identify no species that were making the sounds. Then again, I am not a naturalist, so that is not altogether surprising. We could see far-off aerial creatures wheeling and diving into the fog—presumably fishing—but none were close enough to identify.

"Many islands have their individual species," Cecile explained, as we halted for a breather for a few minutes. "This is one of the markers that led Charles Darwin to his theory of evolution. What we see may well be the local equivalent of cormorants or herons."

"They look a bit large for that," I observed.

"With no competition, their size may well have increased," she hypothesized. "Or, indeed, they may be a species as yet undescribed by science." She smiled widely. "Isn't this exciting, Roger? We may be the first civilized people to ever have seen such birds." Her enthusiasm and delight made me smile.

We continued our climb, and finally achieved our objective. At the top of the cliff, the entire island was spread out before us. As the members of the first landing party had described, thick forests stretched away into the distance. I could see the rising smoke from the north-east that indicated some kind of human habitation. But none of that really caught my attention at the first; like the rest of the party, I was riveted by the central portion of the island.

"It really doesn't matter what the Tankerdons or the Coverleys decide to name this place," I murmured to Cecile. "It will have only one name to everyone—Skull Island."

Indeed, the central massif was a huge, rocky mountain reaching several hundred feet into the air. There were two large cave-like hollows that resembled eye sockets, and a rounded summit crowned with shrubs and trees. It seemed to me to be a warning of an eerie kind, threatening that anyone who ventured further would end in a similar state. I am not a superstitious man—as an engineer I firmly believe in the physical laws of Nature—but I felt a kind of preternatural premonition of death as I stared at this landscape. I could clearly see why the sailors from the first landing had been unnerved.

And then—from the depths of the thick jungle ahead of us—we heard a roar, one clearly made by some animal. It reverberated about, like the cry of a demon. There was a crashing sound at least a mile away from us, and we could see tremors in the trees there. Some creature—massive and certain of its own invulnerability—was passing through. I didn't have the experience to even guess what this might be, so I turned to one of the hunters. "What is that?" I asked. "A herd of elephants?"

He looked a little worried. "No, certainly not," he replied. "Whatever it is, it is an individual, and a very massive one at that." A smile touched his lips. "I think we should investigate." He took his rifle from his shoulder, and held it at the ready. It was clear that he was envisioning a trophy mounted on the wall of his Milliard City home.

"We stay together," the lieutenant reminded him. "By the time we reached that spot, whatever it is will have passed on, anyway." He glanced around. "We need to find a supply of water and establish a base camp, in case we get separated—one we can all find."

"We are on a slight rise here," Cecile pointed out. "Any water would flow away from us." She gestured ahead. "We will need to descend slightly to seek any pond or river."

"Indeed." The soldier gestured ahead. "This seems to be some sort of a game trail, and wildlife will always seek out water. If we follow it, we should be good." The hunters agreed with his thoughts, and so we plunged cautiously ahead.

Cecile could see that I was worried, and she touched my arm gently to reassure me. "We will be fine, my Roger. Why are you so concerned?"

"Because the last party was attacked almost immediately they reached the top of this trail," I reminded her. "It is unlikely we will get much further unchallenged."

My pessimism wasn't immediately rewarded (or punished!). While we could hear far-off cries and noises, it appeared that any local fauna was more cautious of us than we were of them. How long that situation would last, nobody could tell. We moved cautiously ahead, the soldiers and hunters with their weapons ready, and I kept fingering the gun in my own pocket. I stayed as close as propriety would allow to Cecile. She, of course, seemed oblivious to every possible threat, and was enthusiastically caught up in her adventure. From time to time she would give a delighted exclamation and pluck a flower, which she studied and then placed between the pages of a notebook that she carried. Some of these were rather pretty, whilst others were downright ugly—but, however they looked, she greeted each enthusiastically.

And then there was movement ahead of us. The local growths were more like immense ferns than actual trees, and they came in varying kinds and colors.

I am afraid I have little training in botany, and can barely tell a rose from a lily, so I had no idea what we were looking at, but Cecile, of course, was enthralled. Her knowledge of Science was broad, while mine is more specific. This (among other reasons) endeared us to one another.

She paused beside one immense fern, and pointed. "Something has been grazing on this," she observed. "That is, of course, unsurprising."

"Nature does not allow any potential food source to go to waste," I commented.

She smiled, prettily. "True. Observe the bite marks, though—they are about three to four feet from the ground, so whatever munched on this fern must hold its head at about that height. The marks are wide, suggesting a large head, with strong, blunt teeth." Her eyes sparkled. "Such a creature would not be interesting in biting anyone."

"If it has a large head," I suggested, "it is also a quadruped."

"Your reasoning?" she prompted.

"If it stood on its hind-legs, it would hold its head erect, and it would be the tallest part of its body. For it to be large but only three feet from the ground, it would need a substantial body to hold it erect. A three-foot tall body to hold a massive head would not be mechanically possible—therefore it must hold the head out horizontally, and therefore it is a quadruped."

"Fine reasoning," she approved. I basked in her approval, of course.

And we found one of the creatures a short while later. There was a rustling in the undergrowth, and that an unlikely beast emerged. It indeed moved on four feet, low to the ground, with a relatively small head held the requisite three feet from the ground. Its body was spectacularly muscular and its skin looked like leather armor. But what was most remarkable about the beast was its ferocious tail. Instead of tapering to a point, it was thick and ended in what appeared to be a mace-like appendage. The bony growth had a half-dozen spikes emerging from it and looked to be a formidable weapon indeed.

One of the Coverley hunters aimed his rifle and fired before we had time to even take all of this in. The sound of the shot was like a cannon being fired a few feet from my head, and I was utterly deafened for several moments. As the ringing started to fade, I could see that his shot had been effective. It had torn out a portion of the creature's throat. The poor beast expired as we watched, too stunned to say anything. Spraying blood all over the ferns, it collapsed and died.

Coverley seemed very proud of his brutality, and his companions—even the Tankerdon men—slapped his back and congratulated him. My dear Cecile was, of course, furious.

"Congratulations?" she cried, which silenced the hunters. "That poor creature was an ankylosaur—a herbivore. A ruminant!" From their bemused looks, she growled. "A plant-eater. Congratulations, Mr. Coverley—you've just bagged yourself a cow!"

Coverley had the grace to look—if you will pardon the expression—cowed. I could understand his reaction—there is not much glory for a hunter to claim a cow as his latest trophy! Not that I could comprehend why slaughtering any animal might be considered an achievement, of course. His body slumped slightly, until his companion slapped his back again.

"Or a deer," he said, cheerfully. "You've just bagged yourself the first deer on this island." Really, their self-congratulation was completely absurd! But it cheered the mighty Nimrod, and they immediately began discussing how they were going to get their trophy back to Standard Island. The lieutenant immediately informed them that his soldiers were there as guards and not as porters, and the four hunters were suddenly faced with the realization that they would not be able to transport an ankylosaur with them.

"Maybe just that tail," a Tankerdon suggested. They tried lifting this, but it had to weigh well over a hundred pounds, and they had to abandon even that plan. "It's a deuced shame we couldn't get a photographer to accompany us," the bright one sighed. "A picture, at least, with it would be superb."

Even had a photographer been insane enough to agree to accompany us, our hypothetical companion would have been of no avail. There was that huge roar again, but this time from far closer. The trees a mere three hundred feet from us shook, and a massive creature came lumbering into the open.

This one was a biped, standing on two massive, muscular legs and glaring in our direction. It stood almost thirty feet tall, snorting and opening and clenching two massive claws as it regarded us. It was covered in thick, warty skin and—to my utter astonishment, a crest of yellowish feathers that ran from its brow down its back to its tail. It glared at us again, and issued another of those terrifying roars.

"It's an allosaurus," Cecile said, gripping my arm tightly. "*This* one is certainly a carnivore."

The four hunters had all paused when this monster had appeared. The immense creature was incredibly intimidating, and it, too, had paused as it stared at us. Its head moved slightly from side to side and back and forward as it studied us—clearly assessing the possibility that we might be either a threat or potential prey. I did not like the thought of being cast in either role.

"Perhaps we should retreat slowly," I suggested. It was the wrong thing to say, as both Tankerdons and Coverleys seemed to take it as an insult to their prowess. They all raised their guns and took aim as the allosaur roared out its threat again.

I'm sure that these elephant guns are extremely effective against pachyderms; after all, they tend to be lumbering, and often docile in their behavior. Against a massive dinosaur, however, they were off far less use. The creature didn't even seem to notice them. Instead, it lunged forward, its huge head coming within a dozen feet of us. Terrifying as it was, what really struck my attention was that its breath stank terribly.

Even the hunters retreated from this threat, as they prepared to open fire again. I could not see that it would prove any more effective the second time around, but our eager quartet were clearly more optimistic than I was.

"Wait!" Cecile called, urgently. "You will only anger it—it is not attacking us."

"It certainly gives every evidence of it," a Tankerdon insisted.

"Retreat—slowly!" the lieutenant ordered. He gestured his men back. The militia members all had their rifles at the ready, but if the elephant guns were ineffectual, what chance did their lighter weapons have of stopping this monster? Reluctantly, the four hunters slowly fell back with the rest of us. The officer glanced behind, to make sure we were not being manipulated into a trap, and we slowly fell back, all eyes otherwise on the dinosaur. It had paused, and was watching us with an intent stare.

Then it lunged forward, and its immense, multi-toothed mouth fastened onto the still-bleeding form of the ankylosaur, and bit down, hard. We could hear the shattering of bones and the rending of flesh as we drifted back under cover.

"It's like a lion," Cecile explained. "They hunt when they must, but they do not pass up the opportunity to steal prey from other hunters. We should be safe enough now; after it has finished its meal, it will likely retreat to sleep it off."

We didn't stop until we had put what we felt was a safe distance between us and it, though. Then the lieutenant gathered the hunters. "It might be best to retreat to the launch," he suggested. "Your weapons seemed fairly ineffectual against that creature. And who knows how many more there are like that?"

"Or even worse," I muttered.

One of the Coverleys shook his head. "We can't go back without some sort of trophy," he insisted. "It is expected of us."

"Are you so worried about looking foolish that it's worth risking your lives for?" Cecile demanded.

"*All* our lives for?" I added. "Including that of a lady?"

He had the grace to look a little abashed—but was not about to surrender. "The rest of you may retreat if you wish," he said stiffly. "I shall continue until I have obtained my trophy."

The lieutenant scowled. "We cannot split up; I do not have enough men to protect two parties."

I glared at him. "You'd need an entire army, and cannons to boot, to protect us against another monster like that." I could see that my point had struck home. The pistol in my pocket would be as ineffectual as the elephant rifles had been; the militia's weapons would be of as little use.

Unexpectedly, my dear Cecile interrupted us. "The allosaurs is an apex predator," she commented. "It is the top of the food chain here. There cannot be many of them, because there would not be sufficient prey to feed a large number of them on an island—no matter its size. I do not think we are likely to encounter another of them in the near future." When the lieutenant still hesitated, she added: "In India, a single tiger has a hunting range of many miles, a range he will guard from other intruders. I have no doubt that our allosaurus will have very similar behavior. The fact that we have encountered one already suggests that there will be no more for quite some distance. And the one we *have* encountered has just feasted, so—with care—we should have no further trouble from it."

"See," the Coverley said. "Gal's got more sense than the rest of us."

Reluctantly, the lieutenant allowed himself to be persuaded. While I thought her reasoning was sound, I was not altogether convinced. After all, because one tiger keeps others out of its territory, it didn't mean that different predators were not present... But I could not bring myself to dispute her publically. She clearly wanted to go on, and I could understand this. I did not agree that it was a good idea, but I could understand it. Her devotion to the cause of scientific enquiry was her primary motivation for the moment, overwhelming her good sense. My own primary devotion at the moment was to survival—my own, naturally, but primarily hers. I could not bear the thought of those terrible teeth coming together on her lovely form. So, though far from convinced that our actions were a good idea, I accompanied her as we continued on our rather worrying way.

Cecile was correct in at least one matter: we saw neither that one allosaur nor any further ones that day. There was plenty of evidence of other beasts—spoor, sounds and cries—but we saw only hints of movement for the most part. One exception to this was when we sighted a small flock of what we initially took for birds. There were eight of them, flying high above the jungle.

"Pterosaurs," Cecile announced. "They are flying reptiles rather than birds. They are probably harmless, most likely fish-eaters. They are returning to their roots, most likely. The sun is getting low in the sky."

"And we need to find a suitable camping site," the lieutenant observed. "That is our priority right now."

We moved on, and found a good spot within twenty minutes. We found the small river that the game trail led to, with good, fresh, flowing water. Nearby was a hollow in the ground that would put a wall of earth and trees at our backs, and allow us to build a fire.

"If the local wildlife are all dinosaurs such as the ones we have seen, then they will likely sleep at night," Cecile observed. "Reptiles are cold-blooded, and need the warmth of the sun to stir themselves." It was a reasonable assumption—and, as it turned out, completely wrong. It would seem that a lot of what science thinks it knows about these prehistoric creatures is wrong, starting with the simple fact that they had not all died out millions of years ago, as has been supposed. We discussed the matter, but none of us could offer any plausible reason why these monsters had survived here, along, of all the places in the world. But survive they clearly had, and thrived.

Once we had established a safe camp, the sun had almost died out. The lieutenant sent up a green flare that should be easily observed, both by the launch and at the observatory on Standard Island, showing that we were safe—at least for the moment. We built up a good fire. As on many tropical islands, the air became quite cool once the sun had set, so this was helpful for warmth, although its primary function was to dissuade any nocturnal visitors, Cecile insisted that we would not have any, but the lieutenant agreed with me when I suggested that it would be wise to take reasonable precautions. We also agreed to a rotation of guards. It was swiftly decided that at no time would one person be left alone, given the potential dangers of this island. Watching would be performed by teams of two. As we had six soldiers, four hunters, the lieutenant and myself, it was decided that Cecile should not need to take a turn on guard. She protested that she wished to share the hardships, but was overruled in the matter.

Some of you may wonder how we arranged matters of hygiene, given that she was the only woman and we were never to be alone. My answer is that I would never wish to cause embarrassment to a woman I value more than any other, and will say no more.

The lieutenant and I took the first watch, as the others settled to sleep. Cecile was bedded down close by me, and I observed her try to rest. But she was far too excited by what we had seen, and it was clear that she would get very little sleep this night. I could not blame her—I was uncertain that I would be able to relax enough to sleep myself—though in my case through apprehension and not excitement.

As she had predicted, some of the jungle noises died down as night deepened. But there were, from time to time, sharp cries and still rustlings and even a few crashing sounds in the darkness. There was no moon, but the stars were scattered brightly across the sky above us. There was still that omnipresent fog, of course, but it clung to the shore and waters, leaving the vast hemisphere over our heads crystal clear. The Milky Way sprawled above us, and stars spread like freckles away from it. If there were not the potential danger all around us, it would have been one of the most beautiful places on this Earth of ours. In view of the close presence of my dear Cecile, I trust I can be forgiven thinking that under other circumstances it would have been the perfect spot for a honeymoon.

And then came a roaring sound, far off in the jungle, to remind me that there were no guarantees we would survive all of this beauty.

To my great surprise, I did manage to get some rest after my spell of duty was over. I think that I had been so emotionally drained that I badly needed rest. In the morning, rested and refreshed, we prepared to set out again. Cecile, too, had eventually fallen asleep, and was eager to make further discoveries. She had brought a notebook with her, and had detailed our adventures thus far, decorated with rather accurate drawings of the allosaurus and ankylosaur, along with the pressed flowers she had collected. Our hunters, of course, were all eager to kill something—anything—preferably something that they could bring some trophy from back to our island.

Some of my fears had vanished in the night, though I was far from complacent. I began to envy the hunters for their elephant rifles, though purely for self-defense. After a short breakfast from our rations, the lieutenant gave the order for us to move on.

"We will return here by evening," he stated firmly. "And if, somehow, any of us get separated from the rest, they should make their way back here, where the remainder of us will wait for them. But I want you all to strive as hard as possible to remain together."

"We're not likely to be able to bag anything if we're all tramping through this jungle side by side," one of the Coverleys argued.

"I understand that, Mr. Coverley," the lieutenant agreed firmly. "But I am certain you would prefer to be the hunter and not the hunted. Keep one other man in your sight at all times."

We moved out; I stayed beside Cecile, determined to protect her to the best of my ability. It was still early, so she believed that most of the local fauna would not be stirring until the day was more advanced. Sadly, she proved to be incorrect. We had all slipped into the assumption that since we were in a land where dinosaurs had somehow survived into the modern age—against all odds—that the local wildlife consisted solely of these antediluvian reptiles. The idea that other beasts unknown to modern science might co-exist with dinosaurs simply never occurred to anyone—then.

I cannot, even now, explain how this situation could have arisen—nor how it had somehow survived for millions of years in stagnation while the rest of the world had changed so drastically. I simply had to accept that it had. We had neglected one truly obvious point that occurred to us only afterwards—we knew that the island contained people, even though we had not seen any, because we could see the smoke from their fires on the far side of the island. The most obvious cause for their being here was that some of the natives who had spread to other islands in the South Seas had made their way at some point to this island.

We did not extrapolate from this to the idea that other creatures might also have made their way here long after the dinosaurs.

Our first clue that our reasoning was askew was the discovery of bones. We came across a collection of them in an offshoot from the game trail we were following. It was clear that they were from more than thirty animals. Some were intact, but most had been cracked open to allow some creature to eat the marrow. This had resulted in the scattering of remains, making it impossible to be certain how many bodies we were looking at.

"Victims of the allosaurus," one of the hunters suggested.

"Unlikely," Cecile judged. "These bones have been broken and chewed—the allosaurus would not have been so fastidious." She shook her head. "It would have crushed the bones, not broken them. Something smaller—but equally vicious—did this. Perhaps a small pack of carnivorous dinosaurs…" He voice trailed off as she examined the scattered bones. "These victims are of differing ages—this is a feasting ground. The predator dragged the bodies here to consume them, rather as a big cat would do in Africa. It has been in use for a considerable length of time."

Another of the hunters scowled. "Then perhaps we shouldn't linger and give whatever did this fresh prey?"

"Quite right," the lieutenant agreed. "Let's move on."

"One moment," Cecile begged. She had discovered a skull that had been picked clean, but was relatively intact. "This did not belong to any form of dinosaur. Look at the shape of it—almost human, in fact, but not human…"

She was correct—it was considerably larger than a human skull, but there were distinct similarities. But the brow was flattened, and the ridges above the eyes protruded considerably. The lower jaw was missing, but, based on the portion of skull she had, would have been large. "Grinding molars," she murmured. "This creature was primarily a plant-eater…"

"And, judging by the size of the skull, about twice the size of a man," I pointed out. "Whatever killed it must have been very powerful, then." The hunters clearly liked the sound of that, as it promised them good "sport" . I glanced around, somewhat nervously. "It might be lingering in this vicinity."

"Unlikely," Cecile replied, with infuriating calmness. "First of all, animals would avoid the stink of death about this spot. And second… These bones have all been picked clean. That can't have happened overnight, so all of them must have been here a considerable length of time. The predator involved either moved on…"

"Or…?" I prompted.

"Or it was slain by some larger predator…"

I can't say that thought cheered me at all. Even the hunters started to look a little nervous. They were her to kill, and not to be killed, after all. We managed to persuade Cecile to move on—reluctantly—although she wanted to bring the skull with her. I talked her out of it, as it looked to be fairly heavy, and we didn't yet know how stressful the day would be. I promised her that we could return to the spot before we returned to our camp in the evening, and she could collect it again then. She regretfully gave in.

As we continued our way, she said softly: "That skull belonged to some form of ape."

I frowned. "Like a gorilla?"

"Perhaps. I am not sufficiently skilled enough to determine that."

"But gorillas are found only in the depth of Africa," I pointed out. "And we are in the South Seas. How could a gorilla make its way here?"

"How could an allosaur?" she countered. "And yet, here they are. Besides, there are tales out of Java and other islands of the existence of an ape they call the orang utan—and Java is considerably closer to us than Africa."

She did have a point. “Then it may be that other creatures than dinosaurs inhabit this island?” I suggested.

“Clearly,” she agreed. “And to have survived with allosaurus as its predator would suggest that it is very strong—and capable.”

“You make the hunt we are on sound less appealing by the minute,” I commented.

She looked at me in surprise. “You are not excited by all of this, Roger?”

“I’d be more excited if it didn’t endanger your life, my dear Cecile.”

She patted my hand, like a mother reassuring a worried child. “We have several very able protectors,” she said.

“And several rather nasty predators,” I countered.

“You worry too much, my dear friend,” she said, but she took the sting from this criticism by favoring me with a dazzling smile.

The morning’s hunt did not favor our killers of wildlife. We saw nothing but smaller creatures, diminutive versions of allosaurs, and more far-off pterosaurs. Our four mighty Nimrods were getting frustrated—more so when the lieutenant pointed out to them that we were due back at the launch the following day, with or without trophies. None of them wished to admit failure, of course, so they started to take rather foolish chances. Several times the lieutenant had to call to them, reminding them not to lose sight of one another. The only happy person among us was my dear Cecile. She found pleasure in everything from the flora to even the insects. That the hunters had shot no prey was also a pleasure to her.

“It is not right for us to slay these dwellers in this Eden,” she commented.

I stared at her in puzzlement. “They slay one another,” I pointed out. “And this seems to me far from any sort of Eden.”

“They hunt for food,” she replied. “They hunt to live. They do not kill merely to boast of their prowess, and to hack body parts from some defenseless creatures to display as a trophy. They are innocent; it is only Man who murders.”

“You know I agree with you on that point,” I said. “Which is why I shall be glad to leave this island—which is far removed from Eden as far as I am concerned.”

After a brief recess for lunch, though, the hunt continued. We were almost at the point where the lieutenant was about to announce that we must turn about and return to our camp—I saw him glancing at his pocket-watch—when one of the Tankerdons gave a soft exclamation, and motioned for silence. He had clearly detected some sign I hadn’t that indicated there might be trophy material ahead of us. He gestured to his companions, who examined something on the ground and nodded in agreement. Silently, they spread apart. The lieutenant motioned to his militia to be on the alert, but we all remained silent. I stood even closer to Cecile, who seemed torn between fascination and repulsion. As we moved slowly forwards, I stole a glance at the ground the hunters had examined.

The soil was soft there, and I saw a partial print. I didn't have the experience to know what had caused it, but it was slightly filled with water. I assumed that meant that it was relatively fresh. It was merely one print; I could see no more, but in this tangle of a jungle that was hardly surprising. It was only luck that had left this one exposed—bad luck for the prey, but good for the hunters.

It was impossible to guess what we were tracking. Clearly, something large, but more than that I did not know. The hunters would not be interested if it were not substantial, ornamental or dangerous. Or, perhaps, they were just being hopeful.

Then two of them, slightly ahead of the main party, suddenly opened fire into the bush ahead and slightly to the side of us. A great cry followed, and then a crashing sound. Whatever they had fired at was moving—not away from us, but towards. I gripped Cecile tightly, and we saw the target creature crash from the trees.

It was some kind of great ape, though of an immense size. It was roaring, and thumping its chest in a display of rage. I could see that there was a fresh wound, bleeding profusely, in one shoulder, but it hardly seemed to bother the creature. It was bent over, and crashing through the brush, so its true size was difficult to determine, but it had to be at least twenty or thirty feet tall if it stood upright—far, far larger than any such creature yet discovered in the wild.

As it roared and charged us, the hunters all opened fire at once. The elephant guns made a tremendous sound, momentarily rivaling that of the creature. It staggered as all four shots crashed into it; it was so large that even I could not have failed to hit it. It roared again, but this time there was a catch in its voice, and it stumbled, falling to a crouching position. Once more, the hunters fired, and this time there was silence following the blasts.

The beast was down, bleeding profusely. Supine, it seemed to be even larger than I had imagined. I was in awe, and shock, staring at the dead creature. Even the killers seemed to pause as they regarded the fruits of their action.

And then there was another roar—from the spot the ape had been, and a *second* monster came charging at us. Even our mighty hunters were caught by surprise. They hadn't had a chance to reload their elephant guns, though they struggled to do so as they scattered. The second ape threw itself at us. The lieutenant gave a cry, and his men all fired at this second beast, but their rifle shots lacked the power of the hunters' guns. The animal barely paused, and then employed one immense hand to grip the closest hunter. It crushed the man as he screamed in agony, and then, abruptly, went silent. The ape threw the shattered body aside and reached for another hunter.

I admit it—I was frankly terrified. This second monster appeared to be unstoppable. To my credit, I hope, I was more afraid for my beautiful companion than for myself. I considered the pistol in my pocket, and then discarded the idea. If the rifle fire couldn't halt the beast, a pistol bullet would barely be more than an insect bite to it. Instead, I grabbed Cecile and dragged her aside, out of the way of the monster's charge.

As we plunged into the undergrowth, the sounds behind us grew louder. We heard men screaming, the great ape roaring—and then came the reverberating cry of the allosaur. "That dinosaur is smart," I gasped as we ran. "It has realized that it can rob the hunters of their prey."

"It allows them to hunt on its own behalf," Cecile agreed. "It is clearly no mere dumb brute."

I suddenly realized that we were plunging in roughly the direction from which the two apes had come. And it was not by accident, but because Cecile was steering us. "Why are we going this way?" I gasped, trying to ignore the cries and crashes from behind us.

"The safest place to be is where those beasts are not," she replied. That didn't sound convincing to me, but I had little breath left to argue the point. There was clearly a real battle in progress behind us—along with the roars, there were also occasional gunshots, including the boom of the elephant rifles. I rather suspected that the hunters were no longer very interested in collecting trophies, merely in staying alive. It was an aim I could fully share.

And then we broke into a small clearing, and we both stopped, our feet rooted to the ground in amazement. As I said, I am not really a biologist, but I have done some reading in the matter—enough so that I could understand what we were looking at.

The gorillas of Africa make themselves beds from local plants in which to rest at night. This area was clearly where the two great apes had been before they had been roused by the hunters. A sizeable area had been filled with bedding material, and this had been flattened in place by the immense weight of the apes.

It was still occupied.

There was a *third* ape.

I grasped Cecile protectively, but she tried to shrug me off. I was scared for her, this close to another of the brutes.

"Idiot," she snapped. "It's a *baby*."

I started at the animal, which was roughly our own size, and not the monster the others—obviously its parents—were. But it was still a man-sized ape, and thus potentially very dangerous. But Cecile was clearly correct; for those great apes, this was obviously very small, and therefore young. Probably *very* young.

"We had better move on," I said, fingering the pistol in my pocket.

Cecile looked back to where the battle had been ongoing. "They were just trying to protect their child," she murmured. The roaring had stopped by now, and a very uneasy quiet had settled over the area. There were still sounds of something moving, which I suspected was the dinosaur eating its prey. "They gave their lives to save him." She straightened up. "We have to make sure it was not in vain."

"What are you talking about?" I asked in horror. "We must return to our campsite. We should get off this island as soon as possible. If anyone else has survived this massacre, they will meet us there."

"Roger," she said, urgently, "if those obsessed hunters find this child, they will seek to kill it. *This* is one trophy that they could take back with them. We have to make certain that they cannot find it. The sacrifice of its parents should not be in vain." All this time, she was moving closer to the young ape.

It was staring at us, but it didn't seem concerned. It was probably too young to realize that its parents were dead, and it didn't seem aggressive. Even in my confused state I could recall that apes, on the whole, are peaceful creatures, and this was still a child—practically an infant. Maybe it wasn't altogether dangerous. But the rest of this island was.

"We have to go back," I insisted. "We have no means to protect ourselves, let alone an ape." She frowned. "Your safety is paramount to me," I said.

"I won't leave this poor creature," she replied, firmly.

"You are not thinking clearly," I informed her. "You'll come back with me, even if I have to carry you." I was fully prepared to follow through on my threat. Her life was more precious to me than my own.

Her face softened. "My dearest Roger," she said. "I do understand you, and, believe me, I truly appreciate your desire to protect me. But we stand no chance of getting back at all on our own. We have to go back and see if anyone else has survived, and then group together for protection."

I could see the logic in what she said, and it made me pause. "But it is dangerous to return," I said.

She gave a brittle laugh. "At this moment, my dear, it is dangerous to do *anything*. We have to look for other survivors—it is our best chance. Come." She reached for my hand.

"No," I said, firmly. "Stay here and stay hidden." I eyed the infant in the nest. "I don't believe you're in danger from that creature, but if the allosaurus is still around…" I shuddered.

"My brave Roger," she breathed, and gave me a quick, gentle kiss. Even despite our peril, I thrilled at the touch of her lips. "I shall remain hidden," she promised.

I gave her one last look before setting out. The sun broke through the clouds, and her blonde hair was dazzling in the light. She looked so angelic in that moment, and I loved her all the more.

Then I turned, and plunged back over the path we had taken. I was almost intoxicated, and this stifled my more immediate fears. Still, I remained cautious, listening for any sound that the battle we had fled was still ongoing. There were occasional sounds, but diminishing in intensity. I was almost back at the attack site, and proceeded with greater caution. I crept through the bushes to see what was happening.

It had been a slaughter. The body of one of the apes was still there, with great teeth-marks having ripped the flesh apart. There were human bodies—and body parts—as well, but it was impossible to gauge how many. And there was a cleared pathway, evidently where the allosaurus had dragged the body of the other great ape to dine on it in a more secluded spot. Trees were flattened and shattered, and there were pools of stinking blood and entrails all over. It was a scene out of one of Dante's or Gustave Doré's nightmares.

But it appeared to be our best chance of fleeing. Scavengers would undoubtedly start to emerge shortly, and in this horrific place it was likely that the scavengers would be large and deadly in their own right. It was time to move.

There was the broken, bleeding body of one of the Coverleys close to me. His elephant rifle lay in the grass close by his body. I had never fired such a weapon, but simply carrying it would make me feel safer—even if I wasn't; it had done its former owner little good, after all. I collected the heavy gun, and gingerly took the bag of cartridges for it from the poor unfortunate.

As I turned to go back for Cecile, I had a sudden moment of terror as I saw movement in the bushes, but this passed when I realized that it was the lieutenant and one of his soldiers. My heart started to slow again, and I took a deep breath. "Are you all that survive?" I asked in a shaky voice.

The lieutenant nodded, wearily. "The others were all killed," he said. I could hear pain in his voice, and his left shoulder was a mess of caking blood. "And Miss DuBois?"

"She is safe," I replied. "I came to check for survivors. We can return to her –"

And there came the most dreadful scream from the direction in which I had left my beloved. Terror gripped me, and I whirled and ran, faster than I knew was possible for me. The other two men followed behind as swiftly as they could, but I outpaced them and reached the apes' nesting area in moments.

At first I saw nothing—Cecile and the ape were visible nowhere. Confused, I looked about, and then saw the most horrifying sight yet.

Cecile's pretty dress lay in the bushes, torn, and splattered with fresh blood. It was instantly clear that either the ape or some other predator had attacked her. I recall screaming her name, but there was no response. The realization that I had failed her, that she had been butchered on this island of horror, closed in upon me. A vast wave of agony and despair settled over my brain.

The lieutenant and his remaining man saved me from plunging into the jungle in search of Cecile. They may have tried to reason with me, or they may have been forced to subdue me; I cannot say. My mind was clouded, my despair bottomless. I can recall nothing after my discovery until I became aware that I was back in Milliard City, in the infirmary, being treated for numerous cuts and grazes. I cannot tell you how I became injured, nor how I had made the journey back.

I was still in shock and depression. The only thing that registered in my fevered brain was that Cecile was dead, and I had failed her. Later, Calistus Mumbar informed me that I had been in a delirious state for almost three weeks. The island's doctor had treated my obvious injuries, but there had been little he could do about my mental state. Gradually, though, I had regained some semblance of rationality. Though I was in horrible emotional pain, I was mostly numb. It was as if the fog surrounding Skull Island had settled in my brain. Eventually, though, I started to emerge from my stupor and to be able to think rationally again.

Calistus came to see me; apparently he had been doing this at least once a day since I had been brought in, though I could not recall any of his kind visits. He showed great concern for my well-being, and was pleased to see that I was capable of rational thought once more. "We are back on course for the tamer islands," he informed me. "There was a memorial service for those poor souls who were left on Skull Island, and it was decided by the council—unanimously!—that we will not report our stay there in any way. We would not wish any further deaths that would follow to be on our consciences. That place was forgotten by the passing of time, and it will hopefully be also forgotten by us."

"Not by me," I responded, dully. "I can never forget that terrible place—nor the sweet angel who was slain there."

"That is understandable," he replied gently, touching my shoulder in sympathy. "I am aware of how attached you and Mademoiselle DuBois had become to one another, and to have lost her in such a fashion…" He shook his head, solemnly. "But your life must go on. You must make plans for the future."

"Why?" I asked, bitterly. "What is there for me now?"

"Miss DuBois has a family," he said. "We have wired the news of her demise, but that is so impersonal. The council wishes to send a representative to deliver their deepest regrets and respects; I urge you to volunteer to agree to be their messenger."

I couldn't make a decision at that stage, but in a matter of days I could see that this was probably a good idea, and I finally agreed. There was no way that I could return to my former work now—the thought of making trivial games to entertain the rich people of Milliard City disgusted me—and being the bearer of such a message would give me something to anticipate, at the least. And although I could never see my beloved Cecile again, the thought of seeing those members of the family from which she had sprung seemed to have a certain appeal.

Of course, it was a considerable while before I could reach her home village in France. I was taken from Standard Island on one of the supply ships that delivered provisions to the floating island. This vessel transferred me back to

San Diego, and from there I took a train to New York City. In that metropolis, I booked passage on the *France*, a journey of almost two weeks to the country that had named it. It was another several days before I reached Cecile's home town.

As you can imagine, this journey had given me several weeks to think. I confess that I spent a good deal of those days in wallowing in my emotions, and in the feelings of grave loss and in thinking over what I should have done—could have done!—to save my beloved. It was all futile, of course, but as anyone who has experienced loss can tell you, it was also unavoidable.

Eventually, though, I stood outside the neat little house in the sweet little town where Cecile had been born and grew up. It took me a little while to work up the nerve to knock on that door. The family greeted me with a kindness and sympathy that I felt I did not deserve. They insisted that I stay with them for however long I could, and their kindness touched me deeply. Somehow, they did not blame me for their loss—though I blamed myself constantly. They treated me as almost a member of their family from the start. Her elderly parents were desolate, of course, but so kind and caring. The only other member of the family was a younger sister, Madeleine. She was two years Cecile's junior, and as dark as her sister had been fair. The sisters had been very close, and Cecile had written to her often—many of her letters including references to me.

"I feel as though I know you well, Roger," she confided in me one day in the small garden of the house. "She painted a very vivid picture of you."

I admitted that, thanks to their generosity, I felt a similar attachment to the whole family.

"May I ask you, then, to do something that may prove to be painful to you?" she asked.

"I will do whatever I can," I promised her.

"Then, tell me—how certain are you that my sister did indeed perish on that horrible island?" She reached out to touch my hand gently. "I know how this question must affect you, but I ask that you be brave and answer me."

"I am certain," I informed her. "I… found her dress…" I broke off. "Madeleine, you should not hear this!"

"Be brave, Roger, and I shall be also. Go on!"

"It had been torn and bloodied." I closed my eyes, trying to blot out the memory but, of course, instead replaying it in my mind.

"And that is all?"

"All?" I stared at her in astonishment. "What more would you wish? Her torn and partially-devoured corpse?'

"Forgive me," she insisted. "I know how hard this must be for you. And the images of my sister…" She shuddered. "But—there was no body? Nor parts of a body?"

I stared at her as if she was a ghoul. "I should not wish there to have been!"

"Nor I, truly," she admitted. "But… I do not believe that Cecile is dead."

"What?" I stared at her in confusion. "But I saw…"

"What you saw was a torn and bloodied dress," Madeleine said firmly. "Forgive me, my dear Roger, but you are, after all, rather naïve. Cecile found this rather endearing and amusing about you."

"What are you saying?" I demanded.

She stood up, and then, to my confusion and embarrassment, she raised the hem of her skirt some six inches, showing off a very pretty ankle and a mess of underskirts. "Tell me, my dear friend—how is it that whatever monster was supposed to have devoured her managed to remove her dress and shred it but not to have removed her slips, her stockings or her shoes?"

I confess that I was completely dumbfounded. "But… but… What are you suggesting?"

She sighed. "I am suggesting that my sister led you to believe what she wished of you—that she had been killed."

"But… but *why* should she wish that?" I couldn't follow this reasoning at all.

"Since she was very young, Cecile has always had a strong affection for animals of all kinds. Especially for those who were injured or had other needs." She smiled, gently. "She even found a merchant beating his horse one day and snatched the whip from his hand and beat *him* It was not easy for my father to keep her out of trouble for that."

"What has this to do with her death?"

"Her *supposed* death," Madeleine corrected me. "You have told me that she was afraid that the hunters would target the ape child. Knowing how impulsive and protective she was, I think she quickly improvised a plan to do her best to ensure it would have a chance to live."

"But… but that would be dangerously foolish," I protested.

"It would be my sister."

I stared at her in shock. "You mean that she would *deliberately* allow me to think that she was dead—and that it was my fault—in order to save a monkey?"

"I am afraid so." She reached for my hand and gripped it firmly. "Cecile was not quite the angel you imagine her to be. She was always so beautiful, and she tended to trade on this a great deal in order to get people to give her what she wished. She was fond of you, Roger, but she did not love you. I shall not share her letters with you, but she mentions that you are hopelessly a romantic, and quite easily led."

This was a great deal for me to take in, and I instinctively wished to reject it. Madeleine was wise, and she allowed me time. Eventually, I came to realize that she knew her sister far better than I had, and that the scenario she had described did indeed adhere to the facts.

"If it is possible that she is alive," I said, a few days later, "then I should return to Skull Island and search her out."

"That would be foolish—and impossible," Madeleine informed me. "You do not know where the lost island even is."

"Commodore Simcoe knows. The inhabitants of Standard Island know—well, some of them, at least."

"And have vowed never to reveal the information," she pointed out. "And, besides—you have not been following the news, my dear friend, have you?" She touched my hand again. "Do you even know how long you have been here with us?"

I blinked, and tried to recall. "Well, several months, I imagine." I felt a rush of guilt. "Am, I imposing upon you all?"

"Do not imagine that for a moment, Roger." She smiled. "There are some in this house who would be happy indeed if you were never to leave." And she blushed slightly at that remark. "But you have been here a full year."

"A year!" I exclaimed. It did not seem possible.

"Yes, a year. And it is reported that Standard Island is no more. It has sunk in the deep waters of the Pacific."

"And—my friends? Calistus Mumbar? Commodore Simcoe?" I was seized with shock. I had wallowed in my own grief, completely neglecting them.

"I do not know, but we can undoubtedly find out," she replied. "But—with the island itself gone, and the survivors scattered, it is highly unlikely that you can ever rediscover the location of Skull Island. We must leave my sister to whatever fate she has chosen for herself."

It was a little while before the import of all this news sank in for me. Eventually, though, I felt the overwhelming guilt lifted from my soul, and the affection I had felt towards Cecile… Well, it was not gone, but it was tempered. I began to see her in a slightly different light.

And Madeleine in a very different light…

So—why do I write this memoir now, some fifteen years after my dear wife and I were married? Why do I disrupt our very happy home and make arrangements for our children to have a guardian to look after them and to help out with my beloved in-laws?

Because news has reached us from America. An American film-maker, Carl Denham, has just returned from an undisclosed location in the South Seas, bringing with him what he bills as the Eighth Wonder of the World. (I cannot but wonder if he is related to Calistus Mumbar!)

Rumor has it that it is an ape of unusual size…

Did someone break their word and reveal the existence of Skull Island?

And is there word of a beautiful blonde from that island?

The green-masked Fantômas who starred in a trilogy of French films of the 1960s (starring Jean Marais and Louis de Funès) and owed more to the James Bond movies than the original dark-clad psychopath from Allain & Souvestre's novels, has not been entirely ignored in Tales of the Shadowmen. *We featured him in "The Sincerest Form of Flattery" (Vol. 7) and Nathan Cabaniss used him in "From Paris With Hate" (Vol. 13). It is a joy to see Frank Schildiner re-launch the character in yet another inimitable homage to those 1960s crazy pop art spy films...*

Frank Schildiner: *Only One...*

1966

The telephone buzzed over and over, nobody having picked up the line for the twelfth or thirteenth time. The hand gripping the receiver with white-knuckle intensity shook as the harsh ringing continued.

Replacing the phone to its cradle, Brain Ian "Boysie" Oakes ran a hand across his face. He felt the sheen of cold sweat that covered his skin which he knew came entirely from the growing terror in his heart.

"Where are you, Griffith?" he asked to his empty hotel room, "Where are you, damnit?"

The words of Colonel Mostyn, the erstwhile number two in the secret agency known as the Department of Special Security, returned to him as the echoes of his frantic question died away.

"Action, Boysie, action," the aging former military man said as he slid a folder forward. "We have a lead on none other than the Lord of Terror himself, Fantômas."

"Fantômas?" Boysie asked as he glanced at the pages with a sinking heart, "I thought he was a load of codswallop made up by the Frenchies."

Mostyn, who rarely smiled, grinned quickly and guffawed quietly.

"It does feel that way, does it not? A masked man who steals jewels and other rubbish. Rather ridiculous."

"Yes," Boysie said with a sheepish grin.

Colonel Mostyn slapped an open hand down on his wooden tabletop, sending several pens flying in the air.

"Ridiculous or not, Fantômas is real, deadly, and announced he plans on stealing the Crown Jewels! The Crown Bloody Jewels! Plonkers like Inspector Grice are running about chasing their backsides in hopes of a clue! Interpol sent Inspector Zenigata, and the French offered the services of their two greatest experts on Fantômas and others of his ilk. Would you have the Crown Jewels of our country saved by Commissioner Juve III and Inspector Clouseau of the bloody Sûreté? Would you, L?"

"Of course not," Boysie said, straightening and placing an offended look upon his aging, handsome, face.

Mostyn nodded and tapped the folder.

"We found his latest identity, impersonating Sir Charles Lytton, by the purest chance. His Lordship will be attending a special dinner in Nice in two days. Arrangements were made. A rifle will be in your room. Kill him, with a shot or two to the head. End this plague before he even reaches our shores."

Realizing he only had hours, Boysie reached for the telephone again. He needed Charlie Griffith again; requiring the undertaker turned assassin for such a delicate duty.

"Fantômas! If I miss, he'll roast me over a slow flame… If I don't kill him, Colonel Bloody Mostyn will have me tossed in a hole and throw away the hole…" he thought and clutched his shaking hands together.

A knock on the door followed, with a second knock following a moment later. A key rattled in the lock and the door slowly opened. A feminine backside covered in a black skirt emerged, followed by a large cart.

"*Service, Monsieur*," a gentle feminine voice said.

The woman who stepped around the door was tall, with thick golden blond hair, large blue eyes, and plump pink lips. Dressed in a French maid's outfit, she was a lovely, if completely unexpected, sight. She curtsied daintily and smiled; her eyes downcast as she looked up at Boysie through thick, pale lashes.

"*Pardonnez-moi*," she said and giggled.

Boysie, who was never one to let a little terror get in the way of the ladies, smiled broadly. Forgetting even his rudimentary French, grinned widely and waved her inside.

"Feel free to clean anything you want, miss."

"Oh, you are English!" she said, "How wonderful!"

"Yes, I am," Boysie said and asked, "Why is that wonderful?"

"Because I was afraid I had the wrong room again," she said and pointed her feather duster at Oakes.

A sound like gas escaping emerged from the cleaning wand and Boysie felt a sharp pain in his neck. Reaching for his throat, he pulled free a small dart just as a cold numbness flowed down his torso.

"Do not worry, Boysie darling," the lovely blond maid said, "that was just a drug that shall send you into a peaceful sleep. Fantômas wishes to have a conversation with you in his home…"

Boysie Oakes collapsed backwards onto the bed as the darkness fell over him like a heavy, chilled blanket.

Boysie's eyes slowly opened and he sat upright, glancing left and right. He lay upon a simple metal cot in a rectangular chamber that appeared chipped out of the bedrock of the earth. A steel door lay a few feet away and a pair of large blue eyes gazed through the opened peep hole. With a heavy snap of the lock, the door silently swung open, revealing his captor. Though she was transformed. No longer garbed in the titillating maid's outfit, she wore a form-fitting yellow jumpsuit. Her thick hair lay atop her head in a complex weave and she held a small Luger pistol in one fist.

"Good evening, Boysie darling," she said, her accent sounding vaguely Germanic now. "Did you have a nice nap? Such a wonderful curare mixture with no headache or illness later."

Boysie grunted, disgusted that he fell so easily for such an obvious trap. He knew that women would be his downfall, but somehow when they looked like this one…

"Now, now," she said, "do not grumble and complain. We are in the same business, after all. You are the premiere assassin and agent of the British. I am a professional who rank second only after the legendary Scaramanga. We must be nice to each other. After all, I could be a good friend to you…"

"Oh?" he asked and licked his lips nervously, "How?"

Pulling the cell door closed, she pocketed the gun, and reached for the zipper to her jumpsuit.

"I think we shall find a way," she said, "My name, since you never asked, is Irma Eckman."

Boysie smiled and reached for her.

"Nice to meet you, Irma, I'm…"

Irma Eckman placed a carefully manicured finger across his lips.

"I know, now shut up and show me why British agents are considered… special…"

Irma handed Boysie his missing sock and said, "Hurry up, we must not be late."

Boysie closed his eyes, feeling heat and electric tingles across his face. His mouth spread in a wide smile, a fear response that others took as anger and violent amusement. Having such a reaction was the reason Boysie Oakes was the United Kingdom's top assassin despite being afraid of the sight of blood.

"Do not be angry, dear Boysie," Irma said, touching his arm, "I shall ask the master to spare your life."

Boysie grunted again, rose and followed Irma from the cell. They entered a stone corridor with five other closed cell doors and a small, two-person elevator at the end. Entering the elevator, Irma pressed the only button within, and the chamber rose swiftly, opening a moment later.

The room they entered was an octagonal in shape, with stone walls, comfortable steel chairs with leather padding, and a large teardrop shaped yellow plastic desk. There were rows of black metal switches across the plastic surface and a round chair with red velvet padding sat behind the desk.

"Where are we?" Boysie asked, gazing across the odd area.

A wall slid aside, and a deep voice said, "Marseille, Mister Oakes. Not very far from where the delightful Miss Eckman easily captured you today."

A man stepping into view was tall, broad shouldered, dressed in a perfectly cut dark suit with white shirt and red silk tie. He walked with a silent, uncanny, feline grace and lowered himself into the chair behind the desk.

Oh, and his face and voice were that of Boysie Oakes. He grinned widely at the stunned expression upon the British agent's face, tenting his fingers.

"You," Boysie said, "You… you are…"

"Fantômas, yes, I am aware," Fantômas said, "I simply resemble you thanks to my inventive genius. You see, I shall steal the English Crown Jewels, but I shall do so with your face. I shall transform you from the secret weapon of the English, to their worst pariah. Then, after your name is reviled in every part of the world, I shall release you into the world."

Boysie Oakes shook his head and said, "Nobody would believe it. Everyone knows your tricks, Fantyman."

"Fantômas," the false Oakes said, "and they shall believe it when I reveal that I replaced you months ago. People shall believe you are me and every spy, law enforcement officer, and criminal shall hunt you down. By the time they discover the truth, I shall have committed several more robberies in Paris and the Soviet Union."

"You know nothing about me!" Boysie said, playing for time and edging a little closer to Irma.

Fantômas flicked a switch and a box emerged from the desk's interior to the surface. A red folder lay within and he flicked the cover open with one gloved finger.

"Brian Ian Oakes, Major in the Army of the United Kingdom and codename L for Liquidator employed by the Department of Special Security. You are better known by the rather ridiculous nickname of Boysie…"

"Boysie, tee hee," Irma said, glancing at him and giggling.

"Your actions are impressive, having spoiled many operations conducted by Soviet intelligence. Destroying you shall be as effective an action as Philby, MacLean, and Burgess's betrayals. The British intelligence shall be in disarray for a decade," Fantômas said.

"Not today, Fanty!" Boysie said as he sprang forward and ripped the gun from Irma's jumpsuit and shoved her aside.

Fantômas flicked a switch on his desk and his chair began sinking into the stone floor. Boysie fired twice, the bullets striking the false Oakes in the chest, sending him sprawling backwards with a cry. He fell down the hole that swallowed his chair, vanishing from sight.

Irma stared at him with wide eyes, her arms reaching for him.

"Oh, Boysie! You did it! You killed the monster! Take me away with you! The third switch on the right opens an elevator that leads to the surface!"

"No thank you, Miss Eckman. You weren't that good in bed," he said and shot her once in the chest.

Flicking the switch on the desk, Boysie dashed into the elevator as it opened and vanished from sight. The room lay still and silent for several minutes until a bell lightly chimed. Irma Eckman sat upright and stretched like a waking cat.

"He is gone," she said as Fantômas, still wearing the Boysie Oakes mask, vaulted from the opening in the floor.

"Well done, Miss Eckman," Fantômas said, ripping free the Oakes mask and revealing the green false face he wore daily. "You earned a bonus from your conduct. You may also tell your employer, Mr. Peterson, that I owe him a debt for granting your assistance."

Irma rose and dropped into a chair, crossing one leg as she said, "I do not comprehend why you went to so much trouble. The gun with blanks, the false blood packs. Oakes is an oaf, but he will receive renown for defeating you. You cannot steal the jewels and this base shall be compromised."

"That is the very essence of my plan, my dear. First, this base is not mine. The previous owners moved to an island where they toil daily upon a weather control machine. Second, I never sought the British crown jewels. They are useless to me and it would be far more work selling them than they're worth. However, those are unimportant details. The reason for this farce was Oakes himself."

"Boysie Oakes? What interest do you have in him? He is a coward whose only talents lie in the bedroom!" Irma said.

"Precisely," Fantômas said and pointed a gloved finger. "You called him an oaf and coward… this is true. Which is why I wish his success. It shall do my reputation no true harm if Boysie Oakes is known to have defeated Fantômas. It shall enhance him in the eyes of his government in the same manner as Juve III and Clouseau are to the French. From now on, the foolish British shall believe that the daring and dangerous Boysie Oakes is my better. Which was the point of my every action this day."

Irma's eyes widened and she said, "Oh! That is rather clever!"

"That is why, Miss Eckman, there is only one Fantômas. Now, follow me and I shall pay you. Would you wish your money in Francs, Pounds, American dollars, or diamonds?"

We can always count on David Vineyard to provide a story featuring that wonderful rogue, Arsène Lupin, usually taking place late in the gentleman-burglar's career. This post-WWII criminal investigation is a little departure from the earlier, wilder, adventures, but focuses on what Lupin does best. For the record, Lupin's alias of "Peer Linnaus" was originally invented by Anthony Boucher for a homage story reprinted in BCP's Many Faces of Arsène Lupin *(ISBN 978-1-61227-049-4)...*

David L. Vineyard: *The Dufort Cameo*

Paris, 1949

Commissioner Jules Maigret tapped the tobacco tightly in the bowl of his pipe as he looked up from half-closed lids at the American seated across from him.

"Of course, I believe you, Monsieur Kirby. Indeed, I have no doubts as to both the truth and the sincerity of your presentation, but I fear there is little I can do at this stage. Suspicion that a crime is being committed is not sufficient reason to press forward in an investigation, and no Magistrate would let me go forward based on what you have just presented."

Sitting across from him in a small office on the Quai des Orfèvres, Rip Kirby touched the ear piece of his spectacles and nodded.

"To be honest, Commissioner, I didn't expect anything more," he said. "However, I felt that, if I was going to be operating in Paris, I should let the police have a heads up. As a private citizen, I'm not as constrained as you in such matters."

Maigret applied a match to the bowl of his pipe and puffed, watching the tall and fit American through a haze of blue-gray tobacco. The man across from him was an ex-Captain in the American Marines, well dressed, and the black-rimmed glasses he wore gave him an air of intellectual weight. In the years since the War, he had made some impact as a detective, solving numerous cases, some even with international implications. A mutual acquaintance in the NYPD had provided him with a letter of introduction to Maigret.

"This Sacred-Heart Society you speak of has certainly been on our radar," Maigret said. "Refugee children are all too common in Europe since the War, and many of these charities are designed to provide them with good homes, but not all of them are reputable... This couple you mentioned..."

"The Julians," Kirby noted.

"Yes, them. Their story is not unusual these days. A child is adopted from a less than scrupulous agency, a few months pass as the new parents become attached to the child, and then a supposed relative shows up with some kind of proof of their parentage, but willing to forego their rights if the new parents are willing to pay a certain sum of money..."

"And then they come back for more," Kirby added, "again and again until they bleed the new family dry. I'm here to see that doesn't happen to the Julians. I knew Harry Julian in the War. He's a good man. They are good parents and they love their little Peter. I have no intention of letting them be hurt."

"All the more reason to keep the police out of this as long as possible," Maigret replied, tapping ash from his pipe into a heavy glass ash tray. "The law is notoriously blind to human suffering. To speak candidly, you are better positioned to help your friends than I am, Monsieur Kirby. Provided, of course, that you can do so without breaking any serious laws yourself."

Kirby noted the line "breaking any serious laws."

"Well, as I said, I am here mostly as a matter of courtesy," he said, "to let you know what I'll be trying. My man Desmond is putting me in contact with someone who will assist with my investigation. We are meeting tonight, and I've already talked to a private investigator, one Nestor Burma…"

"Burma is not much liked at the Quai des Orfèvres, I'm afraid, but he's a good man, a good choice for this sort of thing. As for your man Desmond," Maigret tapped a fairly thick file on his desk, "I'm pleased to see he has changed his ways. He was never really cut out for a life of crime, despite his skills with a safe. I suspect whomever he has put you in contact with will be of more use than us."

After a few more niceties, Kirby shook hands with Maigret and left the Police Judiciaire. He hailed a taxi outside and told the driver to take him to the Hotel Crillon.

When he reached his suite, Desmond was already waiting for him. The beaky-faced Cockney looked more like a pickpocket than a valet, but was, in fact, skilled at both. Aside from his friendship, he was invaluable to Kirby in his pursuit of crime and criminals.

"We have a guest sir," Desmond noted as he took Kirby's hat. "Monsieur Burma is here."

Kirby walked into the sitting room. Burma was a burly man in a cheap suit standing looking out through the balcony windows at the city. Without turning, he spoke as Kirby entered.

"You forget what Paris looks like from up here," he said. "It's hard to relate it to the streets and sights I'm used to. Almost as if it were two different towns, but I guess all cities are like that to some extent."

Burma turned around. He held a large square glass in his hand, Bourbon if Kirby was any judge. His battered face bore some evidence of the side of Paris he knew best.

"I'm afraid I don't have anything concrete for you, but then, I don't think you expected me to find anything. What I have is what you probably want, though."

Kirby sat down and gestured to a chair across from him. The private eye sat down, removing a notebook from his pocket.

"I won't go over the information you already have. This Sacred-Heart Society was founded at the end of the War by a woman," he looked at this notes, "one Madame Montbrison, Irene Montbrison, age about fifty, born in Lyon, and married to a Georges Montbrison, now deceased, a lawyer whom I met a few years ago. More rumor than facts on her, though there is some hint she may have collaborated with the Germans. It's hard to tell, really. As you can imagine it's a sensitive subject here…"

Burma flipped a page.

"Her partner in the charity is a bit clearer. His name is Lemuel, Henry Armadale Lemuel, English, something of a con man, but no convictions. Colorful character, heavyset little man, who is fond of flowered waistcoats and affects an upper class accent. He wears a gold pince-nez and combs his thinning hair elaborately over his bald pate. Pyke, a friend from Scotland Yard, says he left England just after the war under a cloud over something to do with the Black Market. And that brings us to..."

Burma flipped another notebook page.

"…Emile Korn, sometimes known as *Le Phoque*, the seal, because of his large seal-like hands. Our Emile is quite a boy, a thug off the Marseille docks, ties with the Union Corse, an enforcer, who hasn't the brains for anything more, possible a deserter from the Legion. Shady to be sure. He likes to hurt people and things. He is big, mean, and sadistic. A bad combination."

"I'll keep that in mind," Kirby said. "What did you find out about the operation itself?"

Burma again flipped several pages of his notebook. "They operate out of old mansion gone to weed on in the 18th arrondissement near the Cimetière du Nord. They keep no children there, and indeed have nothing to do with them. They find refugee children in Eastern Europe—that's Lemuel's job—and arrange for adoptions through one Martin Montbrison, the brother of the late Georges, and also a lawyer. He's another one with a shady history, another possible collaborator. He works with a Sister Marie-Rose, a former nun who still affects the habit and pretends to be affiliated with the Church."

"I'm surprised the police aren't all over this," Kirby said.

Burma shrugged. "Another time, they might be, but Europe is still one big mess right now. Everyone is suspicious of everyone else, there are still Nazis in the woodwork, Reds in the bushes, con men, criminals, opportunists, gamblers, liars, thieves, and grifters at the edge of just about everything, from selling penicillin to children to printing counterfeit dollars. The police are overrun, in some cases corrupt, and too often involved, Everyone is out for themselves."

"Does that include you?" Kirby asked.

The detective smiled. "Maybe. But I have a certain shabby ethic. I hope you get what you want from this bunch, but be careful. I wouldn't want to read about a dead American floating face down in the Seine."

"And I wouldn't want you to. I'm meeting Madame Montbrison and Mr. Lemuel this afternoon as a friend of a couple hoping to adopt a child. I'll keep your concerns in mind."

"Just what is your plan, Monsieur Kirby?" Burma asked as he stood to leave.

"Honestly, I don't have one yet. But I'll know it when I see it."

"There is one other thing," Burma said as he picked up his soft felt hat. "Only a rumor, nothing substantiated, but I've heard Madame Montbrison and her brother-in-law acted as go-betweens for certain well-to-do Jewish families who found France unsafe on the eve of the Occupation. Nothing well-founded, mind you, but they supposedly purchased artworks, jewelry, and other items at heavily discounted prices from families forced to flee in the last days before the Nazis arrived in Paris—pennies on the dollar I believe is the expression. Some say the money they paid was funneled through Swiss connections and came from certain higher ups in the Nazi Party.

"Whether they still hold some of the items—if they ever did—is questionable, but when this adoption charity began, there was a sudden appearance on the market of several pieces believed to have been lost, enough to finance a pretty good racket like theirs. Martin Montbrison has contacts in Switzerland that could help him move money easily, even that kind of money.

"It's something to keep in mind, Monsieur Kirby. Such people would have reasons to be ruthless and little desire to face the kind of inquiry that might lead to the guillotine. A few bodies wouldn't deter them from protecting themselves."

When the private detective was gone, Desmond came in.

"You were listening?" asked Kirby.

"I assumed you wanted me to, sir," the valet replied. "I have to say, I'm curious exactly as to what our plans are too."

"A lay of the land first. I want to get a feel for our friends Madame Montbrison and Mr. Lemuel, get a personal tour of the layout, and some idea how the operation actually works. No business like this can operate without some kind of paper trail—a public one to keep the authorities happy, and a private one to keep the partners away from each other's throats.

"The one thing about crooks is, they can never trust their partners. Someone always gets greedy, someone always gets smart. Find out who that is and the whole sick business will unravel. Once they are at each others' throats, they'll be easy picking for Commissioner Maigret. Our objective is to find the chink that does it."

"Anything in particular you want me to be on the lookout for this afternoon, sir?"

"It wouldn't hurt if you exercised some of your old skills, at least your professional eye."

"Oh, dear, sir. And my rehabilitation was going so well!"

"Needs must, and all that. I'm afraid your rehabilitation will have to take a back seat to this little game."

"Yes, sir. One must think of the children."

"That's a good man."

Their appointment was for three in the afternoon, but they arrived early and, keeping well out of sight, did a bit of scouting. The Society was headquartered in a seedy older house in what had once been a fairly nice neighborhood in Montmartre. On one side, there was a somewhat overgrown garden with several large trees that backed up to the famous Cimetière du Nord.

Desmond noted that his employer spent some time studying the wall of the cemetery that backed against the Society's shabby garden.

Just before three-thirty, they picked up a black Citroen Traction Avant that Kirby had hired with a liveried driver. Desmond, sporting a bowler hat and an umbrella, was posing as a British solicitor hired by Kirby. He carried a slender attaché case which contained nothing but a racing form and a few loose sheaves of typing paper.

They arrived in front of the Society, certain they were being watched. Kirby was sure he'd spied a figure peeking out from behind the curtains on the first floor. Still, as they walked up the steps, noting the iron railings were showing a bit of rust, no one came to meet them, and they had to use the large brass knocker that was turning green on the heavy door. The sound was sepulchral and Kirby half expected the Frankenstein-like butler from one of Chas Adams' *New Yorker* cartoons to answer the door.

He wasn't far off.

Emile Korn, all six feet, four inches of him, broad as an ox, and twice as ugly, stood in the doorway, filling no small amount of the big double doors. He wore a gray check suit and darker gray turtle neck, and grunted something that Kirby assumed was "come this way," as he stood aside to let them squeeze by.

Kirby noted the slight bulge under the big man's left arm and recognized the butt of a Browning 9mm automatic, not the larger one worn by most uniformed police in Europe, but the smaller Detective Special. It must have looked like a toy in *Le Phoque*'s seal-like hands, but still a deadly toy.

The interior of the house was claustrophobic and smelled of disinfectant and musty rugs and wallpaper. It looked as if it hadn't changed much since before the War. They were led through large doors on their right, near the gardens, to another set of large double doors where *Le Phoque* discreetly knocked with his huge fist before a refined voice bid them enter.

The tall room was a library, somewhat better cared for than the parts of the house they had seen so far. It was dominated by a large globe, some faded rugs that had seen better days, several heavy, high-backed chairs, and a large teak desk positioned in front of large windows. Standing behind the desk was a tall, somewhat masculine woman, with sharp ax-like features and razor-thin lips. Small hard eyes were set in crepe-like skin under a thick head of iron-gray hair. With one hand, she fingered a small cameo she wore around her long thin neck in its high old-fashioned lace collar.

"Monsieur Kirby," she said in a raspy voice. "You're on time, I like that. You Americans are always so business-like."

She offered a slender hand across the desk, which Kirby took. Then he introduced Desmond as "Mr. Desmond," a London solicitor whom he had hired to take care of any legal paperwork.

Madame Montbrison looked more doubtful about that, but if it concerned her, she managed to let it pass. She offered them seats and sent Emile Korn for tea.

It said something about the haphazard nature of their operation that they had him to impersonate a servant. This was the sort of operation that could fold up in the middle of the night like a carnival and leave no trace behind, opening with little overhead somewhere else in short order.

"My associate, Mr. Lemuel, is attending to some, er, paperwork and will be with us shortly. Meanwhile, perhaps you could give some idea what the family you represent is looking for? We are always careful to match the children as best as we can to the couple adopting."

I bet you are, Kirby thought.

"Excuse me," he said, "but while we are discussing the details of the adoption, might Mr. Desmond look around your library? He's something of a book collector, and I can't help but notice his eye straying to your shelves. We really don't need him until the paperwork is ready."

Madame Montbrison's eyes narrowed even more, her lips almost disappearing in a thin line, her jaw tightening just a bit. Like most criminals, she liked to stay in control in these situations, but she could hardly object.

"Why, yes, of course," she said with an effort to sound gracious. "I'm afraid I know nothing about books. They were my husband's, but your friend is welcome to browse..."

As if on cue, Desmond thanked her and rose, walking over to the nearest wall to examine the volumes shelved there. Of course, Madame Montbrison knew nothing of the books; they'd come with the house when she and Lemuel had leased it, but it fit her game to pose as the original occupant.

With Desmond's trained eye examining the library, Kirby began his own distraction.

"I must say I'm pleased with what I have seen so far," he said, playing the naive American. "I had heard that there were pitfalls to adopting in Europe, and I admit, this isn't my usual line of business. If my friends hadn't been so insistent, I would never have involved myself, but they are an older couple and not really up for this kind of travel. I hope that won't be a problem—their age, I mean."

"I assure you, it will be no problem at all, though, of course, it could mean a bit more cost… You understand how things are in Europe right now…"

"Oh, of course," Kirby said.

He understood very well how things were.

They talked for about half-an-hour, while Desmond busied himself with the library, taking in every inch of the room while supposedly examining the books. Kirby let himself be reeled in, sipping indifferently at the watery tea Korn had brought. He did not catch Madame Montbrison give any signal, but he was sure she had pressed a button to alert Lemuel to come in for the kill. There was a knock on the big doors and the cartoonish little man, exactly as Burma had described him, entered, carrying a large photo album.

Kirby and Desmond were introduced by Madame Montbrison, and Lemuel seemed even more nonplussed at Desmond examining the books than she had been. That confirmed Kirby's suspicion there was something in the room they hadn't wanted him to see.

"I think I have just the child your friends are looking for, Mr. Kirby," Lemuel said, fussing with the album.

Kirby recognized the misdirection going on here. While the album would be filled with children's photos, only one—the one the villains had selected—would actually be available. A child with well-documented parents, real or not, ready to appear, represented by Martin Montbrison, prepared to give up their lost child—for a price—after Kirby's friends would have bonded with the child.

It was a cruel racket, and Kirby found himself hard-put to not throw a punch in the smiling face of the unctuous Lemuel.

"From what you have told us in your communication, I believe we have an ideal match here for an older couple..."

Lemuel was steering Kirby carefully to the child they had selected, likely the only one they had quick access to. Normally, Kirby might have played along, making him work for it, but for now, he was all too ready to be taken down the garden path.

Lemuel was not to be put off, even when the sale was made. Like an over-zealous magician forcing a card on his victim, he could not let go.

"Your friends should be happy they have chosen a man of such discernment as yourself. These matters are so delicate, as I'm sure your solicitor can tell you…" he said, looking nervously over at Desmond who was examining the spine of a copy of *War and Peace*.

He emphasized again that, while their business was fully legitimate, it was also bypassing certain pointless laws and bureaucratic difficulties that would only complicate the process for Kirby's friends, and end up costing them more money and time to no useful end.

"After all," Lemuel concluded, his small hands busy with the tails of his flowered waistcoat, "it is all about the children in this harried and desperate hour, is it not?"

Eventually, the child was chosen, a dark Italian boy with thick hair and an easy smile. Kirby was assured that the paperwork would be ready on the next day, and after payment was received, the child would be produced, healthy and fresh from the convent. No doubt in the company of Sister Marie-Rose, the defrocked nun.

Hands shaken, and escorted out by the hulking *Le Phoque*, Kirby managed to keep quiet until they were again in the back seat of the Citroen.

"Well?"

Desmond smiled. "Very neatly done, sir. My first thought was, it had to be the globe, but while I was studying the books, I noticed Madame Montbrison kept eyeing one section, and when Mr. Lemuel came in and I edged closer, he nearly jumped out of his skin. It was a section of the Russian classics, sir, Tolstoy, Chekov, Gogol, and I noted one particularly worn edition of *Crime and Punishment*—a simple pivot I should imagine. Remove the volume in question and the bookcase swings out to reveal a wall safe. I'm afraid I couldn't check to see what kind of safe it is, but I am quite sure my friend tonight can deal with it. You might say he taught me all I know."

"Good," Kirby said. "Then we have nothing left to do but rest until this evening. Care to take in a museum or two?"

"As long as it isn't a library, sir," Desmond replied. "I've looked at enough books for one day,"

For Arsène Lupin, the whole affair began much earlier. It began in those wary days before the German occupation of Paris, when his beloved City of Lights was darkened, its shocked citizens uncertain of what dark future awaited them, and so many desperate to flee, knowing full well what the occupation would mean for them.

The Dufort family had been neighbors of Lupin's and friends since his heady days as Prince Renine when that identity had afforded him entrance to the highest of society. At that time, he had made the acquaintance of the family and paid particular heed to their beautiful daughter, Rebecca, she of the dark blue eyes, translucent skin, and berry red lips, a child, but one promising great beauty in later life. He quickly became a favorite uncle.

Though Prince Renine had long since faded among the many faces Lupin had assumed in his colorful career, he had kept an eye out for his friends over the years. Little more than a child when he had last seen her, Rebecca was now an adult woman with children of her own, still living in the house where her parent had raised her, when the terrible news of the German victory had spread.

Lupin had been in Cannes when France had fallen. His first thought had been the Duforts and their married daughter, Rebecca. He was sure they would be trying to escape before the Nazis reached Paris, and that his help would be needed. There would be time enough to plan other things for the occupiers once they were in Paris, but for now, all he could think of was repaying the friendship of the Duforts, and in particular those once flashing eyes of Rebecca.

Even for a man of his resources, it was no easy thing to get to Paris. Roads were clogged with refugees making their way South to escape before the Germans arrived, and no one was sure who could be trusted. The story of the trip alone would fill a volume of picaresque adventure.

But arrive in Paris, he did, only to find the Dufort house empty, its rooms barren of furniture and paintings. Monsieur Dufort had been something of a collector, favoring Degas' ballerinas and some of the minor impressionists. But now. the house was deserted and locked up, though Lupin had little problem entering through a garden door.

He was searching through the lower floors when he heard something upstairs—a woman's sob.

Moving quietly, he climbed to the upper floor, following the soft sound of weeping, and, in a bedroom near the back, he spied a dark-haired woman sitting on the edge of the bed weeping. It was Rebecca Dufort, or whatever her married name now was.

"My child," he said softly from the doorway.

Startled, Rebecca looked up at him, her dark eyes red from the tears, with dark hollows beneath them, but still beautiful. For a moment, she was frightened, then recognition dawned in her shocked face.

"Your highness..."

Lupin raised his finger to his lips. "No need for that my child. I was afraid when I saw the house empty that I had missed you. What happened?"

He walked over and sat on the bed beside her. After a moment, she rested against him as she had when she was a child.

"All gone. Everything. With the Nazis coming, we had to get out of the country. René, my husband, has contacts in England, but without money… We had some in the bank, of course, but it took quite a bit to pay for the travel and we had to sell everything… Oh, your highness… Everything is gone, all the beautiful paintings, the vases, our china, our furniture, my jewelry, even Mother's cameo—that pained her most of all, as it had been passed down for generations, and even with that, it was not enough. There wasn't enough for all of us.

"René argued, but in the end, he had to go with the children. I don't speak English, and his contacts only knew him. I knew they would be better off with him, safer, but oh, sir..." She began to sob again as he reassured her.

There was no question but that he could get Rebecca out of France and reunite her with her children. As always, he had methods of his own, but the idea that his friends, that this desperate woman and others like her, had been taken advantage of by unscrupulous profiteers inflamed him.

Within the hour, they were speeding in a roadster he had "borrowed" to a small aerodrome outside Paris where the Phantom Angel, a friend with her own plane was evacuating people to England and had agreed to fly Rebecca out. For a man with his contacts, Lupin needed only to make the right calls.

While they drove, he questioned her about the people who had purchased her belongings. Of the man, she was vague, only that he represented himself as a lawyer; the woman, however, tall ax-faced, calling herself Madame Montbrison, she remembered quite well.

They said good-bye at the aerodrome and he saw her on the plane. She would arrive in London in hours, and a note he had written had put her in contact with an old friend, Lady Strongborough, who would see she joined her husband and children.

As for the Montbrison woman, there would be time enough for that. For the moment, there were more important things to concern him, more urgent matters.

He did not have reason to think of Madame Montbrison again for several years, though he often thought of Rebecca and her husband, certainly when he heard one of their children, a little boy, had died in the war, until an associate informed him that an old ally, an English lag who had reformed and was working for a well-know American detective, was looking for him in relation with an adoption racket and one Madame Montbrison…

Coincidences like that simply did not happen, in Arsène Lupin's experience. And justice delayed, even by a decade, was still justice in his book.

The *bistro* was in Montmartre; no sense in driving all over the city. It was one of those small places smoky from candles in bottles at the tables, crowded, and always a bit dark. The kind of place one might expect to bump elbows with Ernest Hemingway or trade a dirty joke with Henry Miller, where would-be artists and poets ran a tab the proprietor never quite collected on, rather tired ladies of the evening came when the streets were too wet or cold, and the *avant-garde* were more guarded than *avant*.

Lupin observed from a back room as the American and the Englishman arrived. He recalled Desmond, much younger of course, with a decent ear for the tumblers and good enough hands. No savant, as some of his students over the years had been, like the American Lanyard, the Englishman Mannering, or that saturnine British agent he had trained during the war—what was the man's name, something dull, Pond or some such… But gifted enough, a good student, a good man.

Once the two were seated, and drinking a glass of rather good wine—he was impressed with the American's choice from the limited cellar of this little bistro—he appeared. He had made few changes to his appearance, only enough that the Englishman would recognize his old mentor.

"Desmond, my friend," he said as he approached the table. "How many years has it been?"

He knew exactly how many years it had been, but likely neither of them liked to think about it.

Desmond rose and the two shook hands, but then Lupin drew him close and hugged him. He noted his friend was unarmed, but did carry what he assumed was a sap in his right coat pocket.

Good. They were already in a like mind as he was.

Desmond introduced him to Kirby. The tall American stood up; he was big but not heavy or fat. Solid muscle despite the scholarly look the horned-rimmed glasses gave him. A dry, solid handshake, and then the American sat again and Lupin joined them.

As if by magic, a waiter appeared with a bottle and glass. Lupin's private bottle for those times when he visited.

"First," Lupin began, "since we haven't a great deal of time, let me assure you that, since the other day when I was informed that my old friend Desmond was looking for me, and why, I have been looking into things on my own. Madame Montbrison, you see, is an old concern of mine, one dating back to the start of the War. I had not thought of settling that account, I admit, but from what I have been told, and what I already know, I fear I put this off longer than I should have. Your arrival is therefore quite welcome. This business with the children is as nasty as her pre-War activities, and it should not stand one more dawn."

Kirby seemed impressed. "Then, we should tell you what we learned this afternoon during our interview. I'm of no mind to let this lot continue with this dirty business either, not one day longer than I have to."

Desmond quickly filled him in on what they had seen during their visit to the Montbrison house, then Kirby summarized his conversation with the woman and Lemuel.

"As things stand, we will sign the papers tomorrow, and then the funds will be turned over—cash, of course. The child will be handed over two days after. But, with any luck, I should have what I need tonight. That is, if you are as handy with locks as Desmond says, and we can get in and out undetected."

"You expect to find the incriminating documents in their safe, I assume?"

"Most likely, but we won't be removing anything." Kirby took a small rectangle from his coat pocket. "These were quite useful during the war. They work in low light, and take very good pictures. I want the police to have time to develop and study these without Madame Montbrison and Mr. Lemuel panicking and packing up their operation. If they get away, this nasty little racket of theirs will just start up somewhere else."

Lupin was impressed. "Good! You have thought this through. I, too, have my own reasons to see this lot in jail for a significant time. Have you chosen a method of entry?"

Kirby produced a piece of paper with drawings on it and handed it to Lupin. It was a fair representation of the part of the Cimetière du Nord that bordered the garden wall of the house.

"You are in the wrong profession, Mr. Kirby," said Lupin. "You should have been with Desmond and I in the old days. I could have used a man with your brains."

"I think tonight," Kirby said, "your skills will be more useful."

They laid out their plans and then parted, to meet again after midnight near the Cimetière, dressed more appropriately for the night's business.

Lupin, who knew the area like the back of his hand, showed them a way into the cemetery at night through an unused gate. He then navigated them through the tombs at night under a partially darkened sky of clouds scuttling over the impudent stars and a sliver of moon. A burglar's moon, appropriately.

Kirby and Lupin went first over the wall and then pulled Desmond up. Together, they dropped lightly to the ground in the garden, careful not to tread in the soft soil and leave prints.

The large windows from the library gave way to the lightest turn of a pen-knife provided by Desmond, and they were in, the room illuminated only by their flashlights.

Desmond led them to the section of the shelf Montbrison and Lemuel had been so unnerved about. As he had predicted, when they moved the worn copy of *Crime and Punishment*, the book case swung out.

"I've always found Dostoevsky a rewarding read," Kirby said when the wall safe was revealed.

Kneeling, Lupin went to work. While it was an easy enough job, no safe is entirely easy to crack. Listening for the tumblers, he worked carefully. One of the first things he had learned as a young man, learning the art of safe cracking, was that most people failed to jumble the combination after opening the safe, so that it most often sat on the last number of the combination.

Within a few minutes, Lupin carefully opened the safe. The well-oiled hinges didn't even creak.

They found the books they were looking for easily, and Kirby carried them over to the desk where Desmond cleared a space, and then began unscrewing a bulb from a lamp. He replaced it with a special bulb he had brought with him, then held it while Kirby spread the journal out and began photographing the pages.

It took some time to do it all. Twice, they had to turn the lights off when they heard a noise. Once, they heard heavy footsteps as *Le Phoque* came down the stairs, but he quickly turned toward the kitchen and returned upstairs a few minutes later.

Meanwhile, as Kirby and Desmond were busy with the books of the phony adoption operation, Lupin seemed busy with another older volume.

Soon enough, they were done; everything was returned to its place, and they were back over the wall. They went to Kirby's hotel room where he stopped only long enough to call for a courier to send the film from the camera to an old friend of Lupin's who had developed special films for the Resistance.

Over a whiskey to celebrate the night's events, Lupin spoke.

"I wonder if you gentlemen wouldn't mind playing this game through for me. As I said, I have old debts to settle with Madame Montbrison, and it you would be kind enough to play along, I'd like to see this through to the end."

"After your help tonight I'd be ungracious to say anything but yes," replied Kirby, "and I admit this ending is a bit anti-climatic for my taste. What do you have in mind?"

"Nothing too dramatic, only I should like to see Madame Montbrison's face when the last domino falls. And it strikes me that it would be better for the child in question if he found his way into legitimate hands rather than be left in the hands of her brother-in-law and Sister Marie Rose.

"In fact, I have just the place in mind for our final meeting. A friend's home, well, their home before the war. It recently came on the market and I acquired it. It is quite suitable for our purposes. You can pass me off as a physician you've hired to examine the child to make sure he is healthy."

Kirby agreed, but with a curious expression. There were other games being played here than his and Desmond's, other crimes, perhaps deeper to delve into.

Commissioner Maigret agreed to the extra days; it would take time for the photos to be examined, and he himself wanted to arrest the whole gang, including Martin Montbrison and Sister Marie-Rose in one fell swoop.

Kirby kept the policeman out of it, only telling Maigret he had found someone to pose as a doctor and a suitable house for the final meeting. For no reason he could quite lay his hand on, he thought it better to leave the policeman and the safe-cracker unaware of each other.

In any case, he had no wish to ruin his friend's play, whatever it was.

It was a Thursday evening when Madame Montbrison phoned to inform Kirby that the child had arrived in Paris with Martin and the nun. He gave her the address provided by the Frenchman, who has asked him to refer to him as "Doctor Peer Linnaus" , and informed her to be at that address at one p.m. the next afternoon.

Kirby no more believed Linnaus was the man's real name than Desmond seemed to. For once he had a feeling he wasn't being told everything, but he trusted Desmond to do so when the time was right or if the need was urgent.

The house proved to be an upper middle class dwelling well appointed and showing signs of a kind of elegance and style that spoke of times well before the Great War. Kirby was no expert, but he recognized a few Degas, a minor Manet, and some of the lesser Impressionists on the wall. The rich carpets, heavy curtains, and Victorian era furniture spoke of comfort and wealth of a kind not much seen in Post-War Europe. It occurred to the American it had taken some effort to acquire all this in the time since the war ended.

Lupin met them at the door, dressed in a rather old-fashioned suit, looking for all the world like an elderly doctor. He led them into a room that was laid out as an office and seated them.

"I feel I may have misled you, Mr. Kirby, about my position in this business, but I assure you my own purposes in no way conflict with yours. Today will both solve the problem of your friends the Julians, and settle an old debt owed by Madame Montbrison and her associates. I am in your debt for affording me this opportunity as it was an obligation too long put off.

"I only ask that you follow my lead a bit longer in this, and by the time your friend Commissioner Maigret has this lot in custody, you will know everything. At least, everything worth knowing."

"I'm in your hands," Kirby said. "So long as I put an end to this nasty racket and protect the Julians' interests, I could care less what happens to Madame Montbrison and her associates—so long as it is something like justice."

"That, I can promise you."

At one p.m., Madame Montbrison arrived in an ancient Rolls driven by *Le Phoque*. Mr. Lemuel disembarked first, followed by a middle-aged man who could only be the fourth man in the operation, the lawyer Martin Montbrison, then a nun holding the hand of a small tousle-haired child, and finally Madame Montbrison, dressed in black, resembling nothing so much as a steel and lace knitting needle.

Kirby repressed a shudder watching her leave from the car much as if a black mamba had slithered out. Then, from his vantage point at the window, he noted how well Maigret had managed to place his officers on the street. There was nothing out of place, even to Kirby's trained eye, knowing there were police ready to pounce.

From somewhere, a servant appeared, no doubt hired by Lupin for the day. He was a respectable-looking man who looked more like banker than a butler. He let the party in, as "Doctor Linnaus" walked out of the office and introduced himself.

"You know," he said after greeting the party, "it seems a pity to bore the child with our business. Why doesn't my nurse take him to the examining room and I can join them later. No, no, Sister, no need for you to go with them, please join us, I'm sure you have had a hard trip, and you might enjoy a cognac with the rest of us. What did you say the child's name was? Ah, yes, Dondi, such a nice name! You would like to go with the nice lady, wouldn't you, Dondi?"

The boy seemed happy to be away from the nun, whose red face and hard look spoke of a drinking problem, and whose eyes were black soulless coals.

Like a collie herding sheep, he cut the child away from the nun and, as soon as he had spoken, a dark-eyed woman of perhaps fifty, dressed in white, came forth, took the child's hand with a booming smile and, with the faux butler, led him away.

It could not have been done more smoothly. Kirby had been concerned about the child and obviously the Frenchman had as well.

Kirby shook hands with Lemuel and Martin Montbrison, touched the tip of Madame Montbrison's hand with a nod, and shook hands with the cold, clammy slab the nun presented like a man.

Korn only grunted and placed himself near the door. Kirby couldn't see the little Browning automatic he had spotted before, but knew it was there. He would keep an eye on the big man. Montbrison and her associates didn't employ the thug for his finesse when push came to shove.

As planned, the papers were produced. Desmond fussed over them as if he actually understood what they said, and dutifully Kirby signed them. An envelope full of dollars was handed to Madame Montbrison after "Dr. Linnaus" had briefly excused himself and returned, assuring Kirby that the child was perfectly healthy.

Normally, that would have been the point when Commissioner Maigret would have swooped in; there would be protestations of innocence, and the satisfying sound of handcuffs snapping on wrists, but Lupin had something else in mind. When the formalities were done, he proposed a toast.

"Normally," the Frenchman began, "we would drink to the health of the child and to our congenial business, but being the sentimentalist that I am, I would prefer to drink a toast to our hosts, the owners of this house, my dear old friends, the Duforts."

Kirby saw Madame Montbrison suddenly stiffen, her hard eyes snapping at the mention of the name.

"My friends the Duforts, as some of you know, were a wealthy Jewish family. When the War came, their daughter and son-in-law, Rebecca and René, were living here with Madame Dufort and their children. Like many families, they knew they had to get out of France. And like most people, while wealthy, they were short of cash, and in those days, cash spoke more clearly than credit.

"That was when they were approached by a couple, a woman and her brother-in-law, who offered them money for their home, their belongings, their lives. Such people were not uncommon at that time, preying on those desperate for money, shopping for their Nazi clients…"

"Interesting as this is," Madame Montbrison said, beginning to rise, "I hardly see what it has to do with..."

Lupin raised his hand once sharply and Madame Montbrison fell back into the overstuffed chair she was sitting in. Even Kirby had been startled by the Frenchman's ferocity, and heard a growl and felt *Le Phoque* stiffen when his boss had risen to leave. Now he noted the big man was tense. Kirby stood up as if to stretch his legs and moved nearer to Korn.

"As I was saying, the Duforts sold their property for less than a quarter of its worth, though it still wasn't enough. Rebecca had to stay behind because there was not enough money to pay for all of them to go to England. Luckily, an old friend helped her get out on the eve of the Occupation.

"This friend was determined that his old friends should not suffer more. He could do nothing about the circumstances which cost them a child during the war, but he could, and did set about recovering their belongings. He acquired this house and he refurnished it exactly as it was before the War. It was not easy; he could not recover every piece sold, but gradually, he managed to recover most of them, restoring this fine old house."

Martin Montbrison was looking around nervously. Mr. Lemuel blinked uncontrollably. Sister Marie-Rose looked as if she needed a drink, but that was her normal look. Madame Montbrison compulsively fingered the cameo at her neck.

"Today, my friend has restored something else. You see, poor Rebecca and René lost a child during the War—a little boy. Today, these same friends—you met them earlier in the persons of the butler and the nurse—legally adopted a son… I hope you don't mind, Mr. Kirby? They and the child have already gone on, in case anyone objected to may little drama..."

"Emile," Madame Montbrison barked jumping from her chair faster than Kirby would have thought possible.

The Browning appeared like a deadly toy in *Le Phoque*'s hand, but only for a second. Kirby's hand slashed down on the thick wrist and, with a twist, the gun went flying. At the same time, the American followed through with a right uppercut that caught the big man just under the chin and dropped him in his tracks. Kirby felt the blow all the way up to his shoulder, but the big man went down. By then, Desmond had scrambled and picked up the automatic which he handed to Kirby.

"Sit down," Kirby barked in English. He felt as if he had crossed an English Drawing Room drama with an American gangster film.

"My cameo," Madame Montbrison said, clutching at her throat.

"*Madame Dufort's* cameo," Lupin corrected her, standing in the doorway holding the piece of jewelry. "The last item to be returned to my dear friend. Now, if you will excuse me,… Mr. Kirby and my old friend Desmond, I think it best if I retreat graciously as you signal the good Commissioner Maigret. I don't think he will need me, and my friends are waiting."

And with that, he was gone.

Most of the rest of the day was spent making statements. Commissioner Maigret was interested in "Peer Linnaus," but not overly so. He seemed content with the haul he had made, and as he pointed out to Kirby:

"The law has been served. The adoption, in this instance, is quite legal, if rather unorthodox. The documents you supplied on the Montbrisons are enough to condemn them in any court. In addition, your friend has produced some other documents tying them to wartime contraband and collaboration that should keep them quite busy for the rest of their lives."

It was the next day when Kirby and Desmond received an invitation to the Dufort house. Rebecca and her husband René greeted them warmly, escorting them to a drawing room where they served them tea and sat down to explain how they had been contacted by an old friend of Rebecca's, a man called Prince

Renine, who, it seemed, had also operated as Peer Linnaus during the War, and told that matters were underway to return their property to them.

They had never expected the child, but both had thought of adopting after their own son had died in England during the blitz. It was, Rebecca assured them, her dark eyes shining, a kind of miracle.

"I can only say," Kirby added when she finished, "how impressed I am with our mutual friend. He seems to have orchestrated this whole thing with surprising aplomb. Frankly I'm surprised I never heard of him before."

He looked at Desmond who stared down at his tea disguising a slight blush.

"Oh," Rebecca said, clutching her mother's cameo, her eyes filled with happy tears, "I think I can perhaps clear that up for you, Mr. Kirby, You see, I recall Prince Renine quite clearly as a child, and yet, when I saw him again all those years later in Paris, I was so distraught I had totally forgotten when he had disappeared from our lives. When I was just a young girl, there was a *cause célèbre* involving his highness, one I was too young to understand then, but there was a name linked with him that I only discovered later. Of course, I can't be certain… I wonder with that man if anyone was ever certain of anything,…"

She looked down at her hand clutching her Mother's dear cameo that had only been returned day before.

"Could there be any question that anyone else could have accomplished such wonders? My dear Prince, and your Peer Linnaus, was none other than Arsène Lupin..."

Credits

The Cubic Displacement of the Soul

Starring:	**Created by:**
Professor James Moriarty	Arthur Conan Doyle
The Little Prince	Antoine de Saint-Exupéry
Doctor Omega	Arnould Galopin
Fred	Arnould Galopin
Colonel Sebastian Moran	Arthur Conan Doyle
Co-Starring:	
Sherlock Holmes	Arthur Conan Doyle
Doctor Nikola	Guy Boothby
Professor George Challenger	Arthur Conan Doyle
And:	
Bureau d'Echange de Maux	Lord Dunsany
Baltian Neuralyzer	Ed Solomon

Matthew BAUGH is the author of oodles and oodles of short stories and several novels, who aspires to keep writing until there are no more stories left to tell. He is represented by Rebecca Angus of the Golden Wheat agency and lives and writes in Torrance, CA. In his spare time he is an ordained pastor and serves the Manhattan Beach Community Church. He is also the author of *The Vampire Count of Monte-Cristo*, and a regular contributor to *Tales of the Shadowmen.*

Walking on Foreign Ground, Like a Shadow

Starring:	**Created by:**
Judex (Jacques de Trémeuse)	Louis Feuillade & Arthur Bernède
The Shadow (Kent Allard)	Walter Gibson
Tony Rico (Chris Jorgenson)	Arthur Hoerl & Dashiell Hammett
Otero	W. R. Burnett
Mary Gillespie	Arthur T. Horman
"Rainbow" Benny Loomis	Irving Brecher & Harry Kurnitz
Margo Lane	Walter Gibson
Co-Starring:	
Julia Orsini	Louis Feuillade

	& Arthur Bernède
Benedict Stark	Theodore Tinsley
Colonel Gillespie	Arthur T. Horman
The Black Tiger	Joseph O'Donnell, Joseph F. Poland & Ned Dandy
Adam Strang	Barney A. Sarecky, George Morgan, Norman S. Hall, Colbert Clark & Wyndham Gittens
Reggie Ogden	Gerald Verner
"Sparks"	Barney A. Sarecky, George Morgan, Norman S. Hall, Colbert Clark & Wyndham Gittens
Dr. Houghland	Joseph O'Donnell
Jim Quinn	Arthur T. Horman
Enrico Bandello	W. R. Burnett
Leonard Gillespie	Max Brand
Jacqueline de Trémeuse	Louis Feuillade & Arthur Bernède
And:	
Stanfield-Dorn belt	Basil Dickey, George Morgan, Ella O'Neill & Het Mannheim
Rusterman's	Rex Stout

Atom Mudman BEZECNY is a graduate from the University of Minnesota Morris. Her previous publications include the novels *Tail of the Lizard King*, *Deus Mega Therion*, *Kinyonga Tales*, *Jim Anthony vs. the Mastermind*, *Meta-Terrax*, and *The New Adventures of Flash Avenger*, as well as the online stories *Dieselworld* and *Words from the Inner Circle*. For three years she has served as the editor-in-chief of Odd Tales Productions, and has written movie reviews for a variety of websites, including her own, Atom Mudman's A-List (*mudmansalist.blogspot.com*). She is a regular contributor to *Tales of the Shadowmen.*

Master of the Six-Gun

Starring:	**Created by:**
Robur	Jules Verne
Mordecai Jefferson	Nathan Cabaniss
Irene Adler	Arthur Conan Doyle
O'Neil (The Six-Gun Gorilla)	*Anonymous*

Devil Bob	Nathan Cabaniss
Co-Starring:	
Victor Frankenstein	Mary Shelley
Also Starring:	
Bass Reeves	*Historical*
William T. "Bloody Bill" Anderson	*Historical*

Nathan CABANISS is a writer based in Atlanta, GA, where he lives a life consisting primarily of danger, intrigue and Netflix. His stories have appeared in various publications, in both English and French. 2016 saw the release of his first collection of short fiction, *Mares in the Night*, and in 2018 his short novel *The Mummy's Hand At the Center of the Universe* was released by Pro Se Press. He is a regular contributor to *Tales of the Shadowmen.*

Doctor's Note

Starring:	**Created by:**
Abraham Van Helsing	Bram Stoker
John H. Watson	Arthur Conan Doyle
Erik	Gaston Leroux
Angelus	Joss Whedon
Darla	Joss Whedon
Henry Jekyll	Robert L. Stevenson
Co-Starring:	
James Moriarty	Arthur Conan Doyle
Mr. Dark	Ray Bradbury
Dracula	Bram Stoker
Akasha	Anne Rice
And:	
Cooger & Dark's Pandemonium Shadow Show	Ray Bradbury

Matthew DENNION lives in South Jersey with his beautiful wife and daughters. He currently works as a teacher of students with autism at a Special Services School. Matthew writes giant monster stories for *G-Fan* magazine and he has recently published three giant monster novels, *Chimera: Scourge of the Gods, Operation R.O.C.: A Kaiju Thriller* and *Atomic Rex*. He is a regular contributor to *Tales of the Shadowmen.*

The Doctor of Sarajevo

Starring:	**Created by:**
Dr. Cornelius Kramm (Doctor Malbrough)	Gustave Le Rouge Brian Stableford
Percy Phelps	Arthur Conan Doyle
Countess Irina Petrovski	Arnaud d'Usseau & Julian Zimet
Prince Wilhelm	based on Arrthur Conan Doyle
Baron Von Kuffner	Brian Gallagher
Lieutenant Novotný	Brian Gallagher
Captain Hodžić	Brian Gallagher
Inspector Lovrić	Brian Gallagher
Sergeant Ahmić	Brian Gallagher
Ljubica	Brian Gallagher
General Auersperg	Brian Gallagher
Simon Hart	Jules Verne
Kata	Brian Gallagher
Anar	Brian Gallagher
Lord Burydan	Gustave Le Rouge
Captain Huntly	based on Jules Verne
Captain Jelačić	Brian Gallagher
Co-Starring:	
Professor Moriarty	Arthur Conan Doyle
Irene Adler	Arthur Conan Doyle
Sherlock Holmes	Arthur Conan Doyle
Professor Saxton	Arnaud d'Usseau & Julian Zimet
Doctor Wells	Arnaud d'Usseau & Julian Zimet
Fritz Kramm	Gustave Le Rouge
Captain Nemo	Jules Verne
Thomas Roch	Jules Verne
Also Starring:	
Countess Sophie Chotek	*Historical*
Archduke Franz Ferdinand	*Historical*
Governor Oscar Potiorek	*Historical*
Gavrilo Princip	*Historical*
Archbishop Josip Stadler	*Historical*
Mayor Fehim Čurčic	*Historical*
And:	
Fulgurator	Jules Verne

Brian GALLAGHER has a BA in Politics and Society and lives in London. He works in the media and for many years has written on the politics, economics and many other aspects of Croatia and has been quoted in Croatian and international media. In relation to that he has written extensively on Croatian-related cases at the International Criminal Tribunal for the Former Yugoslavia. He has always been interested in SF, classic horror, comics and is proud to be a lifelong *Doctor Who* fan. His latest BCP collection is *The Return of Captain Vampire*. He is a regular contributor to *Tales of the Shadowmen*.

The Woodlanders in the Desert

Starring:	**Created by:**
Thaddeus Frycollin	based on Jules Verne
Elias Stine	Martin Gately
McKay	Martin Gately
Robur	Jules Verne
The Woodlanders: Sister Avellana, Sister Myrtle, Chef Topage, Carpinus, Artemisia, Grand Pater Platanus, Professor Oxalis	Martin Gately
The Stonerich Cavern Worms	based on Bram Stoker & Ken Russell
The Anu Sinom: Naki	Hopy Legends
The Hopi: Maya, Humeata	*Historical*

Martin GATELY is the author of the official prequel to Philip José Farmer's *The Green Odyssey (Samdroo and the Grassman* in *The Worlds of Philip José Farmer 4—Voyages to Strange Days)*. His writing career commenced in 1988 when he wrote for D C Thomson's legendary *Starblazer* comic. He is also a contributor to the UK's journal of strange phenomena *Fortean Times*. For Black Coat Press, he has provided stories for two collections, *Exquisite Pandora* and *The New Exploits of Joseph Rouletabille*, and contributed to the following anthologies: *Night of the Nyctalope, Harry Dickson Vs. The Spider* and *The Vampire Almanac Vol. 1*. His latest work is an adaptation of Edgar Rice Burroughs' *Pirate Blood* into comic strip form, drawn by Anthony Summey and available on the official ERB website. He is a regular contributor to *Tales of the Shadowmen.*

These are the Voyages…

Starring:	**Created by:**
Yusuf-ben-Moktar	Rafael Sabatini

Doctor Omega	Arnould Galopin
Marcel Renard	Theo Varlet & André Blandin
Shelfin Bundt Arbornoth	based on Jonathan Swift
Sir Oliver Tressilian	Rafael Sabatini
Duke Prospero	William Shakespeare
Isaac Laquedem (The Wandering Jew)	Paul Féval
Lotte	Paul Féval
The Morlocks	H.G. Wells
The Yahoos	Jonathan Swift
Mr. Pitt	Rafael Sabatini
Monoclard	Theo Varlet & Andre Blandin
Cipriani	Theo Varlet & Andre Blandin
Anguirus	Motoyoshi Oda
Co-Starring:	
Professor Helvetius	Arnould Galopin
Fred	Arnould Galopin
Duranton	Theo Varlet & Andre Blandin
Dread Pirate Roberts	William Goldman
Captain Mephisto	Ronald Davidson
The Time Traveler	H.G. Wells
The Houyhhnms	Jonathan Swift
And:	
Lilliput	Jonathan Swift
Paradise	William Moulton Marston
The Nameless Isle	William Shakespeare / Jeffrey Lieber, J. J. Abrams, Damon Lindelof & Carlton Cruse
Caspak	Edgar Rice Burroughs
Borgabunda	Edward G. Montagne / Jonathan Swift
Monster Island	Toho Studios
Villings	Adolfo Bioy Casares

Travis HILTZ started making up stories at a young age. Years later, he began writing them down. In high school, he discovered that some writers actually got paid and decided to give it a try. He has since gathered a modest collection of rejection letters and a shelf full of books with his name on them. Travis lives in the wilds of New Hampshire with his very loving and tolerant wife and a staggering amount of comic books and *Doctor Who* novels. He is a regular contributor to *Tales of the Shadowmen.*

The Phantom Angel and the Dwarves of Death

Starring:	**Created by:**
The Phantom Angel (aka Rose L'Ange, Briar Rose)	Randy Lofficier based on Charles Perrault
Captain Laure Berthaud	Alexandra Clert & Guy Patrick Sainderichin
Lt. Gilles Escoffier ("Gilou")	Alexandra Clert & Guy Patrick Sainderichin
The Nain Brothers (The Seven Dwarves)	Brothers Grimm
Druk	*Himalayan Folk Tale*
Prince Fortunato (The Beast)	Gabrielle-Suzanne Barbot de Villeneuve
Belle	Gabrielle-Suzanne Barbot de Villeneuve
The Tea Pot	Linda Woolverton
Co-Starring:	
Inspector Guillaume-Martin Paumier of the *Brigade des Maléfices*	Claude Guillemot & Claude-Jean Philippe
Doctor Francis Ardan	Guy d'Armen
Joseph Rouletabille	Gaston Leroux
Leo Saint-Clair (The Nyctalope)	Jean de La Hire
Judge Roban	Alexandra Clert & Guy Patrick Sainderichin
Sâr Dubnotal	Norbert Sevestre
Shah Zaman	*10001 Nights*

Randy LOFFICIER has collaborated with her husband **Jean-Marc** on five screenplays, a dozen books and numerous translations, including *Arsène Lupin*, *Doc Ardan*, *Doctor Omega*, *The Phantom of the Opera* and *Rouletabille*. Their latest novels include *Edgar Allan Poe on Mars*, *The Katrina Protocol* and *Return of the Nyctalope*. They have written a number of animation teleplays, including episodes of *Duck Tales* and *The Real Ghostbusters*, and in comics, such popular heroes as *Superman* and *Robur*. Randy is a member of the Writers Guild of America, West and Mystery Writers of America.

The Revolution Begins Tonight

Starring:	**Created by:**
Leo Saint-Clair (The Nyctalope)	Jean de La Hire

Sexton Blake	Harry Blyth
Borel	Arnould Galopin
Fred	Arnould Galopin
Doctor Omega	Arnould Galopin
Ségolène	Nigel Malcolm
President Schasch	based on Vladimir Volkoff
Colonel Bozzo-Corona	Paul Féval
Una Persson	Michael Moorcock
Zenith	Anthony Skene
Judex	Arthur Bernède & Louis Feuillade
Auguste Pichenet (Langelot)	Vladimir Volkoff
The Marchef	based on Paul Féval
Jean-Philippe	Nigel Malcolm
Olivia	Nigel Malcolm
Co-Starring :	
Yves Marecourt	Jean de La Hire
Gno Mitang	Jean de La Hire
Fantômas	Pierre Souvestre & Marcel Allain
Hedwige Roche-Verger (Choupette)	Vladimir Volkoff
Me. Karlsson	Alexandra Clert & Guy Patrick Sainderichin
And:	
SNIF	Vladimir Volkoff
BlackSpear Holdings	Jean-Marc Lofficier
The Black Coats	Paul Féval
Spinners	Hampton Fancher

Nigel MALCOLM lives in Kent, England. He works as a Teacher of English as a Foreign Language. He is a long-term *Doctor Who, Star Trek* and *Prisoner* fan - long before all the new-fangled versions came along. As well as being a regular contributor to *Tales of the Shadowmen,* he is working on various novels and audio plays

The World Will Belong To Me

Starring:	**Created by:**
Fantômas	Pierre Souvestre & Marcel Allain
William Dorgan	Gustave Le Rouge
Bec-de-Gaz	Pierre Souvestre

	& Marcel Allain
Dr. Fu Manchu	Sax Rohmer
Co-Starring :	
Dr. Bauerstein	Agatha Christie
Gilbert Blythe	L. M. Montgomery
And:	
Palace Hotel	Maurice Leblanc
Hotel Majestic	George Simenon

Rod McFADYEN has been dabbling in creative writing for a number of years now, although generally doing more dabbling than writing. While an avid reader of books of history, science fiction and fantasy, he is also a fan of the pulp genre and was delighted to come across the French pulp heroes. He's also a sucker for a good cross-over. He has been following the *Tales of the Shadowmen* since the first volume and was finally motivated enough to submit a story.

Wrath of the Cat People

Starring:	**Created by:**
Felanthus	Christofer Nigro based on Paul Féval, *fils*
Aissa (Puma-Woman)	H. G. Wells / Richard Stanley / Ron Hutchinson
Felifax	Paul Féval, *fils*
Mowgli	Rudyard Kipling
Matthew Challenger	based on Arthur Conan Doyle
Rudra	Paul Féval, *fils*
Durgane	Paul Féval, *fils*
Professor Tornada	André Couvreur
Doctor Moreau	H. G. Wells
Ouran (Beast-Man)	Philip Wylie & Waldemar Young based on H. G. Wells
Lota (Panther-Woman)	Philip Wylie & Waldemar Young based on H. G. Wells
Leopard-Man	H. G. Wells
Co-Starring:	
Professor Challenger	Arthur Conan Doyle
Edward Prendick	H. G. Wells
Montgomery	H. G. Wells
M'ling	H. G. Wells
Edward Parker	Philip Wylie & Waldemar Young based on H. G. Wells
Ruth Thomas	Philip Wylie & Waldemar Young

	based on H. G. Wells
Doctor Pretorius	William Hurlbut
Dr. Cornelius Kramm	Gustave Le Rouge
Sir Edmond Sexton	Paul Féval, *fils*
Professor Moriarty	Arthur Conan Doyle
Gouroull (Frankenstein Monster)	Jean-Claude Carrière / Mary Shelley
Also Starring:	
Dr. Josef Mengele	*Historical*
And:	
Seeonee	Rudyard Kipling
Diogenes Club	Arthur Conan Doyle

Christofer NIGRO is a writer of both fiction and non-fiction with a strong interest in pulps, comic books and fantastic cinema, and a regular contributor to *Tales of the Shadowmen.* He may be known to some by his websites *The Godzilla Saga* and *The Warrenverse,* as he is an authority on the subject of *dai kaiju eiga* (the sub-genre of cinema specializing in giant monsters), and the characters featured in the comic magazines published by Warren. He has recently revived and expanded Chuck Loridans' classic site MONSTAAH, and has since been published in the anthologies *Aliens Among Us* and *Carnage: After the Fall.* He is a regular contributor to *Tales of the Shadowmen.*

The Child That Time Forgot

Starring:	**Created by:**
Roger (The Narrator)	John Peel
Calistus Mumbar	Jules Verne
Commodore Simcoe	Jules Verne
Cecile DuBois	John Peel
The Tankerdons	Jules Verne
The Coverleys	Jules Verne
Colonel Stewart	Jules Verne
Madeleine DuBois	John Peel
Co-Starring:	
Carl Denham	Edgar Wallace & Merian C. Cooper
And:	
Standard Island	Jules Verne
Skull Island	Edgar Wallace & Merian C. Cooper

John PEEL was born in Nottingham, England, and started writing stories at age 10. John moved to the U.S. in 1981 to marry his pen-pal. He, his wife (" Mrs. Peel") and their 13 dogs now live on Long Island, New York. John has written just over 100 books to date, mostly for young adults. He is the only author to have written novels based on both *Doctor Who* and *Star Trek.* His most popular work is *Diadem*, a fantasy series; he has written ten volumes to date. Two collections of his stories have recently been released by Black Coat Press: *Return to the Center of the Earth* and *Twenty Thousand Years Under the Sea.* He is a regular contributor to *Tales of the Shadowmen.*

Only One...

Starring:	**Created by:**
"Boysie" Oakes	John Gardner
Colonel Mostyn	John Gardner
Irma Eckman	Jimmy Sangster, David D. Osborn & Liz Charles-Williams
Fantômas	Pierre Souvestre & Marcel Allain / Jean Halain & Pierre Foucaud
Co-Starring:	
Charlie Griffith	John Gardner
Bill Grice	John Creasey
Koichi Zenigata	Monkey Punch
Juve III	Jean Halain & Pierre Foucaud based on Pierre Souvestre & Marcel Allain
Jacques Clouseau	Maurice Richlin & Blake Edwards
Sir Charles Lytton	Maurice Richlin & Blake Edwards
Francisco Scaramanga	Ian Fleming
Carl Peterson	H. C. McNeile

Frank SCHILDINER has been a pulp fan since a friend gave him a gift of Philip Jose Farmer's *Tarzan Alive.* Since that time he has written the *Frankenstein* trilogy, the *Napoleon's Vampire Hunters* series (3 vols.), *Irma Vep and the Great Brain of Mars,* and has just embarked on a new fantasy series, all for Black Coat Press. Frank has been published in many other anthologies. Frank works as a martial arts instructor at Amorosi's Mixed Martial Arts. He resides in New Jersey with his wife Gail who is his top supporter. He is a regular contributor to *Tales of the Shadowmen.*

The Dufort Cameo

Starring:	**Created by:**
Commissioner Jules Maigret	Georges Simenon
Rip Kirby	Alex Raymond
Desmond	Alex Raymond
Nestor Burma	Léo Malet
Emile Korn (*Le Phoque*)	based on Pierre Souvestre & Marcel Allain
Irène Montbrison	based on Léo Malet
Henry Lemuel	based on Leslie Charteris
Arsène Lupin (Prince Renine,	Maurice Leblanc
Peer Linnaus)	Anthony Boucher
The Duforts	David L. Vineyard
Martin Montbrison	based on Léo Malet
Sister Marie-Rose	David L. Vineyard
Dondi	Gus Edson & Irwin Hasen
Co-Starring:	
The Julians	David L. Vineyard
Mr. Pyke	Georges Simenon
The Phantom Angel	Randy Lofficier based on Charles Perrault
Lady Strongborough	Maurice Leblanc
Michael Lanyard (The Lone Wolf)	Joseph Louis Vance
John Mannering (The Baron)	John Creasey
James Bond	Ian Fleming

David L. VINEYARD is a fifth generation Texan (named for his gunfighter/Texas Ranger great grand-father) currently living in Oklahoma City, OK, where the tornadoes come sweeping down the plains. He has useless degrees in history, politics, and economics, and is the author of several tales about Buenos Aires private eye Johnny Sleep, two novels, several short stories, some journalism, and various non-fiction. He is currently working on several ideas while battling with a three month old kitten for household dominance and the keyboard of his PC. He is a regular contributor to *Tales of the Shadowmen.*

CPSIA information can be obtained
at www.ICGtesting.com
Printed in the USA
LVHW040706241120
672559LV00004B/163